Making the Arsenal

Tony Attwood

MAKING THE ARSENAL

Published by Hamilton House

British Library Cataloguing in Publication Data
A catalogue record for this book is available from the British Library
ISBN: 978 1 86083 759 3

Hamilton House is an imprint of Hamilton House Mailings plc, Earlstrees Ct, Earlstrees Rd, Corby, Northants, NN17 4HH

DEDICATION

To the fond memory of Roger Brookes.

My dearest footballing friend.

CONTENTS

Sunday 16th January 1910

The bill of fare at the Manor Ground is, I would contend, unique. For this is a part of the Empire where fashion dominates, and to arrive wearing anything but the latest style is to risk ridicule and social isolation for months to come.

To begin somewhere near the start, one must be seen initially in the right emporium drinking the right drink at precisely the right moment. My choice, as one of London's young bachelors and therefore lacking the homely comforts of a good lady offering home cooking, is to eat eel pie opposite the Deceived Duchess. After that I partake of a restorative pint of the hostelry's exquisite mild ale before venturing into the ground for the jolly japes of other early arrivals.

Once inside the Manor Ground the real festival of the day begins as we skin our eyes in an endeavour to keep up with the latest fashions and current trends.

This week the Blueberry-Fawcett Flat Cap is top-of-the-league in headwear, and the dandy who sports it is certain to be admired by the man on the terrace behind. True, the Military Whitelace is preferred by those of a certain age who desire more than anything to regale their fellow supporters with tales of 1903 when the club won its first eight games on the trot. But this is not a hat for the younger man.

In the stand one spies the ladies, caressed by elderly caressers, most of whom are unrelated to their womenfolk and (it is rumoured) may be from the aristocracy or beyond. We may say no more.

Glasses are the order of the day, although rarely worn by referee and players, even when needed. As for socks - socks this year are worn inside out. A red stripe denotes the height of fashion and a certain rakishness. Matching gloves are not seen south of the Trent.

The players in Woolwich tend to a brusque coarseness, a disrespect of manners and a general inability to kick a ball more than three paces. Most are Scots.

Shorts are worn low, knees high, the waist is waspish. Elbows touch ribs and eyes, sleeves billow. The mouth is open, the tongue hangs out.

Shirts are art nouveau, and the hat of the goalkeeper should swirl and swoop around the head aided by a lavish brim swathed in flora and plumage.

As for the directors - the fashion is for feathers, flowers and fruit. Those attempting to take a seat in the grandstand without such garb are doomed to be a laughing stock for weeks to come.

In the Woolwich team, Rippon cannot hit a barn door (at least according to the man next to me), Lewis does not know the concept of "ball" (that according the man next to me's mate) and Compton's passing can only be explained by the fact that he is colour blind (according to the man next to the mate of the man next to me).

The game concluded with Woolwich Arsenal 3 goals, Watford nil, and Woolwich progress to the second round of the FA Cup for the first time in a year.

"Gatekeeper"

Wednesday 19th January

"You must love it here," said Mr Holloway without looking up.

"I try and live up to the high standards of journalism established over the years and enshrined in our constitution, reminding our loyal readership of their duty to the King…"

"Shut up," he said. I did. "Sarcasm is my department," he added. I did not disagree.

He picked a box from behind his desk and slammed it down in front of me. "Know what this is?"

"Paper, sir, recognise it anywhere, used in much of the Empire for…"

He looked at me. I stopped talking, but left my mouth open for effect, suggesting that I was going to add comments about pens, ink, pencils, rubbers, the difficulties of communicating with India and my specific experiences in the south of Africa soon to be renamed South Africa.

We play this game, Mr Holloway and I. It is a ritual. As is the fact that editors always interview mere mortals with themselves sitting down, leaving the poor scribbler standing.

I put on a look which I thought was one that showed me to be ready to face the complaints of the established readership (although it was unknown even for me to generate a box full). It was also my look for not revealing that I had had a few too many last night.

Mr Holloway, his glasses slipping to the end of his overlong nose, picked up the first letter, coughed, and adjusted his specs up the said feature fractionally. He looked me in the eye before indicating the pile on the desk. "A selection from the past three weeks," he said, and started reading from the top copy.

"Sir, 'Gatekeeper' clearly knows a thing or two about football in London, but I am sure you will agree he is not knowledgeable about the Association game in the rest of the country, and since most professional football is played outside the capital city it seems pointless to keep him writing about a sport of which he geographically knows so little and on which he has such biased views.

"His deviation into his personal opinion about the local public houses, the commentary of supporters who have imbibed too much prior to the game, and his view of their hats, the dress code of the club manager and popular songs sung in a public house after a game, is to say the least irrelevant, and ultimately demeaning to a publication that I have been purchasing for over ten years…"

He looked up. "Biased," he said, and turned to the next.

"Sir, when 'Gatekeeper' has nothing to write about, surely it is better for him to write nothing, rather than to regale us with tales of what he did on the streets of London the night before… While 'Won't you come home Bill Bailey' is undoubtedly a jolly tune, I am not sure it warrants four paragraphs, when the central theme is supposedly what happened in the football match between Tottenham Hotspur and Liverpool."

He looked up again. "This is a newspaper which carries sport, and not your own personal social diary," said the boss. He picked up a third. "Sir, 'Gatekeeper' may have had a good time playing in his band at a public house on the night before the last home match for Fulham, but do we really need to read about it in your august daily journal? His views on ladies attending matches and his comments on the seating arrangements in the directors' box are irrelevant, and his talk of hearing pins drop is surely erroneous. As for his commentaries on the fish pie, I can only conclude that the writer has criminal tendencies and, as such, should be reported to the police rather than given space in your publication. In terms of the notion that the inside left of Manchester United is a German spy, I can assure you his name is Smith and not Schmidt..."

"I'm sorry sir," I said. "I had the idea..."

"Do you think it is possible," he said, "for me to conclude without you interrupting me?"

I said nothing. The boss grunted, but chose not to pick up another letter. We indulged in a period of silence during which his glasses travelled one quarter of an inch further towards the floor.

"Would you like me to write back to these people and apologise?" I said at last.

"I would like you to get so drunk one night that when one of your musical fellows lights a cigarette near you the alcohol in your body ignites and you explode on the spot, leaving me with no problem other than the need to attend your funeral without doing a jig. The last man covering football in London on a regular basis retired because he couldn't stand the strain. You could do the decent thing..."

Mr Holloway was staring into space as he spoke, and I wondered if he had gone to a land where Mr Wells' Martians stalked the streets before the common cold killed them off. But, against all odds, he once again gathered himself together. "You think you are so bleedin' smart don't you, son?" he said.

I stayed silent for a moment, but when I was sure he was going to say no more, I said, "No, sir, in the face of that box of complaints I feel rather stupid."

"In the name of the Almighty," he continued, picking up the box, bringing it down hard on the table and then pushing it towards me, while his voice simultaneously rose an octave and he tried to turn the resultant sounds into a shout, "those were the only complaints! This is a box of letters from readers so demented that they are saying that they agree with you, think you are humorous, witty and amusing, wish to argue with you about what the best popular songs are, dispute whether the whole of Newcastle United should be deported as aliens, and (in five cases) are proposing marriage." I must have opened my eyes wide because he then told me to stop looking like a monkey, even if I wanted to parade like one.

"Let me remind you, you deviant little urchin who – some of these correspondents seem to mistakenly believe – has learned to write. Let me remind you, the Chronicle is a newspaper. In fact, this is THE newspaper of the working man. And you are hired as a writer on... what are you hired as a writer on?"

"Football, sir"

"Oh yes, the subject of which I am editor. And because I am editor I know that football has nothing whatsoever in any form to do with telling people how to spend their evenings and what flowers they should be wearing, nor the price of a pint in the public houses around Tottenham, Chelsea and Fulham. Nor even how far from civilisation Woolwich is. Or Clapton. You have managed to be insolent not just to me, but to the whole ruddy readership.

"And the mere fact that you get more letters than the rest of this journal put together while writing stupid childish gibberish, which I only let through because I had my eyes closed after a difficult night what with my daughter being ill at the moment, and we sometimes have a blank space because an advertiser pulls out at the last moment, does not make you clever."

"No, sir," I said.

"No, sir," he mimicked, "which in the strange and bizarre world you infest means 'I'm going to do this again,' so let me tell you something...." He paused and at last told me to sit down.

"Listen, listen once, tell me you have understood – and for once mean it - and then go and do as I say. I have a job for you. Can you do it?"

"Does it involve my knowing something about Greek mythology?" I asked, and then seeing his face wished I hadn't.

"You know what I did with that piece you wrote in which you suggested there are more anarchists in London than people who vote Unionist?"

I told him I didn't.

"I took it to the fifth floor and showed it to the old man, exactly as I have taken your previous pieces on 'social reporting' along with a collection of the letters that we have received about your work in the past month.

"I told the chairman of this journal that part of the reason for our rise in circulation last year was that we had added a little background 'flavour' and a little local colour to the sports stories, as we had a writer who liked to write about such things. I said your writing was helpful because it was often something we could hold for a number of days without it going out of time, and then slip in when an advertiser slipped out. And I said that we had some letters from readers who liked your work.

"And then I passed over your little piece on how much GK Chesterton had to drink when writing *The Man Who Was Thursday*, plus your work comparing the boots worn by supporters at Spurs and Chelsea and how it related to the chances of each team of being thrown out of the League for being too boring, and your chat up lines with the local ladies, and what music you were playing at the White Hart with your band this week.

"And you know what he said to me – our chairman? He said, 'At this moment we need a big story – a story that we break, a story that keeps us ahead of the opposition.' He said, 'if this clown of yours can land us such a story, let him write it however he likes. But if we do spies any more we need a new angle, a bigger picture'."

There was another long silence. "I'll tell you how we are going to do this."

I gave a grunt which could be interpreted (by those who know my grunts) as "this could be interesting, so please do go ahead and reveal unto me exactly what it is that you know," or not, as the case might be.

"You wouldn't know a bigger story if it hit you on the chin, so I'll give you one and watch you fall over."

Since I am the man whose English teacher said, "What this street urchin does to the English language should be a criminal offence," none of this was new. Mr Holloway was giving me an assignment.

"Now the distasteful bit," he continued. "I am instructed to give you a pay rise of half a crown a week as of today. I fought against it, of course, but I got outvoted. You are going to Woolwich – your favourite resort – and you are going to cover two meetings there as well as the game on Saturday. There's a shareholders' meeting before the game and an open public meeting after the game – and you will attend both. If you can bring in a couple of German spies while you are at it, so much the better. Is that sufficiently slow and clear for your simple brain?"

"Yes, sir," I said, not sure how to take this. "But…"

"Yes?"

"Woolwich, sir?"

"Woolwich Arsenal."

"But there's no underground out there."

"There's no underground to Tottenham."

"Hardly the same, sir. Woolwich is in…"

"Kent, yes I did geography at school. And here's something else you can do for me. Lay off the public house bit. We are not a paper that supports drunkenness. Come back with proof that half the people in Woolwich are working for the Kaiser, and write up the game under Dick's name and in his style. The report of the meeting and anything else you dig up is you. Understood?"

"Sir, why am I writing Dick's column?"

"Because, dear boy, he read your column, took your advice and played with the Monkey Parade, and his wife has kicked him out, and he isn't at work, and she doesn't know or care where he is. He's probably spent last week's wages and I, fool that I am, am trying to save his job and his life and his marriage. And that is one very good reason why you do not celebrate getting drunk. The other is that we are taking a neutral line on the proposed licensing laws – we encourage a restriction on the time the pubs are open because drink is a social evil, but a lot of our readers enjoy a drink so we are against any restriction on their pleasure. Is that clear?"

I told him it was, by and large, as far as my brain could handle such complex information, clear. He accepted that and looked down at his notes. "Got a report of talking dogs in Birmingham. You know anything about that?" I considered the matter and told him that, upon reflection, I didn't.

Annie, who brews interchangeable cocoa and coffee in the basement canteen, saw me upon my arrival in her domain and made the usual flutter of the eyes saying, "You get the empty?" which she always says to anyone called into the boss's office. The more I try to tell her I am a success, the more she puts the damper on and suggests I am losing my job. I grabbed her and gave her a kiss which took the room into uproar. I was onto the staircase just as the international news editor came down to see what the noise was about.

5

Thursday 20th January

Since Mr Holloway had clearly noted my thoughts on Chesterton, I decided to expand on my new found fame, and worked through the day writing on the "anarchist threat". I used George Barrett (whom I had met last year in a pub in Walthamstow where he was whipping up a crowd while I was discussing dog racing with the daughter of a tipster) as an example of your typical anarcho-syndicalist revolutionary: a great speaker but he always wears strange hats.

That gave me the theme – you can tell anarchists by their headwear which should make it easier for the police to pick them up. (That ought to be true since you can tell the daughters of tipsters by their…).

Ah, I thought. (I often think "Ah".) Take this further. Can you tell murderers by their socks? The more likely a man is to murder a fellow, the more likely he is to wear red socks. Or the other way round. Do red socks cause murder? Or does murder cause the murderer suddenly to put on red socks? There was possibly more in the latter so I ran with that.

As for stiff collars, I decided to take care. Mr Holloway wears a stiff collar. Boots and shoes were safer. If I watched what Mr Holloway wore, cut them out of the article, and then divided up the rest of the country according to footwear, that should give a few laughs and keep me safe in the office.

I could also link it to the general election. A survey of people voting, analysed by their hats, socks and shoes, which will tell us the result before polling finishes next month. No one could complain then that I was focussing on the low life of the city. Only the upper crust go voting.

Maybe the band could do an original song. "You can tell him by the socks he wears."

Friday 21st January

Yesterday I had dutifully put off thinking about my problem of how to get into a shareholder's meeting of Woolwich Arsenal without being a shareholder. I had also manfully set aside the issue of how to get more life out of the story that as a nation we were over run by spies from Italy and Germany. It had been done to death in every paper (including ours) every day for the past three years.

Ever since *Spies of the Kaiser (Plotting the Downfall of England)* had been published in The Weekly News, the Mail had run a daily lead story on its "Spies on every corner" lark, the Post had done its bit about how all the governesses of the children of the rich are German spies, and the Times, which ought to know better, had done "How many Italian organ grinders does London actually need?" My contribution had taken us back to basics with a spoof on the Mail piece called "Pies on every corner".

We'd done our bit too, but truth be told, we'd never had a unique line. Until now that had not been my problem – I just wrote football with a social edge. Now, suddenly, I'd cracked a joke too far and got lumbered with the job of taking the whole load of rubbish in a new direction.

And rubbish it certainly is. On spies I am well-placed (although I doubt anyone in the paper realises it), having been part of Section H secret operations under Colonel Edmunds while fighting the Boers. After I returned from South Africa I'd carried on as a sergeant in the War Office in between sorting out new recruits at Horseguards. The Colonel tried to establish us as a permanent part of government, and for a while I was his runner, supplying operational details concerning what we had actually done, but we never seemed to get very far. I knew, as the Colonel knew and as the government knew, that there was no mass infiltration of German spies throughout England. There might be one or two lurking on the terraces, but that was all.

We'd made our report, the Colonel had retired, and our little team had broken up with each of us left to find such employment as he (or in one case she) could.

So now I had to write up what I knew was not true, as if it were true. And make it original and exciting. And if that weren't enough of a problem, I also had to get into the Woolwich shareholders' meeting.

My family connections were no good – we are Wood Green through and through, and as such dad and my uncle are Spurs fans. I knew for sure that the local Kentish Independent paper didn't have anyone who could do it as I'd been drinking with their football man in the past and he was well known to the board. They'd sooner kick him in the Thames. George Allison, who covered the Woolwich games for half a dozen papers would be there, but he'd be working as a rival, so that was no good.

The best chance I had was my occasional pal, David McKinnon, who worked in the torpedo factory. He and I had met in the army during the war, although he had stayed in the front line when I moved into Section H, and by a further strange coincidence his brother was now getting a few games for Woolwich at right full-back. Better still, he'd mentioned that his father had a £1 share – which his mother had kept on wanting to sell (although no one locally wanted to buy). The old man of the family was now seriously ill – something he picked up in the factory, I suspect. Anyway I generally looked in on David when covering Woolwich and bought him drinks in return for snippets of information relayed from his brother. In fact, now I came to think about it, he still owed me two bob from earlier in the season.

Saturday 22nd January

I found David at the Hen and Basket, just after half eleven, moaning into his beer that his brother had been injured in the defeat against Sunderland back in October and the calf muscle wouldn't heal and so was on half pay. He was also offering the free tip that Woolwich would lose. I commiserated, told him my problem about getting into the meeting, and he said he knew where the share certificate was, and so I could go for his old man, if I cared to help a little with his drinking.

He did the deed. I gave him a shilling and took the omnibus into Woolwich to join the good and great at the Town Hall, waving my share cert as my bona fide on the way in. No one noticed – I may have had five proposals of marriage but no one actually knew what I looked like.

At the meeting George Leavey ran the show – turns out the club owes him a fortune – and he said the Woolwich were bust – which was news. The reason behind the problems, he said, was too many London clubs (Chelsea, Clapton, Fulham, Spurs and Woolwich Arsenal) in the league, with Millwall playing just across the river from Woolwich on the Isle of Dogs and West Ham just along the way, plus all the other Southern League teams like Croydon, Brentford...). And all of them easier to get to than Plumstead – which I could verify yet again following my rotten ride out.

I did the regular: talked to everyone and got some background on Leavey. Turns out he runs a gents' outfitters in town and he seemed well liked. Not one of your high-falutin' top nobs, but just a local man who wanted to do the right thing for his local club. One of nature's decent men, so the word went. Not his fault the club was in a muddle.

A couple of the girls from the pub were there – either they had lifted the share certificates from clients or the doorkeepers weren't doing their job properly when a flash of leg was on offer. I couldn't see a story in them, but I kept watching them all the same. Just in case.

Sadly for the club, the shareholders' meeting had all the usual head-in-the-sand sugary speeches (if you can have sugar in the sand) that I had witnessed occasionally when captains in the army got together to discuss how the war should be won. In this case the talk was of not letting the factory boys down, the loyal workers of the Empire deserving their entertainment, the men who made the guns that beat the Boers, the significant help the club had given to the local flood relief fund last season, the Cup semi-finals two years running...

It had nothing to do with the club running out of money, but it made people feel good.

As a meeting it was getting boring, going nowhere, disintegrating shapelessly (good phrase that – disintegrating shapelessly) and I was not getting inside information, when one stout fella stood up and said, "I'll tell you how bleedin' good this bleedin' club bleedin' is, we're worse than bleedin' Millwall, and they ain't even in the bleedin' league. Bloody Isle of Dogs team, that's what they is. And before that Hull beat us. Bleedin'Hull. I don't even know where bleeding Hull bleedin' is. Second Division that's what they is and that's where we're going."

There was uproar. It was great; I couldn't write it down fast enough. The old duffers at the top of the room were demanding that such language had no place in a civilised shareholders' meeting, especially with ladies present, at which point someone shouted, "Then you bleeding well don't go down the Manor Field do you, squire!" and there was cheering, and one of the tarts said, "What ladies?" and they all laughed as if it were the greatest joke in the history of the Empire. Shouts too of, "Are you a shareholder, sir?" and the stout party waved his share certificate, so there was more cheering.

The top dogs protested that this was an outrage, an impossible situation, unacceptable, beyond the pale, and that nothing was being achieved. Several

8

over-excited gentlemen who had themselves had a glass or two tried to get up on the stage, and the local bobby had to push them back down. And amidst all the carry-on I looked down to find that the stout party had dropped a document out of his pocket when he'd waved his share certificate. I went to hand it back to him but then hesitated.

OK, I shouldn't have, but I'm a journalist, so I stuffed it in my pocket, and eased myself out as the meeting broke up. The paper contained quite a lot more information than had been revealed in the meeting including the really big news that the club still owed the firm of Archibald Leitch for the work they did on the grandstand ten years ago. Is it possible that the board have failed to give the report to all the shareholders? That assumes the stout fellow had somehow got hold of a restricted document – and if it were true, I might just be on to something. Not giving full details to your shareholders is either ungentlemanly or a criminal offence. Either way it is suspicious.

David was having fun in the pub when I got back. I bought him another pint and left him to it, walking round the corner to the match, waving my press card in the flamboyant manner of hacks about to break a great tale.

Woolwich were actually much better than I had expected, winning three goals to none. I thought about Dick's style – fluffy, lots of adjectives – they didn't kick the ball high to avoid the mud, they kicked the brown ball very hard, into the leaden sky to avoid the sticky mud on the grassless field. I played with sticky brown mud and a soft brown ball, knowing that I was on the edge of taking the mickey out of Dick's writing (which wasn't the idea), but feeling the boss would cut the bits he didn't like. Where I come from you never give up on your fellow travellers. Besides I liked Dick even if he was a fruit case. A perfect example of how to drink 10 pints and stay upright.

Middlesbrough were poor and looked to me to be fit for relegation, but I wrote (in the style of Dick) "Let's give Woolwich A their joyful day and celebrate their great achievement for the brave souls on the ever-flowing Thames."

"Even better for the attack-minded Gunners," (I added) "it is the second week running they've got three, having energetically knocked over a battling Watford team in the Cup the week before." (The local support reported that Watford were awful too from all accounts, but I chose to ignore that.)

After the game I checked David Mc, who was now in the King's Head next door to the Hen and B doing his piss and vinegar stunt with a woman on his lap. He was probably doing more than that, and he was offering to share, and the woman seemed happy to oblige, but I left him to it, tucking the shareholder certificate in his jacket pocket – but he said no, keep it for next time. I did. Someone else would take David home – he only lived around the corner.

I ambled back into town for the full blown public meeting, reckoning that with the shareholders' gathering turning into a riot they'd have taken extra precautions when letting the plebeians in.

The meeting in fact was so disorganised that I struggled to think how to write it up. "Everyone screams, no one can hear a word" was a possible headline but it didn't really convey what I wanted to say. My main point was that the board of Woolwich Arsenal who had actually called the meeting must be meandering with Jules Verne if they thought they could use their middle class accents plus stiff collars and upper lips to get everyone to think they should put 6d in the cap for the club.

First off, they had made the stupid mistake of booking the same room for the whole afternoon. It was fine for the shareholders, but woefully inadequate for an open meeting, and people were standing in the aisles, with a lot of pushing and shoving even before the meeting began.

As I had learned, Leavey really had put a lot of his life savings into Woolwich A and he loved the club, had a deep feeling for the men in the factories, and this financial mess hurt him. An officer and gent, as we say, as honest and decent a man as you could meet. But I'd met officers like that, and being a gent did not necessarily make you able to take the right decisions on the field of war. They were the ones who put all the women and children in the Free State into the concentration camps, and then had no idea what to do when the cholera started. Jolly decent fellows – a total menace to the human race.

Being a gent doesn't make you able to work in a crisis, and doesn't make you a financial wizard or a politician on the stump – and what was needed here was both of those. Even after the crazy shareholders' meeting he still seemed to believe that he could just stand up and say his piece and everyone would take his cap off and say, "Thank you, Mr L, your lordship, sir, your highness, you done us proud, I won't buy another pint, you have my money instead."

And it don't work like that Mr Leavey, no it don't. It is just possible that it might have done before South Africa – but it don't work now. Too many of the men who work in the arsenal were soldiers in Africa and saw how we treated the natives and the Boers and they thought, "That's the way you do it. We could do it to them in Africa – so how about a bit of that medicine to the toffs?"

Leavey is not a toff, and quite possibly he did have the measure of working men in the last century when the old Queen was still with us, but he doesn't know that he hasn't got the feel of the men now.

But he was decent – and I determined not to take the easy road by making fun of him. I decided to stay with the shouting and screaming and the comments from a group of girls who wanted the police officers to put on footballer's shorts so they could see their knees. They were touting for business, and it was the girls who made sure there would be no real meeting. Woolwich was getting to be like the West End only without the accent. Another little point to note.

To the main concern: London's oldest professional club is bust, and its major creditor was not going to put a single shilling more into the club. So (I ask myself)… is Woolwich an isolated case? Woolwich crowds are not huge – but they are not the lowest I have seen.

There's also the fact that we know that the Football Association has always hated Woolwich for turning professional, and in the early days they ordered their clubs not to play Woolwich.

I tried an idea: Woolwich Arsenal has been deserted by the men of Woolwich because for some reason the armaments factory is cutting jobs just when (as we all knew) there were spies everywhere.

I wrote it and liked it. I called it "Woolwich and the Spies."

I even found space for a mention of a certain Dr Clarke who emerged as a central man for running a new Volunteer Committee which had the aim of racking up £1000 with film shows, a whist drive or two and something that I couldn't quite hear amid the uproar, but which involved the Theatre Royal.

I thought of the people there – the girls moving around sitting on men's laps, the hardened ex-military who now worked in the arsenal, the shop-keepers and tradesmen whose lives depended on the life in the backstreets of Plumstead and Woolwich and who got their profit every time Woolwich played a home game, and thought, "A whist-drive???"

I added a postscript saying that what was needed was a real leader, someone who understood working men, football and finances. "If he is around, would he please make himself known to the directors of Woolwich Arsenal FC, because they have dire need of him."

Then I went across the road to the Pie and Pig.

Sunday 23rd January

Sundays, when the world sleeps or goes to church, has us sporting types (well us sporting journalist types who are forced to work much of the week playing the piano with a band in local pubs to supplement miserable incomes) getting down to work.

First job, 8 o'clock. It's 8 o'clock because theoretically some of the journos actually catch the C of E service in Fleet Street at 7, but that is of course only in theory. The journalists don't go because they are up too late on Saturday night, and the management don't go to St Brides on the grounds that it is packed with journalists. As a result the vicar has only a small congregation – until someone dies or gets married and then we all pretend to be good Christians. We don't even make it over Christmas, there being far too much football on during the festive days. (I heard tell that Glasgow Celtic had to play two games on one day because they couldn't agree with Glasgow Rangers who got the home game on Christmas Day.)

Sundays, rather than starting with a coffee, sometimes start with a "wee dram" as the Scotsmen at the Woolwich arsenal say, and I met Scrapper Chalfont in the Pie writing up the piece for the Telegraph. We cautiously swapped notes. He'd had a fifth rate local stringer at the public meeting and was now realising that he might have missed a trick. As for the match, I suggested that Woolwich would do better when McKinnon was back in the team. Scrapper thought that sounded ok, and I thought that should make David feel good, and would allow me to either a) get my loan back from David, b) get some more insider information when I needed it, or c) have that woman of his sit on my lap for half an hour one afternoon when I wasn't tied up with the writing lark.

Then I went into the Chron and settled down to type up my story from last night. I threw in a bit about Woolwich's secret weapon in the past being that Woolwich was impossible to get to, and that the northern lads usually took a wrong turn and ended up in Southend before trying to catch a ferry and ending up in Holland. The northern papers called Woolwich away "The annual trip to hell" so I was just getting my own back.

There was talk that Manchester had actually come to London and stayed in a Woolwich hotel the night before. (I meandered a bit here and talked about the high quality of Woolwich and Plumstead hotels which I felt my readership would expect.)

Whither Arsenal? Whither Woolwich? I liked it. Sounded up-market.

Just to wind the boss up I added a footnote suggesting that I ought to stop being "Gatekeeper", which is a bit man-in-the-street, and start using one of these classical names that everyone else at the rag – including the boss – has. I chose Phoebe – although I wasn't sure why.

I gave the piece to the boy who scuttled over to the editor's room and did that funny knock that the runners always have. Having seen my piece safely delivered I went to grab breakfast in the canteen.

Half way through the eggs and bacon the boss came out and personally dragged me into his office. I brought my cup of tea with me (me being on special assignment and all I thought tea might be allowed).

"Ha ho bleeding tiddly dee," he said. "You know what I am going to do with this?"

"Print it?" I asked.

"Smart arse," he said. He had put some red ink through bits, as he always did, crossed out Phoebe and changed it to "The Highwayman".

"There's a story that people who have bought phonographs are going mad listening to the same music over and over again. Have you got anything on that?" he asked. I said I didn't.

After he had finished with me I went and picked up one of those big reference books that the Chronicle has on the far wall of the copy room – which I suppose are there because the owners think that we sports writers need a classical education – and discovered that Phoebe was one of the giants who ruled Earth in the time of the Greeks. She was the daughter of Uranus and Gaea, the mother of Leto, and she performed lewd acts with Artemis in front of all the animals just to show them how it was done. Maybe I'd have enjoyed university.

Monday 24th January

The deal is that I work the weekend, mornings, noon, night to help get the football copy ready for the Monday edition, and then I go and play music with the boys on Sunday night.

We're a five piece called Harry's Band – I play piano and lead the singing. I can also take over on clarinet if necessary. My grandfather set up a family piano-making business – that's where I get it. My dad enjoys what I do, as he played light music in bands before, and playing in the regimental band in the army helped me get my promotion, which he approved of. Dad now likes Bach and Beethoven.

We have a simple trick – we take the popular songs of the moment, and play the first half minute dead straight (or as straight as you can with a Sousaphone, clarinet, saxophone, trombone and piano) and then take the mick. We've got bells, whistles, rattles, comb and paper, drum sticks…

The crowds like it, we enjoy it, and we make a few bob each, plus we get free drinks. And meet some nice ladies.

I did Sunday night with extra vim – for I had something to celebrate. I'd done Dick's piece and my own, covering a game and two meetings. I didn't expect to be woken at 9.30am by my mother saying I had a visitor. I don't do visitors. I meet my mates down the White Hart, Harry's Men practise Monday nights in the George at Turnpike Lane and none of the girls ever know where I live.

But today, in an unprecedented move, the boss had sent out a runner to get me up and into the office. I managed to tell him (the runner) to bugger himself (although not in front of my mother) and sent the scruff-bag back to the boss saying I'd be there shortly. I tried a coffee, and just about got it down, and then walked and took the bus – there was no way I could manage the bike. In the works I had another coffee, and took a third up to the boss's office, and listened to him tell me I looked terrible. I told him my mother had already told me, and he'd never outdo her. He told me not to get cheeky, and asked if I'd seen this week's Athletics News.

I said no, suddenly going into a cold sweat in case they'd had someone at the shareholder's meeting too. I had just assumed they hadn't – I hadn't checked. He smiled, seeing my discomfort, and told me they had not only not run the story but also they'd not even covered the Woolwich game. Then he threw a copy of today's Chron at me. My piece was the second football story of the day. The Telegraph had nothing on the shareholders' meeting, and just a basic report on the public affair.

When the boss got up and slammed the door shut while I was still admiring my work in print he only did it for effect.

"Something interesting in today's edition?" he asked. I told him I didn't remember what I had written, and for a half second I swear the old boy took sympathy on me. "Been monkeying?" he asked. I nodded and wished I hadn't.

"The band plays Sunday night."

It was his turn to nod. "I had a phone call. Nine o'clock," he said. "From Henry Norris."

That was interesting. Fulham's man about town. "About…" I asked.

"About your piece, of course, what do you think it's about – your state of mind?" The boss had returned to his more normal frame of mind.

"I may have a hangover," I said, "but Norris runs Fulham, he builds houses in Fulham, he's mayor of Fulham, he's a possible MP in Fulham, he probably owns the roads in Fulham, and I suspect he does not even know where Plumstead is."

My opinion was ignored. "Henry Norris telephoned this office to say that he was interested in our piece about the 'Senior club in London'. Those were his words: 'Senior club in London'. He called us a highly regarded source of news in the footballing world."

"Senior club in London was my phrase," I protested, catching on rather belatedly.

"'Highly regarded' my arse," said Mr Holloway, still ignoring anything I might contribute. "He's probably never seen the Chronicle before today."

"And he's quoting me?" I asked just to make sure I was getting this right.

The boss nodded, something he was able to do with more aplomb than me at this moment in the history of the Empire. I gathered a few more wits. "While I like people to recognise my turn of phrase, I don't see why this is significant. With Fulham he's got enough on his plate – especially with Chelsea up the road with a much bigger stadium. There's nothing for him in Woolwich – unless he's moving his house building business out east – which I doubt because it's a wasteland of factories. If Woolwich go down it won't make a difference to Fulham's crowds, and it won't get Fulham into Division One. That's why the 'Too many clubs in London' bit is all tosh. The men in Plumstead and Woolwich would never travel to Fulham or Tottenham to watch a game."

"But leaving that aside," he continued, "Norris is not just chairman of Fulham football club, he is also a commentator on the game."

"And I know and you know that that column of his in the Fulham Evening is just a pile of excuses after another for Fulham's inability to score," I replied.

"Ask me," said the boss, "and I would agree that local politicians and property developers should never be allowed near a typewriter. And yet I just have to wonder why, of all the people in the world, he would want to meet Gatekeeper?"

"He what?" I dropped my coffee mug, and the remains of the drink went all over my trousers.

"Is it, I wonder," the boss continued, "to discuss politics? But he is a Unionist with a very big U, and we are a paper that – at least most of the time – writes about the daily life that interests the working man who votes Liberal, or as we may find out shortly, Labour. Perhaps he wants tips on how to make an arse of himself spilling coffee all down his leg. If so, he's asking for the right man.

"Besides which, Norris writes for the West London, not the Fulham Evening as you suggest – although that is hardly going to mean that you should refuse a meeting with him. Even if he is a prize carrot." His tone changed suddenly. "He wants to see you today, so you see him today. Fulham Unionist Club for lunch."

"Can I tell him I don't do lunch?" I suggested, but it didn't make much difference. In fact I wanted to go – I just didn't know how I was going to keep lunch down – or get my trousers clean.

"The instruction from the fifth floor," the boss said, "in case you have forgotten after your night of riotous behaviour, is to find a story. A big story which does not include mention of the general election or the Paris floods, since both are being handled elsewhere. What you have got at this moment is a little story. A good story I'll grant, but still a tuppeny ha'penny story.

"But the sudden decision of the Mayor of Fulham and owner of their local club to follow up just such a story that appears in a paper which he would not normally wrap his fish in on Friday night, and then to ask to see the journalist

14

who 'wrote' it (I use the word lightly), might turn this into a sixpenny piece. You go, you don't reveal more than you have to, and you try and find out what said Norris is up to – especially if it is far more than football – and on the way you buy a new pair of trousers. Understood?"

I understood. And it was good news – except for the trousers. And my heaving stomach. Mr Holloway took a final look at his notes. "Got a report that says the Archbishop of Canterbury is really a woman. Can you follow that up?" I suggested that I would check the details with Mr Norris, and took my leave.

I was feeling slightly better by the time I got to Fulham, and did manage steak and kidney for lunch. I'd only glimpsed Norris until now from the press row when doing a Fulham game. Up close he is a bigger man than I thought – big nose, big moustache, big hat, big presence. The restaurateur and the waiters were clearly in awe of him, hovering in the background for his every whim. I think they believed I was a waif – I'd ignored the bit about the new leggings.

To me Norris was affable, friendly, man of the people. What he clearly wanted was to know what happened behind the scenes at the Woolwich meetings. He also wanted to know how I got into the shareholders' meeting. I told him a journalist never pays for his meals and never reveals his sources.

But I did give him a trifle more on the financial problems of the club – stuff that the boss had thought too boring for our sporty readership. He listened, spouted more twaddle about Woolwich being London's oldest professional club (which he had clearly already forgotten was the line I had invented) and asked me to keep in touch if I heard anything else about Woolwich. I said I would, which meant I would not unless there was something in it for me.

I then asked him what his interest was, and he came out with even more guffing and guffawing about what a fine bloke Mr Leavey was, and the munitions workers were the men who had done the Empire proud, and how it was important to retain the sense of being a Londoner. Capital of the Empire. Half the trade in the world flowing past our doors.

So I took my life in my hands and pointed out that it still didn't make any odds, and that he was involved with Fulham, so what was he worrying about Woolwich for?

From that point on Norris was definitely travelling on a ticket that didn't include me, and he became more evasive. If ever there was a man with a plan that was evolving before my eyes, he was one sitting opposite me. The trouble was the steak and kidney was starting to rebel.

I told him I needed a story, and was Fulham going to be doing something interesting? Was Fulham going to sign someone? Was Fulham going to merge with Chelsea? At that point he got uppity, saying it was a private lunch, not a press briefing. I said, "I know that, sir, but my boss is a difficult man. Top sports editor, and he expects the minions like me to ferret out something from every meeting. What can I say, beyond the fact that you are concerned about the demise of the senior London professional club?"

And then he said, "Working men need their entertainment." So I asked why he didn't take over Chelsea. He told me that if I wanted to write a piece about there being no point having two teams so close to each other, and that Chelsea

15

ought to move since he was there first, and that Chelsea had fixed their way into the league without even having a team or playing a match, he'd be very pleased to supply the background, providing of course he could review the piece before it went out. I said that there was already a reviewer of my work, and that was the editor.

We left the notion hanging in the air that I would do some sort of piece about the imbalance of the geography of the capital city. It was clear that humour was not his strength.

Back in the office I wrote up the meeting and left it for the boss, with several suggestions for articles that could come out of it. I felt better by the end of the day, and the band rehearsal went well. *By the light of the silvery moon* played in the second half with sousaphone plus four of us on comb and paper is an interesting development.

Wednesday 26th January

"Jones – Buckingham, Buckingham – Jones."

It was a typical introduction from Mr Holloway. We looked at each other. Me in my usual scruffy attire and Buckingham, maybe a couple of years younger, with a flop of blonde hair and a really eager face and clothes which I judged by their cut to have cost three times my annual salary.

"I say!" he said, in a toff voice, "I say!" and all by way of introduction.

"Buckingham is a photographer," said Mr Holloway, then turning to Buckingham said, "I have no idea what Jones does." Then back to me, "You know what photography is, Jones?"

I reported that I had heard talk of the subject, and that the fact that the Chronicle was advertising itself as being "The Illustrated Newspaper" was something of a clue.

To Buckingham he said, "Try and control him, don't let him take you into any public houses, work hard, don't let me down." With that he turned to me and said, "Seems there's talk of intelligent life on Venus. What do you know of that?" I said I was still trying to find it in Fleet Street, and the boss marched out.

We looked at each other. They had given me a photographer to work with, which was good. He looked and sounded like a toff, which wasn't directly bad, but could mean anything.

"I've read some of your work, Mr Jones," he said, by way of an ice-breaker.

I told him to call me Jacko as everyone else did, and that what he had probably read was my work as re-written by the boss.

"Those pieces about anarchists, spies, football, hats and pubs. Brilliantly exciting. Completely changing the face of modern journalism. My name's Edward, by the way."

"And they have given you a camera and whatever else photographers have?"

"Actually I brought my own – how I got the job really. Father was annoyed at my hanging round the house all day, so I cadged the blighter and he called Uncle Roderick."

"Is that how you really talk, Edward, or are you doing it for me?"

"Sorry," he looked genuinely downcast.

"I'm kidding," I reassured him. "If Mr Holloway thinks you can take photographs, then you must be good."

"He hasn't actually seen any of my work. You see, Uncle Roderick's on the board of the paper…"

I said, "Ah", he said, "I'm sorry," I said, "Not your fault," he said "But the pictures are good," I said, "I am sure they are" and we danced around each other until I suggested we go to the Pig and Whistle for a lunchtime meeting to discuss how we were going to combine his undoubted talents with my own extraordinary ability to reconstitute the King's English. Edward reminded me of the injunction on pub visits, and I told him that was exactly why we were doing it.

And after a few pints Edward seemed a decent enough chap ("cove" in his lingo) who, I reckoned, if kept on reins could probably do no harm and might well produce a few interesting photos (as I learned to call them). I explained my relationship with Mr Holloway (Edward was shocked that such a shining example of early 20th century literature as myself should be anything other than bowed down to, with my every whim answered), and Edward revealed that as well as supplying his own equipment, he was not getting paid.

"If you ever meet the men in the print shop, don't tell them that," I warned. "They are unionised and would probably refuse to touch your work. Demand the money, and then if it embarrasses you, give it to me."

We had another couple of drinks and discussed our first joint assignment. Edward agreed that tomorrow he would show me how the equipment worked and take a few pictures of me. I said that would be delightful. Spiffing.

Friday 28th January

I came in to find that my latest "anarchists and hats" piece had made it into today's paper – a long way back and a bit truncated, but still… I had plans for how I could get Edward to take photographs of behatted gentle folk on the streets, with the slogan underneath, "Is this man an anarchist?"

But the moment I got inside the door of the sports room Mr Holloway took the wind out of my sails. He had a copy of the West London and threw it at me. "Your conversation?" he asked. I read Norris' piece in the paper.

"In part, but it has nothing new save speculation," I replied. "I'd guess that since we met, Norris has been able to talk to a few directors of Woolwich Arsenal and pick up his snippets. I gave him nothing; all he really wanted was for me to write a piece about him. I thought I could do a piece on moustaches, and how much they tell us about the inner man…"

"Shut up!" the boss argued. I obeyed. For five seconds.

"I think he wanted a piece portraying Norris as a senior figure in the world of London football, concerned about the good of the professional game. Oldest club going down, Chelsea getting into the league without even playing a game, Norris as shaker and mover, a man both of the business world and of the people, a man of the times, a man who…"

"Yes yes yes I get the picture," said the boss. "In short, a piece that is about as sincere as the girls in the Monkey."

"You know, we all know, so I didn't mention it. You always complain about me wasting your time with rubbish, and it was rubbish. Everything in the West London is what he already knew or guessed."

I turned to the paper and read it aloud…

"'Of course I have no particular interest in Woolwich Arsenal, my hands are completely full in my push to quickly get Fulham into the First Division. But as a director of a London team, and as Mayor of Fulham, I am sad to see our great city's senior professional club in difficulty. This is the heart of the Empire, and we have a responsibility."

"You're right," he said. "Split infinitive in the first sentence."

I then offered to write a piece about Norris' club, in which every time I mentioned them I would call them "Fulham Nil" in reflection of the way they played, but the boss would have none of it. "You're in there, boy," he said at last, "at least until he realises just how low down Darwin's evolutionary tree you actually are. Play him on a long lead. Find out what he is up to. Norris saying that he has no interest in something translates as 'I am in it up to my neck'. If you give him anything, make it stupid (which you can do with no rehearsal), so we can all have a laugh at the West London."

I took the advice – not least because it was reasonable and confirmed that I was now not only following the apparent demise of Woolwich Arsenal, but also the adventures of one Henry Norris. I wondered if I could portray him as a spy.

"He also said, 'Working men need their entertainment'," I added.

Mr Holloway looked at me. "Then let's have some for a change," he said. "Take that photographer with you." He'd forgotten Edward's name already. He checked his notes. "There's a story running that men are slipping fake sovereigns into the pockets of the crowd at football matches. That's your area, isn't it?" I said I hadn't heard of it, but I'd keep my ears open.

I read up all the notes on Norris in the paper's library. Apart from being (according to some) a pig in pig's clothing, Norris is also (according to others) a jumped up working class lad like me. The difference is, he is very wealthy, owns most of Fulham, owns a football club and he doesn't play the piano.

But in between there were, strangely, a lot of good things about Norris – particularly stories of him helping people out when they had personal problems. That was his style: man of the people, rich man doing good, Father Christmas, private saint in Fulham. Those reports were sincere: he was a complicated man.

Meanwhile the events for tomorrow have been reassigned, and Edward and I are to cover Fulham against Birmingham City under the "Highwayman" moniker. At the same time I have a brief to produce a detailed piece about the finances of Woolwich A as "Gatekeeper". But I have made absolutely zero progress on my new major story. Just how many types of hats and colour of socks can there be?

Jim Steele got the brief to help me with the heavy financial analysis, which showed how seriously the paper was treating this. I dutifully handed him the pages I had removed from the shareholders' meeting and gave him a rundown of all I knew about the club.

The boss had instructed that I write the commentary on the numbers in my own style, "to keep the readers who for reasons that are completely beyond my comprehension like your style in a happy frame of mind." But I needed Jim to tell me what it all meant.

Jim is good – I've done one or two snippets with him before, although football finance was hardly the daily stuff of news. He worked mostly on stocks and shares, government plans for pensions, the cost of rearmament, that sort of thing. He asked me about the size of crowds they got and how much they charged to go in (he was not a football man) and then gave me his conclusions.

"At this rate they might just last the season, but they won't get through the summer. And they'll need to raise more than having a quick whip round in the pub will get them, just to be viable for next September. After that they will still need a serious injection of cash to get them through to the end of next season – unless they get to the Cup Final."

"Would that be enough to pull them through?"

"Extra games and the big income from the semi final and the final itself would do it. Besides, crowds at league games would go up too. 20,000 all the time, not 10,000 is what they need."

"Which still leaves the question, what would a man like Norris want with a ship that is sinking?"

"Public duty?"

I laughed, but Jim was more serious. "Just take a look at the committees he serves on and the work he does. Fulham's finances are ok because Norris supports them, and there's no way he is going to get his money back – at least not from Fulham."

"I still don't see a hard-nosed business man like Norris pouring money into a club out in Kent just because he feels in some bizarre way that it reflects badly on the Empire if the capital's oldest team goes bust."

Jim couldn't answer that, and I developed a suspicion that the boss was putting me up against Norris because he thinks I'll have a go and get a few laughs, which will be a good nudge against the West London evening paper. And if Norris eats me for dinner and spits me out, it will just be a junior whippersnapper that is lost, not anyone Mr Holloway cares about.

Back in the archive I found several stories about Norris before he was Mayor, which revealed friends in both high and low places. But his downfall is that he always likes to give his point of view in the paper, so can't rely on the old boys' reporters club because he is not part of it. I wouldn't be surprised if he also had his hand in protection rackets – but that may also be totally wide of the mark, as well as libellous. He couldn't be running a spy ring could he?

Saturday 29th January

In the morning Edward and I went through the back copies of The Weekly News and read the whole series of *Spies of the Kaiser*. I had to admire the writer, it was a scream – and all without a single item of fact. Full of "the police know that," and "our government won't tell you but…"

It had nothing at all to do with the way we worked in South Africa. We had known that there was no way we were going to defeat the Boers with conventional military tactics, and that got the officers into a right tizzwoz most of the time. The Boer didn't want fixed battles so they set fire to our tents at night.

Edward seemed genuinely interested, so I gave him the run down from the sergeant's point of view. "They'd hit us in quick, unexpected raids. If we changed the guards at one in the morning, they hit us at half past twelve, just as the lads were getting bored and tired. Cut the wire, in, set the fuses, blow the munitions dump, out. We could double the guards and double again, but it never helped. Next time they'd do something different.

"In the end we defeated them with one simple ploy: we intercepted their letters. We behaved like them, bribed the port workers, bribed the postmen, and if needs be killed them. All the natives were with us because we treated them better than the Boers did, and a shilling would buy their loyalty for six months.

"Then we backed up the information we got out of letters by breaking into houses to find the rest. That was part of my work: running one of the Burglary Squads. Never got written up in dispatches, of course, because intercepting private correspondence and breaking into houses was simply "not on." The British do not fight like that."

In the afternoon we dutifully did Fulham against Birmingham – and would you believe it, there were no goals. The biggest centre of attention was Edward who dressed in a flared double-breasted sack coat with silk-faced lapels, looking as if he was either going to climb a mountain or enter a night club in Pall Mall. He surrounded himself with his equipment behind one goal and when a wayward shot hit his tripod the crowd roared. At half time I told him to stop taking photographs of the game and instead take them of the crowd. The crowd cheered their approval and waved at him. (Waved is the polite word). I wrote Edward into my match report, pointing out that never again would the matches at the Cottage be dull because we now had the King of Photography working the games.

In fact, the match was so totally awful that when I wasn't watching Edward's antics I was able to spend quite a bit of time watching Norris'. Interestingly he left well before the end of the game – but not before Edward had a photograph of his back. Highly symbolic.

Woolwich beat Bolton two to nothing. Maybe they are on the way up and won't need a Norris story after all.

Sunday 30th January

All quiet – the stories done, and no one dying, nothing needing re-writing, so I read up on the Norris background while Edward played with his toys. If I could just find that Norris' father was Italian and his mother German…

I didn't find that, but what I found was something almost as odd, and for which there was no explanation at all. It was a trivial detail, and yet it nagged at me.

In May 1903 Fulham got elected to the Southern League Division 1 from Division 2 – despite having lost 7-2 to Brentford in the Test Match. Which is odd, because as Brentford won and won so handsomely, they should have gone up. This was exactly the moment that Norris appeared on the scene – and it looked like a total fix. Did Norris bribe the Southern League, or Brentford, or both? No evidence at all, of course.

In fact our notes in the office said the vote for election to the Southern League Division I was held twice, and even after the second ballot there was a row and a half – and, according to Bob Kendrick who was seemingly our man on the spot at the time, a fight broke out in the offices of the FA.

Then Fulham get the nod, and guess who got up to make a vote of thanks: Norris. Now why did he do that?

By June he was club chairman – which is probably not surprising given what he had delivered in just a couple of months.

There was one other detail I found on Norris. In January 1903 he had left the Fulham Lodge of the Masons Society. Did they kick him out? I don't mix with the Masons (obviously!), but from what I know they never expel you unless you have hurt another Mason. It is some kind of band of brothers.

I also found a note that Norris used Archie Leitch later on to work on the new stands at Fulham – which is interesting because, as I now know, Leitch also built the stand at Woolwich and never got paid. I can't quite see how this fits but it is another link to somewhere. I just wish I knew where.

Back in football, in July 1903 having become chairman of Fulham Norris then seems to have got into negotiation with the Ecclesiastical Commissioners who apparently own the Fulham ground at Craven Cottage – in order to get a longer lease on better terms.

I got stuck at that point, until I asked one of the runners if there was anything else on Fulham – and he said, "Only the programmes and yearbook." Of course. We are all required to bring back and file the official club programme, and Athletic News publish their helpful yearbook once a year. Obviously.

Norris had indulged himself in writing in the programme from the start. And here's the thing – Norris made all sorts of comments about Fulham leaving their ground and looking for better accommodation if the church won't play ball and cut the rent.

And how I love archivists – right there with the AN yearbook were the minutes of the first Fulham Ltd Annual General Meeting in which he made the top dog speech and said he was about to leave the club – he'd done as much as he could, the ground wasn't right – time for another to take over.

But he didn't carry out the threat because there is another note – undated – which has him saying that he was trying to fix up a deal to move Fulham to Stamford Bridge before Chelsea moved in. The crafty bugger.

Edward turned up with his pictures – which I have to say were very good – especially the crowd scenes. He'd already given copies to Mr Holloway who didn't shout at him. I told Edward that was top praise. Then Edward joined in the research, and he proved to be good at that bit too. (If he can write, I'm going to be seriously worried.)

In September 1904 the LCC started legal proceedings against Fulham FC over a grandstand. The argument was odd: if it was a building the LCC had control and wanted it down, if it was a "structure" then Fulham's local council (which Norris controlled) would decide. Norris, with Leitch in tow like a little puppy dog, argued it was a structure, and won.

Moving on to December 1904 we found the first reference in the Chronicle to a "new professional club" to play at Stamford Bridge. The point here was that Fulham were still trying to get promotion to the Football League, and the new club were just going to jump over them, without ever having played a game.

From the moment he found out Norris went crazy. Every week there were articles by him in the West London, the Fulham Evening, his programme notes, and even the letters page of the other papers (although not the Chronicle which he clearly thought was beneath him). Not to mention articles by a whole range of people writing under different nom de plumes who were all probably Norris.

I invited Edward to come to the pub tonight to listen to me play with the band, and on the way he offered a thought. "Getting henchmen to plant stories in newspapers supporting your point of view," he said. "If I was running a spy ring, I'd do just that – most likely in order to deflect interest away from what I was really doing."

Norris the spymaster. I do so love that.

Edward took photographs of the band. Everyone was very impressed with my new friend and his strange fancy dress.

Tuesday 1st February

If I were running a spy ring, how would I run it?

First, I would have very few spies and would target them on key locations. Then I'd use the Erskine Childers approach from *Riddle of the Sands*. Invade by sending their navy across the North Sea.

But before this I'd want to know what ships we had along the eastern seaboard in places like… Woolwich, and up the Thames.

Then I would create a totally different tale, by saying that all the spies were infiltrating the homes of the great and the good, and watching our every-day life by playing barrel organs.

Then I'd take over Woolwich Arsenal football club and use that as my spying base.

OK, the last bit is a spot odd. But it has a certain ring to it…

Athletic News covered the Woolwich financial story although with a version of events that looked like a sanitised re-write of my own report. I was annoyed, but as Jim pointed out, if Athletic News are just copying stories from us, then it means we are ahead of them. They don't think the deal is important enough to put a man onto it, so we are in the clear.

One of Edward's pictures had been used, and he was thrilled beyond belief. He also gave me a "print" (as they call it) of Harry's Men. I told him I would have it framed and he said he had an uncle who owned a picture gallery and he'd get it done.

We went to the library and read up everything else we could find on spies. It confirmed my thoughts. No one had even been arrested as a spy since the days of Wellington and Napoleon.

In the afternoon Edward suggested that we take tea at the local Lyons Cornershop. He was meeting his girlfriend and her friend and would be honoured if he could introduce me.

Edward's girlfriend Sophia looked at me with a look of distrust mixed with superiority, uncertainty and disgust, and given that she seemed to look at Edward in the same way I wondered how he coped. Sophia's friend, Marie, however, was a different kettle. Not nearly so much of an upper class accent as the other two, it turned out she worked across the road from me at the Times. She had a sweet smile, and I told her everyone can be judged simply by their smile. She said, "You can't judge me at all, Mr Jones," and I said, "I am sure you are right, Miss Cortney, but it gives me pleasure to try." Silky, or what?

Edward had clearly talked me up before the meeting to sound like Fleet Street's finest, which was embarrassing, but somehow I coped. Sophia expressed anger at one stage as to the low-grade work Marie was being given just because she was a woman, but she didn't elucidate, and the conversation moved back to Edward's revelations of what people get up to at football matches.

In the end we moved into the Pig, a destination which the ladies accepted without blinking. Modern women, eh?

I fixed up to see Marie again tomorrow for lunch – given that she worked across the street from me and us being in the same industry.

Wednesday 2nd February

Nothing new on Norris, nothing more on spies, nothing on Woolwich Arsenal. Edward had no exciting new pictures, largely because when I wasn't directing him, he seemed to want to take photographs of old buildings.

At lunchtime I met Marie at Lyons Corner House at the end of Fleet Street and realised that in daylight she was... well astonishingly attractive. I hardly realised it was her. In fact, I was quite bemused at not having remembered how good looking she was and how...

We got to talking, and listening to her voice in the cold light of day I began to get the feeling I might have jumped in and was now seriously out of my depth. Here is a woman with class. Which, of course, I should have guessed given that she was introduced to me by Edward. (Edward I can cope with because he wants to be in my world and he thinks I'm a hero, but with any other toff I'm on soggy ground.)

And slowly it tumbled. When Marie had told me yesterday that she worked for the Times and Sophia had talked about low grade work, I'd somehow thought that she served in the restaurant or something like that. Talking to her now, it is clear she is another journalist. Obviously I know all about the fight of women to hold jobs alongside men, but I suppose I'd never quite seen it, and so didn't believe it. We'd had Eggie (I never did know her real name) in Section H but somehow I'd stopped thinking of her as a woman. Eggie was just so obviously good at what she did – including being a natural linguist – that the question of her doing the job never arose after the second day.

We don't have women journalists at the Chronicle – but there she was at the Times – which I had never considered a forward looking paper. I asked what she'd been working on, and she told me, with a dead straight face that she'd been writing up the life and times of one Thomas Crapper who died last week. I asked what he did, and she said he was an inventor.

"Oh yes," I said, not knowing at all how to play this situation, "what did he invent?"

"The water closet," said Marie. "Hence the phrase."

I wasn't at all sure where to go from there. We talked about my work in following up Norris, and about spies, and she asked what I'd done before the writing, and I told her about my time in the army, and gave her a summary of Section H.

"So I should call you captain, Mr Jones, or was it major?" she said. She was serious.

It would have been so nice to have said "major" but I confessed I was not an officer – just a sergeant – and she looked a bit embarrassed about what she had said. So I told her to forget titles, everyone called me Jacko, and then I asked what she had been doing before working at the Times.

"I was at university," she said.

"But I thought..." And she knew exactly what I was about to say. I curl up inside at just writing that gaff down.

"London University admits women," she said seriously, but without annoyance. "In fact a third of the degrees that will be given this year will be given to women."

"What did you study?" I asked. The answer was English, and something called psychology – whatever that is.

She said that she covered the lives of the famous for the paper – sometimes for obituaries, sometimes for background on their everyday work. She also wrote book reviews.

And she lives in Dorset Square – in fact I suspect her family probably own Dorset Square but I didn't get close to asking her about mum and dad. She probably refers to them as mater and pater.

And then, just when I should have been backing off, I did the opposite. I asked her if she would like to come to an extra gig that we were doing that night in the Nag's Head. And to my amazement she agreed.

I started to tell her what she might like to wear, but she gave me a look and said, "You think I have not been in a pub before – apart from last night?" That was exactly what I was thinking, but of course I denied it. Maybe not admitting errors is something to do with working for the Chronicle.

She was, as far as I could tell, suitably impressed by my singing and playing, and the antics of the band. At least I like to think so. In between she gave me her thoughts on how spy rings work.

Thursday 3rd February

With the aid of some of Marie's ideas I wrote a piece suggesting that the spy rings based on governesses, organ grinders, and German waiters in restaurants (Marie goes to better restaurants than I do, and she assured me this was true) were not the main deal.

"It is a deliberate ploy to lead us off the track," I announced in my piece. "The real issue is the navy – and Germany is more anxious than ever to know what ships we are building, and what speeds they are capable of.

"The real spies are watching our naval bases..."

I stopped at one point and asked Edward to go and take photographs of some people in Fleet Street who looked like spies. He did, so I had to call him back and tell him it was a joke, although by then he had photographs of a man with a huge beard and a walking stick which looked rather good, so I added it to the article suggesting that he had been identified as the deputy commander of what the German Spy Command calls "Sector 7".

Friday 4th February

Having kept the spy side of my brief happy for a day or two I went back to Norris. I reckon there's evidence that football can be manipulated (the promotions of Fulham and Chelsea are perfect examples, and I am sure there are others). The Football League is widely thought to love Woolwich because they brought the

League and professionalism into London, so we can expect some kickbacks there too.

If Norris is seriously trying to rescue Woolwich Arsenal he could be doing it to keep in with the Football League because he wants another favour, such as another fixed promotion for Fulham perhaps.

Dick, now back at work and looking clean and fresh, listened to my tales and suddenly said, "Have you talked to anyone at the Fulham Chronicle?" I noticed his hands were shaking. He stuck them in his pockets. I grabbed Edward and we set off; it was an obvious move and I'd missed it.

They were far more helpful than I had expected – not least because they had in the past run a whole series of anti-Norris stories about Fulham being boring, under-funded, badly-managed, and recruiting the wrong players.

Like the story that in 1908 Norris (having been involved with Fulham for five years) took over Croydon Common and nominated them for membership of the Southern League. Croydon got in against all the odds and is still there, with Norris the main shareholder – which means Norris clearly has had a long term plan to set up a second team alongside Fulham.

I searched for more on Croydon, while with each paper I looked at Edward flipped to the front page of each edition for no particular reason. And then he discovered that on December 7th 1909 the paper had run the most extraordinary story. It seems that in September last year the LCC had given British Petroleum permission to build a collection of oil storage tanks on land in Stevenage Road, Fulham which the oil company had either bought or leased from the Ecclesiastical Commissioners.

No one had raised a fuss originally, but by December 7th half of Fulham was ready to go to war over the issue. There was a story about how hundreds of residents had marched on the Mayor's parlour, demanding to know why he had let this happen. (The Mayor being, of course, Mr Norris.)

Edward raced through the subsequent papers – and then found what we were after. On December 17th the issue was resolved when the Commissioners suddenly changed their minds and decided not to let British Petroleum have the site after all.

Now, of course, it might have been that the Godly Com had simply listened to their parishioners and done the right thing. But the fact that Norris had negotiated the land at Craven Cottage from the self-same Commissioners couldn't be ignored. He had blown hot and cold with them, threatened anything he could and eventually had got the oil terminal lease rescinded.

So he had negotiated with the church over Craven Cottage, and now here he was mixed up in another event with the same bunch of bishops.

Could it possibly be that the Church owes Norris a favour? Now that would be a story! I continued rummaging and sent Edward to go and find the site in Stevenage Road and get some photographs. Apparently I should call them photos.

Saturday 5th February

Cup day. I suppose they make so much fuss about it because they keep hoping one of the London old timer teams like Wanderers or Clapham Rovers will win it again. All we've had since the old days is one win by Tottenham Hotspur when they were in the Southern League. Worse, as far as I know Wanderers and Clapham are gone to a football graveyard.

(My dad goes to see the Corinthians sometimes – but of course they won't enter for the FA Cup – it is against their charter to play competitively. Dad told me that he watched them play Dulwich and half way through the second half the Cors got a penalty and instead of shooting for goal just tapped it back to the Dulwich goalie. Corinthians never believe that a gentleman would deliberately commit a foul and so they wouldn't take advantage. Can't see that working against those Scots playing for Woolwich.)

The fact is that since they moved the final to the Crystal Palace it's been mostly Midlands and Northern teams that get through – and anyone who thinks Woolwich is hard to get to gets a surprise with the Palace. True, Bristol City got to a final last year of course, but which self-respecting Londoner is going to go down to the Palace and see Manchester beat Bristol 1-0?

I had taken my latest findings on Norris to the boss on Friday night. He wasn't too impressed, but told me to keep going. He said my piece on spies was on the fifth floor and they were thinking about handing me over to the Tower of London, but they were very taken with Edward, and that meanwhile I should do a piece on the discovery of coal in the Outer Hebrides.

He then sent us to see Chelsea 0 Tottenham Hotspur 1 which was as boring as Hebridean coal and left me thinking I ought to have opted for a reserve game. Or something in the Southern League. Once again, however, Edward saved the day. At the turnaround I got him to take "photos" (I tried to say the word in inverted commas just for him) of the crowd in the stand. They looked at him in bemusement, and as a result the pictures were great.

Even the second half wasn't totally useless – in fact there was much ribald laughter in the journalists' section when there was a commotion on one of those huge terraces that Chelsea have. There was a lot of movement, and then a rush out of one section. When the dust settled, we could see that a whole chunk of terracing had sunk about three feet and become uneven rubble. No one seemed to be hurt, but it shows what a state the place is in. Edward hasn't quite got the swing of all this because he sat there gawping for a bit until I virtually threw him out of the stand and told him to take pictures.

I'd finished my write-up back in the office by the time the news came through of Everton 5 Woolwich 0 – which will put a lot of extra pressure on the Woolwich Volunteers Committee – it's not as if Everton are a semi-decent team.

Sometimes I wonder why we have a national league – certainly not for the benefit of London. Fulham were slaughtered by the Geordies 4-0. I then heard that Norris had not even bothered to go to watch his team.

Truth be told, once he gets out of streets that he has built he gets lost. (I doubt that I'll ever get away with printing that but it is quite amusing).

Sunday 6th February

I wrote the Chelsea piece up, including some questions about what was wrong with their ground, plus a note about the need to call the architect and builders to account.

Edward suggested that it would be nice if Sophia, Marie and the two of us got together. I nodded vaguely, wondering how to handle that, and switched to the issue of spies. Edward was still perfectly willing to take pictures in the street – and I thought, why not? "But not now," I added. "Let's try when it gets dark."

Which we did. I don't think Edward has seen the Monkey Parade before, nor met the sort of people who go on it. He certainly wasn't used to the street fighting, drunks and being propositioned every two minutes, and it was clear that if we were going to try this again we would need an army of men to keep the onlookers away.

Monday 7th February

My spy piece is on page five. They hadn't told me yesterday, so it must have been another pulled advertisement, but at least it keeps me on the move. Edward hit the high spots again with his photographs. According to Mr Holloway, Edward is the talk of Fleet Street. He also wants me to cover the story of an oak tree in Nottingham Forest that, according to the natives, has moved one hundred paces west in the past year.

I spent another lunchtime with Marie. Enjoyable – but am wondering just how far out of my depth I am getting. She… well to be open about it, she knows more than I do. OK she knows nothing about Woolwich Arsenal or how to play a clarinet, but she knows about politics, about the Boer War, and even about that drunken journalist (Mr Churchill) I teamed up with at the end of the War. She knows about the Suffragettes, and confirmed that Sophia is committed to that cause, although she (Marie) is not…

So she knows virtually anything and everything – including rugby football, women's football (chiding me for not knowing that a crowd of 40,000 turned up for the women's international last year), hockey, netball, and all the women's stuff that men don't know about.

We talked about the Times. Despite being the great publication of record it, like every other paper, was falling for the German spy nonsense. I told Marie more about Section H and my belief that it could be the anarchists who are the real threat.

"What about the vortex?" she countered.

Fortunately I was all right with that one – at the start of the general election campaign last year Labour had talked about little other than the "pit of poverty from which there is no escape". We all knew it by heart. But to put the vortex next to spies and wars?

To lighten the occasion I did my Kaiser impersonation, saying "Vot more can I do zan I unt done?" which everyone believes he said when asked by Edward the Caresser if Germany is about to invade.

Tuesday 8th February

Marie told me that we have a new secretary of state for war called Winston Churchill. I gave her a look of disbelief and told her more about the Churchill who was war correspondent for the Morning Post when I was a Sergeant for Her Majesty and the Empire, and how he earned more in a day than I did in a year.

"He was in a prisoner-of-war camp in Pretoria," I told her. "He told the Boers he was just a journalist, but he kept on getting involved in harebrained schemes to break into officers' houses to steal plans which was Section H's work. So eventually we tipped the Boers off as to where he was, just to get him out of the way, and they dutifully picked him up and put him in a POW camp. He was on parole – which meant he gave his word of honour as a gent that he would not escape – and so then first chance he gets he escapes, leaving behind the officers banged up with him in the camp. The Boers went mad and started torturing our officers, which of course the old boys protested is not cricket. Apparently they can torture up to the rank of sergeant but nothing above that. So then they scrapped the parole system, which meant our officers were put in the regular prison camp with the men. Caused a huge amount of fuss. 'It's the toilet situation,' Colonel Peterson said. It became a huge phrase in the war and everyone said it all the time after that. 'Anything wrong, sergeant?' 'It's the toilet situation, sir,' and we all creased up just like sniggering schoolboys. The officers hated it.

"But it was out of all that mess that Section H was formed, and I put away my rifle and trained as a thief. Churchill continued to be a total embarrassment so I broke into the local Boer colonel's house one night and left papers that showed that Boer secrets that were leaking out through our postal intercepts had actually come from Churchill. The Boers said they'd let his dishonour pass if we took him out – and Colonel Edmunds handed the honourable gent over to me. After that I had the job of keeping Churchill drunk until I could put him on a boat home."

"And he really did escape and abandon the officers knowing they'd be tortured?" she asked going back to the origin of the problem.

"Churchill's version that he told me was that he went through the defences of the prison camp first – which would be an act of bravery and bravado – but as he slipped through the guards came round and caught the officers. Who knows if that is true or not? But his decision to break parole did increase the reprisals and torture. Eventually we rounded up all the women and children and put them in the concentration camps, where they caught cholera and died."

She looked chilled, but we all knew the story, and let it pass.

"And what did you think of him – Mr Churchill?"

"He's from a different league from me – he could be from the sun as far as my life is concerned. Main thing I remember was his enthusiasm and recklessness. We did breaking and entering as planned military operations with routine checks for days before, look outs, back ups, fall back positions, everything. The idea was to fool the Boers into thinking they had a traitor in their own ranks who was passing information to us – and it worked. Churchill on the other hand would say, 'What fun – what absolute fun' and just go rushing in, flick a lock and shout 'Yeeee" at the top of his voice. Amazingly he got away with it, but it was nerve racking. Funny thing is, he always said he'd put a word in for me when we got back from South Africa, but I'm not sure he remembered."

"Are you saying he got you promoted?"

"No, but he was decent in his own way, and did his bit to help the ranks. That's why the officers disliked him – he was concerned about the living conditions of the privates and corporals. No one else was."

"So you worked as a thief?"

"I was a thief, when the Empire needed a thief," I corrected her. Somehow I got the feeling that all the rest of it was irrelevant. Maybe she had a thing for thieves.

Wednesday 9th February

If I am going to find a long-term series of pieces that the Chron wants, if I am going to follow the Norris story, if I am going to develop my career, and if I am to develop a relationship with Marie, I think I am going to have to calm down on the street life. Stick to playing with the band – which is becoming quite a local success story. I'm not stopping the Monkey Parade totally, but maybe if I cut the drink a bit...

However... there was an amusing situation at the White Hart where a fight broke out as usual about 8 o'clock. Five doors down at the Green Dragon there was also a punch-up going on, and by chance something blew up between some women in the Red Lion across the road.

Without warning all three merged and the whole of the Lane exploded as a single fight which spread outwards in all directions – down the road, through the gardens, up the walls, into Devonshire Hill Lane... A few of us got up onto the railings in Empire Parade and you could see the whole thing flow into the Cambridge Road. Charlie from the band was there so we started singing Bill Bailey and banging the railings. Got the whole crowd going.

Eventually the peelers turned up – late as always – took a look at it and blew their whistles for a while. One of them – name of Don – climbed up next to us, and turned out to be a character I'd met when covering a game or two at Tottenham. I already had him down as a decent bloke with a sense of humour, and he enjoyed the spectacle as much as I did. He even joined in the singing and banging until his sergeant turned up and told him to behave himself. About midnight we went to the Dog and Duck for a nightcap, and I told him what I was working on.

He said he thought Woolwich would close down – and he didn't hold out much hope for Fulham, given the rise of Chelsea. He thought the Ironsides over at West Ham stood a better chance than either of the clubs I was interested in and would get out of the Southern League in the next year or so.

And I thought... Supposing the police know all about the spies, because they are fairly obvious and inept. But maybe with the anarchists they are really in the dark... And the anarchists use the spy stories as a cover for their activities...

When we left at two o'clock there was still fighting going on up and down the Lane and I had to take a detour to get back home. Late night again.

Thursday 10th February

Marie told me at lunch that Norris will try to stand as an MP for the Unionists. He won't get a seat this time, but will do eventually.

My news to her was less exciting: I said that Fulham had announced that they will play a friendly against Woolwich on Saturday "to help raise funds for the club." Put one and one together and Norris is edging towards making Woolwich his third club.

I persuaded Marie to sneak me into the Times so I could see Jimmy Craig. My story was that I might have something for him in return, although in truth I didn't know what.

Craig's a good guy. He could look down on me, of course, because I didn't do the university thing, but he doesn't. He's straight, treats me like a regular writer, and a while back when he introduced me to one of his seniors he mentioned my doing important and "rather hush-hush" work with the War Office on coming back from southern Africa.

Once I got in to see him I came clean: I told Craig I was trying to put together an understanding of Norris the man.

Craig's view is that Norris "wants to conquer London". He wants to be the biggest property developer in London, the man who can talk to the top people, the biggest fixer in the place, the man they call on when they need something done. "A friend of knights, lords, bishops and the common man," were Craig's exact words. "The number of people in the capital is going up year on year, most of the world's trade runs through the place, and it's too easy for those of us who live here to forget that this is the capital not just of Great Britain but also of the world. But Norris knows that simple fact. Hence his philosophy: be King of London, and you are King of the World.

"He imagines that, in a crisis like the current one where the Lords are blocking the budget, Mr Asquith will call him and say, 'Have a word with them and strike up a deal, will you, old man'?

"Norris sees everything as being up for sale – from the girls in the West End to government office; he's in the market and he's buying – although in saying that, I'd better qualify it to say there's nothing to suggest he is not faithful to his lady wife – he's not like Asquith or Lloyd George. He'll buy his place in Parliament, and he'll probably buy himself a stately home when the next bubble bursts and the next bunch of lords go bust. Eventually he'll seriously ask for the King's telephone number so he can give him a ring after lunch and ask His Majesty to see to some small spot of bother he has with some houses he's built. He wants a knighthood first, then a peerage. And he'll either make a total fool of himself and be laughed out of the country or he'll get everything he is after.

"What he has worked out (and many have yet to realise) is that the old families used to go on for centuries – but now they are lucky if they get to hold their place in society for one hundred years before getting knocked down by gambling debts, bad business ventures, income tax...

"The old world changes – they're all squeaking and I'll bet you he'll be in there picking up the pieces. The world belongs to people like Norris and you, Jacko, and you'd make a better fist of it than he would." (He meant that both Norris and I had left school at 14.)

Then he gave me the final spike that made me forget his compliment. "He'll buy the Archbishop of Canterbury if he needs to – and probably get him at a reduced price for being used goods."

I told Craig about the oil terminal and Fulham's ground. He made a note about it, but then shrugged with a look of, "That's exactly what I've been telling you," and let me draw my own conclusions.

"He won't last – none of them ever do," he added. "London eats the people who try to eat London," which I thought was rather neat. He saw me write it down, and told me to lay off! I apologised and said I had no intention of using his phrase, but I didn't make much of a fist of it and felt embarrassed.

I then asked about spies and anarchists, and he said he'd seen my recent pieces. (Two conversations, two readers. I am getting famous). He told me to carry on with it. "I don't know where you are taking this, but you are talking sense. If the Germans invade they won't bother to sail along the Channel where everyone can see them. Out in the North Sea no one will know they are there. They could be there now for all we know. Same with the anarchists. Put them in a cellar and they will sit there for months plotting, planning and making bombs."

I thanked him profusely, and paid for the drinks.

Friday 11th February

Despite my earlier resolution I stayed out on the town last night and had something revolting at Pie Corner and then had to buy a Lilly and Vinegar to try and calm myself down.

No more of that from now on – it's mum's cooking and the Lyons Corner House with Marie.

Through the upset stomach I tried to think: if Norris really wants to be the top dog in the top city, what is he doing playing with the likes of Fulham, Croydon and Woolwich? Does he really think that this buys him power and influence?

Maybe it will give him the look of one in touch with the common man. Ask anyone what the working man does and the answer is drink and watch football. Being a brewer is not good news these days, so becoming Mr Football in London might imply you have the ear of the common man, without annoying the temperance groups. Also he must reckon that eventually the London teams are going to take on the midlands and the north – and knock them off their perch. Being Mr Football and a Unionist MP could be an interesting (if unexpected) combination.

So far he has Woolwich Arsenal in Division 1, Fulham in Division 2, and Croydon Common in the Southern League, the ear of the Football League and of the Church of England and is planning a seat in the Commons.

I took out a new sheet and tried a different line. Assume most of Germany has already moved to England to spy on us, Germany would then be empty and thus representing a great opportunity for expansion – which our folk would have taken. I liked that – the invasions are over and we have swapped sides. We are now German, and so are presumably about to invade Austria-Hungary.

I wrote it up.

Saturday 12th February

England played Ireland in the Home Championship in Belfast and got a 1-1 draw. For me it was back to Woolwich with Edward for the utterly awful Arsenal 0 Blackburn Rovers 1. I wrote…

Woolwich Arsenal met with Blackburn Rovers in the Football League Division I on Saturday. With a fierce wind blowing across the pitch, it was too cold for standing on the terraces, so the majority of the fans gathered in a hot air balloon hovering just over the centre circle. Both teams were weak in shooting throughout the game and, although it appeared nothing could be worse than the opening session, after the turnabout it was so awful I lost consciousness and had to be revived by our trusty photographer.

It then got worse again.

Then a little while later it got worse.

Towards the end of the game one of the Blackburn men scored, but by then most of the crowd had departed. However, those who remained were so outraged and so cold that they jumped down from their flying machine, invaded the playing field and attacked the referee, who walked off the field, returning only after five minutes when order had been restored. Hot punch and rum were not served, so the death toll among the hardcore fans is likely to be high.

If it is true that there are German spies on every street corner, the simplest way to defeat their dastardly plans is to force them to watch the next game at Woolwich Arsenal. Their pleas for mercy will be heard across the North Sea, and the German fleet will arrive, not to invade, but to take its advance guard home.

I persuaded Edward to take a picture of the empty ground after everyone had gone, and gave it the caption, "one of the highlights of Saturday's game", but just in case Mr Holloway had not suddenly discovered the notion of humour I also included the picture of the on-pitch riot.

Given the chance I think I'd sooner write about Thomas Crapper.

In the evening Marie gave me a copy of "Our Waifs and Strays", a quaint monthly which supports homeless children. Apparently her family are strong supporters of the organisation which is run by a friend of her mother's.

I can imagine what my mother would say if I showed it to her. "We've enough problems looking after ourselves, no time for others". Or, "God helps them that helps themselves." Or some such.

Sunday 13th February

"So now you know better than anyone," said Mr Holloway. A good opening line, I felt. He was on form.

I said nothing. He was reading my piece on spies. We hadn't got to yesterday's game yet.

"Apart from anything else, you are telling our readership that you have got this spy business sorted."

I said nothing.

"However, that was not the main thing that concerned the people on the fifth floor. Rather it is your assertion that you can tell an anarchist by the hat. If it weren't for the fact that you have just made that up I would say you couldn't make such rubbish up.

"I would also say that you could not sink any lower, were it not for the fact that you then went on to say that the people we should be wary of are not Germans but Latvians. Do you know any Latvians? Or, come to that, any milliners?"

I admitted that I did not.

"Overall this is probably the most stupid piece of writing I have ever had the misfortune to read, until I read your report of the Blackburn game at Woolwich."

I said nothing.

"Go away," he said eventually.

"Can I hand in a replacement slogan for the picture?"

I slid across a picture of the game in progress with the caption on the reverse saying "Our waifs and strays".

He threw a book at me. As I ducked he said, "There's a tale doing the rounds that Edward the Caresser died last year and has been replaced by a bookcase." I said that this one had passed me by but I would ask my informants down the pub in case they had heard.

Monday 14th February

I made page 13 with my spy story. It was chopped around, and they cut the bit about Latvians, but spies and hats were still there.

Come to that, so was the Woolwich report and Edward's picture and my new caption.

Tuesday 15th February

Edward spent the morning saying he still didn't understand why the picture of the match was funny.

Marie brought yesterday's Times to lunch and showed me the report on the international just to prove that they do carry some football – even if they don't do club games. What I like about the Times is that they call the game "Association Rules".

"England and Ireland drew at Belfast on Saturday, each side having scored one goal. The game was watched by a crowd of 25,000 people. The match was not a great one, and there were several comparative failures...."

It read as if they had had as boring a day as I had.

"Tell me about you," I said.

Wednesday 16th February

Back to Woolwich with Edward in tow, following a report that there was disquiet among the working men at the factory. Mr Holloway said he chose me because I knew the area so well.

We found several hundred disgruntled men and women standing in Dial Square being harangued by, of all people, my old anarchist mate George Barrett. Edward looked in amazement, having never seen a factory before, and I pointed out the Yellow Men, with their stained hair and skin, who worked in the TNT rooms.

Barrett was putting up a good show talking about the need to remove the apparatus of the state, but it was clear that the men wanted to talk about one thing and one thing only: their jobs. It seemed that they had just been told that the torpedo factory was going to be closed and moved to Glasgow.

Barrett told them that the government never thinks about the ordinary man and women, but the men and women of the arsenal were not in the mood for theory. When one firebrand leapt up, pushed Barrett aside and demanded that they "march on the bosses' offices and demand a change now", it got a roar of cheering, and the march was on.

I went over to see George – and consoled him on his failure. He took it all in good heart, as always. Talk to him privately and he is the mildest of men – and he has a twinkle in his voice which is what makes us friends.

"You're still with the enemy," he said, as I introduced Edward, who duly obliged by taking George's photograph.

"Undermining from within," I told him, and we settled on that.

Edward was for following the riot indoors, but I took both of them off to the Hen and Basket and bought a couple of rounds and some pies from the stall in the roadway. Being an anarchist doesn't pay too well apparently, and following rioters indoors usually results in a biff on the head. In return for sustenance, George gave me the story.

The torpedo factory was going to the Clyde, and removals were starting at once. 500 workers would go with it as fast as new accommodation could be found. The rest would lose their jobs. As to why the factory was moving, no one had a clue.

After an hour we wandered back to Dial Square to find a new meeting in progress. The management had called the police, who had assumed that their role was to protect the bosses. This was achieved by restricting the workers' movements to the square and threatening that if the workers didn't go back to work the cavalry would be called in. The masses (in retaliation) were now debating strike action. I told Edward to take two pictures and then, no matter what, to get back to Fleet Street and get them printed. "No matter what," I shouted above the hubbub.

Barrett immediately started edging his way to the platform, but as he made it onto the steps two constables pushed forward and arrested him, quickly hustling him out and into a police wagon that had pulled up outside.

I found a more leisurely form of transport in the form of the horse-drawn cab and ambled into the police station ten minutes later. After a further half hour a sergeant came out, said he didn't want any trouble-making journalists in his station, and then arrested me when I wrote down what he had said. Rather amusingly they threw me in the same cell as Barrett.

"You are in for…" I asked.

"Raising questions," he said with a smile. "And you are in for…"

"Asking questions," I replied. "Between us we make quite a pair: the questioning men. We should be on the music hall."

"Bring your new friend Edward along and we could be Two Questioning Men and a Toff," he said, and we spent the next hour alternatively working out our routine, and falling about with laughter. "I say," said George, "What's the difference between a soldier and a policeman?" I said I didn't know, and George said, "You can't slip a policeman into a boiled egg."

In the end it got too much for the police, and they shouted at us to shut up, but we just put that into the act, and George asked if laughing was a crime. We became a pair of song and dance men.

Ultimately we were called into an interview room where George worked himself into a diatribe on the need for constables to resist the reactionary forces which were keeping their salaries so low and their hours so long. Property, that great English tradition, was the root of the evil. It was not so in other countries such as France where property had been abolished in 1789 and everyone shared everything (including the women) for the common good. Here we had the dictatorship of the incredibly stupid, so that intelligent people like these police constables, men who would work for the common good, were subverted into a system where they were set against their fellow workers – such as the good men of Woolwich – whose only crime was to try to secure their own jobs when the government, on a whim, decided to move the factory to Glasgow.

Not surprisingly, with George still working on his theory, I got called out first – and was told to be on my way but to avoid the munitions factories in future. Dutifully I stood in the entrance lobby while saying that I was just gathering material for a music hall double act, and asking for the exact reason why I had been detained. I thought we were going to go through the routine again when an inspector who had a slightly better idea of how to handle the press came out.

Mr Barrett was being questioned about his speeches, I was told, which were thought to be liable to cause a breach of the peace, not to mention undermine the well-being of His Majesty's police force and disrupt the protection of the nation. I had been arrested through a misunderstanding, and I was thanked for my co-operation. It was likely that Mr Barrett would be released shortly. Thank you and goodbye.

I didn't leave. Instead I asked if the inspector had noticed Mr Barrett's hat. "He was not wearing a hat when in his cell," said the inspector seriously.

I suggested that it might be worth checking if it had got knocked off during his arrest. Inevitably the inspector asked why this might be of significance, and I feigned surprise that he had not read the article in the Chronicle which analysed anarchist activity and revealed how the hat worn was a signal to other anarchists relating to the plans and the way they were going. The inspector thanked me for my co-operation and said he would investigate further when other duties permitted.

On my journey back to north London I sketched out a new piece noting that the Kent Constabulary were confirming the importance of hat-wear in the tracking down of anarchists by sending out special hat squads under an officer of inspectorial rank. Plus a review of George Barrett's activities with the constables when the hierarchy were off having muffins. "Who guards England when it's time for tea?" was the question of the day, I felt, and I noted that the anarchist's greatest weapon was the fact that he didn't stop for conventional meal breaks. "If we are to survive," I wrote, "we will have to learn from this frightening experience in the Woolwich police station." I also suggested that the anarchists were about to start putting their message across via the music hall stage.

I handed in my piece on anarchists, the Kent police, the hat squads, music hall and tea-time, but kept back the story on the torpedo factory. That seemed like harder news, and I wanted to consult with Marie before I produced the final copy. And I needed Edward's pictures, but he seemed to have gone home.

Two hours later Mr Holloway told me that I was to go to Manchester with Edward to cover the opening of the new Manchester United ground. As I let the notion sink in he told me he also needed someone to investigate a report that the Astronomer Royal had said that the earth really is made of poetry.

I have no idea if my trip to the north is a reward for a brilliant article which set the beacon for a new standard in English journalism, or if the boss is so fed up with me that he's decided to get us out of the office as much as possible.

The trip takes out Friday and Saturday nights: no Parade, no Marie. But it has the compensation of giving me a chance to chat with the men from Athletic News and the Manchester Guardian, who will all be there in force.

Thursday 17th February

I enlarged my piece on the removal of the torpedo factory and turned in a serious article reporting on the trouble at the gunnery, while suggesting that this sudden move confirmed that the real danger in the government's eyes was from the German invasion across the North Sea – exactly as Childers had predicted in *Riddle of the Sands*. The government clearly does not want one of its main manufacturing bases taken out in the first wave of attack, I postulated, although I couldn't help wondering if there was something else going on in the background. After all, if they were moving out the torpedo shop, why not the rest of the works?

At lunchtime I managed to get to see Marie and gave her the rundown on yesterday and asked for suggestions (other than the Riddle of the Sands explanation) as to why they might be moving the factory.

"There's been trouble in Wales with the mines and trouble in Scotland, the Suffragettes are always causing mayhem and if your anarchist friends get their act together there's more from that quarter," she said. "So they move manufacturing from the untroubled areas to troubled areas to smooth things down – forgetting that that probably causes more civil unrest in the area that loses the jobs. The theory is that people in work with decent pay don't join revolutions, and the workers they move back to Scotland have Scottish roots. I suspect it is a step on the way towards widening the franchise in Scotland."

We walked along to the Times offices and started to check their archives. What we found were two full scale riots, both taking place on New Year's Day (a big holiday in Scotland apparently) in 1898 and 1905. What was interesting was that the reports of both events were also football stories. They involved the Glasgow clubs Rangers and Celtic. The newspaper stories blamed not the supporters in the ground but the police – quite a radical stance for the Times. There was also some talk of beer being a problem and, presumably because it was Scotland, scotch.

After that we found the Hampden riot last year. What was interesting was that both our papers covered the story with a similar emphasis – that the problem was with the officials and the police not being clear about whether there would be extra time or not after a draw – and the feeling locally that the match had been fixed in order to play another game and so get extra gate money.

It was also clear who won. (Marie didn't like using the notion of winner or loser in a riot, but then she hasn't been in the army where the facts are recorded for all to see.) 7,000 members of the crowd beat up the police, attacked the fire brigades, and burned large parts of the ground. 1-0 to the audience.

"What must worry the officials is that the Times is openly blaming the authorities," said Marie. "Also it looks like they had a riot, and then went home to sleep it off. But supposing they had decided they had other grievances and had not gone home."

"Such as what?" I asked.

"Rule from England. High taxes. Bad housing. Low wages (which is the cause of the problems in Wales). The fact that the rumour went around that the game was fixed suggests that anything could happen. Supposing your anarchist friend at Woolwich had been there, whipping up the cause…"

"But games are fixed," I said. "Everyone knows that."

"Are they?" she said. She seemed genuinely surprised.

I gave her the look, and she realised I meant it and that I was surprised she didn't know. I then gave her the lowdown on the football pools, and she added that psychologically (a word I was starting to get used to) that meant that the people at the game would feel they were being used by the betting rings, and that was as good a reason for a riot as losing your job.

We kept digging through the archives, and found an article in the Times that said all football matches in Scotland should be policed by soldiers with fixed bayonets.

Marie wanted to know what I, as a solider, thought of that. I told her that, as far as I had seen, the notion that soldiers were an organised unit that killed the right people in the right place at the right time was a total fantasy. Soldiers would obey, for not to do so was treason. The problem was that the officers were generally incompetent and gave the wrong orders at the wrong time, so the soldiers generally shot the wrong people at the wrong time.

"So what are we saying?" I asked. "That the torpedo factories are being moved to Glasgow because…"

"Because the government is scared of rioting in Scotland, and they think that a group of Scottish working men who have been civilised in Kent are going to calm everything down, and that they believe Germany is about to invade across the North Sea. Both or either or neither."

Marie was still flipping through archive newspapers as she spoke, but then suddenly stopped and shouted, "I remember this from my studies. It was a headline that read, 'The workers of Clydeside are imbued with a 'spirit of revolt'."

We looked at each other.

And then she said something utterly remarkable. So remarkable I wrote it down there and then. She said, "Supposing this is the start. Supposing the government has the plan that if they do this often enough – if they move enough men from one place to another – they can stop rioting and regain control of the country. Maybe there is a government department for disrupting society to preserve law and order."

I looked at her, and then kissed her.

"I could run this as a story," I said. And then realised what I had said. "I'm sorry – it is your story, of course I can't run it."

"You can," Marie said, "for the simple reason that it is not a story the Times would even consider for a second. Especially when written by a mere woman."

"I could put you down as co-author," I said.

"And lose me my job! Do you know how hard it is for a woman to get a job in Fleet Street? Since the Daily Mirror ran its all-woman edition and failed to sell anything at all, no one will use a woman anywhere other than in the canteen. If they saw I had worked on anything that the Chronicle was running I would be out of the door. 'Given the empty' is the saying, I believe."

So it was my story. I went back to the office and wrote it up. The torpedo factory. Forget the popular reasons why they might move it and think instead of the rioting in Scotland, Wales, and indeed Ireland. Think of the suffragettes, and then think on this: a government policy of displacement, to stop anarchists, miners, factory workers and even suffragettes taking control.

I handed it in, went home and prepared to get the Friday train to Manchester with Edward.

Saturday 19th February

Having spent a journey with Edward, who proclaimed in a loud voice that he had never travelled third class before, and then spent the night in one of the dirtiest "hotels" (I use the word in its widest sense) in the Kingdom, I did my job by covering the social side of the first match at Manchester United's new ground, Old Trafford, where the home side dutifully lost by 3 goals to 4 against Liverpool.

Edward took pictures of the impressive new ground before, during and after, and I explained to him why this was a perfect example of a fixed match – the Manchester team couldn't put two passes together.

The hacks handout says the ground cost £60,000. It has a capacity of 80,000 and looked just about full to me, so I guess they will be making quite a packet on each game. And, would you believe it, it was designed by none other than Archibald Leitch: the man who worked on the stand at Woolwich, who designed the crumbling ground at Chelsea – about which I wanted to write something anyway – and who worked for Norris at Fulham.

And would you believe it (again) Mr Leitch himself was there and I got an interview and Edward another picture.

First surprise, the chap is Scots, although I suppose with the name "Archie" I ought to have guessed. His first big job was Ibrox Park for Glasgow Rangers in 1899. I wrote down a lot of stuff about balustrades and pediments which I didn't understand, but trusted that we would have someone in the office who could decipher it, and maybe use as a separate piece. It was only after I had finished the interview that Alfie Jardine from Athletic News (yet another man who said he was enjoying my new approach to football) tapped me on the shoulder and told me that in 1902 one of the terraces at Ibrox fell down and over 20 people died. Given that, I am amazed that anyone would ever use Leitch again – and that throws the crumbling terrace at Chelsea into a new light.

Anyway, Alfie turned out to be a source of all knowledge about Manchester, especially in return for a few drinks. I wrote it all up and, as a bit of a joke, called the ground "the most handsomest, the most spacious and the most remarkable arena I have ever seen. As a football ground it is unrivalled in the world, it is an honour to Manchester and the home of a team who can do wonders when they are so disposed."

I thought that was quite funny, although I expect it will get cut, so I then did a piece on how ugly most footballers are. "Put them out on the streets," I said, "and they would look like huge louts. The police would be on their tail, and they would not have to look at the footballers' hats for their ears and flat heads would give them away. That is why gentlemen do not play football. It is not that they cannot – because there is nothing in the class system that says that a gent ain't got the muscle power to kick a ball. It is the look. If you look like a gent, you go into the arts and write books that no one can understand about other books that no one has read. Look like a thug with flappy ears, and you end up playing professional football. Indeed the situation is so bad that footballers now have to carry identity cards so as to assure the local constabulary that they are not German spies."

That should teach him to send me to Manchester.

At Edward's insistence we travelled back second class. I told him George and I were going on the stage and wanted Edward as part of the act. Wouldn't you know it, he'd acted while at school, and said he would love to.

Sunday 20th February

I went into the office to file my report and catch up on the other results. Tottenham had lost by 3 goals to 2 at Swindon. So much for my family's views of them being the great London team.

Apparently it was even worse at Woolwich where Mr Norris' grand plan of a friendly seemed to have come unstuck. It wasn't the score which really attracted my attention (Woolwich 2 Fulham 2) but the attendance. While I had been sitting with 70,000 people or so, the attendance at the Manor was a grand 950. The gate money (according to our source in the counting house) was £30 2s 6d, although that was probably over the top.

What Norris, Leavey and that Dr Clarke who is running the appeal committee at Woolwich have not yet grasped, is that Woolwich is a working man's club, playing a working man's game.

I think I'm fairly tough about town, and I know I was tough when fighting in the Orange Free State, but sometimes I sit in the journalist box at Plumstead and look in the faces of the factory workers and I can feel my knees shake. How Edward has managed to put his fancy costume on and take all their comments when he's photographing the game is beyond me.

I finished my articles from the weekend and added notes about two other articles that I wanted to research: one on Leitch, linking Ibrox with Chelsea, and whether Leitch should go on designing grounds, and the other on the power that football gives the working man.

I was still working on this when the boss came over and told me that the torpedo article would run tomorrow. "They liked Edward's pictures," he said, just to wipe the smile off my face.

Monday 21st February

I got up late to the sound of noise in the house. Wandered downstairs and found that half the street was in the sitting room. Mum was serving tea and cakes. I was still wearing a dressing gown and was very much unshaven. My entrance caused a riot – mostly emanating from mum.

Ten minutes and I was back, bright and jolly, because as I had turned to walk back up the stairs I had caught site of the Chronicle. Actually not just one Chron, but about twenty. And on page one was the giant headline:

Government moves gunnery to Glasgow
Fear of German invasion
By our Woolwich Correspondent, J. Jones
Special photographer, Edward Buckingham

41

I smiled at everyone and took in the spirit of the occasion, graciously acknowledging their kind regards and good wishes while mum announced that she had always said I would be a success, and how the English teacher at school had told her that I showed great promise, and now I was the top reporter in Fleet Street, and how every paper wanted me to write for them.

Occasionally neighbours went out as others arrived, while children stood in the road and made faces at those inside the house. And then suddenly there was a commotion – a knock at the door followed by my mother walking back in saying "'Ere, there's a toff at the door asking to see you. What's 'e want?" I told her I would not have a clue without actually setting eyes on him, and perhaps if she might just step aside a little I would go without and investigate. She was about to cuff me round the ear when she remembered she still had half the street in the house, so she pretended she was adjusting her hair and returned to offering more tea and cakes.

Outside it was Edward, not in his work clothes, but in his even more expensive and spiffing top-hole top-hat top-drawer leisure clothing.

"I'm terribly sorry to bother you," he said, "but I wondered if you have seen the paper?"

"Paper?" I said, gently closing the door behind me so he couldn't see inside. "Today's paper?"

"Yes, you see…"

"Do you mean the Chronicle?"

"Yes, because…"

I turned back to the house. "Mother do we happen to have the Chronicle in the house…." And then as I turned back he saw me laughing, and we grabbed each other and swung round and round and danced in the street and screamed "Yes yes yes" and then for absolutely no sane reason, and with no explanation, we suddenly started singing…

By the light, of the silvery moon,
I want to spoon,
To my honey I'll croon love's tune.
Honey moon, keep a-shinin' in June.
Your silv'ry beams will bring love's dreams,
We'll be cuddlin' soon,
By the silvery moon.

And then we found the party from inside the house was now outside the house, with mother looking ready to call the bobbies except that half her guests were now joining in, so she couldn't stop us. And at the end of the second verse we all cheered, and mum was forced to look as if this was all part of the celebration she wanted.

Eventually we went back inside, and I said, "Mother, this is the Rt Hon Edward Buckingham-Fitzurse," and mum nearly fell over and called him "Your Grace", and Edward said, "I say, how did you know my name – I'm sure I never told you," and I confessed I had got the inside track from Marie. Then I told everyone that Edward was England's most famous photographer, and he had taken the pictures of the anarchists' meeting at Woolwich, and Edward said, "I say, steady on!" and everyone thought he was great and asked us to sing again, so we paraded up and down the street in front of the house, arm in arm, like a music hall act, and sang "Silvery Moon" one more time.

And then Edward blushed, said, "Oh I say," and "Steady on" quite a lot, apologised several times for arriving unannounced and for interrupting our busy day, and yes a cup of tea would be most charming, thank you Mrs Jones, and on, and on, interrupted every twenty seconds by the two of us bursting into laughter.

Eventually we decided we had to go into town. By tomorrow there would be a new paper and a new headline and (we feared) we'd be forgotten. I wanted my moment and I guess so did Edward. Edward insisted on calling a cab when one passed us in Green Lanes, and we arrived in time to gather the troops and call them into the pub. Edward went into the Times to collect Marie who had already called Sophia and they joined us moments later and gave us kisses, which led to huge cheers.

At 3 o'clock Mr Holloway sent a runner into the Nag's to demand our immediate attendance within.

There was a formal-looking man sitting with him who was introduced as Charles Willis, from the Labour Party. He told me my work was a brilliant piece of writing, complimented Edward too, and then asked me for my sources.

Fortunately (since I had no source for the displacement policy story other than the gossip at the factory, Marie's theory and my imagination) I was saved the embarrassment of a confession by the boss's intervention. "I've told Mr Willis that journalists don't reveal sources," he said. "But he is interested in you following up the story – finding out more examples of this government's policy."

I had to think, and think quick – as well as ensuring that Edward remained silent. That was tough, given the alcohol consumption of the last three hours.

"Mr Willis," I said with all the formality I could muster, "I have a feeling that there may have been more moves like this, but I don't as yet have the exact evidence. I was rather hoping that a Member of Parliament might follow up our work and would ask a question about how many other factories have suddenly been removed from their natural base. It is possible that this is the first in a campaign…"

"I see, I see," says he. "I will get my Parliamentary colleagues to ask, of course, of course, yes, of course. But if you can find another episode… Ramsay McDonald is planning to make a particularly powerful speech on the issue of government employees in a debate on the 7th of next month, and I know he would be most grateful if you could supply more evidence. Most grateful."

"I will see what I can come up with," I said, and with that we were dismissed.

Once Mr Willis had left I went back to Mr Holloway and confessed there was nothing more to the story. At least nothing that would get past the fifth floor.

"I know that," said the boss, much to my relief. "Every idiot knows that. But politicians make idiots like you look like university dons. They believe anything, and you'll know if you really have a story, right enough."

"How's that?" I asked.

"Because a member of the government will come knocking at the door, demanding to know how you found out. If that happens you are on to something. If not, we got extra sales, extra publicity, you two got a party in the pub, and people will be looking for your next article. You had better make it good. There's a report of a dead zebra that has turned into..."

"Next article?" I stammered.

"Dear boy," he said in his top patronising tone. "You have just accused the government – our beloved leaders whom we all hold in the highest regard – of deliberately moving men hundreds of miles across the kingdom, disrupting their families at goodness knows what cost to the Exchequer in terms of houses and allowances, in a secret plot to stop civil unrest in Scotland. More, you accuse them of covering it all up. Your next story is going to have to beat that. Now what can the famous Jacko Jones write about? I know – 'Government moving to Mars to avoid anarchist hat problem.' Or 'Street urchin and toff sing By the Light of the Silvery Moon so loud in cab that driver puts them out half a mile from destination for being drunk.'"

"How do you know that?" I asked.

"This is a bleedin' paper, you moronic imitation of a flower seller's bucket emptier. We're supposed to know what goes on."

"But I don't have another story," I bleated, not even bothering to correct the point of detail as to how far we were from Fleet Street when the cabbie threw us out.

"Then find one," he said. "Or pray that the government comes knocking. Meanwhile, there's a report of a wild boar terrorising office workers in Oxford Street. Can you cover that?"

I decided to pray.

Tuesday 22nd February

Still worried about the next story I went to the Times offices across the road and asked for Marie. She was not there. Apparently she was working on a piece about a man called Houdini who had flown a plane across Australia.

I went back to the Chronicle and scratched my head for a bit. The only story I hadn't worked up was Leitch – and that was not really headline news unless I tried to suggest that a significant number of our country's football grounds were unsafe.

To stay with the factory removal theme I needed another armaments workforce on the move, and the only factory like that which I really knew about apart from Woolwich was the Royal Small Arms factory at Enfield Lock. And I only knew about that because we went out that way once on a family trip from Wood Green.

I looked them up and found they made the Lee Enfield rifle that we had used in Africa. Trouble is, last time I'd read about the place in the Wood Green Herald it seemed to be expanding, rather than being moved somewhere else.

And then the world fell in. A messenger came in and said that I was required in Whitehall and that a motor car was downstairs. Edward said, "What fun!" and so I picked up my coat and went with the boy, and there was a motorcar outside with a driver.

I had never been in a motor car before in my life – the moment will live with me forever. I got inside, and was transfixed, amazed, and just stunned as we drove to Whitehall through the omnibuses, hansoms, and, of course, other motorised traffic. Everywhere along the way people looked and I looked back, trying to find an expression that said, "My man drives me around in one of these machines every day." It was only as we arrived that I realised I had no idea what I was stepping into, who I was seeing, why I was seeing whoever it was, and that I didn't even have a notebook with me.

The only government building I know is the War Office, and I knew we weren't there, so I just meekly sat down in a corridor. Then I stood for a while, walked up and down, and sat, and repeated the routine maybe 200 times, or maybe I was only there for a couple of minutes before I was ushered into an office.

Two men stood talking at the window looking down into Whitehall, their backs to me. The flunky introduced me and left. One man turned but stayed by the window. The other walked over to me with his hand outstretched, and said, "Jacko. How are you dear boy?"

I shook the hand and looked at him, stupidly, with mouth agape. He burst into laughter. "Don't ya recognise me, old man?" he said.

And of course I did. Who could not? His picture is regularly in the paper. I work for a paper. I read a paper. I ought to know.

"Winnie," I said, and then I clasped my hand to my mouth in mock horror, stood back and saluted. "Sir, I do beg your pardon, I meant no offence…"

And he just laughed, knowing I was playing the game, while the fellow at the window stayed where he was, looking stern. He had a long thin face with tight lips that looked as if they never smiled.

Mr Churchill on the other hand had got his lisp more under control, and still had that ability to switch between easy familiarity and the hard authority of an aristo used to getting his way.

"Compared with what you called me in Pretoria," he said, "that is the mildest word under the sun. Come, come, we are friends." He turned to the older man. "Captain Vernon Kell," he said, pulling me forward, "Sergeant Jack Jones."

"Now, Jacko, my boy," he continued, turning back to me, "come and sit down, and let's talk man to man, as we did before." I took my place opposite him by the desk. Captain Kell did not sit. "You helped me in Africa, Jacko," he said, "and I'm dashed ashamed to say I need yer help again. Can you do it, boy? Can yer?"

"It depends what it is, Home Secretary," I said.

"See," said Mr Churchill, "it's that dashed story of yours. Story about the moving of the torpedo factory to Glasgow. Where did you get it, boy?"

I thought on my feet or rather, since I was sitting, on another part of my anatomy, and for once that part of me came out good. (Mr Holloway would not have been surprised.)

"You told me, sir."

He looked at me quizzically. "I did?"

"You did, sir. I asked you about being a journalist while we were waiting for your ship – on that day at the docks you gave me some tips. That's why I entered Fleet Street after I left the War Office. I said to you, 'What makes a good journalist?' and you said, 'He follows his nose.' That is what I did. I asked myself, 'Why should a Liberal government start moving workers out of Woolwich, when I know that this will cause problems to the local life of the shopkeepers and people like that? And why should they go to Glasgow?' And I went sniffing – just as you said, sir, "Sergeant Jones, you said, go sniffing. So sniffing I went. Sir."

"And what else did you sniff out, Jacko, besides a story about Woolwich and Greenock?"

"Possible explanations, sir, nothing more."

"Now listen here," said Mr Churchill, his mood suddenly changing. "I need to know what you know about this case and what else you intend to publish. It is a matter of national security, do you see? There's enough rumour and misinformation. Words are weapons in the war now, and they must not be misused."

"When we debriefed in Section H after the war, we looked at all the options," I said. "My job was to read what everyone was writing: *The Battle of Dorking*, *Spies of the Kaiser*, *Riddle of the Sands*, *War of the Worlds*… I looked at stories and tried to make sense of them."

"Battle of Dorking?" said Kell. "Don't recall that campaign."

"Written by George Chesney for Blackwood's Magazine," I said. Blackwood's was the weekly of the political classes – I was making the point that he should have read it. "It tells of the invasion of England by Germany with a band of loyal citizens defending Dorking without news of outside events and with very little food. The story ends in 1920 when England is still devastated from the invasion and unable to recover. These days among the ranks a minor injury or a knock is always attributed to the Battle of Dorking. It's a long term joke, sir."

"So," he replied, "We are being told how to run our defence by a short story from forty years ago."

"I believe Jones is saying that he read *The Battle of Dorking* to see if it might have a relevance to the situation in Africa, and he's reviewed the torpedo story to see if it has wider implications here." I nodded agreement to Churchill, and he gave me a look which said, "the man's an idiot, let him hang himself."

Kell had the look of a man who had read a manual on how to interrogate a junior and was putting it into practice for the first time. The result was comical. I pitched my look straight into his forehead just as we were taught. "What else did you spend your time reading while you were in Africa?" he asked. I told him about *Spies of the Kaiser*.

"Who wrote *Spies of the Kaiser*?" asked Captain Kell with the air of a tired schoolmaster extracting knowledge from the school dunce.

"William Le Queux," I said.

"Can't you arrest him?" He turned to Mr Churchill. "And his publisher."

"Publisher is the Daily Mail," I said much amused. "And you might like to go for the German publisher too. In the German edition the Huns win. In the English edition we win. There's probably a Swiss edition in which they win. Perhaps we should raid every house and remove all copies and have them burned," I added.

Mr Churchill obviously decided to rescue his captain from further punishment. "Even the Home Secretary has problems shutting down newspapers, Captain," he said,

"But we need him to drop the subject and repudiate that story you ran about the torpedo factory," Kell insisted.

"I'm sorry, sir, I can't do that," I said, heart thumping. "I am not sure of the exact laws, but I think the newspapers do have the right to seek out news and to comment on the government, sir."

"God damn it, Jones," shouted Captain Kell. "Mr Churchill told me you were impudent, and by God he was right. What sort of a man are you?"

"A journalist, sir," I replied, and I swear I saw Mr Churchill smirk.

But Kell would not back off. "You will tell me, as a superior officer, what your source for this story is, and I will decide what you do and don't print."

"Proud soldier, sir," I said, "but now demobilised. I don't think you can order me to do anything."

"Once under orders, always under orders, what?" said the Captain. "Sergeant Jones, I arrest you for treason."

There was a moment's silence, and then Mr Churchill spoke. "I disagree with what Sergeant Jones has written, Vernon, but I have the advantage over you. I was with him in Africa, and this young man served his Queen and his country perfectly well. More than perfectly well. He may be an insolent upstart," (I looked up suddenly, but his face beamed back at me) "but it is men like Jones that the Empire is built on – and I'll tell you why.

"When we were under attack in Pretoria – and not an officer in sight – after the first shot Jones was on his feet, he shouted two orders and his men were in place, protecting me as a civilian and protecting the Queen's property. Jones acted without thought, because that was his duty. And the men did it because Jones said do it – which tells you everything you need to know about Jones. Then they stood down and sang a song."

"Sang a song?" Kell was outraged to find that singing had a part to play on the battlefield. "What song?"

"I came to Africa for our dear old Queen," I said, causing Mr Churchill (who had himself heard the lyrics and knew what happened in verse three) to burst into laughter, which he subsequently disguised as a fit of coughing.

"Jacko," he said, upon regaining his composure, "You were right to refuse my request for information. But I would like to talk with you further. Could I offer you a glass at my club?"

I could hardly refuse. We left Captain Kell still fuming at the desk, and got a government car in which we were driven to Brooks's in St James Street. "I'm not actually a member, but they seem have given me an honorary position here," he confided in me, as we were greeted with deference, and led me into what appeared to be the lounge, although it could have been a bar. I ordered a scotch – it was all I could think of having.

"Can we talk totally off the record?" he asked, once the drinks were in place. I agreed – what else could I have done? "I've said I don't want anything else on this story published. I don't know how you got it, but if you are half as good a journalist as you are a soldier you'll have found a way to get more."

I said nothing, unsure of where to take this.

"So how do I persuade you to drop it? Could I appeal to your patriotic duty, to your sense of loyalty to our king, Edward the Caresser?" We both laughed. "I am not sure I can count on you as a supporter of the Liberal Party…"

I would not be drawn on that. "I am a patriot, sir, as you well know, and I am loyal. But I also have a job to do."

"Well," he said, clicking his fingers for more drinks, "what can I offer you? How about I give you a replacement story and you agree to drop this one?"

"That is possible," I said. "But I have an editor who only half believes in me, and I can't chop what has already gone…"

"An editor who gives you as much room as you have had with the torpedo story, thinks you are the gift of God, fallen unto the press. Take my word, he loves you. Demand a pay rise! Tell the old man that the trail is cold, and I will give you something that makes your reputation and does something for me too, eh?" he said. "Is that the deal?"

I agreed it was, and we sat in silence savouring our drinks.

"You know what makes this country great?" he asked at last. I said I didn't know. "It is quite simple – it is people like you. Good, honourable men, who know what's right, and who have imagination. That's what it is. Makes me proud to be British."

We drank to that, went back to his car, and he was dropped back in Whitehall. But then came the wonderful part, for he told the driver to take me home. As we drove up Norfolk Avenue the neighbours came out to look. Mum came out to look. The world came out to look at ordinary, regular Jacko Jones, the man who wrote yesterday's front page news, getting out of the smartest car in the world, and thanking the driver in his uniform, and… oh this is the best bit… him, the driver, calling me "Sir".

My life is complete.

Wednesday 23rd February

I briefed Mr Holloway. He listened in silence and then said, "Now we know the government is anxious. Find out what Captain Kell does. It must be important if he's in an office with the Home Secretary."

And that was it. No telling me to go back to work. Nothing. I just sort of got up and started to wander out of the office. As I got to the door he said, "You have any inside information on this ten foot tall duck they've found in Nottingham?"

I sat down in the typing room and a boy came up and said….

And said…

"Would you like me to get you a coffee or a tea, sir?"

And I said "Yes, a cup of coffee would be good."

Oh, how my life changes.

At lunchtime I met Marie at Lyons and told her everything, and she kissed me and hugged me, and everyone sitting at the other tables cheered, apart from a couple of spinster ladies who tutted and some elderly gents who pretended not to notice but who kept looking over their newspapers.

We took the afternoon off.

After all I am Jacko Jones, confidant of the Home Secretary.

Marie took me to a bookshop in Charing Cross Road and bought me a copy of a novel by George Glendon called *The Emperor of the Air*. "Anarchist rubbish," she said with a smile. "We can't have you getting too carried away."

Friday 25th February

For all the fuss Norris made about making The Chron the place to release football stories, he showed today that he was certainly not going to give up dropping the news anywhere he could get it published. He has a piece today in the West London on the scandal of how much footballers are being paid.

It was, in my opinion, a dozy piece of writing which had no structure and no argument save, "I want to cut my players' salaries so I can make more money."

I wondered if Norris co-ordinated his piece with the Kentish. They said that last weekend's attendance for the game against Fulham was an utter disgrace, and the Woolwich club should shut up shop now, given that there was no local support.

They mentioned how the "big teams" in the north could get 20,000 for a friendly, while Woolwich struggled to get 10,000 for a First Division game.

"Woolwich does not deserve a top team," they said, "Woolwich does not need such a team, because there is no interest in professional football in the area. The owners of this club should allow it to return to the honourable Kentish amateur leagues and play in the FA Cup and the London Challenge Cup. To go further is to betray our heritage as men of Kent."

Saturday 26th February

There being nothing more on the Norris front Edward and I were sent off to Woolwich again – which was a relief because I certainly didn't want to follow Norris to Bradford – wherever that is – for his team's game.

On the train to and from Woolwich I read *The Emperor of the Air*, while Edward read the Times and then the Financial Times. It (The Emperor, not the Times) mainly concerned a bunch of anarchists who speak an international language called Esperanto and build a sensational airship and use it to declare war on society. The leader of the anarchists then makes himself Emperor of the Air (which to me seemed odd for an anarchist) and ignores everything about anarchism. So then all the anarchists who were not in the airship now join forces with the police, whom I thought were their opposition, to fight the Emperor.

At the ground Edward and I tried out some new ideas. He took a few photographs of the Hen and Basket and its clientele, and while he was doing that one old timer told me that Woolwich did have one brilliant player – Charlie Buchan, a 17-year-old apparently playing in the reserves. This old boy claimed to have watched the reserves against Croydon Common. He said that Arsenal won 3-1 and Buchan scored one of the goals.

Back at the ground we found Dick Bartlow, the groundsman whom I'd bought a few drinks for last season, and I asked him. He certainly knew Buchan and said he had played at least three games for the Woolwich team, and had trained twice a week with the team as an amateur – which is fairly common.

But Dick then said the story he had heard was that young Buchan had given the club a bill of 11 shillings for his travel costs to and from the ground. That, I could imagine, would have gone down like a lead sandwich given the state of the Woolwich finances. Dick said the club had refused to reimburse him. As a result, Buchan refused to play any more games for the club. Edward took Dick's photograph but chose to do it just where the players come out – just as they came out. Everyone and everything went flying, and there was a great roar from the crowd.

One of the Sunderland players cut himself on some broken glass and needed to be patched up, so they had to start with ten men. Immediately Edward was the hero, and after he'd sorted his equipment out there were huge cheers as he started to walk around the pitch to take up a place near the goal Woolwich were attacking. Sensing his moment of fame Edward waved imperiously and they all waved back – which was much more fun than the match. I ran over to the crowd and shouted "Take your caps off" mimicking the move with my hat, and as they did Edward got the picture.

Sunderland scored while we were larking about, but it didn't matter too much.

I stopped at the bookshop in Fleet Street before we went into the office, and they sold me a copy of *Anarchism and outrage* by Freedom Press. Edward wondered why I was so interested in anarchism, and I just said, "Knowledge – it's all knowledge."

"You should come round with Marie, and get to know Sophia better," he said. Then seeing my face added, "She just takes a little getting used to."

Sunday 27th February

While waiting for any comments on my piece on yesterday's game Edward and I followed the Buchan story back through the archives. Turned out that for the rest of last season after his bust-up Buchan had played for Northfleet in the Kent

League. (Not more Kent – I can't stand it.) But then scouts became aware of Buchan, and Bury offered him wages of £3 a week.

And then, would you believe, my old pal Norris had become involved. According to Athletic News he offered Buchan a deal which meant that Buchan could be a teacher (which he wanted to be) and a footballer. They offered him £1 10s a week but Buchan wanted £2, and the deal fell through. After that we found him on the books at Leyton in the Southern League. That was a stroke of luck because I'd occasionally bumped into the correspondent at the Leyton Times when doing Clapton Orient pieces in the early days, and Edward and I took the underground to Finsbury Park followed by an omnibus to his offices.

Derek Widlow was indeed duly at his desk, as he always was seven days a week, and had the Buchan story ready and available in return for a drink or three. Buchan, he thought, was paid £3 a week at Leyton and at the same time as playing did teacher training at a college. That was significantly more than Fulham offered, and he was playing in a lower league. I began to wonder about Norris' ability to see the world straight.

The Leyton files showed Buchan had first played versus Plymouth Argyle in September last year and had continued playing ever since. According to my man on the spot, he was the best thing that had ever happened to Leyton, and there was no way in which Buchan should be playing at this level.

"Someone should take him on," he said.

Edward took Derek's photograph.

Wednesday 2nd March

I fear my stock is declining – but I am at least trying to bring a little illumination to the winter game.

Nottingham Forest 1 Woolwich Arsenal 1. It was… terrible. The local journalists don't like the London boys because they think we think we are superior – and they are half right. We know that we are. So there's no conversation, I get cold, I get hungry, and I get no sharing of insider information, no sharing of the hip flask. (I had assumed Edward would have one, and he didn't).

I know nothing about the Forest team, no one will tell me anything, and I ended up buying a Forest yearbook and taking information from that. Apparently this is the town where Robin Hood lived. 5000 turned up, Gray was missing at left back, so the right back played left back and Donny McDonald who is a left back played right back. It was as much of a mess as that makes it sound.

But Edward was the only photographer on site, so when he revealed himself in all his wonderful clothing, which I swear is getting more bizarre game by game (yellow and green today), there is always stunned silence and none more so than here. I got him to set up in front of the stand and photograph the journalists as well as the crowd who had no idea how to react – until Woolwich scored, that is. Then they reacted so much that the referee took the teams off. I ran round to interview the ref with the rest of the pack, and apparently it was because of the "unacceptable nature of the crowd's language."

The teams came back on after five minutes and played out the rest of the match, with me sitting next to a local oaf who was supposed to be reporting but kept shouting in favour of Forest and screaming abuse in my ear about Woolwich being the team from Hell. When Forest equalised with a very soft goal he put his face within inches of mine and screamed in an incoherent (but probably very Nottinghamish) manner. At the end of the match the journalist put out his hand to shake mine and said, "No hard feelings."

On the way back in the train we went third class (it was my turn to buy the tickets) and so Edward and I had a little sing song, centring mainly on "Yip-I-Addy-I-Ay!" – and "I wonder who's kissing her now?" much to the enjoyment of those with us in the carriage, most of whom joined in. There was talk of us doing a music hall act, and I suddenly thought it would be amusing to do that with Edward saying "I say!" and suchlike every time I said anything. Or maybe it's not so funny after all now I write it down.

Back in the office I wrote that football is now coming to an end. There are too many games, it is too boring, and we should be put out of our misery. Failing that, the Woolwich approach of playing players in the wrong position should be extended, so that the goalkeeper plays centre forward, the manager is outside left, and the ref is right back.

Edward had a picture of a Forest player who was so covered in mud it was impossible to recognise him, and we put that in, to make some point or other (I can't remember what).

Thursday 3rd March

Lacking direction I wandered around the building and (for no reason that will become apparent at this time) went to the Letters' Department on the second floor. As I entered three elderly spinsters looked up in shock, and rose to their feet as one. I don't think they've ever had a visitor before.

The eldest, a charming woman in exquisite clothes and with grey hair tied in a bun, came forward, peered at me through thick glasses and said, "Why it's Mr Jones from sports! We have so enjoyed your little pieces on hats and shoes, Mr Jones," and turning to her colleagues added, "haven't we, ladies?"

And they agreed. I checked that I was not disturbing them and whether it was all right for me to enter, and they said it was an honour, as they didn't get many visitors. And thus I entered a strange new grey world.

"You… deal with the letters people send to the paper?" I asked.

They agreed with much enthusiasm that they did, going through every item that the Chronicle received from its readers.

"And what do you do with them?" I asked. "I mean, do you answer them?"

"Every one," said the leader who introduced herself as Miss Mountview. The others nodded their agreement. "Although I have to confess, the readers don't get individual replies, of course," she said. "We wouldn't have time."

They invited me to come into the room, offered me a cup of tea (they had their own kettle and stove) and explained the system.

"Every letter is read in case it is suitable for publication on the letters page, and those that are get sent up to the editor for his consideration. The rest are divided into four groups." ("Four groups" concurred the others, scurrying around over my cup of tea.) "We split everything into Pile A and Pile B at first – Pile A is written to the editor or one of the section editors, and Pile B is written to one of the journalists… like yourself," (adding this presumably in case I had forgotten who I was).

"Then we split these piles in two – those which are supportive and positive go into A1 and B1, and those which are negative or rude go into A2 or B2. And we have four letters to send back. One for A1, one for A2, one for B1 and one for B2."

"And you get lots of letters?" I asked.

"Hundreds every day," she said, "and all of them answered."

"So how can you answer a rude letter?" I asked, revealing at a stroke that I was not a gentleman, for no gent would every have asked such a question of such delicate elderly ladies.

And I was shown A2. It thanked the writer and apologised for not being a personal reply, but hoped the writer would understand, what with the Chronicle getting so many letters each day. But, it continued, the letter had been read, and its contents noted. The editor was sorry the writer did not approve of the current policy, and the writer could be assured that the policy of the paper was kept under review. If it became clear that the majority of the readership shared the views of the writer then the writer could be further assured that the paper would act at once and change its policy.

It was a masterpiece of doubletalk, promising something by saying nothing and vice versa.

"I wonder," I said, having sipped my tea and found it infinitely more digestible than the nonsense served in the basement, "do I, that is to say, do I, as it were, do I…"

"Do you get many letters, Mr Jones?"

"Well, the point is that one day Mr Holloway showed me a whole clutch that were for me, but I never got to see them as I had to write an article…"

"Mr Jones!" she said, and I noticed the other two elderly ladies had their hands to their mouths. "Mr Jones! You get more letters than everyone else put together!"

"I do?"

"Of course you do, Mr Jones. Our readers think you are wonderful – all your stories about the people you meet, saying that men in brown boots are all anarchists. But, you know, I shouldn't really say this, but it is most amusing, some people do take you very seriously – I have just had one letter to reply to where a dear young lady writes to say that she is sure her grandfather of 82 years is not an anarchist, but he wear brown shoes every day. She was most put out."

"Oh dear," I said, "I didn't know people would take it like that."

Miss Mountview lowered her voice conspiratorially. "Don't worry, Mr Jones – we are not supposed to, but we slip in a little note saying that the piece is only meant to be a joke."

"And I really get lots of these letters?"

"About two hundred a day, Mr Jones. Isn't that right, ladies?" and she turned to her colleagues to back her up, just in case I thought she had suddenly decided to make up a number. But no. The word in the Letters' Department was that I got two hundred letters a day.

"What do they say?"

"They say they love your work, Mr Jones, and it brings a little ray of light into their world. They ask why you don't have a regular column about your life. Some of them are a little rude, but we get that everywhere. A lot of young ladies ask you out, and we have such fun saying that you would love to go, but you can't because you are married, or just about to climb the Himalayas, or digging a hole under the football ground at Woolwich… You have had a great influence on this office in terms of what we say."

"Digging a hole…." I repeated, unable to believe what I heard.

"Well, it just seemed the sort of thing you might suggest, Mr Jones. I do hope you don't mind too much. You see, we do love our jobs, but you have given us all a lift, because sometimes answering all the political points can be a little bit tedious."

"Tedious," echoed one of Miss Mountview's assistants.

"Ladies," I said, "would it be breaking too many rules if I had a look at one or two of the letters that came for me?"

"I don't see why not," said Miss Mountview. "Of course you can't take them away as they are the property of the newspaper company, but no one has ever said you can't look."

"No one," said the ladies, so that seemed to settle it.

So I looked, and noted that I was (according to some) an imbecile who should be put in the Bedlam, while I also read that certain ladies would like to step out with me (and once or twice I blushed to think that Miss Mountview had had to read some of the things that the writer suggested we might do). Many wrote to say I was right or wrong on some point of detail, but much more interesting were the few who made suggestions for other pieces I might write. There was the correspondent from Accrington who believed that the anarchists secreted their messages of destruction inside popular songs and that a careful study of such would reveal all, while a gentleman from Penzance told me that he had developed a piano that was twice as long as the conventional seven octave instrument (he didn't say how it might be played). A hat manufacturer in Luton offered me £10 if I would suggest in a future article that his produce was what all upper crust people were now wearing, while two brothers in Brighton suggested that if I mentioned their town again I would find myself falling from the cliffs at Peacehaven (although they didn't say why).

"I haven't written about Brighton as such, have I, ladies?" I said, and they confirmed that no, I had not mentioned Brighton, Sussex, or the English Channel, as far as they could recall.

Friday 4th March

I am getting the feeling that Norris's use for me had more or less ended and that Mr Churchill's story is never going to materialise.

There was a piece by Norris in the West London and Fulham Times predicting that Arsenal, "The capital's senior professional club," is about to go down. In a sense this is interesting, because I would have listed Chelsea as Norris's obvious club to knock, but maybe he just thinks that too many attacks on them was a step too far. Or maybe he's got bored with Woolwich. Or maybe he's putting the pressure on.

I offered a short piece on Charlie Buchan, and Mr Holloway growlingly agreed that I should write it and he'd consider it, especially if I could come up with something on the man-eating sheep that have now spread across Salisbury Plain.

Lunch with Marie, Edward and Sophia was a lift. Everyone was bemused by my interest in anarchism, but I think I impressed them by the fact that I had gone out and bought a political pamphlet of my own accord, read it and understood it. And that Edward and I had been to Nottingham, a city that the girls have had no cause to know exists.

Then Edward and I did our routine from the railway carriage and had half of Lyons complaining to the management and the other half telling them to be quiet so they could listen or join in. We went through the two songs again and then... my hand is shaking so much I can hardly write it... and then Sophia joined in by... playing the spoons!!!!! And not just playing, but playing brilliantly. Little Miss Sophia Sophisticated Suffragette!!!!! Everyone cheered, even those who complained about the songs. I told her she should be on the music hall stage.

(Apparently she had had a nanny who was stepping out with the boot boy whose dad had taught him to play and she had taught Sophia.)

In passing Marie said she has managed to find a contact in the War Office and hopes to be able to tell me exactly what Captain Kell does. This could take me in a new direction. But then so could the music hall.

Monday 7th March

There was a Woolwich Arsenal match today in Liverpool against Everton, and thankfully I have not been dragged out of my bed to cover it. I was doubly pleased when I heard the score. Everton 1 Woolwich 0. 6000 there, and Woolwich did their left and right back reversal game again. I sketched a piece about the reversal of full backs being a political signal.

I continued to rifle through the copies of Athletic News that we had from the last few years and there, just before lunch, I found an article from exactly three years ago by one Henry Norris proposing merging the Football League and Southern League.

So I have a new theory. He put forward this proposal for a superleague with promotions and relegations throughout, and that was rejected. Now he wants to be King of London – and to achieve this he's taking London out of the Football League – and the capital shall stand alone.

I went back through my old notes. I knew there was something from that period – and I found it. England had played against Wales at Croydon Common (the other Norris club) in March 1907. How did he manage that?

According to Athletic News, Croydon was a church team – that fitted with the Norris profile. Turned pro in 1907, one year before Norris took them over, when they were in the Second Division of the Southern League. Since then they seemed to have had quite a bit of difficulty with fires. Their original ground had burned down, and so they moved to Crystal Palace's ground (the Nest) when they got into the First Division of the Southern League.

And then, would you believe it, the stand at The Nest was blown down. Two stands wrecked in two seasons, and immediately after that Fulham apply to move up from the Southern League to the Football League (just while Croydon Common is going the other way to Division 2 of the Southern League.)

And, meanwhile, this hopeful reserve – Buchan – on whom I was now writing an article, played for Woolwich against Croydon when the two sides met in the Cup.

Of course, everything might be a coincidence, but Marie was telling me only yesterday that our aim as civilised people is that we should make everything connect. Apparently that is the key thought of our age. I suggested that we might be better off if our age was known as the time when everyone learned to play the spoons.

Tuesday 8th March

Marie told me her contact at the War Office would talk to me, providing I gave an absolute assurance that it would be a secret meeting. I was out of the door before she finished telling me.

To be fair I won't write his name here – let's just call him "Smith". Smith met me in his room and told me a simple story. Captain Kell was a paper-pusher of no ability, who believed the country was in danger and who was trying to set up a new department in the WO which dealt with the threat to our security from within.

Trouble is, he was useless as a negotiator, didn't know his background, and did little but put people's backs up. The navy had downright refused him access to their files, and the word was they were setting up their own division to cover the threat of invasion.

"Until a week or so ago, Kell was just a nuisance, always asking for meetings, always trying to find someone new to bother with his story," Smith said. "But then, suddenly, he changed tack and is now talking about Section H, claiming that the army had just such an organisation before and should have one again. He particularly wants to track down the Colonel who led Section H."

Wednesday 9th March

I wrote an article under the headline "Britain to get secret police force", claiming that the War Office is working on a plan to develop a department that would spy on the 20,000 German and Italian spies within Britain. (I made the number up. Why not? Everyone else does.).

The idea of a secret police force had been tried out in South Africa during the Boer War, I suggested, and the lessons learned there were now to be used to counteract the spies in this country. Since an invasion was now imminent from across the North Sea, it was important to know exactly when Germany was going to launch its attack so that we could send out our fleet to meet theirs and stop them reaching the Thames.

Head of the new service is the highly respected Captain Vernon Kell, veteran of the Pretoria Campaign (another invention), who is expected to have a staff of 20 providing secretarial and administrative support in spacious rooms in the War Office. I made no mention of the torpedo factory being moved – as promised to Mr Churchill.

That done, I noted my other possible stories: the extraordinary case of the Woolwich hole; how anarchists send messages inside popular songs; Brighton: the city that dare not speak its name; how to play an elongated piano. Which to choose?

Thursday 10th March

A junior called me into Mr Holloway's room at 10.30. I expected a meeting on my "Secret Police Force" piece to be the order of the day, but instead was told that the directors of Woolwich Arsenal had put the club into voluntary liquidation under Section 182 of the Companies Act 1908 (whatever that is).

They had finally run out of money, and I had to start work on a new story at once – it was going to be national news tomorrow. A First Division club, indeed London's oldest professional club, going bust.

So, casting spies and Section H memories aside but holding fast to the idea of the Woolwich hole, I turned myself back to the world of business and summarised the news coming in...

The shareholders of the Woolwich Arsenal Football and Athletic Company (Limited) have been told there will be an Extraordinary General Meeting of the club to be held at the Town Hall, Woolwich, on Friday, March 18.

This meeting will look at the present position of the company and adopt or otherwise deal with a proposal for the continuance of football on the Manor Ground next season. The club will continue for the present and complete its obligations to the Football League this season.

The heart of the matter is, who will put up the money for the new club? Will it be the people of Woolwich? It is certainly unlikely to be the existing shareholders, who looked to have been more than honourable in supporting a club that cannot support itself.

Could it be that Mr Norris, who already owns Fulham and Croydon Common, will now also seek to add a third club to his stable?

And, I concluded, there is talk that even the pitch at Woolwich is unstable and that a significant hole has opened up near the centre circle. Several workmen are looking into it.

Just to make life even more varied in the middle of the afternoon while still waiting for the fifth floor to stir themselves, I got a message that the players at Leyton were issuing a statement condemning the new arrangements on player transference. That led me back to Charles Buchan. I used one of the new phones in the journalist room to try to phone Clapton, but found they didn't have a phone at the club. (What's the point of this new device if you can't use it when the person you want to speak to doesn't have one?) So I had to beg a quote from Derek in return for all I had on Woolwich's demise. A fair swap.

Friday 11th March

Mr Holloway called me in, telling me that while I still resembled something that had just crawled out the woodwork, I was the only person who had linked up the Woolwich event with Norris and also the only person who had ever pointed out about Norris and Croydon. He congratulated me.

I asked for permission to sit in order to take in such praise and he thwacked a ruler he holds just for moments such as this on my hand which was stupidly resting on his desk. I said that he had just assaulted my typing hand and I would thus not be able to write again, and he said that was the general idea and asked whether I would be attending my leaving party. After several more moments of similar banter I asked about the secret police. He said he had heard nothing, probably because it was a secret. He found this amusing and was so encouraged by his own humour that he asked if I could look into the report that we would soon have talking pictures at the cinema.

Marie and I compared the coverage of Woolwich Arsenal's demise in the Chronicle with the Times. We were similar in terms of the notice of the announcement, although her lot were much more formal, as always. As Mr Holloway had said, the Times had no one independently working the story, and that was another point in my direction. What he had not said was that only the Chronicle covered the strange case of the hole near the centre circle. It took Marie two reads to realise it was a spoof.

Marie then said that she had to go because Sophia had been arrested and it was important to get her released before Sophia's family heard of the story. I assumed this was because they would be annoyed but she said that it was more because if it came to the ears of Sophia's uncle, Lord de Broke, he would blame Mr Churchill for the arrest and probably start a civil war.

Saturday 12th March

With matters hotting up in Woolwich and going stone cold on the secret police, I didn't object too much to yet another trip to Woolwich with Edward to see... Woolwich Arsenal 0 Manchester United 0. 5000 people there, and not only did the left and right backs swap position, but the inside left (Bentley) played inside right, and Lee (the inside right) played in Bentley's position.

It was probably meant to confuse Manchester but only succeeded in confusing Woolwich. However, outside the ground there was a itinerant hat seller who was shouting that brown caps were all the rage – and that this bloke in the Chronicle had recommended them. I said that in that case I'd better have one, and Edward took a photograph of me standing by the hat stand in my new cap. Then at the half time the hat seller turned up walking round the edge of the pitch flogging hats to the crowd, shouting "as recommended in the Chronicle". Edward and I then did an impromptu display of my cap in front of the main stand. I put it on my head and Edward shouted, "I say!" and then he put it on his head and I said, "I say I say!", and then back onto mine while Edward took a picture of me and then of the crowd who were roaring.

This was too much for the management who then sent the police round and they arrested both of us (but not the hat seller) which annoyed the crowd who started throwing anything they could find at the police. The referee then refused to restart the match until we were out of the way, and that was the last I saw of that.

Edward had never been inside a police station before and kept saying that Sophia would be so impressed that he (like her) had been arrested. We settled down to a sing-song in the cell with the phrase "I say!" at the end of each line, and when they couldn't make us shut up they let us out.

Edward showed me how to take a photograph, so I could get a shot of him posing outside the police station (which led to us being arrested by an eager constable, and instantly thrown out by the desk sergeant to whom we kept saying "I say!"). Then we toddled back to the Hen and B, but no one had any more news on the club or anything about the extraordinary general meeting (which I found is called in business circles an EGM). I learn something new each day. It wasn't that people were being quiet – it was that no one knew anything, and the directors were not saying anything. Edward said, "I say! A pint of your best bitter, Evie," and she threw a dishcloth at him, and so we did our song and dance act in the middle of a very crowded bar. I think we're getting quite good at this.

When we finally got back to the office I was given a copy of the West London and Fulham Times which had an article taking up half the front page and all of page 2, saying that the editor of the Fulham match programme had resigned because the directors (a code word for Norris) had interfered with the articles he wrote. That won't do Norris much good as Mayor of Fulham.

I wrote up "Woolwich 0 Manchester 0 – first half only" and covered such diverse issues as the fact that the hole in the Woolwich pitch has now been filled in, the colour of the paint and the faintly unpleasant smell in Woolwich nick, and how the local hat seller is clearly both a Chronicle reader and a fantasist. Plus a bit about inside lefts and inside rights. Edward then suggested we could do a second article called "My first arrest" – the story of a toff being done by the police for the first time in his life. I wrote it up and slipped in a note that, as everyone knows, many popular songs are coded anarchist messages, and that the occupants of Anarchist Cell 4 had been distributing anarchist propaganda to fellow travellers in pubs in Woolwich.

Sunday 13th March

We are running the "Britain to get secret police" story tomorrow, but with changes. Firstly, my name won't appear. "Your contact with the Home Secretary is too important," I was told by the fifth floor via Mr Holloway. ("They don't want to admit that they are still employing someone as clearly demented as you are.") The name of Kell was removed as well, to make it look as if someone else had done the research. Instead he became "a senior and well respected military figure." And finally the reference to South Africa went and was replaced with talk about "experiments during the most recent of the empire's wars".

At the end of the fifth floor briefing I was asked to stay by the political editor. When they had all gone, he told me my work was good and highly valued. He appreciated that I would be disappointed not to have my name on the piece, but I had to accept that for the higher good. And I could have a ten bob a week pay rise.

For the first time I used the paper's phone to call Marie. The butler answered, and went and found her. We fixed up to meet in Trafalgar Square with Edward and Sophia (all of us now safely released from the clutches of the law), and it was, what shall I say... a rather fine evening. They eventually took me to a night club on Park Lane (I was admitted only after they persuaded the doorman that I was in fancy dress and had just come from a toffs' "street urchin" party) and while there Edward and I sang which got us a warning, and then I persuaded Sophia to play the spoons again, which got us all thrown out. The level of ice between Sophia and myself is reducing. We are not exactly on best terms, but I can certainly hear the trickle of melting ice.

Monday 14th March

George Leavey has been grabbed by Athletic News and did their match report on the Manchester United game from the directors' box. (I'd been too busy larking around to notice. Black mark to me.)

In his article he said that the actual ground where the Gunners play has money against it, and they cannot pay the interest on the debt. He also said the players have not been paid this month and added that there was hope, but that crowds of under 10,000 were not enough.

I was depressed about the article – from being top of the pile for my story connecting Norris with Fulham, Croydon and Woolwich I have been outdone by Athletic News. (On the other hand I have the pay rise and a direct conversation with the political editor, who now thinks I am one of his. So some compensation there.)

Besides, Athletic News has nothing on hats.

Tuesday 15th March

Here's some fun: in July 1908 Norris was part of a consortium that bought "Football Chat" – a chronically awful magazine that tried to rival Athletic News but failed miserably, largely because it was the gossip of one writer, Charlie Crisp. Charlie was a football ref who fancied himself as a businessman and who changed the name of his magazine every other week to avoid having to do proper circulation or advertising figures. He simply nicked gossip from us (but without having the benefit of my stunning inventiveness) and then filled up the rest of the paper with stuff that was neither believable nor amusing. Charlie even had the nerve to buy me a drink a few times to "Check on some details" when in fact he just needed some story to fill a page.

What was really funny was that Norris, the grand businessman, was conned over the magazine which never had the advertising or readership it claimed for itself. Which is interesting in itself, because it reveals how Norris always wants more outlets for his views – no matter how crummy the outlet. It also shows that, hard-nosed business man that he is, he can still be taken for a ride.

Could he end up buying Woolwich Arsenal in the same way without actually knowing quite what he is buying? Is he a man who buys on emotion?

It is hard to imagine, but maybe, just maybe, he is so full of his own ability that he actually thinks no one can con him – so he doesn't bother to check. Now that is a thought and a half. Norris so full of himself that he doesn't bother to check…

Strangely, and quite unconnected, at exactly the same time (according to the ever-helpful Fulham local press) there were arguments about building a tram line in Fulham Palace Road about five years after every other minor suburb had got the trams. Norris was chairman of Fulham Works and Highways committee at the time of the debate on trams and, for a reason that I can't quite make out from the records, refused to let the council have a full discussion on the issue. So Fulham didn't get its trams.

I was still contemplating these issues when a runner came up and said that I had a visitor – and there was George Barrett complete with a purple coloured trilby.

"The piece in your paper about the secret police," he said, straight off. "Is that true?"

I asked him how long we had known each other, and had he ever known me to make something up. He said, yes, and I said that to the best of my knowledge the story was real but my knowledge was never quite as complete as it should be. "Stories like this always cover their tracks so as not to reveal sources," I reminded him, and Barrett's view was that this development would help his cause no end. "Once the people see the lengths the state will go to they will flock into anarchism," he said. "The state will go on strengthening its stranglehold on everyone in the country. We'll turn the people who were not born here into monsters, and once that is done the secret police will start arresting ordinary folk like you and me."

I told him he could be right, and wondered if he had anything new he could tell me about the developments in the anarchist movement, but apart from an assertion that support was growing by the day and that every meeting was better attended than the last, there was nothing to tell. "We don't live for news," he said, "we are a movement of the people."

I guess that's why they don't do press releases.

I grabbed Edward, persuaded George to sit still, and Edward took his photograph. Edward said that we should move on from the hat issue and say that ear trumpets were now "de rigueur". After I obtained the translation I have to admit I rather liked the idea. Maybe we could get the girls to be photographed using one in a night club.

Friday 18th March

Today's West London article by Norris is mostly concerned with who gets relegated from Division One and why London clubs are not faring well. Nothing about Leavey in the piece at all.

Edward and I were delegated to cover the meeting to wind up Woolwich Arsenal Ltd back at the Woolwich Town Hall. Before we left the political editor dropped by to tell me he'd have a new assignment for me shortly – but in the meanwhile was there anything I could do to get Mr Churchill to give me a new direction to work in sooner rather than later? I said I doubted it but I would ask.

Edward got an ear trumpet, and we larked around with it on the train. At Woolwich it was clear that nothing had been learned from the shambles of the previous meetings. I used the share certificate once again, brazenly claiming to be a proxy holder. I put the ear trumpet in my ear and said that as I was deaf I needed the Rt Hon Edward to relay information for me. The doorman looked extremely dubious, and then told Edward not to relay information too loudly, to which I said, "What did you say?" over and over.

George Leavey was in charge, and for once was heard in respectful silence as he stated that he had put as much money into the club as he could, and that either someone else had to put cash into the club or the club had to go into liquidation. He gave the usual explanation about what liquidation meant – adding that if the club did not follow this route it would be wound up for good.

On the positive side, the bank, the players and other clubs Woolwich have played recently, the people who had designed and built the grandstand (which is now publicly confirmed as Archie Leitch – as per the information I had got back in January) have all said that they will wait.

Although that was good in itself it was not good enough, because there were only a handful of matches left to play before there was no income at all through the summer. Although the players would be on reduced salary in the close season, the current situation would mean that the club would enter the 1910/11 season with a huge debt, and the same problems as this year. And there was no telling how long the bank and other creditors would let this drift on.

It was at this point that someone from the floor – I couldn't see who – started shouting about dear old George Morrell, the club's disaster of a manager, who had spent over £1000 on players all of whom had turned out to be useless beyond expectation, and who was now playing half the team out of position. Without that expenditure the club would have been ok, he shouted.

Actually I agreed with him. I have never been one to say that I could see things that managers can't – after all they work with the players and see them in training, so they must know more than I do – but Morrell must be the biggest golderned idiot of them all.

Morrell made a sad little speech saying that such disrespect would never occur in other teams and he didn't see why he should have to put up with it – which brought the inevitable cries of "You earn respect, not demand it" and, "If you don't like it, resign."

Poor Morrell has never quite got it – he is dealing here with a lot of people who have served their country – it is the ordnance factory of the empire after all – and they know about leadership and respect in a way he doesn't. He would have done better to keep quiet, and I suspect his time at the club is over.

I stood up and asked if he was thinking of buying anyone from Brighton, and he looked at me curiously and simply said, "No, sir."

Then we had all the usual hopes for a better future – better luck on the pitch, a good cup run, completion of the tramway out of London, extra trains on match days. Each point made by small-time shopkeepers with one share, none of them making an impact on Leavey. Inevitably the plan to move the club out of Woolwich to Blackheath (which the Kentish Independent had mentioned a couple of times) came up. It was the one plan that plainly irritated Leavey, and he made it clear that he was a Woolwich man, his shop was in Woolwich and his home was in Woolwich, and if the club moved on, he would pull out. Given the amount he was owed that would be that.

Revolt was now brewing, and it was clear that the £1 share men were unhappy because if it was Leavey's liquidator that ran the show Leavey himself would probably get bailed out first, which they thought unfair – although it's hard to follow that argument since Leavey is the one who has risked his personal earnings for the club.

Leavey let the argument ride and then came up with his winning point. He said that he had had discussions with a buyer – someone who would bring new money to the club. (I nearly fell off my chair. If he had had meetings with Norris without me knowing I was going to look a fool and a half in the paper, and that would be the end of my rise to fame – at least on the football front.)

This new money, when combined with the new transport system and the fundraising that was already underway, would surely set Woolwich Arsenal back on its feet, he said.

There was a stunned silence – for about three seconds – before everyone started to ask who it was. Leavey made it clear he was not going to tell us – but did let slip that he had met with the parties that very evening,

To salvage my position as the man at the pulse of Woolwich I needed to find out who Leavey was talking to. As the meeting broke up I worked the shareholders, but none admitted seeing Leavey in discussion with anyone from outside the meeting. I was on the edge of giving up and drowning my sorrows when I realised that I had forgotten the people most likely to remember – the officials of the town hall.

Edward and I went through them one by one to no avail… until I hit on a doorman who looked like a real veteran from the Arsenal factories – and that is what he was. I told him about my time in the war and how we relied on the big guns from Woolwich (not true, of course, but he didn't know) and how terrible the news about the torpedo unit was, and after a drink or four he had no trouble telling me.

A smart cab had turned up with two men in top hats half an hour before the meeting started. They'd asked for Mr Leavey and had been shown into a private room. They'd left by the back door just as the meeting started.

I pressed for a description, relying on Edward to empty his pockets of change, and gradually I got them. One was tall, big whiskers, big nose, "A real gent", big tipper, big tall hat, so with hat and man he was about six feet six. The other shorter, always a pace behind "Big-nose", shifty-eyed, looking around to see who was watching.

I was so stunned I needed a drink – except I had used up my money, including my fare back to town, on the old timer. Somehow Edward had vanished after buying the last round of drinks.

William Hall (one step behind) and Henry Norris (big nose). Both directors of Fulham. Both at a meeting with the leading creditor of Woolwich at which said creditor announced that the club had to be liquidated and that he had new buyers. If it hadn't been for the fact that it was Norris it would have been hard to believe. Fulham (who already owned Croydon) were about to take over Woolwich Arsenal, just as I had suggested.

Penniless, I wandered back to the Hen and Basket. David Mc was nowhere to be seen, which was a shame because I was hoping to kip down on his floor. So I went to find Evie and told her I'd used my last pennies to bribe my way into the shareholders' meeting, told her all I knew with the exception of the bit about another club taking over, and assured her that Woolwich Arsenal would survive in Plumstead because Leavey had said it had to be there, and so her Saturday trade was assured.

Oh, and by the way, could she open up a tab for me to sleep somewhere, open up a loan of some money for the train back to London in the morning, and open up a loan for a nightcap? And breakfast.

She swore at me, told me it was not a doss house, told me where to go to (but not in those words), called me a whippersnapper (which I thought was rather cute coming from someone as tough as her) and then agreed in return for a mention in the next piece I did about Woolwich.

I said I would further enhance the image of the Hen as the place to drink before during and after every Woolwich Arsenal game and made use of her facilities. It was just about two in the morning when I was getting ready to slip to bed when Edward burst in through the pub doors, looked around the suddenly silent room and said, "I say!" He walked straight up to me and told me in a loud voice (Edward doesn't do *piano*) that he had met this charming young lady who in return for a most modest sum had shown him some very interesting locations in the backstreets of Plumstead.

I turned to Evie and said, "Make it the two best rooms, clean sheets, no cockroaches, and we'll pay in the morning."

I thought Edward might be about to say, "I say!" so just in case, I bashed him round the back of the head. He said, "I say!" and we all laughed.

Saturday 19th March

We got into the office by 9am, asked for the boss, and saw him ten minutes later with the story (my story that is, not Edward's).

He told me I smelled of beer and something worse, that I looked like an East End tramp, and that if I ever dared come to work dressed like that again I would be out, and the mere fact that I had been on the case was no excuse at all.

We stood, apologised, and he said, "For God's sake sit down before you fall over."

We sat. He asked if Edward had had breakfast (presumably on the basis that the average aristo dies if not fed every five hours). He said, yes, and the two of us were ordered to get washed and be back in his office in 30 minutes.

We did, and I was – Edward suddenly feeling very queasy and preferring to sit the next meeting out in the gents.

Mr Holloway asked me, as he had before, if my source was accurate. I gave him the full story and said, first Norris is making noises, second Norris had done this before with Croydon, and third there was absolutely no one else on the scene, and I knew because I had questioned everyone. No one else wanted to buy Woolwich Arsenal. In fact it was hard to see what Norris was doing – but that at least was in keeping with Norris the football man. We couldn't see what he was doing with Croydon either.

Mr Holloway instructed me to write up the story for the Monday edition on the basis that we will shortly and exclusively reveal the identity of the new owner of Woolwich Arsenal. Once I had written the piece I was to go home, and get back to Woolwich tomorrow to find out anything else I could. He needed confirmation of the story from another source, pronto. If I could stop Edward throwing up, that would be a bonus.

Oh and the 5th floor were asking when the next story from Mr Churchill was coming in. Oh and would I look into the report that the Shetland Isles had just been sold to Norway. Oh and don't forget to clean up the gents because the regular toilet man is off.

I did as I was bid, (except the last bit, and the Shetland bit) and sneaked past mother into the house around 1pm.

Sunday 20th March

Story in Woolwich is that our sturdy lads yesterday beat Bradford City one goal to nil. No one told the guys up north about the left / right reversal game.

I sat drinking in the pub, when in walked none other than Dr John Clarke – the man supposedly at the head of the great fundraising committee. It quickly became clear that Dr Clarke was working the local people. In each case he was laying out some papers, and talking in that earnest way that the professional classes think they ought to talk when addressing the working man. I wanted Edward to say, "I say!" but he was being nursed by Sophia.

Edging past the table, I glimpsed the paperwork, and then pushed into the street just in time to find Shady Flintock and pal strolling back to Woolwich.

Shady is one of those guys who hangs around the edge of things, pretending to be part of it but never quite making it. I never understand how these guys earn their dosh – but somehow they do.

"You joined the ranks of the well-off?" I asked him, falling in step beside the two. "Buying the shares and all?"

Shady introduced me to his mate with more build up than I normally expected – until I realised that Shady was using me to build up his credentials with the other man.

"Dr Clarke is taking over the club," he said. "Asked me to be on the board." It was as likely as a turnip being appointed as manager – but then judging by the manager they had that probably would be an improvement.

"So what would that make you?" I asked, "A shareholder in the new company, after it is liquidated."

"Aye, that's right," said old Shady, clearly lacking any knowledge of what I was talking about.

"Did you discuss your shareholding?"

The other man spoke. "Early days," he said in a more refined accent than Shady's. "Opening discussions, possible opportunities you understand. Nothing for the press as yet."

I assured him that I was one of those highly responsible press men who never ever went to the editor with anything at all that was not 100% cleared and ok, and that even if I did, the editor of the Chronicle – a serious paper if ever there was one – would certainly not consider the story. I had my fingers so firmly crossed that my knuckles went white.

"When might there be an announcement?" I asked the unnamed man, but he just told me it was early days, and that they would probably meet next month to "thrash out the details." He bade me good day and I wandered back to the pub where Dr Clarke was just finishing off. I introduced myself properly as I retrieved the remnants of my drink.

"I was wondering," I said, "who will take over Mr Leavey's shareholding for the new company after the current company is liquidated."

"We have one or two parties in mind," he said.

"You mean Mr Norris and Mr Hall of Fulham."

The good doctor denied it. But really there was no point. Not after he knocked his pint and all his paperwork all over the floor, spluttered and flustered, turned bright red, tried to loosen his starched collar, and then coughed. Overall he is not quite the man you want handling top secret negotiations on behalf of your troops in the war zone where you pretend you have ten times the artillery you actually have, and thus are just about on an equal footing with the enemy.

"Any other club want to buy some of the shares?" I asked innocently, piling on the pressure.

"Tottenham Hotspur are in for £100," he said.

I showed him how the delicate art of camouflaging feelings is done, knocked over my pint, bumped into the door, and ran to the railway station.

Monday 21st March

The Woolwich story was not run in today's paper, the boss being dissatisfied.

"More," he said. "It is all too circumspect. I need more."

And I was about to go digging when the news arrived that Kell had made a statement about the secret police. If my view of him at the start of the day was somewhere around absolute zero, it was now lower. Firstly, he named himself (which we had carefully not done). Secondly, he said that his department was not a secret police force at all, but a department of government charged with responsibility for investigating the claims that the press had been circulating about spies – and that it would be irresponsible of any government not to undertake such an investigation in the light of "so much evidence". (That actually was the clever bit – Fleet Street could hardly deny the spy story having been running little else for years.)

Then he denied the notion that anything he was doing was based on the Boer War experience. "The fight against some poorly resourced Dutch farmers is hardly relevant when considering the spies of the Kaiser," he said portentously. So that's what I had been doing for three years. Fighting a bunch of Dutch farmers. Oh Captain Kell, I am going to get you for that.

I was still reading the summary that had been dictated over the phone by someone in Whitehall when Mr Holloway came by to see why I was "standing around". He told me with varying degrees of graphic detail that he needed me to cover Norris and Woolwich and that if he needed an office loafer he would choose Edward. I said, of course, but then turned back. "Can you do something for me, Mr Holloway?" I asked. I had never spoken to him in this way before. "This rubbish from Captain Kell is disrespectful to every soldier who died for the Empire in South Africa. I'd like to write an article on it. Now Kell has named himself..."

"I'll go and ask," he said, but suggested that in return he would like me to look into reports that the Duke of Cumberland is actually a tree – no male issue having come through the family and their lordships not wanting the ancient line to die out. I went to White Hart Lane, where a man in the office (who might have been a cleaner) confirmed that they had offered to take £100 in the new club, just to show support for football in London.

Back in the office Mr Holloway said that the men upstairs would look favourably on a piece about Captain Kell and his jumped-up War Office team – along perhaps with a piece about a boy in north Wales who had turned into a fish. I sat down at the typewriter and knocked out the first draft.

Tuesday 22nd March

My story about Norris buying Woolwich Arsenal and Tottenham putting money in as well was the lead in the football page, despite Mr Holloway's dismissal of my work. Two months ago I would have celebrated all day and night, but today I just settled down and wrote.

At lunch time I met Marie. I can't ever remember as a journalist being as angry as I am about Kell's "farmer" comment. But I determined not to attack Kell with facts, for to do so would just open up an argument. Instead I decided to make him a figure of fun and to punish him (at least in my terms) for what he said about my fallen comrades. We all know the Empire got bored with the Boer War. But even so, you do not disinherit those who gave their lives in your Empire's name.

What I did was simple. I took the characters and plots out of some of the invasion novels, mixed them with a touch of reality, and came up with a story of my own. I thought I might as well have a bash at Norris while I was at it, so I suggested that the secret police knew that there were no spies, but were simply trying to get more government money by pretending there were spies everywhere. Besides, there was an invasion on the horizon. It was the takeover of the playtime of the working man. The new enemy, I said, was not coming with guns and boats, but with money and power. And he was using that money to buy up the one thing that working men valued more than anything else. Their football clubs.

"Take over the working man's football club," I said, "and you take over the working man's spirit. You buy his soul. Because the working man believes in his local team, and more than anything he wants it to be his, not part of some other club."

So what we have now, I wrote, are two protagonists. On the one side The King of London, who is taking over that which the working man holds most dear. On the other side we have Mr Dandy Ffopp who is running his invisible secret police force, arresting every hurdy-gurdy player in sight.

Mr Ffopp is recruiting his army to help him in his fight against an enemy that does not exist, while the real invading Terror (i.e. Norris) is biting deep as football falls under the black boots of the invader. As I wrote I portrayed the King of London as an ultra-efficient monster – a cross between a Martian and the Kaiser. It was quite a creation.

Each side was preparing for a great battle, I proclaimed. Mr Ffopp had rallied the Swiss Navy to ensure that the Thames Estuary was properly protected, and had formed a parliament of advisers, all of whom were veterans of the Battle of Dorking – many still carrying injuries gained in the battle.

The King of London, however, had cunningly purchased thousands of copies of the German edition of *The Invasion of 1910* by Le Queux, in which the Germans actually win the war, and was planning to throw the books at anyone who dared resist.

Next I threw in Digby Digweed. Digby was a Boy Scout who had endless experience of fighting. Besides, if the gas lights go out in the dark days ahead, he can rub two sticks together.

Ffopp would win, I suggested, only if the rural working classes don't join in and use the occasion to demand better working conditions. If that happens Ffopp is in trouble, for the only people who have any experience at dealing with farmers are the Boer War veterans, and sadly Mr Ffopp has so insulted them in the past that they would never lift a finger to help his battle.

I read it, checked it, proofed it, and added a note saying that maybe there could be a cartoon by Robin, in which he had the King of London in football shorts and boots and wearing the Kaiser's distinctive helmet, stamping on Stamford Bridge with White Hart Lane tucked under his arm, while little Mr Ffopp, his secret police and the boy scouts stand at his feet raising their fists and saying "give us back our souls". In the distance I suggested a group of farmers watching on, pitchforks in hand.

I read it again. It was… well, nonsense. And yet it was so stupid that maybe it was funny. I called Edward and gave it to him to read. He said he'd never seen anything like it, and I said that that was obvious. But was it funny? Edward had no idea.

I took it upstairs before going with Edward to meet the ladies for a meal.

Marie had been working on the John Nisbet story – the latest murder case to excite the nation. Yesterday a fellow called Dickman had been arrested for the murder of Nisbet – but apparently had not been found with the huge amount of cash that Nisbet had supposedly been carrying with him at the time he was killed. I wasn't really on top of that story, but Marie said she was going to try and cover the trial.

We talked about why I was angry, and Sophia talked about her anger regarding the way women were treated and how she had had to nurse Edward when I'd forced him to drink too much. It was that kind of night.

Wednesday 23rd March

In an effort to calm down I wrote a piece about a man in Brighton who has invented a piano with 14 octaves and wears arm extensions to play it, and how he has been arrested by the police on suspicion of being an Elongated Anarchist (the worst kind there is).

Edward said I needed cheering up, so took me to the pub, and I have a recollection of us walking along Fleet Street in the early hours of Thursday singing something. Made a note to avoid Sophia.

Friday 25th March Good Friday.

Feeling a little calmer, I reported for duty. Woolwich Arsenal were away at Newcastle (they drew one goal each). Maybe there is something in this left/right formation after all. Newcastle are a good side.

Mr Holloway required my presence.

"You think you're funny, don't you?" he said.

I told him I thought we had had that conversation back in January.

"Trouble is," he said, "the fifth floor think you might be funny, but they aren't sure. The cartoonist does think you are funny – but he is certifiable. Your piece will run, carefully tucked away where no one will see it."

"You mean about the man in Brighton with the long piano?"

"About the King of London, you idiot – and believe me, we are going to watch the letters from readers as never before. Now please give me something that explains why Tottenham Hotspur want to buy part of Woolwich Arsenal. And while you are at it, look into this business about a new civilisation being discovered at the South Pole.

I tried to find an explanation (for Tottenham, not the South Pole), but got nowhere other than the obvious notion that if Spurs were watching Fulham buy up clubs they might think they could scupper Fulham's plan by throwing a bit of money at Woolwich themselves.

At midday I went to Lyons to find Marie. She said I was exploring a new art form – which sounded grand – although in truth I was simply trying to be amusing and satirical, turning Kell into the booby and Norris into a booted monster.

Saturday 26th March

I took Marie to watch Woolwich Arsenal against Sheffield Wednesday. She used her Times press pass to get a seat with me. The talk in the press box (George Allison, representing half a dozen papers, the two Kent dailies, and the Fulham and West London) was that Woolwich Arsenal might yet stave off relegation. It was by no means certain but it was possible.

Trouble was, as the man from the Kentish Independent sitting next to me said, "You can always rely on the Woolwich Arsenal." He meant they always messed it up – and indeed today they lost at home to Sheffield. A win could have been the big breakthrough, but it wasn't – and so relegation stays a possibility. Where they went wrong was that the left winger played on the left. An obvious error.

The ground was empty – well 8000 – as it always is at this time of year. Despite the gloom everyone was happy to talk to me, especially as they realised I had a lady from the Times by my side. Dr Leavey was there, and I grabbed a word, but he remembered his bad move last time we spoke, and he would say nothing of importance.

Back in the office Mr Holloway grabbed me and threw a piece of paper in front of me. It was the cartoon – just as I had wanted it. I looked up. And I swear before Almighty God, for one second a smile passed over his face. "What do you know about the face of Christ appearing on a piece of toast in Liverpool?" he asked.

Sunday 27th March   Easter Sunday

Marie and I both took the day off – I because I was working again tomorrow covering the Chelsea vs Woolwich match, and Marie because she doesn't work Sundays. We made a clear decision to talk about each other and our respective families.

Marie's view was that her father would like me and admire my style. As she explained, "He's an Edwardian at heart – just like you. His motto is 'Never be dull', and, Jacko Jones, no one could ever accuse you of being dull."

As I had guessed, the family were completely upper class – although I hadn't realised that her family, like Sophia's, were in the Lords. The only difference between the two families was that Marie's were Liberals and the supporters of reform, while Sophia's were Unionists and as backward as they come.

I told her about my family, how small the home was, how basic the education of my parents, and how my mother would probably drop dead of a fit if I ever took Marie home. "It would be embarrassing," I said.

"For me?" she asked.

"No, I said, "for me."

Monday 28th March

I was hanging around in the canteen when a note came across from Mr Symmonds saying that the King of London story would run tomorrow.

The game at Chelsea was awful; it finished Chelsea 0 Woolwich Arsenal 1, Woolwich reverting to the left/right technique. If football goes on like this Norris will have nothing to buy because it will never survive. There is talk of changes to the rules – restricting the goal keeper so he can only handle nearer his goal, or changing the offside rule so you only have to have two players instead of three between you and the goal. As far as I am concerned, yes, I'll have all of that.

As far as the Chelsea crowd is concerned everything is disaster, for they are down to Division 2. Woolwich could still go down with them, but they have a fighting chance to stay up. That was the theme Edward and I tried to develop, as I directed him to get contrasting pictures of the hardy group of Woolwich fans who had ventured upstream, and the bulk of the crowd supporting Chelsea, who looked as morose as a moose.

Parts of the terracing on the far side from the grandstand – the huge area that is supposed to hold 50,000 people – are again roped off, although some people were right up against the ropes. After the game, with the crowd gone, we wandered over to have a look. More sections of the terrace had collapsed – the holes were not great but they were significant, and it looked to my untutored eye as if other parts of the concrete were breaking up. It was clear that running repairs had been done to the holes I'd seen elsewhere: a patch and mend stadium.

I wrote it up: Patch & Mend 0, For Sale 1.

Wednesday 30th March

Mr Symmonds invited me into his office at around 11. Whereas Mr Holloway shouts at me, Mr Symmonds requests me to join him and asked me to sit down.

He had a pile of letters which he pushed towards me. "They liked it," he said simply. "Some thought it incomprehensible, some thought it childish, some wanted us to print an explanation, and some demanded an apology. But most who wrote said they thought it was different, interesting, illuminating and amusing – although not always in that order. There's one here," and he paused to find a particular letter, "which says, 'Sir, I was shocked, amazed, amused and annoyed to read the article,' which I rather like.

"This paper would like you to shock, amaze, amuse and annoy its readership for a little longer. Carry on with the story of the King of London. Do two more, please, and quickly, and we'll review the situation again." Then he thanked me politely, said he personally thought it was very good, and that he looked forward to the next instalment.

I went and found Robin the cartoonist, told him the news, and thanked him again for getting the drawing so right. He thanked me for giving him something interesting to work with. I said that no, his picture made the story and I hoped he would be doing it again for future editions, and he said that I was being too kind, and I said, "Can we stop this, and simply have a drink to celebrate," and he agreed.

I caught up with Marie at lunchtime and asked her out for a meal in the evening. She agreed, but then I had to admit that I didn't know where would be proper and smart enough to go, and where I would be allowed in with the clothing at my disposal.

"Bring your press card," Marie said.

It wasn't until Edward arrived in the sports room in the afternoon and pointed it out to me that I saw that the Patch & Mend piece with its happy and sad supporters pictures had appeared completely without cut.

We dined out at The Southgate in Royes Row, off Oxford Street. It was magnificent. As we entered the waiter looked me up and down and was about to show me back outside when I presented my press card. He slipped away, and then the maitre d' (as it seems the top waiter is called for reasons that I completely failed to get when Marie explained) came over, said he was pleased to welcome me, and it was an honour to have me, and if there was anything at all that I wanted, just to click the finger.

It was embarrassing of course, since I had no idea what the menu meant, but Marie was wonderful about it all and helped me. Two diners, one of whom worked at the Times with Marie, came over and shook my hand and said my piece was "a lesson to editors that taking a risk was sometimes worth the candle and that it would teach the government a thing or two." I had no idea my article meant that at all.

It was only after they had returned to their own table that Marie told me that I now had to write a review of the restaurant. It appears the manager of the establishment has mistaken me for the food correspondent.

Thursday 31st March

At lunchtime I strolled into the letters office on the second floor. Miss Mountview was out of her chair and greeting me before I was half way through the door. "Oh Mr Jones, Mr Jones, what have you done?" she said. "We've had to ask for more help, we can't cope."

"With the letters?"

"With the letters about your article about the King of London and Mr Ffopp. I've had permission to write two new reply letters – they have had to be approved, of course, and that is holding us up – but the current letters were just not suitable."

"What do the new ones say?" I asked.

"One says thank you we are glad you liked the story, and there will be some more episodes."

"And the other?"

"It says that we're sorry you feel like that and it may be that you will find the story becomes a little clearer in the next episode."

Then one of Miss Mountview's assistants approached, wringing her hands but with eyes beaming and said, "Mr Jones, we are all wondering. What happens next?"

"I was hoping that some of these letters might give me a clue," I said, and they all thought that was a wizard joke.

Friday 1ˢᵗ April

Of course these days we all know of Digby Digweed. Come to our great capital city, and you will pass down Digweed Street, to Digweed Circus, and journey along Tottenham's Digwe Parad (where, sad to say, the signs are in need of some repair) and back in the West End go to the Palace, where Digby himself is probably having tea and crumpets, while entertaining His Majesty. The great head, the short legs, the ever-ready elbow – these are his trademarks: the signs of Britain Victorious, no matter what the odds, no matter what the opposition.

And so I continued the story, with Digby, the great boy scout and saviour of the nation, against whom the might of the rest of the world is as nothing.

I had no idea if it worked or not, but I couldn't think of anything better so I handed it in.

Saturday 2ⁿᵈ April

I grabbed Edward upon his arrival. "Do you know how to write a restaurant review?" I said, and explained what had happened on my last date with Marie.

"Have you got a menu from the place?" he asked. I produced the copy I had removed, and he proceeded to write words next to various dishes. One was "exquisite", another "slightly overcooked for my taste," The pudding was "divine", and so on.

"Now," he said, "describe some of the people there."

I went through those I could remember and in each case he called out questions. What was his hair like? Was her face round or oval? Were the ears big or small, flat or crinkly? Did he wear glasses? Did the mouth smile or look sour? Did I hear the voice? Was it smooth? Was there an accent? What was the attitude towards the waiter – arrogant, downtrodden, untrustworthy, deferential? Were there mannerisms? Did the person sit with fingers interlocked? How was the fork held? Was there a shrug when spoken to? Did the head rotate? Was the hair scratched, or the nose? Was the person fat or thin? Were the legs long or short…?

"Stop," I cried, "I need to write a bleeding restaurant review, not an anatomy piece."

"That's how you do it," said Edward, who was more forceful than I have ever seen him. "Shall I write this for you?"

"Be my guest," I said, and he went away as happy as a fellow who loves photography but also secretly wants to be a writer.

Sunday 3ʳᵈ April

For once I had no football report to rewrite. Woolwich Arsenal are secure in Division 1, having beaten Bristol City one goal to nil in Bristol. And this despite the fact that by far their best player of the season – Andy Ducat - had been playing for England at the game in Glasgow.

Scotland beat England by two goals to none. According to our report the match "was fast and interesting".

Tuesday 5th April

I handed in my Digby Digweed story to Mr Symmonds, completely unsure of what to make of it or where it was going. When I got back to my desk there was an envelope for me. There was no letter inside, nothing to indicate who it came from, just a handwritten note, headed "The Parliament Act". It said that if the government was elected by the people in January and the Lords continued to defy both the constitution and the will of the people by stopping the government's budget – the "People's Budget" passing into law then there would be a new act that would prevent the Lords from stopping any finance bill – like a budget – for more than a month, and any other bill for more than six months. If they tried, then the finance bill would go straight to the king. For other bills, if the government brought the bill in twice and it was rejected twice, then after six months it would go straight to the King. MPs would be paid £500 per year, and parliaments would last only four years and not seven as at present.

I read it twice, but was not much the wiser – it seemed to me a dull and technical matter, and not at all what I was expecting from Mr Churchill.

I took it to Marie at lunchtime at Lyons. She read it, and her mouth, which started opening with the first paragraph, was wide open by the end. I found it strangely attractive. "This," she said at last, "is dynamite. Where did you get it?" and I duly explained how it had arrived, before confessing that I didn't see what the fuss was about.

"Have you ever listened, even once, when we have talked about politics?"

There was an awkward silence. Truth is, when she and Sophia get going, I tend to switch off. I find Edward easier company. Eventually she relented and explained. "The government wants to spend money on building a new navy, because it thinks we are going to go to war at some time with Germany. You know that?" I said I had gathered as much in passing, and that was the origin of the torpedo issue.

"But it also genuinely wants to make this country a better place to live. Do you realise my whole family are Liberals?" I half nodded (although I had never really believed that. The wealthy were Unionists, as far as I knew). "Our party wants to help people not to be poor. It wants to give money to old people who can't work so they can live in dignity. It wants to build proper roads for cars, so they don't just rip up the countryside and turn everything to dust. And to do all that it needs money. And it gets money by passing a bill in parliament that allows it to tax the rich, particularly the landowners. But the big landowners are mostly Lords, and the Unionists have a huge majority in the Lords and they have voted down the Liberal budget.

"A bill like this would stop them ever doing that again. It would cut the powers of the Lords to shreds. In fact it would end the Lords."

I thought about it. "But surely a bill like this would itself have to get through the Lords – and they would never vote for it."

She was excited. I had never seen her so excited. It made me interested. "If the Liberals and Labour along with the Home Rulers in Ireland whipped up the masses into thinking that the Lords were stopping them being supported in their old age, having better homes, in fact having better lives altogether, they would riot and ensure that the Liberals stay in power. The Liberals don't want riots in the cities, but riots on the land of the aristocrats, with workers throwing the landed gentry out…"

"The government would never support that."

"Not support, true, but they would be saying, 'Look we tried to stop this happening with the Parliament Bill, but you wouldn't have it… it is your fault, we can only stop this if you agree to this Act'. They would make this bill, which you think is the dullest thing under the sun, into a cause for the common people."

"So you think this is big news?" I asked, still not sure.

"Bigger than anything. Bigger than torpedoes. Mr Churchill has given you something bigger than you could ever imagine. Of course, he is doing it for his own good…"

"Because…"

"Because the government is unstable. Do you know who is running this country?"

"The Liberals," I answered, hoping it wasn't a trick question.

"Just, but only just. They have a majority of two over the Unionists, but there are also fifty Labour members plus the eighty Irish Nationalists and a large number of independents, so even if they can get their own party to vote for something (which is rare) they can readily be defeated. There will be another election soon – in fact as soon as they can get the budget issue sorted. This is all about power."

"And will the rural masses really rise up?"

"The Third Reform Act gave everyone with money the vote, irrespective of where they lived – except women, of course. This is about the power of the government to govern, as opposed to the power of the landed elite to run the country for ever through the Lords."

"So we write this up?"

"You write this up," she said. "If you want my thoughts, you know I will give them, but don't diminish yourself – you are the one who manipulated the Home Secretary into giving you this story. You use it. It will make the Chronicle the biggest selling paper in the land."

And on a promise like that there was nothing else to do. We started turning the note I'd been sent into an article. Marie had to leave at 2.30, but by then the whole piece had taken shape.

At half past four I gave the piece to a boy who took it to Mr Holloway, since nominally he was still my boss and Mr Simmond's commission was merely to write the occasional humorous piece. Five minutes later I saw Mr Holloway leave his office and head for the news editor's cubicle.

At five o'clock I took a coffee and a sandwich in the canteen.

At quarter past five I was back at my desk. There was some coming and going, but nothing seemed to relate to me.

At half past five Mr Holloway came back, beckoned to me and, as I got up, turned away and led me upstairs. We went to see the editor.

For the next half hour he grilled me. He didn't ask about the source, but he did ask things like, "Are you sure about this or is it a guess?"

I told him I was sure.

"And this comes from on high?"

"Very high," I said. They could all work out who but protocol meant they could not ask.

"How much of this is you, how much the original source?"

"The source gave me the information in writing," I said.

"In writing, by gad!" says he. "Your friend in very high places trusts you enough to give you information in writing! You must have a singular grip on your source's throat." I thought it would be amusing if Edward could come in and say, "I say!" but I kept quiet.

The Editor looked at me with a glare. I did the standard army trick and looked at a spot slightly to the right of the top of his head.

"Army man?" he said, recognising the look.

"Sergeant in the 2nd Duke of Cambridge's Own Middlesex Regiment. War Office Section H," I answered formally.

He waited for a moment. "Keep that quiet," he said. "It says too much," And of course it did. You didn't need to be a journalist to know who the most famous writer in the area was during the Boer War.

"Thank you, Jones," said the editor. Mr Holloway showed me to the door in case I had forgotten where it was, pointed me to the stairs and asked if I could look into the reports of a band of Benedictine monks who had declared war on the Isle of Man.

Wednesday 6th April

The menu at The Southgate is varied, with dishes ranging from the divine to the slightly over-salted, but on the whole "exquisite", that much overplayed word, does fit the bill. We started with shrimp cocktail, a little on the shallow side for my taste, and followed with a magnificent steak Diane – do be sure to ask for it rare. But highlight beyond highlight was the Divinity Fudge. Music was played by Gilberto and his South-West Venezuelan ensemble.

Of the clientele, one may say that one does not go to The Southgate for the food as much as to observe and be observed. Propriety forbids me to mention names, but from my descriptions you may perhaps deduce our fellow diners for the evening.

In one corner sat a gentleman of serene military bearing and advanced years, his white hair swept back in gay abandon. Beside him sat a bright young thing with an oval face, far, far too young to be the gentleman's wife, so we must hope she was his daughter (or perchance niece) and enquire no further. Two couples, who through age and a tendency to ignore their partners most certainly were married, sat near by. Most interesting, one male member of the party had the largest ears seen outside of the circus while the other's were tiny – and yet it was Big Ears who seemed to have the most difficulty in hearing. Glasses were worn in abundance both by women and men, and one wonders if everyone wearing them is truly deficient in eyesight, or whether there is now a decision to wear just for effect.

But, of course, it is the mouth that distinguishes our already distinguished guests, and, you will be asking, did the mouth smile or look sour? The majority of guests, I can assure you, have adopted the proper smile this season (aside from our two married couples who only parted their lips when speaking from their right molars). Voices were smooth and gentle, lilting and gracefully curving up and down the range with a gentle drop at the end of the sentence. Deviation from this mode was frowned upon by the waiters.

Attitudes were less certain. The military gent and the married couples were brusque towards the waiters, while everyone else was polite and kind, showing up the uncivil for their lack of manners. The waiters themselves sported fashionably foreign accents (one cannot tell from whence) and a look of superiority, as if judging that being British means that one cannot tell one's Steak Diane from one's jellied eel à la Bon Turk.

Forks are held low, knives high. Fingers are locked when speaking, knees bent. Elbows touch ribs and are never out.

I laughed, clapped Edward on the back and asked him where he learned to write like that. "We used to review lectures at Cambridge for the college magazine," he said. "I was the editor in my final year."

He wanted me to take credit for the piece, but of course I told him to go and select a Greek name and to hand it in as his. I wondered what Mr Holloway would make of it all.

Thinking of the devil, the boss came along and said that on Thursday I should go to Woolwich where there was going to be a meeting being held by Dr John Clarke in order to set up a takeover company.

I sat down and tried to emulate Edward.

Digby made his way home and was horrified to find a troop of German soldiers outside the door. He pushed past them and went inside.

"Ah, Digby," said his father, welcoming him in, "this is the Graf de Graf de Coborg Helslingford. He is here to buy football clubs. Help him out would you?"

"Football clubs?"

"Seems they want football clubs in order to help develop manly attitudes and keep the workers happy," said Digby's father. "I was just negotiating a price for Spurs."

"But you don't own Spurs," said Digby

His father looked down at him and scowled, but then in a pleasant voice said to the German, "Minor details, not important to a boy of his age who doesn't understand high finance. Now, Captain, do you want to take the terracing and the ground, or is it just the players and surrounding streets?"

Given that I have no idea where this story is going, it seemed to be working out quite well.

Thursday 7th April

Picked up the Chronicle at breakfast, and there was my story of the King of London written by "Sentinel". I showed it to mum and dad. "Do they pay you to write this?" Mum asked dubiously, adding that she didn't understand it and that if she didn't get it then nobody would.

I took the omnibus and ferry to the Woolwich meeting as instructed.

Dr Clarke said he wanted to form a group that would make a bid to the liquidator, Charles Branna, for Woolwich Arsenal. They would then issue shares in a new club to be called Arsenal Football and Athletic Company, and take over the Woolwich Arsenal's place in the First Division, along with the players and all the other assets.

The talk was of the secured creditors and the unsecured creditors – much of which is beyond me. The totals for the unsecured were given as £4,676, which included £1,630 owed to Mr. Leavey and £1,347 owed to Archie Leitch for the grandstand. Most of the rest is owed to the bank. Mr Gray is owed £232, Mr Ducat, £260, and a certain C. Satterthwaite £150.

So that was the downside. But they had assets of £12,000 – which is the value of the ground. The players must also be worth something, but it seems they don't count.

Back in the office I asked Dick how much it would cost Norris to buy the club.

"He could certainly have it for £4,676," said Dick. "That's enough to ensure that all the secured people get paid, and the liquidator would consider that a reasonable deal. Add another £1,600 to pay the rest of the Leavey loan, and no one would blink."

"So the other unsecured people get nothing?"

"That's how it goes."

"And is the land really worth £12,000?"

"Probably not, but it has value, and they could build more factories for the arsenal there," said Dick. "That would increase the value of the land. But it all depends whether anyone wants to build there. The land is only worth what someone will pay, and if no one wants it, it is worth nothing. If they really are moving the factories away it will be useless unless they want to put houses there."

"So Norris could move Woolwich Arsenal to Fulham, take the team with him, play on the weeks Fulham aren't at home, and have two teams – probably just to annoy Chelsea and have a plot of land that might be worth something in the end. Or, alternatively, he could set up a new club in Woolwich and get it into the Southern League. The crowds would be enough for that."

And then I remembered something that had struck me as odd in the meeting, but I had missed the significance. "Bugger," I said, "that's it. The new name of the club is Arsenal Football and Athletic Club. Not Woolwich Arsenal. It half struck me at the time."

"They need a new name for a new company," he said.

"But they could have Woolwich Arsenal Football and Athletic Club. Why drop Woolwich – unless you are not going to be in Woolwich."

I went back to the office and wrote the story.

"I can't run it tomorrow," said the boss. "We're full."

Friday 8th April

My story on the Parliament Act is front page news. Edward's restaurant piece is on page 12.

I sat in the office being congratulated by everyone, and in turn I congratulated Edward who brought in a bottle of champagne to toast me.

Marie came in at lunchtime to look for me, and everyone but everyone stared at her. Some knew her as a Times woman. None knew her as my girlfriend, but they did when she took me out arm in arm for lunch. Even Mr Holloway failed to ask me about the volcano in Liverpool.

By the afternoon it had become even more exciting. At three o'clock the editor came in and announced that the House of Lords was in turmoil, with their Lordships waving copies of the Chronicle around demanding that the editor and I should be arrested for treason for making up such a tale.

"Don't worry," said Mr Holloway, patting me on the back somewhat harder than protocol normally dictated, "we'll visit you in prison. But before you go in, I'd like you to investigate these stories about people making forged sovereigns and handing them out to Suffragettes. And do the Woolwich Arsenal tomorrow, and we'll link it with your piece on Norris. We've just destroyed the House of Lords, so we can bring down a jumped-up Unionist too."

At home I suddenly felt rather down. No one I knew would have a clue as to what the Parliament Act piece was about, so I sat in the kitchen (to mum's great annoyance) and wrote out another piece.

The invasion of England by a foreign country seeking to steal this proud nation's football clubs did not go unnoticed in the national press or in government.

The Daily Review covered the intrusion onto our native soil on page 16 (just below "Chelsea attendances down as club falls into foreign hands") while the Herald News placed it below the classified adverts for secondhand roses.

Only the National Express, however, took the matter more seriously and said in a leading article that the removal of our football clubs was an inevitable consequence of free trade as it ordered its readers to vote Unionist...

Saturday 9th April

I am the great correspondent of the Chronicle, ranging across the humour of the Theft of Football, covering the great political moment of the Parliament Act, discovering the torpedo factory scandal, and also revealing the changes taking place at London's oldest professional football club.

And what do I do this fine Saturday? Woolwich Arsenal 0 Bury 0. Crowd – 5,000. Awful. The only thing that saved me from total depression was the fact that in the second half a Bury played fell over, stayed down, and refused to play on, claiming that he was injured. He was carried off the pitch, and then, when he thought he was out of sight, he started walking into the changing room under the stand. Fortunately, Edward was on sharp form and got his picture both on the ground and then back on his feet.

I wrote up the story, integrating it with a revised version of the Norris-buys-Woolwich-Arsenal affair, saying that he was going to build a new factory on the site of the old ground, move Woolwich Arsenal FC to Fulham's ground, and drop "Woolwich" from the name of the club.

Then Edward and I went to meet Marie and Sophia. Edward, it seems, has been commissioned by the fifth floor to do another review, and (he said) he needed us there to help him. He very specifically asked Sophia not to play the spoons.

Monday 11th April

I dropped into the office to see if there was any news and got waylaid by Mr Symmonds who patted me in what I felt was too familiar a way on the back and said "Dear boy" all the time.

"We have letters," he said, when we made it into his enclave. "Letters. About your little story about, ah, the, ah, King of London."

"Ah," I said, hoping that the word conveyed my profound understanding of the gravity of the situation and an excited anticipation of what was to follow. I didn't tell him I had discovered the letters' room on the second floor.

He got out a box. "The readership is divided," he said portentously. "About a quarter thought your little piece was" (he consulted some of the correspondence and said ah a few times) "childish, drivel, pointless, idiotic, and…" (he paused searching for a choice comment) "the meanderings of a deranged and dangerous lunatic who somehow gained access to the press overnight – his father or uncle may be an employee of yours."

"Ah," I said.

"A quarter wrote to say they didn't understand it and could they have a translation. A quarter thought it quite amusing, but would be better if we covered…." Another pause. "Well anything that they had a beef about."

A pause.

"Ah," I said.

"And a quarter said it was the funniest thing they had read in years and would we make sure that the series continued."

"Ah."

"So," he said, beaming at me, looking over the top of his thick spectacles. "Carry on, dear boy. Next episode to me by Monday afternoon. We'll go over it, and see if any, ah, adjustments are needed. In the light of readers' comments."

"Each week?" I said, horror creeping into my voice. I wanted to write, but I was still covering the Norris story, and who knew what was going to come up out of the Parliament piece? I hadn't exactly been sitting on my arse before all this started.

"Is there a problem?"

"Errr…" This was what I wanted, of course, so I could hardly object. "Do I get any extra payment?"

"Oh, didn't I say?" He beamed in an absent-minded way, and then began to clean his glasses on an immaculately pressed handkerchief. "Two pounds a week additional salary has been voted by the board."

"Thank you, sir," I said, shocked, amazed, amused (not sure why), annoyed (because to him it was a nothingness, to me it was a huge step up), and, overall, numb.

"Oh, not 'sir' please. It's Clarence."

I left.

And dashed to a shareholders' meeting in Woolwich and got in just in time waving "my" share certificate. I thought I might also get thrown out, but everyone was so excited that no one noticed me. The meeting lasted 15 minutes, and basically Mr Leavey said he had agreed to the takeover. There was no mention of the Tottenham shares.

Back at the Manor we had Woolwich Arsenal 1 Aston Villa 0 – crowd 8000 – which was marginally better than Saturday's game. What distinguished this event was the singing. You get some singing at games these days, but not that much, but if someone wants to make a deal of it they can. One bunch behind the goal chose Silvery Moon and just kept singing it all the way through the second half. Then the other end joined in. "By the light" said the north end, ("By the light by the light" echoed the south) "of the silvery moon" said the north, ("the moon the moon") said the south. It was one hell of a lot more interesting than the game.

Back in the office Mr Holloway said that he had had Norris on the phone, with Norris demanding an apology for my outrageous piece about him buying the club in order to build a factory, and also demanding a personal meeting.

Mr Holloway said, "I told him that you were an esteemed political commentator and investigator, and that before Norris could get his hands on you half of the members of the House of Lords wanted to ring your neck first."

"And he didn't mention the King of London piece?"

"Of course not, you puerile urchin," said Mr Holloway – he does have a way with words. "If he says the King of London is in any way related to him buying clubs he draws attention to it. We'll then say Norris is not the King of London, and run it again so the readers can decide. He might guess it is you, if he studies the non-existent mindless style, but he won't know for sure. Are you doing more?"

"Mr Symmonds has just asked for one a week."

"And a pay rise?"

"Yes, sir."

"You have the luck of the devil, and the breath to go with it. The editor wants another political piece from you too."

"I can't do that," I said in even greater horror than I felt when facing Mr Symmonds. "Mr Churchill gave me that story in return for not running the piece about the closure of the torpedo factory. I can hardly go up to the Home Secretary and say 'I say ol' fella' give me another exclusive, what?'"

Mr Holloway shrugged. "You dig your quarry pit, you eat the gravel," he said. "You can't mix with the nobs and then expect to walk away. Anyway, from my perspective – and may I remind you that for all your fancy bonuses you are actually employed within the sports department – keep annoying Norris. Norris will always reply in his local rag, and that will give you something else to go on and me an alternative to your pathetic match reports."

"Anything you particularly want me to do to annoy him?" I asked.

"You'll think of something, I'm sure," he said. 1-0 to Jacko. Seeing me smirk he added, "There are reports of a man in Bristol who steals jewels, makes imitation copies out of them, and then hands the original back to the owner. Interview him would you?" One each.

Tuesday 12th April

Having told us shareholders what was what at the meeting yesterday, Leavey held an open session in which he said he had now changed his mind! The reason he gave was that he had read my piece in the Chronicle and wanted to make it clear that he was not selling his shares in the club if that meant that the club was going to move away from Plumstead. (At least this means that I don't have to make up the next episode of the King of London story – I can just run the real events. Newspaper influences football club!)

It was the strangest feeling, to be at a meeting where my own article was being given as the reason why things would happen. I kept my hat on, pulled down as far as I could, turned up the collar of my coat, stuck my hands in my pockets and made no comment.

Clarke's new approach was to make the new company directors personally liable for paying the rent etc on the Manor ground, and that means that the directors will not be able to walk away from Plumstead. The meeting did not like the news and broke up in uproar after 20 minutes. There was no sign of Norris or his men – I guess they must have known what was coming and didn't want to look stupid.

Back in the office I worked on the next episode of the King of London.

The main news confirmed that many of the clubs of the English First Division were being bought up, but not just by the Germans. Some Young Turks had landed and joined in the invasion, along with some Even Younger Turks, and some Turks who were So Young they hadn't been born yet. These had started to remove Chelsea, and had already floated away a considerable part of the ground into the Bay of Biscay.

A set of Russians had been allowed to buy Bury and were even now being aided in taking up the pitch by locals who claimed that they owned the mineral rights. Meanwhile, in the west country, the Swiss naval forces had sailed up the Severn estuary and taken Bristol City. A detachment of the Pope's personal protection division were reportedly occupying Manchester United aided (it was reliably reported) by several thousand Manchester City fans who were holding off all attempts to take the ground back...

Wednesday 13th April

Norris called the paper at five minutes past ten with a simple piece of news. If I could meet him at the Unionist Club in Woolwich at midday he would give me a story. I looked at the boss for guidance. He looked back at me in surprise. "Go," he said simply.

"But a couple of days back he was screaming that he was going to drag the paper into the gutter where it belongs," I protested.

"That is Norris. He shouts and screams. We didn't buckle. He won't know if you really wrote the Parliament Act story or the King of London drivel, but he realises he might have an enemy with a little more power than he previously imagined. So he thinks again and decides to buy you a round of soft soap. Quite possibly he thinks he can butter you up, get you into his camp, and fight the rest of the papers through you."

I must have looked uncertain, because he went on. "People who used to dismiss you as nothing – and that would include Norris – now think maybe they were wrong. Of course, I know you are a long piece of pig's belly, but as for the rest, they just haven't discovered yet."

"You really are a fine motivator of men, sir," I said.

"Thank goodness you are not being sarcastic," he said. "For that is a flogging offence. You will, of course, be out of your depth, because you are still an urchin, but that will make Norris believe you are bright and intelligent, which should throw him off the track. There's also a story about Loch Ness being moved to Sheffield. Find out about that, will you?"

I met Norris as agreed, and he was full of good wishes, bonhomie, slap on the back, and saying, "Jacko Jones!!!" as if I were his favourite circus act just come into the ring. Then there was the offering of a cigar and drinks prior to a meal at the club and things like, "I don't know where you get your stories," and laughing as if it is the funniest thing under the sun.

Next Mr Leavey and Dr Clarke turned up. We did the introductions and Norris made a funny speech about how I am a leading political journalist, and how I wrote the Parliament Act story – "Whole party is in uproar, landowners building the barricades to keep out the masses, ha ha ha. All a bluff, eh, Jones? How much the Liberals pay you to run that?" and so on.

Leavey and Clarke were clearly not expecting me to be there (Clarke said at one point, "Really Norris, you could have told us the press would be in on this") nor were they sure what to make of Norris' gibberish, but could do little more than ask me if I was going to write any more. I told them I would write more when there was more to write, but that I was here because Mr Norris had invited me to be here.

So there was some chitchat about the deadlock over Woolwich Arsenal, about the need to protect football for the local people, the need to protect the investment of the owners, the need to carry on the great tradition of London's oldest professional club (that was Norris, of course, nicking my phrase again).

Next thing I knew, as we all finished our meal (which I have to say was rather fine and I wished Edward had been there to do a review) and were back on the drinks, Norris was saying that he could certainly find a way to do a deal with Leavey. I couldn't make notes, of course, but I am certain he said, "I can sort the debts if you will let me take on the club."

Mr Leavey looked at Norris with narrowed eyes, as if to say, "What are you up to?" but before he could say no, I asked if I could put this in the paper. Leavey was really taken aback, but Norris saw where it was going and said, "if it is written by you dear boy, of course. It would be an honour. Ha ha ha."

"I'm not sure," says Leavey. "Nothing is agreed…"

But Norris had said that it would be an honour to have me, the famous football AND political writer, write a piece about little Norris and little Woolwich Arsenal. Ha ha ha. But then Leavey found his voice and said that there was no deal without an agreement that the club stayed in Woolwich, and Norris said, yes, yes of course, of course, it will be Woolwich Arsenal. Ha ha ha. Oh yes. Never any thought of anything else. Of course. Ha ha ha.

And I was thinking, "Like hell it will." Because Norris will hold all the aces once he gets control of the club. "I did want to keep it in Woolwich," he will say, "but the support is so poor, I was forced to move it… Just look at the recent attendances. Not my fault."

We carried on in the same vein, with lots of jolly-good-fellow stuff from Norris, and total uncertainty from other parties, and then I judged it the moment to get up and bugger off, although not before I asked if Tottenham were buying some of the shares, but Norris said, "No, no, of course not, just a silly rumour, we thought you started the story, Jones. Ha ha ha."

Once more back to the office, and a last minute write up of a story. The boss said it would do, I thought it was good, and I even got home in time to change and go out and play with the band, who treated me like a celebrity and expected me to pay for all the drinks.

Thursday 14th April

I was sitting in the office, having read the latest episode of the King of London and thinking that there was nothing more to be done on the Norris story and wondering if I would ever get any further on the idea of a story about football grounds designed by Leitch when a runner announced a call for me in the Sports' Office. It was from a man on the Reading Standard, asking if I knew anything about Norris of Fulham taking over Reading FC.

I said I hadn't heard anything about it, but please would he tell me. He put the phone down on me.

Mr Holloway looked at me with a look of dismay and pity. "It's a good job," he said, "that I am the only person in this room to witness our star sports and political reporter, who even now probably has a great story from Mr Churchill up his sleeve, not even knowing how to handle a rookie provincial hack."

"What should I have said?" I would have bristled but I knew there was no point. Mr Holloway would best me, as he always did. And besides there was no denying that I had got nothing from that phone call.

"When a story comes in from another hack, and you know nothing, you tell him you know all about the story and offer to share your knowledge with him. All he had was a whiff, and just wanted to see if it was worth putting energy into, otherwise he wouldn't have called you. You've told him you don't have it, which means that if he gets a story he's going to have a scoop – which you have just given him. If you'd told him you knew, and you'd then got the train to Reading, he would be in awe of you – the famous football reporter from the Chronicle. You make up some story – which as far as I can tell is what you normally do – and give it to him, and then see what he has got.

"You know Norris, so whatever this is it involves calling in favours or property deals. If it involves spending real money it's not Norris."

"Sorry," I left as the phone rang again. He was right, I had screwed it.

Mr Holloway listened and then he called me back in. "You, young man, land on your feet too often for my liking. The Reading Mercury."

I took the phone.

"Good to talk to you, sir," said a voice that sounded older than mine. Called me sir. A good start. "We read your work on Mr Norris of Fulham, and well, we were wondering, perhaps, if you know about him being interested in Reading."

"Strange you should be on the phone," I said. "I'm actually in the office of Mr Holloway, the sports editor of the Chronicle, just at this moment, and we were in fact discussing Norris and Reading."

"So it's true then," said the voice, going up an octave and sounding very enthusiastic and excitable and a lot younger.

"I can't say that," I said. "With Norris you simply never know until you do the leg work, but the story is out there. We've picked up bits and pieces."

"Oh... could I ask, bit of a cheek I know, but perhaps I could, well, ask, what you have got. We'd acknowledge you of course..."

"Difficult to say," I said, "like I said, it is no more than bits and pieces, hard to separate fact from rumour, and Norris is the master of saying one thing but meaning another. I had lunch with him and some of the Woolwich Arsenal grandees yesterday and he spent the whole meal trying to divert my attention. But I tell you what. I was thinking of coming to Reading to see what I could dig up on the story. If I came over could we meet up?"

"Oh that would be an honour, sir," he said. "A real honour. I read all your work, all the stories about the pubs and what people wear at the games... Plus your political work too... Will you be coming to the game?"

The game? I had no idea what game. I said, "The Game", hoping the boss would miraculously help me out, but he just raised his eyebrows and looked the other way. I tried my luck.

"I was hoping to, but am running late. Will you be there?"

"Of course," he said. "Look, I'll meet you in the press box,"

"Fine," I said and put the phone down.

"What was his name?" asked Mr Holloway.

I swore. I had forgotten to ask. I called back, said the line had been cut just as I was about to ask the name of the reporter who had called me, and got it sorted. I then took a long shot and tried to call Reading FC but they didn't seem to have a phone. I tried the longest shot of all and called Fulham.

I introduced myself and said, "I think you have a game today."

"There is a friendly away to Reading," said the receptionist who clearly had no idea who I was, and she gave me the details.

"So what do you know of Reading?" asked Mr Holloway when I put the phone down.

"Southern League Division 2," I said.

"And?"

I said nothing. He said, "Go and get the bleedin' Athletic News Yearbook."

Five minutes later I was back in the office. "Top man in Reading is Mr Joseph Sydenham," I said. "And before you tell me that I am useless, that you don't know why you pay me, that I really should be on the street picking up horse shit, and that it would be helpful if I knew how to write, I looked him up too. He is a Mason and a Unionist – exactly as is Norris."

"Good enough for me," said the boss. "Go to Reading. Third class, mind. And while you are there, find out if it is true that the United States of America have agreed to Edward the Caresser becoming their King."

And go to Reading I did: a train from Paddington, a hansom from the station to the ground. The game had been going for 20 minutes by the time I got there. The crowd was sparse. A typical Norris friendly.

My contact, a Mr Wrigglesworth, was just a bit younger than me, and continued calling me "Sir" which after a while got on my nerves, so I told him to stop it and call me Jacko, which seemed to impress him enormously.

I told him I had watched Norris' footwork vis-à-vis Woolwich (Mr Symmonds says vis-à-vis – I don't quite know what it means, but it sounds good and probably means 'kiss my arse') and he had arranged a friendly there.

"Exactly as he is doing here," said Wrigglesworth. "Fulham are in the all white."

I told him I knew. "I hope this goes better than his friendly at Woolwich," I said. "That didn't even cover expenses. But I suppose Fulham are a bigger draw here, with them being in the Football League."

"People have been talking about it for days," said Wrigglesworth, who had a strange accent that sounded a trifle west country.

"And your club needs the money?" I asked.

"That's the story, but it is hard to get straight facts."

"It's Joseph Sydenham who keeps the books?"

He was duly impressed. I made it sound as if Sydenham was known at the Chronicle.

"He pretty much runs the club, although he's officially the 'secretary'. But he's secretive, and those who aren't in his circle say he treats it as his private fiefdom. To put his side of the story, he's devoted years of his life to setting up and running Reading FC. I suppose if you start an organisation it is hard to let go of it."

The conversation stopped, and I realised I needed to do a little more to get out of Wrigglesworth anything else that he knew about the Reading / Fulham situation. We watched the game for a few minutes.

"I'll tell you what I've put together," I said generously, "and then if you have anything else, you tell me. After that we can both use all of the story. How about that?"

Once more he looked impressed by my largesse (another Symmonds word) so I added "Let's do it at half time," which at least gave me time to make something up.

At the turnaround we dutifully began talking. By then several people had recognised me – presumably because the man on the gate had thought it odd to have someone from the Chronicle turning up late, in a taxi, covering a friendly. We had to walk away from prying ears.

"Norris and your man Sydenham will have met either through the Unionist party or through the Masons, or both," I said. "Norris is up and coming – Mayor of Fulham, aiming to be Fulham's MP and looking to expand his wings. Sydenham moves in the same circles but doesn't have Norris' connections.

"Norris is a genuine football fan, but he wants to own the game in London. He had a chance to move Fulham to Stamford Bridge, and when he turned it down the owner of Stamford Bridge set up Chelsea, and that annoyed Norris beyond belief. What especially annoyed Norris was that Chelsea also used the promotion for money tactics. In Chelsea's case, however, they went even further than Norris, getting the club into the league before they even had a team.

"In fact Norris couldn't move to Chelsea because he had just signed a deal with the Church to rent their land at Craven Cottage – and I think he needs to stay sweet with the church – he's certainly buttering them up.

"So he's trying to outflank Chelsea – and the rest of football – by taking control of most of the other clubs in London. He also believes he can build a team to win the league, and bring football power to the south.

"So he's on the look-out. He's got Fulham and Croydon Common, and soon Woolwich Arsenal. The Arsenal are obviously bust, and a new company is being formed to run the club, but that's not the end of his search. If Sydenham has told Norris that Reading has financial troubles then Norris will be looking to buy Reading as well – and his first step is to order his team to play a 'fund raising friendly'."

Wrigglesworth swallowed the bait and jumped straight in (a reversal of sequence I know but Mr Holloway isn't reading this). "It all makes sense. Sydenham has been having private meetings all over the town, trying to find new sources of money to keep Reading going. We don't have other clubs on the doorstep, so that's good, but it's a small town, and second division of the Southern League is a long way down the ladder. With the trains running so well people are actually starting to go to Chelsea to watch football, rather than staying in Reading. Not many, but there's a few.

"Two weeks ago Sydenham went public and said that the club will close unless we can get bigger crowds to support the local team, but the crowds won't come unless there is success, and all we have here are local players.

"Then just after Sydenham made that announcement, the Fulham friendly came up, and Norris and Sydenham were seen together at the Unionist Club and then at the ground. Since then we haven't heard a word."

I shook my head and made it look as if this was nothing much more than I already knew.

"Do you think it's true that the club will go empty in two weeks?" I asked. He said he thought it probably was.

"And are there any other bidders?"

"Talk of a new consortium – but it is just talk. This town is full of talk."

"And can you see anything else in the story?" I asked. I tried to make it flippant.

"Sydenham is very thick with the Unionists in town – he's always out campaigning, writing pieces for the papers about how we need the Unionists, how the Liberals are killing the country, that Labour will take over and the Irish will kill us in our beds."

"How does that fit with football?" I asked.

"Search me," he said. And although I didn't say it, you could search me too. I can't see the connection, unless Norris is simply after power. Unless there is something else: something to do with connecting the working man and the toffs in the Lords. Could it be that the Lords are thinking that maybe they should learn more about the working man, rather than treat him like a creature from the abyss? As far as I know most Unionists think anyone in the vortex is there because he's lazy, and should simply get off his backside and work.

Norris is a political animal. So is Sydenham. So is Mr Churchill, and he is prepared to feed me what Marie and the political people on the Chron think is one of the biggest stories of all time. The problem is, I just can't see what, where, how, who, why, when or come to that anything else.

Friday 15th April

My story about the new Woolwich Arsenal, owned by Norris but staying in Woolwich, is in today's Chronicle, plus a few choice bits about owning Fulham. Nothing about Reading, of course, because there wasn't time to write that up – but it will make another good story.

My angle is simple – nothing has happened yet on the Woolwich front, and Norris might not take on the club if he can't move it, but if the current round of setting up a new company fails, Woolwich Arsenal will become part of the Norris Empire followed by (I predicted a little cheekily) another club from the south east that runs out of money. Perhaps a Southern League club…

It wasn't a great article, but it was ok, and it made second billing in the sports section behind a piece about rugby union that I didn't understand.

In the evening there was a meeting at the Royal Mortar in Woolwich. News was spreading like wildfire, this time to the effect that the deal to save Woolwich Arsenal had gone down at the last minute because of Leavey's change of heart over the threat to move the club. Everyone who had been ready to put their 20 shillings in was now ready to pull it out.

Leavey, of course was there, as was John Humble – which was really odd because he had been a director and had left a few years back. (I couldn't remember exactly when, but I grabbed a word with him at the end and he said he had left in "1906 or 1907 – I can't recall which".) Bringing back an old director smacks of desperation to me.

We were here (we were told) to set up the Woolwich Arsenal Football and Athletic Company (Limited) (note the "Woolwich") following the dissolution of the provisional board of directors formed some days ago for the same purpose which itself followed on the liquidation of the Woolwich Arsenal club. There was no explanation as to why the previous attempt at resurrection had failed. (I suddenly thought, wouldn't it have been funny if Jesus Christ's resurrection had failed a couple of times and that he had intended to rise from the dead on the first day, but they couldn't make it happen until the third day. I giggled – everyone looked at me, and Leavey said, "The gentleman from the Chronicle will do us the courtesy of remaining quiet.")

Mr Leavey then gave us a list of the people who had agreed to take on the onerous responsibilities of the new company and would be the opening board of directors (who could be replaced later on if needs be) – Messrs. Crick, Lamly, Titlow, Bailey, Grant, Coombes, and Evans.

We duly noted the omission of the Norris gang.

Contracts for the purchase of the old company had been completed and the liquidator was happy. The articles and memorandum of association of the new new company as opposed to yesterday's new company, drawn up by the board, had been lodged with the FA – although I suspected that these were the ones drawn up for the first replacement company with one or two bits scratched out.

So now the plan is to issue a prospectus early next week, with local people taking up 2000 £1 shares. I couldn't see it happening.

The creditors of the old club should be paid in full, Leavey said, and a certain Mr. Squires proposed a pledge that the meeting would support the new company and take up the shares. Everyone voted in favour.

Saturday 16th April

Tottenham Hotspur 1 Woolwich Arsenal 1, England 10 France 1

I took the bus from the Wood Green Town ground (where an amateur match was also taking place in front of a few hundred) to the Spurs' end of the Lane where there were sixty times as many people, although no one ever seems to talk about numbers at Tottenham. I wondered where the money went.

I got the usual jokes about my name in the press box – there having been a captain of the Spurs with my name apparently about ten years ago. I told them I was fighting for Queen and Country at the time, although I am not sure they believed me.

Tottenham looked as if they have risen too far, too fast, and were a sorry bunch, and only got the draw because Woolwich were nearly as bad and couldn't care less about anything having already arranged their survival in the First Division. It was interesting that the Spurs' match day programme had a list of the

90

club's triumphs on the front – including, of course, the FA Cup victory. Woolwich didn't have that – but then they had never won anything. The Spurs goalkeeper was wearing a hat and gloves and had a habit of rushing up towards the halfway line to catch the ball. It broke the play up quite badly, and would have been dangerous for Tottenham if Woolwich had had a decent centre forward. I liked the hat and gloves, though, and made that the focus of my piece.

In the evening I gave Marie a full update on Reading and the latest at Woolwich, and we asked the same question: if Norris is going to buy Reading and/or Woolwich Arsenal, what is he getting in return?

She said, "You should talk to my father." It was just about the most frightening thing anyone has ever said to me in my entire life. I am getting very fond of Marie – very fond – but talking to her father.... On the days we didn't meet I missed her. But her father... I can just about cope with Mr Holloway and Mr Churchill, but a member of the Lords...

Sunday 17th April

I went in to the Chron, wrote up the Hotspur game, read up the reviews of the jamboree of England against France, and then went to see the boss. I explained that I hadn't got evidence, but I could now take a broader guess as to what was going on.

He said, "A broader guess?" and laughed a lot.

When he'd finished and had done the mock wiping of the eyes thing he does, I told him my argument. Woolwich Arsenal is truly bust, Leavey is a true gent, but he isn't a negotiator and he can't keep the club going much longer. Which means that, although he would love local people to take it over and believes the local man will support him, it won't happen.

Leavey feels a "connection" with Woolwich and Plumstead and with the working men. He wants to look after them and give them something. But they feel no connection with him. They pay their pennies and want to watch a game, no more.

"And what do you know about negotiations and connections?" said Mr Holloway. I told him I had sat in at several of the Transvaal meetings as the war drew to a close, because I was the most senior person to have rounded up some of the enemy – most of the officers being drunk or absent without leave at the time. I also told him that when Section H moved into the War Office I was included in the debriefs and we talked about such topics, trying to work out why we had been given such a runaround and what lessons should be learned. No one on the British side really understood the Boer, and until Colonel Edmunds came along no one was able to find new tactics to beat the Boer. (Most of the officer corps had been trained in a totally different type of warfare and hadn't the foggiest notion what to do.) It was gaining that understanding of what the Boer did and then turning it on themselves that turned the war around. Colonel Edmunds, I said, made connections.

"Leavey has just got one way of thinking about the club, which is to sell shares to local people. He thinks he sees connections but he doesn't. When the latest share offer fails Norris will come in behind and rescue the club – mostly just to hit back at Chelsea. And he may also buy Reading – and it may be that he is jumping both sides of the fence at once – he might even have Reading as a preferred choice." I looked at my boss. He was sitting patiently, allowing me to spill it all out. Quite a change I thought.

"Quite the political analyst these days, Jones," he said, with less malice than usual. "How much of this is fact?"

"The early bits," I said. "On Reading, we know Norris was there, we know Reading are in financial trouble and have an owner looking to sell. We know he and Sydenham are both Unionists and Masons, but we have no evidence that Norris is looking to take over."

"We run with Norris, Woolwich Arsenal, possible move to Fulham, and he's been seen in Reading, but don't – I repeat do not – suggest he is buying Reading."

I protested, saying that I had speculated before and come up trumps, but Mr Holloway was having none of it.

"This story will run for a few weeks," he said, "quite possibly right the way through the summer when we have a dearth of football. So we don't want to ruin it now. Take your time, and wait for some reaction. With a story like this someone is going to make a move at some time, be it the FA, the Football League, Chelsea, Leavey, Norris, Reading or someone else we haven't even thought about. That statement or act or disclosure, whatever it turns out to be, will give us the next stage. Learn patience if you want to make it big in journalism. Meanwhile get yourself off to a vegetable farm and find out if there's anything in this story about carrots making you see in the dark."

Maybe he was right. I still felt sure I was still missing something. As things stood the story had a great big hole in it which was: why would Norris be willing to spend a lot of money buying one, let alone two, loss-making clubs outside London? Getting back at Chelsea was possible, but it wasn't really enough.

Monday 18th April

The story ran as a minor piece in today's paper, and no-one replied instantly – no Norris, no Leavey, no-one. In one sense this is not surprising since I reported facts and then made a prediction – it is hard to argue with that. Especially if everyone was getting ready to do the big deal.

I was still thinking of such things when a runner came into the sports room announcing there was a car at the door for me, and calling me sir, and treating me with even more respect.

Mr Churchill took me for lunch in the Home Office guests' restaurant. (I am getting used to be taken out for meals – it could become a very enjoyable habit, although I seem to be putting on a bit of weight. Either that or mum has shrunk my trousers in the wash.)

Once we had settled he asked what I knew about Norris wanting to buy the Plumstead ground for a new factory as I said in today's article – perhaps for a new government contract being placed in the area. My heart skipped a beat.

Surely I couldn't have stumbled on a real story again. I decided not to push my luck. I gave him a run down on Norris, Woolwich Arsenal, Reading, Croydon Common, Chelsea, Fulham. I said most of what I was writing was "just a guess."

"Just a guess?" said Mr Churchill, as the flunkies hovered behind. He didn't believe me. "Just like the torpedo story was just a guess?" I wondered if I had him rattled.

"Did you appreciate the Parliament Act piece?" I asked.

He admitted he did. Called it "excellent" in fact. I didn't tell him that half the newspaper's political team had had a hand in editing it.

"So you think Norris is not buying Woolwich Arsenal's ground?" he asked.

"No sir, I think he is going to do that. What I can't work out is why. To go to all this length to move Woolwich to Fulham in order to spite Chelsea seems a bit much, even if collecting football clubs is his hobby. Mr Astor is said to have given $100,000 to help the Empire fight the Boer War and the Chronicle said it was so he could have a baronetcy. Do you get knighthoods for buying up failing football teams?

"I am aware of Mr Astor," the Home Secretary said icily. I decided to shut up.

Eventually he said, "Who told you to write the King of London piece?"

I told him that I wrote it because I was so annoyed with Captain Kell's comments, and it just came out that way. The paper thought it worth a run, turns out some of the readers do too. So it continues, for the moment.

"Norris has friends all over the place," said Churchill at last, "and even as a political opponent I have to admit that at times he does good – both in the broader sense and for the ordinary voter. He comes unstuck only when he tries to pull in favours in a way that makes his one-time friends find him an irritation. A gentleman will honour his debts – up to a point." He leaned back, signifying a more expansive phase to his discussions. "Politics is war, except in war you can only get killed once. Norris and I are similar in one way – shoot us down and we'll come back from the dead. You know he has friends in the church, of all places?"

I confirmed that I knew and asked if he wanted to stop Norris taking over Woolwich Arsenal.

"Good heavens no, let him have the club. He won't get permission to do anything with the ground – I've already spoken to Kent County Council, and they won't give him any rights for anything other than a football club. They weren't going to anyway, but now they certainly won't. And I can tell you, you scallywag, that the government has no plans for a new venture in Woolwich. Off the record – and I mean that strictly – we are pulling out of Woolwich."

"Does he know that?"

"Not unless you tell him!" Mr Churchill said.

"I don't think I want to spoil the fun," I said, and we had a chuckle and another drink, just like old friends.

"See here," he said, as the meal drew to a close, "Norris has a wild imagination and he'll try any trick. More money is irrelevant to him. But he doesn't yet have power, which is what he craves. Do me and your government a favour: give him some rope, encourage him if you meet him, if it helps, mention that you have a friend in high places, but for goodness sake don't say who. Let's see where he goes. The government's only concern is the Lords, not the Mayor of Fulham. Help him hang himself and I won't forget to say thank you."

"So there is a political line," I said, still searching in the mists within my head for some sort of connection.

Mr Churchill nodded and lit a cigar. "There is always a political line. My job is to see what will happen next month and then to make sure it doesn't."

"May take a while," I said, "to bring him down," and we laughed and toasted each other. Me and the Home Secretary. Just like old pals.

And then suddenly I had an idea. "Does the government have a view about football?"

"A good thing indeed," said the Home Secretary. "Keeps the working man happy, stops him spending his money in the pub, develops loyalty to the home town, aids civil order."

"Even when they riot in Scotland?" I asked.

He gave me a stern look, and I backed off. "So I can take it that the government is happy for there to be a First Division club in Woolwich?"

"Delighted," he said. "The more football clubs there are, the more the working man is entertained. Bread and circuses. Have a First Division club in Southend as far as I am concerned. Build a stadium on stilts in the estuary. Anything that keeps the men happy on Saturday."

I didn't get the bread comment, but I noted it so that I could ask Marie later.

"The political question is always the same," he told me, leaning back in his chair. "Lenin raised it, if you know who Lenin is." (I nodded, hoping he wouldn't push. So far I was only clear on the anarchists; my notion of Lenin was vague.) "Who does what to whom? Who persuades the working man to work for £2 a week? Who encourages people to vote, rather than overthrow the whole state? That is Lenin's question. Who persuades the man in the street to accept the police as authority, when in fact on any occasion the crowd could rise up and see the police off? Where is the real power to run the whole operation we call Britain?

"Is it with the landed gentry in the Lords? Or is it with people like me, elected by a minority of men but at least elected? Or with the industrial barons? Or the workers? Or the King?

"If the Lords turn against the Commons, the Prime Minister will go to the King and ask him to create hundreds of new Lords overnight, and their job will be to vote down all the Unionist Lords and get the budget through. If the King refuses, we are all in trouble.

"And what if these stories about the German invasion across the sea are true? And what if, just as they invade, all the workers in our steel works, our boat yards, our coal mines and our railways go on strike?"

"You could pass a law saying, no strikes, I suppose," I said. "And send in the police to break the strikes."

"And would the workers obey it?"

"Or would you, Home Secretary, order the troops to fire on the working men on the railways or in the coal mines?" I asked. "Or would you give the workers the pay rise they demand and tax the rich to pay for it. So, tell me, who does what to whom?"

"Do you know," he said, "I haven't the slightest idea."

I didn't believe him, and we left it at that.

Tuesday 19th April

I met Marie and we went over the implication of what had been said by Mr Churchill. I had no new story – just a new way of thinking.

"Churchill is an able man, but his point of view is how to stay in power. You need to meet another politician to get some balance."

I asked who, and to my shock she said Lloyd George. She saw the look on my face, and I explained that the army hated him because he spoke against us while we were in Africa.

"I think you are mistaken," she said. "He was against the Boer War on the grounds that the British had no right to be there, but he was not against the army. He certainly never demanded a mutiny. He just criticised those who made the decision to send you out there. He also criticised Kitchener for the concentration camps.

"You know the saying: if you are going to hunt a tiger don't take Lloyd George with you - he'd be on the side of the tiger. He is the man who wants to bring down the Lords by taxing their income and land. I thought you'd approve."

"So – should I read something of his?" I asked.

"No – we'll hear him talk. He does a speech somewhere every night – he travels the country. He'll be in London within a few days – he always is, to fit in with his time in Parliament."

We left that and I returned to football and Archie Leitch, the architect. "All I have at the moment," I said, "is that there was a disaster at Ibrox, that he has worked at Chelsea and there is clearly a problem there too, and I believe he worked on the grounds at Woolwich and at Fulham."

"When I work on a story about a person," she told me, "I start with dates. Get the dates all set out and quite often a pattern appears."

So we worked on the problem, came up with a cascade of dates, and then narrowed them down to...

August 1900, Woolwich Arsenal's stand was built to Leitch's design. It was quite possibly his first job – although odd that a man based in Scotland should be in Kent – except of course that at that time Woolwich was predominantly a Scottish town in England with the workforce recruited from Glasgow – where Leitch was based.

April 1902, the wooden terracing of the West Tribune Stand at Ibrox Stadium (built to Leitch's design) collapsed. The Times report says that there had been rain the previous night which had damaged the foundations. 25 people died and over 500 were injured, mostly because they fell from the terracing which collapsed to the ground nearly 50 feet below. There were enquiries and Leitch gave evidence. The Times revealed some interesting issues: the question of whether the right materials had been used, and the fact that Leitch had never been paid for the job (interesting, given that he wasn't paid at Woolwich either).

July 1902, the first reports came out of enquiries into the disaster, suggesting that Leitch's specification for the building was not followed.

November 1902, the Times reported a recommendation from the Scottish Football Association that it was not safe to put wooden terracing on top of a steel girder frame because of the danger of collapse, and that the builders had been wrong not to use concrete.

January 1903, Norris was removed from the Masons.

June 1903, Norris became chairman of Fulham.

July 1903, Norris started negotiating with Leitch over a new stand at Fulham. "Remember," said Marie, "that Norris is a property developer. He'll know about structures, plans, architects and everything to do with building."

July/August 1904, a second bank of terracing at Woolwich Arsenal was built and opened for the new season. We could find no record of who prepared the design.

September 1904, LCC started proceedings against Fulham for keeping the "temporary" stand too long, and Leitch gave his evidence about the difference between a building and a structure.

June-August 1905, Fulham's new main stand was built to a design by Leitch – exactly at the same time as Leitch was working for Chelsea just across the road.

"Let us suppose," I said, "that the first Woolwich Arsenal stand was built using the same method that was used in Glasgow."

"There's nothing wrong with that," said Marie, "no one knew it was unsafe at the time."

"But by 1902, Leitch would be a person to avoid – the man who had been designing football grounds that could be unsafe. You wouldn't expect people to be rushing to him saying, 'Could you design a ground for me?' And yet a year later Norris is approaching this man whose stand fell down and killed all those people, and saying 'Build a stand for me'."

"If he were cleared, and if he had worked for nothing at Ibrox and effectively at Woolwich Arsenal, I'd probably give him a shot," said Marie.

"Do you think Norris would have told Leitch to use the Ibrox system?" I asked. "And what about Chelsea? Was their ground built using the same system? It is certainly falling apart – although in the Chelsea case it's the terrace concrete, not the structure that holds the terrace up."

"We'd have to get hold of the plans to find that out, but if Leitch did still believe that his original system was safe he might be willing to build it again – especially as it would be cheaper than concrete. And if he was not getting any other work, he'd jump at Norris' offer. Even more, if the man who was asking him to build would promise that no one would ever know that the old discredited system was going to be used again." I said.

"But there's another approach," said Marie. "Supposing Leitch's design for Ibrox, and indeed Chelsea, was fine. Supposing the report suggesting the builders cut corners at Ibrox was right – and suppose the same thing happened at Chelsea. If we argue it this way, Leitch is a great front man. He's qualified, he's articulate, and he can fight his corner. But – and this is the big attraction to football club owners who want a big terrace or stand put up quickly – he is not a man to keep a close eye on the builders. He rushes the plans through, gets them accepted by the planning authority, tells the builder what to do and moves on to another job. Everyone knows you don't trust the builders – they will have their budget, but they make their profit cutting corners. And Leitch is so busy he never checks."

"Is that part of his job? To check?" I asked.

"I'm not a builder," said Marie, rather obviously I thought, but I took her point. "But surely someone has to check that the builder is following the specifications. If no one was appointed to check on the builders independently, then it must be Leitch. And this fits with Chelsea – he would find it hard to keep an eye on their ground while he was working on Fulham's at the same time."

"But none of this explains why he was not paid for the Woolwich stand," I said.

"Maybe it does," said Marie. "Supposing he did a botched job – a quick design and then leave it to the builders. Leavey might have realised that he had been tricked. Leitch was to blame, but maybe it is hard to prove – without digging up the foundations of the stand. Leitch denies it, the builder denies it, everyone denies it, but someone must be guilty. So he says to Leitch – I am not paying you unless you can produce records and evidence to show you supervised the construction step-by-step as per contract. Leitch can't, and doesn't want a big row, so he backs off. Life is tough after that, because the word in England would be around that there is something 'iffy' about Woolwich. So he goes back home, finds that his home town team of Rangers want a ground, and says, 'I'll do it for nothing.'

"Then that goes wrong too, so he comes back to London - a long way away from his home ground, and a long enough time for people to forget about one little stand in Kent, and starts touting for work again. He finds Norris, who knows about every building trick under the sun, and does the design job there and at Chelsea (who need a stadium at full speed because they've been given a place in the League if they build the stadium quick enough). In short he becomes the specialist in speed building. And all we have to do is find some proof."

"When you go to Woolwich, could you go somewhere else in the ground?" she asked. "Not in the stand?" It was a real sign of concern about me.

More silence.

"We need the plans," she said at last. "The plans of Fulham and Chelsea must be in the planning department for the LCC. That's the only place to start."

Wednesday 20th April

Today the Leader has an article in which Norris denies that he is about to merge Woolwich Arsenal with Fulham. No mention of Reading.

I was sent to yet another shareholders' meeting, the purpose of which was to put Woolwich Arsenal Ltd into liquidation. I was about to present the shareholder certificate as usual when I saw two familiar faces in the lobby of the Town Hall. One ducked away quickly into the office before I could get a clear look but I swear from the size of the man it was Norris. The other looked like William Hall – the co-director of Fulham. He remained in sight for longer, until the big man dragged him into the office by the collar.

By the time I had barged through the crowd of onlookers both men had vanished, and I could hardly push my way through the private council offices looking for them – not least when I had no right to be in the meeting myself. So I gave up the chase, presented my certificate, and sat through another exposition by the honourable Mr Leavey on what liquidation means and why it is better than bankruptcy. He tells us we are going to pay all the creditors and sell all the assets.

My guess is that Leavey really entered the meeting thinking that this time he'll push it through. After all, he's done everything under the sun for the club; he's arranged meetings, set up the new company, held off the Norris interest as far as he can... He even had some good news – the London and Provincial Bank that runs the club's overdraft are still not pushing for payments. Knowing the way the banks treat most people I thought that was a coup worth a round of applause, but no one seemed to notice.

Instead, all Leavey got for his pains was an argument over who the liquidator should be. The argument was that if the liquidator was Leavey's man then Leavey would tell the liquidator who should be paid first.

Then we were back to moving the ground nearer to London – even though nothing remotely like that was on the agenda. Someone said, "What about Fulham?" but it wasn't followed up. I looked for Norris and Hall in the public gallery but there was no sign of them.

They voted for liquidation and I managed to get the last train back to town and wrote out the next Digby episode.

As the troops of all the invading countries marched to and fro removing football grounds, the surrounding areas (including the hedges, of which the Swiss in particular seemed very fond), the players in the teams and the supporters, it was inevitable that some damage was done. In particular the cricket ground at the Oval was scuffed, while in the shires their lordships were unable to hunt because the foxes had all run away, frightened by the invading forces.

Inevitably Parliament was suspended. "You cannot expect us to sit around all day in central London," said Sir Hardly Anyone, spokesman for Lord A'Leaping, "when the fox population is being destroyed..."

Thursday 21st April

Marie sent a note saying that Lloyd George was speaking at – of all places – the Houndsditch tonight and making arrangements for us to meet. LCC planning office confirmed that they held the plans for the football grounds at Chelsea and Fulham, and it turns out that Mr Leitch has an office in the West End, although he is rarely there. I made an appointment to see him on… 7th June.

So, in the evening, to the Houndsditch. Marie and I presented our press cards and got decent seats. Lloyd George used no notes and delivered a speech so exciting and moving that time and again I stopped writing just to listen to his voice. I actually applauded several times, which got dirty looks from the other hacks.

But there was one bit we did get word for word (or "verbatim" as Mr Holloway is training me to say), although only because both of us were taking it down in shorthand and compared notes at the end to make sure we had it. He was talking about visiting the mine owners.

"When the Prime Minister and I knock at the door of these great landlords and say to them, 'You know these poor men who have been working in your mine, risking their lives digging up the coal that earns you the royalties you live on? Some of them are very old – they have survived the perils of the mines, and now they are broken and can work no more. Won't you give them something towards keeping them out of the workhouse? Just a penny, just a ha'penny, even a farthing.' And they scowl at us and say, 'You thieves.' And they turn their dogs on to us."

At the end of that sentence there was silence for a second and then suddenly the house erupted. There were shouts of "shame" mixed with shouts of "nationalise", and much applause. And I must admit that Marie and I were on our feet too, our notes forgotten, shouting and cheering for this man with his beautifully lyrical voice (my God I sound like Dick) and a new vision of how we can live our lives. And I noted that either Marie has no sympathy with her family, or her family does not make its money out of coal.

Friday 22nd April

On the way home after hearing Lloyd George, Marie and I debated his message, while looking at the newly visible Halley's Comet. She said it takes 76 years to go round the sun and spends most of that time out in deep space. And, she said, the Earth is going to pass through the tail of the comet for the first time in a thousand years.

Today the papers are running stories about the comet and the end of the world. Although not the Times, of course – they are treating it as a straight scientific event. My paper is telling everyone to stay indoors and jump under the bed when it happens. We are also covering Lloyd George. I handed in my report on the Houndsditch speech to the surprise of Mr Symmonds who, of course, had no idea I would be there ("I like to stay in touch" I said imperiously), and it seems it might be used.

Back on the football front everyone is full of rumour, mostly that the latest bid to set up a new Woolwich company is failing, and Norris is going to take over the club at last. Seems also they will pay off the football debtors (but I suspect not the rest) to keep the authorities happy and then move to Fulham. I had call after call through the morning from people wanting me to confirm the story – there is a half-baked version in West London, while the Kentish Independent is saying that shares in a new company go on sale next week and Norris will buy them all up.

After the third call Mr Holloway started to shout at me, demanding to be reminded which newspaper actually paid my salary, when a boy rushed in, said, "Sorry, Sir," to Mr Holloway, and then said, "Sorry, Sir," to me (oh I do like that) and handed over a wire. Leavey had put out his own statement saying that he would only agree to the new company taking over Woolwich if it stayed in Woolwich. One nil to Leavey.

Eventually Mr Holloway did something he had never done before. He left his office, told his deputy to cover the phone, and walked me to the Pen and Sword next door. I thought he was going to buy me a drink but he instructed me to buy him one.

"What is no one else saying which might just be true?" he asked.

"No one is talking about Reading," I said, "no one is talking about Leitch."

"Then where is your story saying that Norris is in the market for any and every football club in financial trouble? Where is your piece about Tottenham's directors buying Woolwich?

"Everyone else is going to run what you have been writing, in your unfortunate manner, for the past few weeks and I expect you to stay ahead of the pack. We don't say Norris is going to buy Woolwich, we don't say he ain't. We don't say he is going to buy Reading, and we don't say he ain't. We just lay trails, false leads, talk about Croydon Common, blame Tottenham, throw in someone else."

"You mean make it up?" I asked.

"As normal," he said. "Try Chelsea, they are always on the make with their dog racing track. Or what about Millwall? Or West Ham? Maybe he wants to buy the lot! A monster on the prowl who wants to take over London football."

"So, Mr Holloway, if I have understood this situation correctly, you have asked me into a public house, for the first time ever, and required me to buy you a drink, so that you can tell me to make things up."

"Don't be ridiculous," said the boss. "You know I'd never willingly spend more time with you than is necessary. Just get on and write it. And also I want a piece about that woman from France who has just swum the Channel under water."

So I did as I was told (except for the underwater swimming bit) suggesting that rather than this being a Norris ploy it was a football issue, and Tottenham were at the heart of it. The starting point, I suggested, was the friendlies – like Fulham against Woolwich and Fulham against Reading. Watch the friendlies, I suggested.

After writing the piece I shuffled down to County Hall to look at the plans for the grounds of Fulham and Chelsea, and that turned out to be worth a visit and a half. Chelsea had been put in first, followed within a matter of weeks by Fulham. The Fulham application was sketchy in the extreme, saying that the stand was of the same design as that which the LCC had accepted for Chelsea just a few weeks before, and the terraces would be built in the same way – again as recently approved.

That confirmed Leitch as the speed merchant. If he was so busy he didn't even have time to put in any information on the building of Fulham, he was just as likely not to be checking on the way the builders were doing the job.

Besides, Fulham's new stand was nothing like Chelsea's – I knew because I had done reports from both. Which implied that either the LCC were not doing their job or Leitch was paying them off – as well as not supervising the builders. Corruption or incompetence? I'd go with either.

Saturday 23rd April

My future of football story is in today's paper and I busied myself on the Leitch research. The reports say that after the collapse of the terracing Alexander McDougall, the timber merchant who supplied the terracing, was charged with culpable homicide on the grounds that against the orders of the architect he had used the wrong wood. Leitch was called as a witness in the trial, and he admitted to having been employed to supervise the erection of the ground, as well as design it. It was also believed that Leitch's design was accepted because it was stated that he could get the ground built more quickly and more cheaply than anyone else.

Leitch admitted in court that he had found McDougall using cheap wood and had written to McDougall to complain, but had never received a reply and never followed up the matter in person. He said that he was forced to trust the integrity of the contractor – which is tantamount to saying that we don't need to have an army or navy because we trust the Kaiser.

When Leitch examined the construction after the collapse he said that it was all built using the wrong wood and it was cut to the wrong length. McDougall's foreman, however, said that Leitch knew about this and approved it, simply to keep the job on schedule – and anyway there was a shortage of the right sort of timber.

As the trial went on it looked to me as if Leitch was only staying out of trouble because the ground was technically outside Glasgow, and there was virtually no control over design in the country areas. A whole string of expert witnesses came along to show that Leitch's design was faulty. It all got rather technical at this point (to do with safety factors, live loads and dead loads) and although I don't know about all this, it seems Leitch got the worst of the exchanges.

Worse for Leitch, after the disaster Rangers had written to the architect responsible for their earlier stadium asking him to work out a plan to strengthen the new ground – clearly a vote of no confidence in Leitch. Then the court saw a letter Leitch had written asking that this approach by Rangers to their original man be kept quiet for this very reason: it would show no confidence in him.

It got worse as Sir Benjamin Baker, the best known architect of the day who had designed the Forth Bridge, gave evidence and said Leitch's designs were "dangerously light" and "I would not approve it for a moment". The contractor for the Forth Bridge also gave evidence – seems he also did Tower Bridge – and he too laid into Leitch.

At the end the Ibrox contractor was found not guilty, and no one thought it worth prosecuting Leitch. So it looks as if Leitch was offering to do the job on the cheap – with no fee to him. Maybe he was planning to take a cut from the contractor but there's no evidence on that. Certainly all the experts concur that the designs were shoddy and the contractor cut corners – with evidence suggesting that at best Leitch turned a blind eye to this.

By 1905 Leitch was back working at full speed and cutting corners, although so far it looks as if only Chelsea's ground has problems.

I pondered my findings as I made my way once again to Woolwich to cover the game against Preston North End. I paid to go in the ground, rather than using my press pass, and watched from the terraces, making notes as best I could.

Preston won 3-1, and I wrote up a story about the commentaries of the men around me. Trousers are worn long this year, drinks are brought into the ground, and there is a lack of lavatory facilities, I reported. Mr Norris was not present.

No sooner was I done writing than Mr Holloway's runners said I was needed, urgent. "I need a story to round up this Woolwich business for Monday. Feeling is that it has been going on too long – readers are getting bored, we want an end."

"But if the story is still running…"

"I am the editor, you are the snivelling journalist. I say, you do," he said. "But I'll be kind. You can bring in something so big that it replaces Woolwich, so you can come back to it later, or you can resign. Alternatively, investigate the story of this man in Newcastle who claims he knows all the horse racing results in advance by studying the colour of seaweed."

I said nothing and went off to meet up with Marie. We took the underground to the Angel and sat in the park. It was crowded as always, but somehow much of it seemed to pass us by. I updated Marie on Leitch and Woolwich and we pondered how to find the end of a story.

We'd finished our meal at the fish restaurant, and were walking hand in hand through the gardens gazing at the comet, when Marie said, "What would you have done in South Africa? You must have had situations where a Captain told you to sort something, but didn't tell you how."

"Every day," I said with a smile. "Captains are the lowest of the low – no knowledge how to fight, no knowledge how to command. Some of them just say, 'See to it, sergeant', and some ask nicely, but none of them know how."

"So here we are in Transvaal. The upper class, public school, university educated captain says, 'Sergeant, we need to wrap up the Norris story. See to it, will you?' What do you do?"

"In Africa we would have broken into the enemy's house," I said. "Found the plans, papers, maps, anything that might tell us what he was thinking, and got out fast."

"You never got caught?"

"No, I was a good thief… and the thieves I trained were good thieves, but I am not sure about being a thief here. I've got a career going…"

"So go and find yourself a sergeant and get him to do the deed. Or better still, I'll go…"

I ignored the last comment, not taking it seriously. It was only when I looked up at Marie on the bench beside me that I realised that she might just do it. Naturally I told her that there was nothing doing, but her mind was racing.

"First, I am light on my feet, which means I can get in and out of spaces easily. Second, I'll have a good idea what I am looking for. Third, if I am caught…"

"If you are caught…" I said not believing I was hearing this.

"If I am caught I will plead temporary insanity. No one will believe a respectable woman of class and background would suddenly for no reason break into the house of the Mayor of Fulham."

"No, they'll know that you have been seeing me, the judge will believe I forced you to do it, and I'll go to prison for white slave trading."

"I am going to do this," she said. "Norris' house – something fishy. Piece of cake."

"Where do you find these quaint phrases?" I asked.

"You mostly," she said. "We will speak no more of this until I am done – if you know nothing of it, you can't get involved."

"But I am involved…" I protested, but she looked away and would say no more of it.

We moved the discussion onto Marie's work. She told me about Samuel Clemens also known as Mark Twain, who was born during the last appearance of Halley's Comet in 1835, and who predicted he would die when it came around again. Apparently he did exactly that and died on 21st April.

That night I convinced myself that it was just a jape – Marie could not in any way undertake such a venture. She was just winding me up and, besides, if she did try she would fall over the milk bottles or wake the maid some other way… And Norris would be at home. Or at least his wife would…

Monday 25th April

I went to the dinner held in the Town Hall to launch the new company taking over Woolwich Arsenal. (Quite which "new company" this is, I have no idea, having lost count. But it was organised, so either Leavey was learning how to do it or Norris had laid on the show.)

Norris was there, of course, as a "friendly observer" and he nodded to me in passing. There was much toasting of the team for its survival in the First Division, and then the formal launch of the great rescue plan. One new idea came forward – if you wanted a £1 share you could buy it over 20 weeks at a shilling a week. Football on the never-never.

No one wanted to talk to me, and who could blame them? I'd been running stories which disrupted their efforts from day one, but I didn't tell them I had been ordered to drop it.

The players were dressed in their best suits, and were cheered and slapped on the back as if they had won the cup. I stayed until the party broke up around midnight and cadged a room at the Hen and Basket. Mrs B even put me out a razor for the morning. They were used to me by now, and I had, after all, mentioned the inn in dispatches more than once.

"Next thing you know," she said, "we'll be getting tourists."

Tuesday 26th April

Mrs B and I sat and chatted over the egg and beans. The local postie arrived with half a dozen letters for the pub. "I didn't know your guests could read and write," I said, trying to keep up the jollity.

"Not the ones that stay here," said Mrs B. I let it pass. My head was still aching as I caught the train.

"Get down to Fulham," said Mr Holloway as I finally walked into the office. I had admitted already that I had no final winding up story.

"Norris' house was burgled last night," he added as I looked at him quizzically.

I must have stood there with a stupid look on my face for a good five seconds. He was looking at me and doing the finger clicking business in front of my nose that he does whenever he thinks I am not paying him enough attention. "And cover the piece about a volcano going off in Preston," he shouted as I hit the door.

The stairs vanished beneath me (Edward who followed more sedately suggested that I was taking them five at a time) and I called a taxi. I didn't have a chit for it, and the paper probably wouldn't cover the cost. Edward had the sense to stay quiet – checking his equipment.

Norris' house had a fine garden and looked almost like a mansion – except it was in Fulham – which to most Londoners meant that there would be wild apes swinging from the banana trees and penguins grazing by the river. There were two police constables on the gate, and I waved my press card at them, but to no avail. Journalists were being kept in a pack to one side.

As we joined the mob I started to ask them what had happened, but then realised they were expecting me to tell them. "He's your man," said a stout party from the Telegraph, "what's he up to?"

"This time," I said, thinking on my feet, "I have no idea. Norris was at the launch of the new Woolwich Arsenal company last night," Several of them wrote it down, as if it were a press conference.

I told Edward to stay put and get whatever he could, while I grabbed a taxi back to Fleet Street. I had a total alibi for last night having been with Norris and co in Woolwich until midnight, and then at the Hen, but that would just make it look as if I had set Marie on the job on a night when I had the total alibi.

Marie came to meet me at the Times office foyer, and I was just about able to avoid shouting at her. Instead I simply asked if she was in Fulham last night.

"I think it is unbecoming of a gentleman to ask a lady where she spent the night," she said primly, and then before I could continue she said, "but it is equally unbecoming of a politician in the 20th century to try and buy votes."

"Who is buying votes?" I asked, unsure about this turn of events.

"Someone who has lists of voters in his house with ticks by certain names. Page after page of printed lists covering various constituencies."

"These are the official lists of voters?" I asked incredulously. No matter what his position or rank, Norris should not have access to those, and certainly not in his house. And then before Marie could answer that question I added, "what constituencies?"

"Oh, different parts of London, such as Fulham – as you'd expect since it is his constituency. And Woolwich – of course he has spent time out there too. And Croydon. And Reading. And Tottenham and Wood Green."

"He's…" I still couldn't get my head around the idea – although all my outrage at Marie for breaking into the house had gone. "He's buying votes?"

"He owns the football team," she said "or in the case of Reading and Woolwich, soon expects to own the team. And if he puts money into the team, that might make him popular. And if he becomes popular then people will probably want to say thank you by voting for him."

"But he can't stand in every constituency," I protested.

"But his man can," said Marie. "You can just imagine Norris reminding voters of who saved their club, and therefore who they should vote for. He doesn't have to be the MP himself – he controls the voters so he controls the MP. He gets extra power – he is his own power block. His own party. Word is that with a balanced parliament with no majority, as we have now, some MPs are selling their votes to the highest bidder. You can buy a knighthood for a few thousand pounds. But supposing a whole raft of MPs owed allegiance to a private gang of Unionists operated by Norris – then he'd be able to swing their votes. And maybe he's only just started – he could buy even more areas. And he'd be able to get any office that he wanted. It is like having a private army."

"But not everywhere is going to vote Unionist. I can't imagine Woolwich and Plumstead being Unionist," I protested. "They are Liberal – or maybe even Labour."

"Now you are being slow," said Marie mocking me, "which famous would-be owner of a football club wants to get in and move it?"

"Oh my," I said, feeling utterly stupid. "If he can establish the moving of clubs from one place to another as perfectly normal, he'll take the club to a unionist seat. Except that this means there's no point in going to Fulham."

"More likely he'll move Woolwich Arsenal somewhere else," she said. "This is not a three month plan – this is a long-term assault on the ideals of democracy. While the rest of the kingdom is heading towards votes for more people – and you never know, votes for women eventually – Norris is taking us back into the 15th century with rotten boroughs."

We sat in silence for a while, each deep in thought. Then I said, "What are you doing to do with the story?"

"That is what you and I have to work out," she said. "I took about half a dozen pages of the electors lists from each area – items from part way through each collection so it won't be too noticeable that they have gone."

"If you go public," I said, "Norris will demand to know the source – and I am not sure you would want to lie on oath."

"I'm not a Christian," she said simply, and I looked at her in surprise. "The oath is not a problem. What is more interesting is that the pages have notation on them against some of the names – comments about the voter. And that writing looks to me like the same writing that I found in a diary that I also removed."

"You have Norris' diary?" I was shocked. She nodded. "And…"

"And it is private and personal, and not something that Norris will want to have distributed."

I was excited now. "So do you run the story?"

She shook her head. "No, the Times won't take this. You run it."

Wednesday 27th April

"We hold the story," Mr Holloway told me.

I protested, but he would hear none of it. Instead he wanted a detailed report on the man in Brighton who could play the Moonlight Sonata with his big toe.

The electors' lists had been found in Norris' house, annotated with his handwriting. Better still, I hadn't stolen them. My source had. Since it was technically a crime for anyone other than the returning officers to hold lists of electors (a leftover from the Reform Acts which stopped the practice of buying votes) we had him for attempted gerrymandering in Fulham, Reading, Woolwich, Croydon, Tottenham and Wood Green.

"There are two big reasons why we won't publish today," the boss said. "The first is that today the House of Commons is going to pass the People's Budget."

"Taxation of the Unionist rich and their rural property. Set up a proper hospital service, pensions and better roads," I recited.

"My goodness, the boy is well versed in public matters," said the boss, with heavy sarcasm. "And what that means is that tomorrow there is just one story, which is that the Commons have approved the bill and will the Lords turn it down again and thus allow the Commons to turn on them with full gusto. Who blinks first – that's the story.

"Alongside that your piece about the Mayor of Fulham stealing election lists is tiny. We wait until the political storm is dead and then, with every other newspaper looking for a new venture to follow, we pop up and give it to them."

"And the second reason?" I asked.

"The second reason," and here he coughed like a bad actor, "is that it is just possible that your story will hit Norris by not being published. He knows he has had a break-in. He knows there was incriminating evidence all over the parlour. So what does he do?"

"Sit tight and hope that the thief was an ignorant twirp who didn't know what he was looking at?"

"He'll guess it was you behind it, and he'll guess you don't know your electoral list from your toilet paper. So you interview him, tell him that stories are circulating that there was sensitive material in the house and that people are offering information for sale. Would he like to say what was there…?   That might just get him moving. By the way who did the business?"

I said I couldn't say. He nodded knowingly, but I have no idea how knowing he really is.

"But Edward, under oath, said that you shot away from the scene of the crime and came back to Fleet Street. You didn't come in here, so where did you go. Across the road?" We had a moment's silence. "If Norris says that if you publish he will sue, then we know we are on to a winner."

Thus it was that once again Edward and I made the journey across town and ended up at the political office of Norris in the Conservative and Unionist club. The Telegraph man, Scrapper Chalfont, was there, but no one else. He reminded me that I owed them, so I invited him in with me. Since he didn't know all the background he wouldn't know where I was going with my story – at least I hoped not.

I ran the story that Mr Holloway had outlined, and, as predicted, Norris exploded. And what an explosion it was. Scrapper had backed out of the door before I had got even half way through, and Norris certainly wasn't listening. I guessed that most men would never have seen anyone as angry as Norris – unless, of course, they had served in the armed forces and had to answer to a major who had just been turned over by a captain who had just been turned over by a colonel who had....

Outside Scrapper asked what these famous rumours were that everyone else had heard about except him. "Oh everything," I said nonchalantly. "Forged sovereigns, cigarettes without duty paid, beer from Belgium, stolen copies for Liberal Party meeting notes, letters in which he is attempting to buy a knighthood... Do you know what he's doing tonight?" I threw the question in as lightly as I could.

"He's making the after dinner speech at the annual dinner of the Fulham Philanthropic Society," Scrapper told me. "Asking people to give help to the needy, that sort of thing."

Thursday 28th April

At the office we got the details of the Cup Final – replayed after last Saturday's draw. Newcastle beat Barnsley two to nil in Liverpool. Newcastle's fourth final in six years. Second Division Barnsley apparently played like a load of thugs. Must be taking lessons from Woolwich.

What interested me more was the fact that Lloyd George's budget went through the Commons and entered the Lords. All the political writers rushed off to do their bit as the news came through, and I went into Mr Holloway's office with a junior reporter, Josh Kelvinside, whom I had always liked because he had been one of the first to indulge in calling me sir.

"Josh here has something to tell you," said Mr Holloway.

"Sir," he said, looking anxiously from side to side, "Sir..." (I think he said it twice as there were two of us.) "Mr Norris didn't go to the Fulham Philanthropic meeting last night. I was in there for the paper, sir, and his wife was there on the top table, but not him. Every time someone new came through the door she looked up – I'm sure she didn't know where he was. Eventually one of the other members got up and apologised for Mr Norris not being there, and made a brief speech." He consulted his notes. "It was Mr Gilbert, and he thanked the people of Fulham for their generosity of spirit, and..."

"The speech isn't important," said Mr Holloway, "at least not unless it mentions Norris."

"No, sir," said Josh. "Mr Gilbert just said Mr Norris had been detained on important business."

Mr Holloway thanked Josh and led him out of the door, carefully closing it, and turning to me. "Got him," he said."

"How…"

But I needn't have asked. It should have been obvious: Mr Holloway, old hand that he is, had put half a dozen runners on look out front and back of Norris' house and he already had their reports. He read them to me, "Lady wife left the house at 6.30pm - in good time for the meeting, but looking a little agitated," he said reading the note. "No sign of Norris. Five minutes later, gas lamp is illuminated in back parlour. Twenty minutes later – that is ten minutes after Norris should have been at the Philanthropic meeting, a man of Norris' size and build is seen leaving the house carrying a large heavy object."

"The electoral lists!" I announced, rather obviously.

"I had reached a similar conclusion," said the boss dryly. "He takes a cab, and returns 20 minutes later, wherein he repeats the trick."

"So where did he go?" I asked.

"Fulham Football Club."

"Oh no!" I couldn't believe it. "You had the boys follow him?"

He looked at the ceiling, emphasising my stupidity.

"And they saw him go in with the bags?" I persisted.

"They did."

"And they went in after him?"

"They did."

"And what did they observe?"

"They observed a man, about six feet tall, having what one of the boys called 'some kind of bleedin' fit'."

"Why?"

"Because in between his delivery of the first heavy bag and the second, the boys, acting on their own initiative you understand and absolutely not in any way whatsoever under instruction from the newspaper, happened to find themselves inside the club house at Fulham – I can't quite see how or why but there it is – and found on the committee room table a large bag stuffed with paper. Thinking this odd – as one might do – and indeed thinking that all that paper left lying about might be used by an arsonist Chelsea supporter to start a fire, they removed it. Then they waited for the return of Norris, who on seeing that the first collection had indeed been removed, became multo agitato."

"What?"

"Visibly upset."

"Isn't this theft?"

"Technically yes," said Mr Holloway, clearly enjoying himself no end, "but (and this is the key point I would like to emphasise here, your honour) it is not breaking and entering, because there was nothing broken. You see, Mr Norris, in the agitation of his activity, forgot to lock the doors to Fulham Football Club in between the first and second visit."

"So the boys who wandered in after him…"

"Saw this scurrilous-looking man carrying papers in the dead of night…"

"Eight of the clock…"

"The dead of night, and fearing that he was planning to burn down the place, went in to investigate and removed the objects in question. Far from being theft, I'd say it was a public duty. Then finding the papers to be of a questionable nature…"

"Election lists…"

"…they brought them to this newspaper. Strangely there was one other coincidence that evening. Edward – bless his soul – happened to be hanging around in the area, complete with his kit, and, when he saw a dubious character rushing from the Norris household carrying a box of tricks, he took a picture. Night-time photography is difficult but apparently can be done, and by a stroke of luck he got a picture. And as I happened to be the only person not covering the budget at the time he brought it to my attention…"

"And now?"

"The front pages of tomorrow's paper will be full of the Lords' vote. Our readers who are less concerned with party politics will be looking for us to lead them somewhere else after that. Saturday is the last day of the season – seems a good time to run your piece don't you think? After that you can investigate the doctor who apparently ate the first three volumes of Encyclopaedia Britannica and now speaks Arabic."

We spent the rest of the day working and reworking it – me writing and Mr Holloway warning me when I went too far, edging me on when I was too cautious – in between his being abusive, rude, down-putting, hair-splitting, and generally obnoxious.

Friday 29ᵗʰ April

The final touches were made to the article, and it was cleared by the fifth floor and the solicitors. The West London and Fulham Times was delivered, and everyone in the office who knew what we were planning devoured Norris' regular football article.

He wrote nothing about the break-in, Woolwich Arsenal, Reading, or in fact any of the story that we were running. He talked solidly about Fulham, about the problems with low crowds, the difficulties of running the club financially, and all the usual "I am doing my bit but you are not doing yours" stuff that marks him out so strongly in comparison with the infinitely more honourable Leavey who would never flinch from taking responsibility for the club as long as he was part of it.

After that, Edward and I took Marie out for lunch and gave her the update. At half past one she went back to work and we sat in the pub. We were still there when she returned at the end of her shift. She was very forgiving, understanding that tomorrow was going to be our big day.

And then suddenly she said something else and I became completely sober. "What did you say?" I asked, putting down my glass and looking at her face on, not having caught her last phrase.

"I said I'd like to do it again."

"And by 'it' you mean breaking and entering."

"Yes."

I paused for a moment. "Anyone in particular?"

"Not especially."

"I take it you got a feel for this thieving lark."

She gave me a look that could have meant anything.

"We are talking of a criminal offence here. Prison, that sort of thing."

"If I am caught."

"Yes – that is true. They tend not to bang you up for not breaking into the house of a politician of some repute."

"I'm glad about that," she said. "But you did it, you told me."

"In the Transvaal – yes, and that was just a little bit different, because it was a case of my responsibility to the country whose uniform I wore. I broke into the homes of rebel leaders to try and find out what they hell they were up to because that information could help stop my men – and possibly me – getting killed in an ambush. You seem to want to do a break in because you like it."

"Didn't you like it? When you did break ins?"

I paused. The truthful answer was that I knew exactly what she was talking about. The adrenaline rush, as the doc called it. So powerful could it be that I found I had to be careful who I took on a house raid – some men could become overwhelmed by it and stop obeying orders. The fact that Marie had it was something else entirely.

She went and bought us drinks, and I turned to Edward and asked him his view on Marie's latest activity. "Seems like a jolly good wheeze to me," he said. "Sophia gets arrested all the time with the Suffragettes. Got a black eye last week."

Saturday 30th April

The last day of the season. The day of the latest official take-over of Woolwich Arsenal by whichever of the various new companies was now supposedly taking the club over.

Woolwich didn't have a game – which was probably why they chose today to try to get the new club up and running. Chelsea went down, as we all knew they were going to do (at least those of us who had learned long division knew), and Aston Villa won the league several weeks ago.

All in all it was feeble for southern clubs – the three London teams in the bottom five along with Bristol, the only other representative of the south. Fulham drew with the O's at Clapton – 0-0 – I presumed Norris was there. We didn't hear a word from him.

Edward had another gastronomic review running, complete with his own pictures. If I don't watch out he'll be running the whole paper soon. Apparently he is still not being paid.

Lyons Corner Café in Trafalgar Square is the five storey eating house of the West End connoisseur who has failed to make a booking at the Ritz. The menu is standard, the dishes unchanging, the options uncertain. The choice on the ground floor moves smoothly from the ham sandwich to the spotted dick, with everything slightly under heated, but always over egged. Passable is the word one uses if one doesn't notice that which passes between the lips.

Yet one must be fair and admit that the place is engaging with the waitresses whizzing at full speed, always jolly, always on the go. This is not the establishment in which one raises the hand and clicks the finger – if one does one is liable to get a sharp slap round the wrist from the manager.

We started with the sandwiched egg which had the slightest whiff of hen followed by tea cake (although my companion opted for scone) with moderately warm tea. Music from without was played by the Ex-Serviceman's War Heroes Band while we had Reggie Black and his orchestra within. Dancing was the Turkey Trot, involving as always, the couple plodding around the room in the manner of a large bird with a fan-shaped tail.

The clientele is Trafalgarian – the mobile classes on the move, out for a spot of food, no questions asked. But one must be fair – by the third floor the menu is more interesting, and apparently by the fifth one could be in the Ritz itself (although I cannot confirm this, my companion lacking the constitution to climb the stairs).

Next week: The Alhambra, Brixton.

Monday 2nd May

My day off, but I went in. Athletic News had an advertisement for the shares in the new company to run Woolwich Arsenal. It was clearly Leavey's last throw of the die – a new company made up of men from north Kent, with not a touch of Fulham anywhere near it.

At half past nine I was called into the office of the editor on the fifth, along with Mr Holloway. They went over what we knew about the Norris break-in.

I confirmed that I had not taken part in the robbery and would swear on the Bible that I had not known about it in advance, but that the robber had shown me some of the pages and still had those pages.

Mr Holloway confirmed the story of the runners and that Edward would swear the whereabouts of the taking of the photo. There had been no mention in the article about Norris' botched attempt to move the pages from his house to the club, so at this stage he would be focussed on what we had revealed – that we knew what was in his house.

"So," said the top man, "he knows there was a break-in but has no reason to believe that it had anything to do with the pages of the election lists." We nodded our agreement. "Which suggests that his decision to move the lists to Fulham was based on the mistaken thought that the break-in was what is known as a "near thing". On that basis, he still thinks no one knows about his scheme."

We agreed again.

The editor spoke. "Norris' solicitors have just issued a writ for libel against this newspaper. Mr Jones, you will consult with our solicitor Mr Beckwith over the gathering together of the evidence. Thank you everyone."

Mr Beckwith took me into an office on the 4th and got straight to the point.

"You know who the thief is?" I confirmed I did. "You will have to reveal the name of the thief if this goes to court – does that give you a problem?"

"It certainly does."

"I imagined it might – a thief who knows what an electoral list is when he looks at one is not your common or garden thief. A person of education I'd venture."

I said nothing and wondered where we go now.

"Norris' solicitor may think that the thief just happened to give it to the paper, but that seems unlikely without knowing the implication, which means we have to play a better game. He is using Cattermole and Young – a good firm but they think they are cleverer than they are. We'll try and lead them a dance."

He then proceeded to tell me how he would run the case.

"We'll make it clear that the thief was a person of breeding and education who knew what Norris was up to and wanted to expose him as someone involved in electoral fraud. We'll tell him that this person is so concerned about this that he will go to prison for theft if that is what Norris wants.

"A little later we'll tell him about the trip to Fulham and the evidence from that. They will assume we are talking about the same thief, whom we've already said will stand up to him, and faced with all of Norris' actions coming out into public, they will back off." He stood up. "Good day to you," he said, and with that was gone. As we walked back to the sports office Mr Holloway indicated that he would be grateful for a report on the man who jumped from the top of the Eiffel Tower yesterday into a cup of coffee.

Tuesday 3rd May

I finally caught up with Marie after work and told her the position about having to reveal my source. I said she need have no fear since I would refuse.

"But you'll go down for contempt of court," she said.

I agreed that was a possibility, but having served in Africa I had seen worse situations, and besides I suspected such an eventuality would do my journalistic reputation no harm. We moved on to other matters.

Marie has been given the job of writing up the life of Lottie Collins who had just died. Seems she had started out in a dance act with a skipping rope with her sisters as The Three Sisters Collins and had then gone into the music hall as a solo act in America.

What I knew her for was her song Ta-ra-ra-Boom-de-ay, which we'd even played in a jokey manner sometimes with the band. Lottie Collins had done the song as half skirt-dance and half can-can at the Tivoli, and I'd even heard my father mention it, much to my mother's disgust. Marie gave me a full run down of the dance including some of the more outrageous elements. By the end I felt sad that I had never seen Lottie. She was 44 – and had been performing until last year. Such is life.

"Her daughter is on stage too," Marie told me, "and I'll try and find her. Plus her husband who is a musician – you might have heard of him. James Tate."

I said I hadn't. Then I asked, "Is the Times going to run this piece? It doesn't sound like them to me."

"No. I've been calling around – the Telegraph will take it," she said. So now she was stealing information for me – and writing for our biggest rival. Was there no end to what this woman would do?

Wednesday 4th May

Mr Symmonds came to me. "We have a telephone enquiry," he said. "The War Office want us to confirm who writes the King of London story, and they wish to meet him at once. There is no reason for us not to tell them, so we did. They asked then for you to be sent to the War Office. I said you were busy. The speaker, a man with a rather shrill and childish voice, said he would come here. Maybe you should find something to do."

I found Edward and dragged him off to the pub.

"I need to do something new," I said after the third pint. "I think they might cut the "King", and I've been warned that the Woolwich issue is running into the sand. Got any ideas?"

We came up with doing a tour of the pubs of England, taking pictures and writing about the beer and whether it was safe to take ladies in.

Thursday 5th May

George Leavey came to the office and talked with Mr Holloway. After a few minutes I was asked in and I told him I admired his commitment to the club.

"That has not come across in your articles," he said.

"That is not how we like to do it," said Mr Holloway. "Jones' personal feelings are not what he is supposed to focus on. He's writing what our readers are mistaken enough to want."

"The prospectus should be available tomorrow," said Mr Leavey, ignoring the internal politics. "You must write what you wish, of course, but it would help the survival of the club if you could be positive about buying a share in Woolwich."

Once Mr Leavey had left we went to see Mr Symmonds who filled Mr Holloway in on yesterday's events with Captain Kell and the Captain's complaint about my story. The piece was, in short, undermining public morale, causing problems for the preparation for war, making public that which should not be public, and generally mocking his position which, as an officer in His Majesty's forces, was intolerable and probably treason. The column must stop, and I should be handed over for interrogation.

"I'd agree with that," said Mr Holloway, rather unhelpfully I thought.

"I told him to bugger off," said the effete Mr Symmonds, smoothing back his hair. Apparently the fifth floor concurred. My story should continue – along with something on the fact that a sprout had just been declared King of Andorra.

Friday 6th May

Dick Park came in with the news that Punch McEwan at Fulham was trying to sign amateur players in a big way. Seems they had tried to get Charlie Buchan, and Norris himself had conducted the interview which, according to the way Buchan told it to Park, had not gone well.

Fulham were offering £1-10s-0d a week and allowing Buchan to continue training to be a teacher. Buchan had said that he'd been offered double that to play for Bury. He'd then circulated his story to the press – presumably to talk up his worth but also to show what a bad negotiator Norris was. Norris had clearly upset him.

A copy of the Woolwich Arsenal prospectus was delivered, and I wrote up a little piece saying what a great guy Leavey was, and how it was an honour to have a First Division team in Kent. I even had a little dig at Fulham saying that not every club that wanted to get into the top division can manage it and announced that "this writer" would be buying a share.

It seems that when a company is set up the shares can only be offered on sale for a while. So there's a closing date of 10th May. They don't have long to sell £2000 worth.

In the evening Marie announced that it would be very helpful indeed to know what Kell was up to inside his office. "What," she said "does he have in the drawers of his filing cabinet?"

Very stupidly I said that I forbade her to try breaking into the War Office. Naturally I had to apologise, and apologise again, and again. Eventually she gave in and accepted my grovels and I said that yes it would be rather amusing if those filing cabinets turned out to include nothing other than a lunch that had been packed up by his mother.

Saturday 7th May

And suddenly we stop thinking about football and all the other trivia of life, and have to change editions half way through the print run to announce that King Edward VII (Edward the Caresser as everyone knows him) has died and will be succeeded by George V. I know I am not supposed to think this way, but it just made Mr Leavey's job even tougher. How do you sell something when a King who has epitomised the last eight years has just popped off? Suddenly we all loved the old King with his "Don't be dull" speech, and his inability not to put his hand up the skirt of any lady within groping distance.

With their being no sport, nothing humorous and no politics in the paper I took the day off and went to see Marie.

Seems her department carries on as usual – people still need researching and all of it can be held over. The Prime Minister is on holiday in the Mediterranean somewhere and they are trying to get a message to his ship.

That evening, in sombre mood (even though neither of us feels anything special for the monarchy), we watched Halley's comet get ever closer and drank a toast to fat royal lechers.

Tuesday 10th May

We're all still in mourning, but you'd never believe it. Josh Kelvinside came racing in and was so excited he shouted out his message without finding the right person. Mr Holloway was about to tell him what for when the enormity of the message became apparent. Leavey, the man whom I had held up as the man of honour, was in Fulham trying to flog off the shares in Woolwich Arsenal to Fulham FC. What we had been talking about for weeks was now about to happen.

It sounded as if they had failed to sell the shares locally and were trying to find someone – anyone – to prop up the offer before it ended tomorrow.

I was about to rush out onto a bus when Mr Holloway called me back and told me to get a cab. He also asked if I knew anything about the story that a man calling himself Sherlock Holmes had been arrested in Liverpool yesterday. I took Josh with me.

There was already a crowd of hacks outside Fulham FC when I got there – apparently Norris and Leavey were inside. "Now we'll find out what's going on," said Scrapper Chalfont, as we got out of the cab.

"Don't bank on it," I said, "I think I've been given the run around." But still they pressed me for news I didn't have, which meant part of my reputation was still intact.

After an hour a highly disreputable old boy emerged from the side gate and said that for a certain consideration he'd tell us what he'd overheard. Turns out he is the groundsman with a grudge. Thank goodness for groundsmen with a grudge – where would we be without them? This old fellow's annoyance came about because Norris only pays him every third week in the summer and the old boy has noticed that the grass grows faster in the summer.

We all chipped in 6d and dangled the half sovereign in front of him. He told us the tale. It sounded good enough to me, and looking around, everyone else bought into it too.

Mr Leavey had offered to sell the majority shares of Woolwich Arsenal to Norris and company, with no restrictions at all – and they were talking about moving the Woolwich to play at Craven Cottage. But there had also been a man from Tottenham wanting to get to Leavey and continuous calls for Mr Leavey from Chelsea, which of course Mr Norris refuses to allow him to take.

"Fulham made a loss last year," said the groundsman feeling perhaps that if he kept talking he might get some more money. "Norris says the rent from a second club and having a ground in use every week would make money."

I told Josh to find me a taxi and told him to stay there until some big news happened. God help me – the old boy got it quite right.

Back at the office I suggested we get someone out to Tottenham and someone to Chelsea to check if they wanted to make a bid, while Jim Steele checked the annual return of Fulham. They had lost over £700 last year, so the groundsman was right. Josh came back with the news that Norris had an open meeting of the council at 6 o'clock, and I got there in time to catch him read a proclamation of loyalty to the new king and regret on the death of the old king. Then he got a couple of his men to walk over and remove me. I shouted, "So much for the freedom of the press" and there were one or two shouts, but mostly people wanted to express their feelings to the memory of the king. No one really gave a toss for some wretched journalist making a fuss.

I went to the West London's offices and used their phone to see if there was any need for me back in the cockpit. "Someone broke into the War Office last night," said Mr Holloway. "The story is he bit all the guards on the neck."

I had no way of contacting Marie, so went to the White Hart.

Wednesday 11th May

Leavey has done an interview with the Star, saying he had failed to get the company going from the prospectus and now needed to sell to anyone at all – including a takeover by another club – with a tailpiece saying that this would not be against FA or FL rules. I was glad I didn't work on Mondays.

Playing with the band helped a little.

Thursday 12th May

Back to Woolwich – and thinking that at least if Fulham do take over Woolwich it will be an easier journey next season. If they ever built the trams into Fulham it would be easier still.

There was a meeting of the Board of the club, followed by a public meeting in the late afternoon. Leavey got up and said that they had only sold 1200 £1 shares and could not proceed with the new club.

I stood up as one of the people who had put up my £1 and asked what he was going to do now. He said he didn't know. "When it was clear we would not meet our target the board tried to arrange for people at Fulham who have been friendly to this club to buy the remaining shares,. But we were unable to reach an agreement, so it came to nothing. Chelsea and Tottenham have shown an interest so we'll talk to them too. We don't have enough sales of shares to set up the new company and I have to pay the liquidator £900 by tomorrow. Quite simply, I don't have it, which means no liquidation, and effectively Woolwich Arsenal comes to an end at five o'clock in the afternoon. If I have offers from other clubs I will take the one that gives the best chance of Woolwich Arsenal staying in Woolwich."

Eventually I went back to Fleet Street and was able to see Marie. "Did he just have sandwiches?" I asked.

"Just a paper wrapper – I suspect his mother makes them," she replied. "There were a few files and bits of paper with a list of names on that I copied down, but in essence nothing. There's his desk, an unlocked set of drawers, place for a secretary that looks like it has never been used, and that's it. Oh – and there was a book."

"Which one?" I asked, not because I really wanted to know, but because I was trying to take it all in.

"*The Napoleon of Notting Hill*," she said. "Do you know it?"

"I read it about four years ago when it came out," I said. "I just can't imagine Kell reading metaphysical humour."

"I've never heard of metaphysical humour," Marie replied.

"You should read more," I said, and felt rather pleased with that. However, seeing that she was lining up a quick slap to the side of my face I changed the subject. "So there is no Section H."

"I have been to see two of the people named on Kell's lists," Marie added, suitably distracted.

"And…"

"They don't exist."

We looked at each other – and at the comet. Bigger again.

"How did you get in?"

"It wasn't locked. Said hello to the cleaners, walked in, looked around, walked out. And don't tell your readers about the stunningly amazing lack of security. I might need to go back some time. But why would anyone have a list of people who don't exist?"

I had no idea, just as I couldn't understand why he was reading *The Napoleon of Notting Hill*. At every turn everything always got murkier.

Friday 13th May

Back with Marie in time for lunch.

Marie said that she had picked up a copy of *The Napoleon of Notting Hill* in one of the second hand shops in Charing Cross Road. I was embarrassed knowing the sort of things they sold in those shops. She saw me redden. "You are such a prude," she said. "But you are right. If he is going to read GK Chesterton he'd read *The Man Who Was Thursday*, because at least it is about spies. *Notting Hill* is just…"

"Odd," I said. "Set in 1984."

She did not disagree.

Saturday 14th May

The Times are now writing that the new Woolwich Arsenal company has failed, and the liquidator is about to sell off the assets – which basically means the ground and the players. Their piece, however, does not mention Norris.

I went to the liquidator's office. Mr Brannan was not there, but his junior was. He was actually quite willing to talk, and he gave me a story. From the horse's mouth. Fulham FC were definitely buying Woolwich Arsenal FC. (Again.) The new company had failed because it hadn't sold enough shares, both Chelsea and Spurs had pulled out when the price went up. So only Fulham were left in the show and that is where Mr Brannan was – doing the deal with Fulham.

The assistant liquidator could not say anything as to where the club was going to be based. That, I guessed, would involve the issue of whether they could sell the ground, whether Norris had to sign a deal with Leavey not to move the club, and whether the League had a view on moving grounds.

I got back to the office, wrote up my news piece and went to see Marie in the Times office. No one seemed to mind; I suppose everyone took it that the coverage of the two papers was so different, it didn't matter.

Marie was working on a piece called Pauperism in London. The number of people receiving poor relief in London at the end of April was down slightly on last year. Marie had worked out that out of every 1000 people in London 25 were paupers. Greenwich was one of the few areas to show an increase in the paupers. I wondered if it was an omen.

"And I joined an anarchist group," she said, "since you seem to have lost interest. George Barrett gave me an introduction."

I think I did my mouth-falling-open bit, because she laughed and shut my mouth for me. "He's actually a gentleman."

"And an anarchist," I said.

"Which means…"

I had been about to say something about her being suited to anarchism what with her breaking into the War Office and rummaging through the files of the secret police, but kept my counsel. If the Times won't run her piece on anarchists, she plans to take it elsewhere.

"Did you tell George Barrett about what you found in Kell's office?" I asked.

"No," she said. "Not yet."

Tuesday 17th May

Halley's Comet now blazes so bright you can see it in the day sky as well as at night.

I spent the day bribing members of the Imperial Hotel over a meeting planned for tomorrow which will apparently sort out the future of Woolwich Arsenal. As always, everyone has a price.

In between I worried about how much I understood of Marie. Do I want her getting friendly with anarchists? No – at least not if I am not with her. I wish I hadn't read *The Man Who Was Thursday*. Somehow I have a mixture of worry that she might be finding another man who is more fun than I am, and a feeling that I am going to miss out on some fun. Childish or what?

Wednesday 18th May

The Imperial Hotel, where there now can't be a single worker who has not been bribed by one paper or another.

We watched them go in: the board of Woolwich Arsenal and some of the Football League management toffs. And, break-through number one, Mr Norris and a couple of the nonentity directors of Fulham turned up too.

Every ten minutes or so one of the waitresses or room guards or bell boys, or whatever they were, would pop out and give one of us the details while the rest of us had to wait for our man or woman to come out with the same story.

So, Josh and I waited outside in the warm spring sunshine and amused ourselves playing cards with the Telegraph team. A certain ability left over from my soldiering days gave me a good return and also reimbursed me a little from the fact that I had decided to pay three insiders to tip me off.

As always the results were mixed – but that is why I went for three. One was serving drinks, one was clearing, and one was on hand for any emergency issues.

Two of my sources came up with the goods. The third defected to the Star, but I had only paid him 3d retainer, so that was not much of a problem.

Norris (I was told in quick gasps by the informants, anxious not to be seen outside for too long) was proposing that he and one other director buy all of the shares in Woolwich Arsenal FC and that the clubs merge under the name Fulham Arsenal. They would play at Craven Cottage in the First Division.

There was then a pause before the next ringer came out – this time saying that the first plan had fallen because the representative of Chelsea had opposed another club in the area and Bolton had opposed Woolwich Arsenal's place automatically going to Fulham Arsenal. Apparently the League ruled that the first issue (too many clubs in one area) was outside their remit, arguing that if a club wins promotion it would not be stopped from going up just because another club was next door. Bolton's point was accepted – Fulham would stay in Division 2, and an extra club would go up from Division 2 to replace the defunct Woolwich Arsenal. At this point Norris withdrew the suggestion.

I sent Josh back to Fleet Street for the first edition, and told him to send back another runner, and then come back himself.

Scrapper and I waited some more as we picked up news of another point being debated: this one allowed Woolwich Arsenal to share Craven Cottage with Fulham and keep its own identity. There was a pause until the League said there was nothing in their rules to stop this, but apparently this time Mr Leavey would have none of it. As he was the major creditor of the club, that deal was off.

I looked at Scrapper who had got the same news from his ringer. "Why would Leavey allow the club to cease to exist in the first option, but not allow it to share a ground in the second?" We were bemused.

As the meeting wore on I watched the sky. Halley's comet was growing brighter. This is the day when the earth passes through the tail of the comet – the day the end of the earth was being predicted. It could well be the end of Woolwich Arsenal.

We waited. No more ringers emerged, but eventually Leavey, along with Hall, Allen (a business pal of Norris) and Norris himself from Woolwich Arsenal, came onto the steps. Norris spoke while refusing to look my way. He said, "Agreement has been reached and the four of us here have been given the task of setting up a new company to run Woolwich Arsenal. The club will play in Division 1 at the Manor Ground, Plumstead this coming season."

Josh's replacement runner turned up, and I gave him the story. Scrapper and I went to find a pub.

Thursday 19th May

Norris and Hall were in Woolwich as I guessed they would be, and Edward and I followed them around, much to their annoyance. It seemed they were trying to find local buyers to take up some of the shares – and after an hour of cat and mouse Norris asked a constable to move us along as we were impeding them in our lawful business. Edward took a photograph of me being pushed by the forces of law and order which captured Norris in the background. After that we meandered to the pub to pick up some local chit-chat.

By the afternoon Hall was offering five shares for the price of four, and then five shares for the price of three – with a guarantee buy-back clause if Woolwich Arsenal moved their ground. He turned out not to be a very good salesman, so I got Edward to give the man three sovereigns for five when Norris wasn't looking. Edward and I went back to the Hen and B and tried to work out what we might say about the place in our proposed review of the public houses of the Kingdom. The Hen as the leading trading house of stocks and shares was rather a nice concept.

In the evening there was a meeting of the fundraising committee with Hall and Norris, but I had no one on the inside and was refused entry until Edward – bright lad that he is – asked why shareholders in the new company were already being excluded. Norris scowled at me, and let both of us in as we proudly waved our share receipts.

The chair of the committee asked Hall and Norris for assurances about the future of the club and where it would be – Norris was on his feet before poor Hall could even breathe in and said that since at the moment there was no club, because not all the shares were sold, there was no assurance he could give on anything. He would return to the matter as and when the good people of Woolwich and Plumstead started to buy shares.

"But why," I said, "were you offering five shares for the price of three with a guarantee of buying them back if Woolwich moved in two years, if you now can't give assurances because you don't own the club."

"Hypothetical," said Norris, and after that he sat down, glaring at anyone who caught his eye.

The meeting didn't get too far, and Edward and I spent the journey back to town seeing if we could invent pubs so that we didn't actually have to travel around the country. "The Doting Duck, on the downside of Dunstable..." It might work. Unless we had any readers just outside Dunstable.

"Where is Dunstable?" said Edward, who found it hard to keep up after five pints in the course of one day.

I said I had no idea.

Friday 20th May

The funeral of the old king. The pubs were open all day and everybody started out by drinking solemnly and toasting "Edward the Caresser" and "Georgie Porgie Pudding and Pie", and then someone nudged someone else, and then there was some pushing, and by half past ten in the morning (as opposed to the evening) a fight had broken out. There were no police anywhere – probably all on duty along the procession route in case anarchists tried to steal the coffin or the king's lovers tried to get inside with him – so the fights just went on until everyone was too drunk to swing a fist.

The band played a gig in the evening. We had talked about toning it down because the audience might want respect, but it was clear by lunchtime that the day was a riot and no one was sober enough to remember anything about what the day was for. We played the usual funny stuff and got a huge reception. "Georgie Porgie" got an even bigger reception, and we had to play it six times.

The big turn was Edward, who had been threatening to do a show with us for weeks. We did "The Daphne Jig" – the one where we all shout out "The Daphne Jig" and then clap four times. Except we replaced the clap with Edward standing up saying, "I say! I say!" in his fruitiest voice, and again it brought the house down. When we finished they wanted it again, and again. I then got them quiet and said, "M'Lords, Your Grace, Ladies and Gentlemen... May I introduce the Right Honourable Edward Bucking-Fitzurse," and there were cheers, and a number of ladies of dubious merit got down on their knees before him, while one rushed straight up and gave him a very prolonged kiss. "More, more" screamed the crowd, and we had to do The Daphne Jig twice more – and another Georgie Porgie.

Gerry said we should change the name of the band to the House of Lords.

Saturday 21st May

As I tried to recover from my headache I wrote up the story of Thursday in Woolwich, and did a piece about wild parties across the nation in celebration of the king's death. Mr Holloway called it "truthful but disrespectful" and spiked it. Same happened with my next episode of the King of London. Suddenly no one wanted my writing. The series about pubs was getting closer by the day.

In the afternoon we got news that Allen had left the board of directors of Woolwich Arsenal, leaving them with just Norris and Hall. I tried to get information on the share ownership of the new club – after all, as shareholders Edward and I had certain rights (at least we claimed that we had) – but no one was talking.

Marie and I met up with George Barrett at the Angel and went for a meal. Marie promised me she had not told Barrett about her work inside the War Office and had reassured me in a non-verbal way about her feelings towards me, so although I was still fed up about the lack of Jacko Jones in print I felt better about the rest of my life.

During the meal Marie quizzed George about his views and activities. Was he a bomb thrower? Did he believe that the only way out of our society into the anarchist world was through blowing the old world up?

Basically he came across as he always does – as a peaceful, rather nice character who, politics aside, I'd say was a good mate, and as always I have to admit (having seen him at work at the arsenal) that he was quite a speaker. I also think he might be more socialist than anarchist.

Eventually George said that he was surprised that the Times were interested in him, and couldn't imagine the Times giving him anything remotely like a fair coverage. Marie told him that it might not be the Times – she was able to work freelance on any story the Times turned down as long as she didn't do it during her hours of work. Then Barrett suggested that the powers that be – the government, the Lords, the Church – will do anything to hold onto power. Some of the outrages that have been blamed on anarchists were, he said, simply the work of criminals trying to rob banks and jewellers. Some were undertaken by parts of the power base of the state and were part of an eternal war between the estates of the church, the Lords and the Commons.

He turned to me. "You have the gift of writing, just as I have the gift of oratory. We each use what we have, and you should not underestimate what you can do, Jacko. Instead of being trivial or covering football, you should be writing serious political pieces. Use your humour but use it to hasten the end of this evil society and put an end to poverty and the vortex. Don't use your talents to keep the old estates going."

"So what should I do?" I asked. "Start writing a comic piece about the anarchists, so that no one takes you seriously?"

"That's the logical response to Mr Barrett's point," said Marie, suddenly taking my side (I think).

"Make a laughing stock of anarchism, and then no one will believe it is us when we do the next bank job – that could work. But then no one takes us seriously at all – when I stand up they all think I'm a music hall act. It doesn't really help my cause."

We carried on talking for another hour, and George's Barrett's words stayed with me. Although I don't agree with him, I do like him, and at the end of the evening I tried to tell him so. He's honest and straightforward, and the world he foresees is a world so much better than this one.

Monday 23rd May

A call to Norris' solicitors revealed that they were handling the Woolwich Arsenal share issue – if he had his own solicitors running it, it meant he was paying for the legal fees, which meant he definitely intended to get his hands on the show.

According to the legal crew Norris and Hall each had 240 shares, Leavey, God bless the old fellow, had 100. Allen was not listed, which was probably why he had left the club. (They didn't mention that Edward and I had five between us.) There were still more on sale, the statement said. Athletic News ran a story saying that the local people were angry with Norris and Hall and that's why they wouldn't buy shares. That seemed a bit steep – not least because I hadn't seen an AN reporter anywhere near the club of late. The greater truth was that the local population was asleep with apathy or, in the case of the armaments men, trying to work out if they had a job left.

I got Robin to draw a cartoon with the whole town of Woolwich sleeping (along with the players while the opposition scored) and with Norris standing on a soap box waving share certificates with the line Your Football Club Needs You. We both signed it and sent it to Mr Holloway.

"More like it," he said, and took it upstairs. On the way up he looked over his shoulder and said, "Try not to mention dead kings too often at the moment. Go to Dunstable – they've got a plague of dead ducks and I need a report."

I looked at Edward and he at me. We each denied telling anyone the Dunstable story.

Athletic News were also claiming that there would soon be more people on the board of the all-new all-exciting soon-to-be-appearing-near-the-West-End Woolwich Arsenal. Actually I made that last bit up, and then thought of doing a sketch about the Woolwich Arsenal as the latest musical – linking George's comments about anarchists and music halls. Robin and I thought about doing another piece in which an Athletic News reporter was asleep with dream bubbles coming out of his head leading to a board room full of Woolwich Arsenal directors, but we knew it wouldn't get through.

I grabbed Edward and got him to write a letter putting himself up for the board of the club and using his family name. We didn't tell anyone that idea.

The Kentish Independent says that Hall and Norris are running the club – which is because no one else is on the board. Morrell is confirmed as manager ("Relegation assured" I told anyone who would listen) and the ground staff have jobs too ("Good for them," scowled Mr H).

"The new owners have promised to make significant transfer signings to strengthen the first team," trumpeted the Kentish, and everyone cheered as I read it out.

"Norris spend money on footballers?" asked Mr Holloway.

It was the craziest story yet. None of us could see it.

Tuesday 24th May

Marie and I sat down for a serious talk about anarchism. I confessed that beyond the novels, one pamphlet and my chats with George, I hadn't got too much grasp of how it worked.

We established the basics. Anarchists believe the opposite of Christians. They believe that man is basically good but is corrupted by society. Get rid of society and we return to our state of goodness. Society (meaning politics, the church, and the class system as defined by Marx) is to blame.

Marie outlined her ideas for an article explaining the views to the untutored world after which we moved back to the implications of Captain Kell having nothing much in his office.

"You should see him, as he asked," said Marie. "I think you should offer all the skills you had in Section H, so that his department does what it is supposed to do. It finds there are no German spies, it finds there is no anarchist threat, and it stops the government wasting money on such ventures."

"Kell would never allow his own department to report on something that he doesn't believe to be true."

"But you have the ear of Churchill."

"No – he has the ear of me."

"But if you were in Kell's division…"

I stopped her. "Kell will not allow me in. I have ridiculed him, comparing him to an incompetent idiot called Ffopp. What's he going to say? 'Oh jolly funny, Mr Jones – and please come and work for me'."

"Not if you say, 'there are no German spies, there is no anarchist threat, but there is another much deeper much more insidious threat lurking in our midst'."

"The Loch Ness monster?" I asked.

"The House of Lords," she said.

I suggested she had been listening to George too much.

Wednesday 25th May

Marie's concept is that we should take the speech that we had heard Lloyd George give and combine it with a warning about the network of spies and undercover agents in our midst: the backwoodsmen of the House of Lords who had thrown out the elected government's budget.

I can see it as an article, but I can't see it as something that Kell would go for. Still it is was worth pitching to Mr Symmonds.

Marie told me that there is to be a formal service of remembrance for those who fell in the Boer War this coming Saturday – just ahead of the independence of the new state. It was advertised in the Times. Took me by surprise, but I said I wanted to go to honour the fallen, and I asked her rather tentatively if she would accompany me. It would be our first formal occasion out together – rather solemn, but it would be nice to be with her. To my delight she agreed.

Friday 27th May

Apparently Fulham played a game of netball at their stadium in front of 100 curious spectators and five journalists yesterday. Norris at his most weird, I thought.

Mr Symmonds came back to me on the thought of running pieces that said the enemy was the Lords. "Possible," he said. "Write me something. And do me another King of London piece, but we still can't say anything about the king. He's dead you know." I told him I had heard.

Ultimately, the good Captain Ffopp was reduced to calling on Digby Digweed for help. "It is not in the papers," he wailed to the young lad in his all-brown uniform, "and the government don't care. What are we to do?"

It was embarrassing for young Digby, our hero of the future, to have such a senior member of the secret service police blubbing in front of him, but he did his best to console the officer and gentleman.

"It may appear that we are falling under the boot-heel of the Duke of St Dennisburg and the Even Younger Turks, but you are forgetting the basic make-up of the British people," he said. "Have you noted the situation in Birmingham?"

Saturday 28th May

The first formal occasion for Marie and me. We had the service, and then the reception addressed by, of all people, Mr Churchill. Still, he had actually been in Africa, even if he did cause mayhem.

No one else from my regiment turned up – I was demobbed in 1906 and by then most of my troop had moved on and vanished. (Indeed I was only around that long because of the War Office interest in Section H).

Mum had cleaned the old uniform, and Marie wore a frock that is beyond my ability to describe. I realised that until now I had only seen her in her work clothes. Mr Churchill made his speech in Westminster Hall in which he declared that, "By an act of the British Parliament, the Cape Colony, the Orange Free State, Natal, and the Transvaal are joined to form the Union of South Africa and granted dominion status in the British Empire."

We cheered, and after that there was mingling with drinks the likes of which I had never had before. Then the buffet meal – which I think I coped with rather well.

Indeed I thought it was all going fine until suddenly Marie stood up and introduced me to Lord Cortney – and if that were not enough (meeting a member of the House of Lords) it turns out that Lord Cortney is her father. The woman I am going out with, who is writing about anarchists and encouraging me to write on the subject of the Lords being the enemy within, has a father in the House of Lords.

And she never told me.

I stood to attention and saluted – I had no idea what to do – and he said with a smile, "At ease, Sergeant. I don't think the constitution requires that an ex-member of the armed forces salutes a member of the House of Lords. Rather the other way round I should think. Marie tells me you fought the Boers."

"Yes, sir," I said, and then realised I had got it wrong again, stumbled over my words and eventually managed to say, "Yes, my lord."

Lord Cortney put his hand on my shoulder and said, "This is going to be a very difficult conversation, Mr Jones, if you keep trying to treat me with formality. Stick with 'sir' if you must, and I will call you Mr Jones. Is that agreeable to you?"

I told him it was, of course, yes sir, absolutely, of course, and we talked. Seems he had spoken in the debate in the Lords about the problem of not giving the vote to the natives in the new Union – hence his attendance here. "I think they should have put it in the South Africa Act, but it got taken out again. Can't force the Dutch to give the natives the vote if they don't want it, I suppose. What do you think?"

What did I think? I had no idea. To me the blacks in Transvaal were the underlings – the carriers. We weren't fighting them; we were fighting the white men, the Boers, who were in control. I didn't think that was much of an answer, so I took a jump. "Should we then give votes to women?" I said.

"Of course we damn well should," said Lord Cortney, and then turning to look over my shoulder said, "and here's someone who thinks exactly the opposite. What do you say, Winnie – votes for women?"

"Afternoon, James," said Mr Churchill, obviously on familiar ground with Marie's father – another thing I didn't know. "And my old drinking pal, Jacko Jones. Did you know, James, that Jacko and I were in Africa together?"

"So I gather," said Lord Cortney. "Mr Jones here has a ... what's the phrase... (he paused and smiled) a 'working relationship' with my daughter, Marie. She's with the Times."

Mr Churchill bent forward and kissed her hand and said, "Charmed ma'am," before turning back to Lord Cortney, saying, "Fine man Jacko Jones – did the Queen's service in Africa, and now holds the government to account back home."

"Ah – the piece on the Parliament Act," said his lordship, "trying to remove all the landowners' money with more tax."

"Re-wrote it for us, in fact," said Mr Churchill. "Don't know how he got the story but when it started out it was a notion and by the time Jones had written it up, it was set up as an Act of Parliament. We had to present it to the other house," and here he bowed with mock formality to Lord Cortney, "after what Jones did to it."

And everyone laughed, with Lord Cortney slapping my left shoulder and Mr Churchill my right. Then suddenly there was a flash, and I realised my photograph had just been taken – and for the first time in my life it was not Edward behind the box. As my eyes cleared I could see a huge crowd gathered around a member of the House of Lords, his daughter, the Home Secretary, and…. me. People seemed to be looking at me, and I stood straight and tall as if on parade, with what Marie told me later (and what I discovered the next day) was a particularly stupid grin on my face.

"Strange how popularity can change," said Mr Churchill. "When they made me Home Secretary no one wanted the job. Now I'm seen with Jacko Jones and everyone wants the job!"

Monday 30th May

The Times carried the picture of man with stupid grin, Lord Cortney, Mr Churchill and Marie. At home the entire street is in uproar over it. The kids in the road keep playing knock-down ginger on the door, saying "My lord" if they see me, and my mum organised a tea party in the garden for the neighbours at which I had to make a guest of honour appearance.

The article made no mention of me (no reason why it should) but the picture had the sub-text which called me a highly regarded veteran of the Boer conflict and political commentator. Nothing about Marie or about my relationship with Mr Churchill, which was fine.

In the evening the band was playing as usual at the White Hart – and there… there was no difference. No one had seen the paper, so no one knew the news. I was operating in two worlds.

One of the regulars said, "What do you guys do when there's no football?" I said it was tough but we had to find other news.

Tony Attwood

Wednesday 1st June

Mr Holloway greeted me as I emerged from the stairway, bowing and saying, "Mr Lord, your tongue is hanging out and you are dribbling. May I have the honour of pushing it back into your mouth…"

I said, "It's Sergeant, if you need a title, although Mr Churchill calls me Jacko…"

"Then he's a bigger fool than I took him to be," he said, leading the way into his office with a scowl and perhaps just the slightest hint of a smile, although only regular Holloway watchers would notice it.

We sat down. "You have a miserable knack of falling on other people's feet," he said. "All you need now is to avoid being thrown into prison on account of the Norris affair, and you are made for life." It seems the solicitor would be in momentarily. As we waited Mr Holloway drew out a copy of the Times and made fun of my expression.

The solicitor's news was interesting. "Norris has sacked Cattermole and Young", said Mr Beckwith, "and moved to Frown Robertson Tarr."

"Is that good?" I asked.

"To be expected. Cattermole and Young will have told him that we would not have printed anything without some evidence, and that meant that if there was even something in our story he would be in trouble. Norris will have reacted to that, and Frown Robertson Tarr will not make such impertinent suggestions. They are your total yes men."

"So what happens now?" I asked, while Mr Beckwith admired my picture on the editor's desk.

"We give them a few days to get to grips with the situation, and then we let slip that we have just gathered in information from another source that suggests that the election documents were moved on the night of 27th April to a different address, that Mr Norris was seen by several different people, none of whom were implicated in the original theft, and the documents have been examined. Would he like to comment? And how are things going with taking over Woolwich Arsenal?"

"And then what?"

"He'll sue the newspaper for breaking and entering to deflect the story. He'll not go through with this, but our job is to make sure now that he thinks twice next time around."

He looked again at the picture. "Who's the woman, Mr Jones?" he said.

"His fiancé," said Mr Holloway, and I nearly fell off the chair. "Jones will soon be our first titled reporter. He already writes like a half-baked imbecile, so he's well-equipped for hob-nobbing with them. He's currently working on the story of a stoat who can recite the Lancashire Evening Telegraph verbatim."

Thursday 2nd June

Mr Holloway called the "summer meeting" which we have each year at this time to discuss what those of us who write about football will do during the non-footballing period of work. We are expected to put in proposals for other articles and research. Or else take a holiday. Unpaid, of course.

"Woolwich Arsenal is still running," I said, "and with Edward and I both being shareholders now, we ought to be able to stay with that."

Mr Holloway was unimpressed. "You've already been told to wrap it up once. The locals will handle it, the intricacies of who owns what shares is not of national interest unless it turns out to involve the King. Unless the FA refuse to allow both Fulham and Woolwich to be in the League at the same time – and even then you can only run that once. One story and it's over."

"What about Leitch, the architect-engineer?"

"Corruption is good, so are collapsing football grounds. Anything else on architecture you can give to your ladyfriend at the Times."

"And I was going to do some social pieces," I added ignoring the jibe. "Such as going to the pictures."

"The what?"

"The cinema, sir," I explained although I knew for sure he wasn't unaware of such developments.

"So you are not going to do the Monkey Parade, or the pubs of London, or hats, or the quality of the pies in the east end, any of the things you were doing before?"

"I certainly could…"

"No, I want something new. Turning back to your picture…" He still had it on the desk – Churchill, his lordship, Marie, and Sergeant Jones. "I think we should do some high society – how the other half lives…"

"I can't prey on them, betray confidences… not the Home Secretary of all people."

"Remember who pays the salary, Jones. You go and talk to your new friends, tell them that our readers would be interested in how such people live…. Edward takes a picture or two…. All nice and summer like."

"But I want to expose the Lords as the real threat to our society."

He looked at me quite blankly.

"I could do a thing on dog racing…"

"Hasn't quite got the same verve, the same flair, has it?" said the boss. "Go and do something about your mates in the Lordship, and chance the ducks."

"What about anarchists?" I pleaded, "or the secret police?"

"Anarchists are done, unless they are blowing up places. Secret police yes, if you can do a totally factual and truthful report that shows we have them. Otherwise do something on that woman in Gloucester who is advertising for a man to come in and give her a wash three days a week."

I skulked out. Edward stayed behind, and I could hear him talking about who his mother knew.

Friday 3rd June

I saw Marie and told her about the meeting. Didn't give her anything special, didn't beg, just said what had been said to me. Ending with an apology.

"Stop that," she said. "We're journalists, we get asked to write things we don't want to do. That's the game. The Times has asked me to get football news from you."

"What?"

"They said that if you talked about anything big happening in football or from your old contacts at the War Office that would fit in with the ethos of the Times, I should pass it on."

"Damn cheek," I said. "So what do I tell Mr Holloway?"

"Tell him that you'll do it, but that in return you are having to pass on information on Woolwich Arsenal that your paper doesn't want. After all he told you to give me the architect story."

"But there is no real architect story. Besides I can't meet your circle of family acquaintances and practise steganography."

"I think steganography is writing in code. You mean writing things down in secret. I'll fix up a time when you can come and meet my family – the whole crew and you can lionize them."

"But…"

"Don't you think my father and mother have read some of your work in the Chron? They'll know you are going to write it up – it is just up to you to make it positive. It is easy to poke fun at families like mine as being indolent fools, just as it is easy for the upper class to make fun of working men spending all day in the public house, then going home to knock the wife about. You'll just have to come to terms with the fact that in reality my family is more in favour of political and economic reform than yours is, from what you say. My father supports the Parliament Act and the reform of voting and taxation, plus health provision and pensions for everyone. Some of my more radical friends would go much further."

"Your father supports the end of the Lords?"

"Don't you?"

"Yes, of course," I said, hoping I hadn't paused too long. "We'll give coverage to your father's campaign and show that not everyone with some wealth is against the Liberal reforms."

Saturday 4th June

Illustrated London Review have the picture of Churchill, Marie, her father, and me, and stated that Marie and I were expected by "those in the know" to announce our engagement this summer.

Which meant… Mr Holloway knew before this came out. Did he tip them off? Money? A house? It was impossible. On my salary? With my family. Anyway, she'd never say yes.

Of course someone in Norfolk Avenue found it and showed it to my mum who ran around the house screaming, and my dad had to be called back from work to calm her down, and I was blamed, and no one believed me when I said I didn't know and that papers always made things up. They ought to know that, seeing what I write.

Eventually I went to work, explained to Mr Holloway what was going on, asked if I could go back home because my mother was in hysterics, and then I looked on in horror as I saw tears of laughter rolling down his cheeks. He couldn't even bring himself to tell me to go away; instead he just waved me out of the door. As I turned I saw he had a copy of the Illustrated on his desk. He looked up and said, "While you are there, can you cover the story that half of the members of the House of Lords have got anthrax?"

Tuesday 7th June

Edward and I met Leitch in his West End office for the appointment made nearly two months ago. It was a less impressive setting than I had imagined – illuxurious even. A couple of those fancy tilted drawing boards, a junior and a secretary looking very prim and proper, and that was it. He gave us some preliminaries about the fact that he worked in various parts of the country and rented space when he needed it.

Leitch was in town now because he had been doing the deal with Leavey over the debt for the work on the Woolwich Arsenal grandstand – ten years on. I guessed the deal had to be that if it hadn't fallen down by now it was probably safe, and so the debt was now due. Also the FA don't like clubs not to pay "footballing" debts.

I asked Mr Leitch where the money that was paying him was coming from, and he said that the "new owners" of the club were putting it up. I asked if that meant Norris, and he said he couldn't confirm that – which means yes.

He also told me that I was the second in the queue to be asking these questions. The other questioner, it turns out, was the Football Association who were concerned about clubs running into debt and going into liquidation.

When I pressed Leitch he said his impression was that the FA would accept a new Woolwich Arsenal as proposed, but if Norris was involved too closely or was suspected of trying to buy many more clubs then they would come up with some quickly invented rule that said that the original Woolwich Arsenal were in the FA, but not the 1910 Woolwich Arsenal which would screw up all of Norris' plans. Whether such a ruling was legal or would stand up, I doubted, but as yet no one had sued the FA.

"My guess is that it will go through and the FA will demand a couple of internationals at Fulham with no ground fee – in return for their turning a blind eye," he said.

I then asked him about working on both Fulham and Chelsea at the same time in 1905.

"It happens," he replied, seemingly unmoved. "I've designed a number of football grounds, so it is natural people should talk to me. Chelsea wanted the design done quickly, and so did Fulham."

"But there are problems with the Chelsea ground," I ventured. He said nothing.

"You built the stand at Plumstead," making my deliberate error as a way in.

"A common misconception, Mr Jones," he said, swallowing the bait, "I am an engineer and a designer, I do not build."

Even with Edward now making a devil of a noise clattering around with his equipment, he continued to focus on me. One up to him. I'd read that in the court enquiry into Ibrox he had been as cool and sharp as a lemon.

Edward knocked his tripod over. I swear he was doing it deliberately. Leitch still did not bat an eyelid.

"Mr Leavey is a good man, and I would count him a friend. The financial troubles of Woolwich Arsenal meant that I was not able to be paid, it is true, but Mr Leavey pointed me in the direction of Mr Norris, and I have reached an arrangement with Mr Norris, for whom, as you have realised, I designed the Fulham ground."

"Did Mr Norris pay you extra to build some poor design into the Chelsea design?"

"That is a wholly outrageous statement."

"But you know," I continued, doing everything I could to keep the argument running, "how things can go wrong when structures are not put up according to the architect's wishes. The issue of red pine and yellow pine, for example. You repeatedly said that at Ibrox the builders were cheating on the quality of materials, and you had to keep pulling them back into order. Surely, working on two grounds at the same time in London, you would not have had the time to check that the builders were doing it all to the right standard. I am just saying that maybe you gave more time to one than the other, and didn't notice if the Chelsea terraces were built to specification."

"And I am answering that this is untrue, and I have had enough of this outrage. Print any of this and you will hear from my solicitors."

"How did you meet Mr Norris?" I was trying the tactic I had seen in South Africa, where we would fire questions from all directions on the internees and trip them up.

"We are in the same Lodge…"

And so I had it.

"And Mr Norris will be paying off the long overdue bill on the Woolwich Arsenal stand?"

"Woolwich Arsenal is paying its bill, which I have said three times now."

Edward, with perfect timing, announced that he was ready to take a picture. Mr Leitch agreed – he must have thought it would be good publicity despite all I had said. He posed, the camera flashed, there was smoke, the secretary ran into the room to see if everything was ok.

"Have you had the cash yet?" I asked while everyone was still blinking and waiting for the smoke to clear, "for Woolwich?"

"I am getting shares, not cash," he said.

"And the stands you have built since Ibrox," I said. "No problems?"

"Miss Mayhew," he replied, "the gentlemen are leaving." And he turned away.

"Got him," I said to Edward as we trooped out, Edward having to pause on the pavement to sort out his gear. Several urchins gathered around to look. A prostitute approached. I shook my head.

"You see that," I said to Edward. "It's not even noon and the girls are working."

Edward finished packing his kit bag. "A working day is a working day," he said. "We started at nine, why shouldn't they?" He packed everything away, and we walked towards the underground at Tottenham Court Road.

"Masons," I said. "Norris is a Mason, the top man at Reading is a Mason, Leitch is a Mason. I wouldn't be surprised if Leavey is a Mason, although I've always thought he was straight."

"My brother-in-law is a Mason," said Edward.

"Explain that," I replied.

"My sister's husband, the Honourable Richard Fox."

We walked for a few moments, deep in thought.

"Fulham, Woolwich Arsenal, Tottenham, Chelsea, Manchester United, he designed grounds for all of them," I said, "and we are finding Masonic connections. Is all football run by the Masons? At least it would explain how Leitch gets so much work despite one terrace falling down and another cracking up. But I still don't understand the money. Leitch clearly isn't a toff – begging your pardon, Mr Edward – so how did he afford never to be paid a penny for Ibrox and the same at Woolwich Arsenal?"

"And why is it he only works in football?" Edward asked very reasonably.

"I wish you had asked him that," I said.

"You're the reporter," he said with a smile. "I'm just a toff." I kicked him, harder than I meant, and then had to help him pick up the equipment he dropped as a result. Fortunately nothing broke.

Back at the office we started on the files trying to find anything on Leitch. One of the assistants found it just before we gave up for the day – in The Scotsman (of course). Archibald Leitch designed the Sentinel Works in Glasgow, in 1904. Reinforced concrete construction.

"That is what they turned to after the Glasgow football ground disaster," I told Mr Holloway when we took the findings to him. He looked at me blankly. "If Chelsea used that technique on the terraces, then Leitch is in the clear. If he went back to the Ibrox technique of designing or continued not to oversee the work properly then we have the start of a chain around him. All we then have to prove is that by working on two grounds at once he didn't oversee the quality of the work on one of them. But I still need to know if there have been problems at other grounds. Manchester United hasn't fallen down, has it?"

"Not that I know – and I find this all rather tedious, Jones," he said. "So please run away and cover the first Edwin Beard Budding National Lawnmower Racing Competition in Enfield. Bring me back twenty or thirty words, would you?"

Wednesday 8th June

George Morrell must be the first ever manager to have his job confirmed twice in one summer. Norris' press office put out a notice saying that Morrell was staying at Woolwich, forgetting that the same thing had been done on 23rd May.

I went to Woolwich and got myself inside the ground and talked to the groundstaff. One gentleman, Mr Gently, was rather thirsty, so we took a little break at the Hen and Basket. I told the staff that I would appreciate it if cracks about my pictures in the Illustrated were cut from general discussion, at least while I was in the building.

As we left the pub I left behind the counter a little "contribution" to Gently's drinking fund and said there would be more if he could get a message to me concerning anything interesting. Back at the ground I asked him if he could read, and finding that he could I showed him how to use the telephone and gave him my number.

Coming out of the ground I met Dr John Clarke, head of the fund raising committee, and reminded him of my status as a shareholder. "Are you supporting the new company?" I asked. "We need that money to keep the club running." I liked the use of "we" in that sentence.

"We are not happy with Mr Norris' bona fides," he said. I had no idea what bona fides were – but the "we" was obviously the fundraising committee. I made a note to get a translation from Edward. (If I asked Mr Holloway he'd tell me they were a new type of goat that was being built in Stoke on Trent.)

"So you are not paying up," I said.

"Not for now," said Dr Clarke.

Thursday 9th June

Extraordinary. Mr Gently phoned and said that Leitch had been to the ground and had a meeting with Mr Leavey. Gently had "overheard" some of it, and from what he said it sounded as if Leitch had changed his mind about accepting shares and was now asking for his money.

I phoned the liquidator. He was in his office, and I said I would be there in two minutes. I made it in seven.

"I am a shareholder in Woolwich Arsenal," I said.

"Congratulations," he replied. He knew exactly my game.

"Is Mr Leitch a creditor of the company?"

"Your being a shareholder does not give you the right to such information," he said, still smiling.

"Would you care for a drink?" I asked.

"Don't mind if I do," he said.

After the third scotch he confirmed what Mr Gently had said. Leitch had changed his mind and was now asking for the full amount to be paid to him in cash not shares, and was suggesting that he would report the matter to the League and the FA if he didn't get his money. It sounded as if I had given him the idea. As the longest standing creditor he was first in line – and that meant £1300 going out of the company before anyone else could get a farthing. As we left, the liquidator told me he had also been bought a drink by a man from the Kentish Independent. How low can these provincial journalists sink? Bribing a liquidator with drink!

It was at this point that Digby Digweed, saviour of the nation, decided to take action. That very night he marched into the War Office, strolled nonchalantly past the cleaners, got directions to Captain Ffopp's offices, and rummaged through the files, looking for details of the nation's spies, with the intent of galvanising them into action.

In horror he discovered the Captain's secret: the filing system was empty save for the bag that held the remains of yesterday's sandwich. Searching the offices high and low he found, beyond any doubt, that there was no secret police force save the incredibly well paid Captain Ffopp...

In the evening Marie told me that the Times did not want her anarchist story, and she wasn't having much luck anywhere else. What she really wanted was for me to get a job in the War Office and then become her source of information so she could do an exposé and tie that in with her piece about anarchists not being a danger.

But that wasn't how I saw my career developing. Besides which, having refused the request of a meeting with Kell and just sketched out an episode of the King of London, I certainly couldn't expect him to give me a decent interview.

Friday 10th June

The Kentish Independent contains an article by Norris demanding more support from the locals in his imperious chairman style.

According to his piece he has only sold around 500 shares in the latest new club, and the rest are now being taken over by himself and Messrs Hall and Leavey. Which clarifies one thing – Leavey has not walked away. That also means that Leavey must know something about Leitch's change of plan in terms of wanting money instead of shares – although I still can't see where that story leads other than round and round the Masons.

"The good people of Woolwich and Plumstead cannot expect the directors of the club to carry the load," continued Norris for another four paragraphs. It was enough to make loyal supporters dive straight into the Hen and Basket.

"If there is to be football in this fine county of our fine kingdom, then local people must support it by buying shares and attending matches. And if anyone else wants to run the club rather than myself and my colleagues, then please do step forward by the 17th and take the club over."

Put another way, everyone is to blame except Norris. It was, as Mr Holloway said, a very local piece now. He also suggested the paper needed someone to cover monkey fighting in Norfolk.

Tony Attwood

Saturday 11th June

Following up on Mr Holloway's statement that multiple ownership might be an issue I went to Croydon to dig up what I could. I found something – but it certainly was not what I expected.

As always there was a groundsman at the ground, and as always he had nothing much to do. "We came here when the old ground at the Crescent was burned down three years back," he said after I promised him a pint. "Here" was the mud heap they call The Nest. There was no stand – but there was what looked like the remains of one on the far side of the ground. "Last year we beat Bradford and took your club to a replay."

"My club?"

"Woolwich Arsenal."

"What happened over there?" I asked, pointing across the pitch.

"Burned down last season. We were in the Southern League Division 1 – our highest point ever. It all looked fair sailing but then it went wrong, the results started going against us, and we went back down. That was the main stand: the roof came off in a gale in April.

"Do we have gales in April?" I asked.

"Well, not quite a gale, but there was a lot of wind that night. Some of the stanchions buckled."

"Must have been a difficult time for the club," I said as sympathetically as I could.

"No we were fine, all properly insured. Mr Norris is very correct in these matters."

"Do you remember who the architect was?" I asked. He looked at me blankly. He didn't know quite what an architect was.

Back in Fleet Street I phoned Leitch's office, but there was no reply.

In the evening Marie and I went to the cinema. She chose the film "Voyage to the Moon" – a fantastic piece made by Georges Melies. Apparently it was a few years old but brought back because of the interest in the Comet. There was also a news piece, and then a really worrying Dr Jekyll and Mr Hyde by August Blom. After the films Marie could not stop talking about the technique, about the books behind the films, and how the films changed the story in order to maximise the technique (which I didn't quite get.) I told her Jekyll and Hyde was really troubling, which struck her as funny.

Then Marie announced that she had a way for me to write a piece about her family. The family were planning to go to Stonehenge for the summer solstice. (Apparently the sun rises over the stones built by the Celts who were here before the Romans, who were apparently here before us. I've heard something of it, but never really taken any notice.)

Seems it is now a fashionable thing to do, and they are going to do it as a family. It involves overnight stays in hotels and the like, and they have invited me to come along and share the fun.

I have no words to describe how shocked, amazed and terrified I am.

Monday 13th June

Meetings, meetings, meetings. The AGM of Woolwich Arsenal and of the FA and the Football League. I was sent off to Woolwich. Mr Holloway had someone else at the FA and at the League meeting.

This was the moment when Norris could not put off his arrangements any more: he needed the new club in existence today. Interestingly there was no mention of Leitch's change of heart, but as a responsible shareholder I waited until the man from the fundraising committee had demanded and got an assurance that the club would not leave the area for at least two years. That seemed enough for them. The committee would have a meeting within days to discuss the offer.

Then I pounced and asked about Leitch. The directors denied that they had heard that he wanted his money. So I asked (as a shareholder) if they actually knew that Leitch had never been paid for his work on the stand.

After some herumphing they agreed that the bill was outstanding.

"So do you agree that as the oldest creditor he should be paid first?"

The man from the fundraising committee was looking daggers, but not at me. No one chose to answer. That was as exciting as it got.

Back at the office Mr Holloway reported that the FA had lost £1300 in the last year which to me seemed insane – they must make a fortune out of those internationals and the Cup Final. How can they lose money?

The stringer telephoned in a report on a terrible line (according to Mr Holloway) but he thought the man said was that Hall was at the FA and Football League meetings representing both Fulham and Woolwich Arsenal, and no one even seemed to think this was odd.

It all went nowhere until I put in another call to Leitch's office. Leitch had been the architect of the Nest – Croydon Common's ground where the stand had blown down. Three grounds, three problems. Croydon was hardly on the same scale as Ibrox or Chelsea, but still…

I sketched out the story, ending with a plea to readers across the country to write to the paper if their local ground has suffered from any problems with its grandstand or terracing. Mr Holloway read it, and asked me how I had written the piece. "I sat by the typewriter and shouted at it," I said.

Wednesday 15th June

George Barrett called in to tell me that the lay-offs were starting, as the torpedo factory move out of Woolwich and up to Glasgow got underway. He said he would be talking to the men and trying to organise some action, and was hoping I would cover it.

I felt a heel and a scoundrel as I made my excuses about already being on a story; I could hardly tell him that I had a deal with Mr Churchill which meant I would not touch it. I told George that I would, however, get back to him and try to pick up the story, or another story from him, later. Meanwhile, I kept my head down and spent the day writing a piece on the cinema. I asked Edward to see if he could get a picture inside a picture house.

Thursday 16th June

My social piece on the cinema appeared and was well received in the office, so it seems I am back in favour. The central point of the piece was the weekly newsreel from the Pathé Animated Gazette. The interesting middle was the story of Jekyll and Hyde, while the deep background was what people got up to in the darkness of the cinema.

Edward had managed to get a picture, which clearly was taken without the clientele knowing. I took the piece as far as I could go in that regard, and found my judgement was getting better because it got through without any editor's cuts.

The insight – that's what the boss wanted – was that people were starting to go to the pictures as a weekly thing – so they were demanding a new film every week. The newsreel showed four or five stories – not the stories I would have picked – but I suppose there are only certain stories that they had on film to show. There was some debate on high about the newsreels challenging the newspaper sales, but the fifth floor wouldn't have any of that. "If we are put out of business by four stories a week, and those a week behind the actual events, then we shouldn't be in Fleet Street," was the official word, so I got the go-ahead.

I ended with a bit about the possibility of showing more football on film. I knew Fulham had done it once, so you never know – it could happen. I didn't say much about the films themselves, largely because I felt I would sound naive – I suspected the readership had been to the pictures more than I had.

Friday 17th June

Having done my duty with a social piece I dared to take my football work back to Mr Holloway. I outlined the new approach: Norris owned Croydon Common and had twice made substantial claims on his insurance on stands that were designed by Archie Leitch – possibly to a sub-standard (and therefore cheap) design.

Leitch had designed grounds here there and everywhere and was a Mason, as was Norris, as was the owner of Reading, and quite possibly everyone else in the story.

My key suggestion was that Leitch was just a cheap-skate – never checking what happened once the designs were put through – and that he used his Masonic connections to get him by when things got difficult, such as when he wanted to slip the plans of Chelsea and Fulham past the LCC, claiming the two stands would be the same when they were not.

"Tell you what, Jones, friend of the Home Secretary, the man what hobnobs with the high and mighty," said Mr Holloway. "Tell you what: let's get rid of the current writ from Norris, before we let him start a second, shall we? I've been told the ravens are leaving the Tower of London which means that the kingdom is about to fall. Do me something on that will you?"

I walked into the newsroom and found one of the juniors who had taken to calling me sir. "What I want to know," I told him, "is who the insurance agents were for the Croydon Common stands and what investigator they employed to find out if the destructions were deliberate."

He scuttled away looking pleased.

Saturday 18th June

It was at this point that matters took an unexpected twist. Calling himself the King of London, a newcomer appeared on the scene, announcing that the only way to overcome the foreign invasion was to amalgamate the nation's football clubs together into one strong fighting unit. Each club, the King said, would retain its identity but would be owned by him so that he could direct the nation's footballing affairs and ensure victory...

I wrote the final two episodes: Digby tells the invading forces that the only way for them to retain the goodwill of the working man is to provide an alternative entertainment to football and sets them all up as music hall acts which is where they remain to this day; the King of London was dismissed as an irrelevance and everyone lived happily ever after.

It all seemed a bit odd, but the readers seemed to like it, and in one story I had taken a poke at both Norris and Kell which made it all worthwhile.

Sunday 19th June

Today was the day. A day I had been hiding from myself, because it filled me with so much dread.

I went to Marie's family house in Dorset Square, a fine grand town house indeed, and presented myself at the door, petrified.

Petrified of wearing the wrong clothes (even though Marie had talked me through it all), petrified of being turned away by a footman or butler or valet or whatever they had, petrified of not knowing what to say, whose hand to shake, who to call sir, who to call my lord (even though again Marie had tutored me). It was like the first day of being a private and not knowing if you call the guy with the stripe "sir" or "corp" or "corporal" or "you stupid bugger".

But... it was by and large ok. There was a butler at the door, Mr Jenkinson as I discovered a little later, and as soon as I said my name he knew who I was. Even better he said, "I enjoy your sketches about the invasions in the Chronicle, if I may say, sir." Talk about being knocked down with feathers.

Marie was there within seconds, calmed me, said I was dressed perfectly well, checked the provisions in my bag, and introduced me to the party – which was in fact her mother, a friend of her mother's called Alyson Fairbright, her father, a chauffeur for the second car, the butler, Marie and myself.

So I travelled, by car, across country, with the toffs, and to tell the truth, at every turn as people paused to look at us, I wanted to wave and shout and say, "Look at me!"

Monday 20th June

After the overnight at Newbury the journey continued, with suitable stops for coffee, luncheon, and tea, before we arrived in our hotel near the Stones – a hotel

packed with other likeminded folk of similar status. Slowly I got into
conversations with the others. Lady Cortney and her friend seemed particularly
interested in my life, and once, when Lord and Lady Cortney and their daughter
went for a stroll, Alyson Fairbright questioned me very closely about my
relationship with Marie – more closely than I would have ever anticipated.
Another surprise.

Marie's view on the class barrier was that if I acted as if I belonged, then I
would belong. "By and large," she said, "people do what you expect them to do.
Expect everyone to see you as a fish out of water, and that is what you will be.
Feel part of it all, and you are. The aristocracy is full of wild eccentrics – in fact
you have to be eccentric to be part of the clan. Just look."

And she was right. There were people dressed in the most extraordinary
fashions and styles. There were young men with older women, and young women
with old men – and no one seemed to notice. There were people who seemed to
have twenty servants, and those stepping out on their own. There were even
people who had apparently bicycled here – even though civilisation was miles
away.

Later Lord and Lady Cortney joined us as we sat after lunch on a terrace
overlooking farmland. Lord Cortney mentioned Norris and asked if I thought him
a crook.

I was about to jump in but Marie got there first. "In terms of the voting
papers, yes. They were in his house, and that is an offence – they must not leave
the council offices. But it is a very minor offence – a bit like standing on the grass
in the municipal park. Most likely to get a word from a policeman, nothing
more."

"After that," added Marie, "it's guesswork. We assume an ulterior motive in
buying up football clubs. We know he is using Leitch who does not have the best
record as an architect, but Leitch has never been proven to be negligent, and who
are we to say he is? And we know Norris has high political ambition. Jack has
also found the connection between Norris and the Church, and there might be an
insurance claim that is not right on the stands at Croydon Common's ground – but
it is all at the edge. We can prove nothing, and in truth it is as likely that there is
nothing. And I suspect we can say that about a lot of people."

"No evidence," repeated Lord Cortney. "And yet…"

He let the sentence hang while he puffed on his cigar.

"Doesn't it strike you as strange that he is suing your paper for libel, Mr
Jones, over the issue of having the election papers in his house. And yet that is the
only thing that is certain. So why sue you on that point?"

"To buy time?" suggested Marie.

"To what end?" asked her father. "Time is valuable if you have some other
stratagem coming up from behind, but he doesn't – at least as far as we know.
The best Norris can hope for is that there is another election and he becomes an
MP – which is far from certain. And even in that case he cannot expect any sort
of immunity. If anything he is an embarrassment to his party. I don't think he will
become a parliamentarian for a long time."

"Doesn't the fact that his is suing the paper suggest to the Unionists that he is innocent?" I asked.

"Not really," Lord Cortney replied, "they are just as likely to say that they would prefer to take on someone else as an MP until such time as this difficult little matter is cleared up. The political parties can be vicious if they think something is going to inhibit their progress. So I ask the question again – why bother to sue over the one thing that is true?"

"To tie Jacko up in knots," said Marie. Her father looked at her. It was a look that I knew she hated – a look that suggested that he was a patient father tutoring a rather dim child who had finally seen the answer that she had been led towards.

"Because there is something else out there, something he doesn't want us to reach, and he wants to slow us down," I said spelling it out. "Except that in the end it is a strategy that won't work."

"I fear you have yet to experience the full force of the solicitors' collective," said Lord Cortney. "The Norris team will probably offer a deal in which they graciously drop their case, offer to pay the Chronicle's costs, and give one or two other concessions of no particular benefit to anyone, and merely ask in return that the story – and all other stories about Norris – are now abandoned. They will say that it is for their client's political life and his constituents. Fighting the case is becoming too time-consuming for such a busy man, they will argue. And quite probably the Chronicle will accept because they won't have a clue what else is in the offing, and they will know that if they keep hitting him with little stories, it will begin to look like persecution. So for a little spot of legal cash Norris gets everything dropped."

Tuesday 21st June

We rose at an hour I had not seen since South Africa and made the short journey by car to the Stones. The scene we found was not exactly that on the postcards as not all the pairs of stones had lintels joining them. Alyson (she insisted I used her first name, without formality) explained that there had been a storm ten years earlier that had caused some damage. The owners of the site, worried about the increasing numbers of visitors, had laid down several stones that seemed to be in a parlous state – but had failed to update the postcards.

We all had tickets – although this, of course, like everything else, had been arranged by the butler who is apparently also the family secretary. Lord Cortney was well enough known to get a doffing of hats from the gatekeeper and the three constables from the local constabulary who were obviously there to ensure that the toffs did not start rioting and knock a few more stones over. Then the champagne was opened just at the right moment, and we toasted the sunrise with much cheering, and everyone checked pocket watches to show it was right on time while Lady Cortney complained that she was cold and Alyson put her arm around her to warm her up.

The back of my ticket (which I duly kept to show mum and dad) stated that, "All persons are requested not to deface or injure the Stones, and to attend to the orders of the Constable on duty."

After the celebrations we started the journey back, stopping en route to celebrate our great achievement in actually getting to the right stones on the right day at the right time.

Wednesday 22nd June

My birthday – spent on the journey back. To my surprise, embarrassment and ultimately my enjoyment there was a party at the hotel for the overnight stay, with a "Happy Birthday" cake.

Feeling more integrated I chanced my luck by asking Lord Cortney what he thought were the big stories of the moment. "From what I've heard from my daughter," he said, "you know them: the war between the classes, the proposed war between Britain and Germany, and the rescue of the old and poor from the vortex.

"Behind all that is secrecy, which brings fear – and that fear has led your friend Kell – most amusingly described as Ffopp I may add – to try to recreate Section H without the slightest knowledge of how to do it. The danger is that Kell might actually start to denounce people as spies when they simply have German names. But you tell me something – what exactly happened when you came back from the Boer War?"

"I was ordered to report to Colonel Edmunds, and he told me he was running MO5, the Directorate of Military Operations. The aim was to apply all the techniques we had learned in Africa to the situation in Britain and elsewhere in the Empire. He said there were reports of "mobile agents" who wandered around the kingdom and "local agents" who had jobs and fixed positions, and we had to check the stories, establish current conditions, and then put in place a permanent force that would meet the security needs of the country and the Empire in both times of peace and war.

"We worked at it for a while, but then quite suddenly it all stopped – and I never knew why. We were all laid off, and I heard nothing more until Captain Kell turned up."

"We have a government that has always been driven by class rather than a rational understanding of the situation," said Alyson unexpectedly.

"Alyson and my wife work on projects to bring the vortex to an end in ways that move beyond politics," added his lordship. "But back on the political front, what happened to you, Mr Jones, was not the end of MO5, although I suspect no one has told you the story.

"Section H wasn't simply wrapped up – it became the Committee of Imperial Defence in 1904 answering directly to the Cabinet. The high and mighty officers running the show (which did not include me by the way) thought that since Section H had included mere soldiers (such as you) it was itself a security risk. 'How can we trust a sergeant?' was the cry, suggesting that anyone less than a captain was more likely to sell himself out to the highest bidder than give up his

142

time willingly to the empire. Colonel Edmunds objected and said he had got more sense out of his sergeants than he had out of his majors, but that was considered sacrilege, so he went off to tend his farm and has not been seen in government since. Alyson and my wife are still friends of the family and visit him occasionally.

"Without the Colonel and your team MO5 had no foundation, but that has never stopped the government, and last year the fools set up a sub-committee to plan counter measures against a possible German invasion. They call it the Secret Service Bureau, it was all undertaken in extreme secrecy, and the only copy of the sub-committee report ever produced was given to the Director of Military Operations at the War Office. It is known as CAB 16/232, and only a handful of people – including me – have seen it, which is why I can recall the number."

I watched him in fascinated silence, using every trick I had learned to store every aspect of the information in my head.

"The SSB was established under Captain Vernon G. W. Kell of the South Staffordshire Regiment, and he was appointed under the Director of Military Operations (5) at the War Office along with Captain Mansfield Cumming of the Royal Navy.

"In the way these people play their childish games Cumming is known as 'C', and Kell as "K" – which should of course fool the Germans completely and keep us safe from invasion.

"By the start of this year it was clear that "C" had realised "K" was a brilliant linguist, a superb administrator and a total fool, who was wholly inappropriate as a person at the top of the Bureau. So "C" marched back to the Admiralty to set up his office for gathering intelligence overseas, while "K" got his room in the War Office working on counter-espionage within Britain. "K" is funded from the secret service vote by the War Office – Parliament doesn't even know he exists."

"Mr Churchill knows," I said, "I met Captain Kell in Mr Churchill's office when we discussed my torpedo factory story. Captain Kell – "K" – was acting as his liaison intelligence officer."

"Well, well, that is a revelation," said Lord Cortney. "Kell, being the good administrator he is, recently submitted a list of his possible MO5 operations labelled MO5(a), MO5(b) and so on to the end of the alphabet. (Don't ask how I know: like journalists, their lordships have secret sources of information.) MO5(t) is the drawing up of a list of all aliens in the United Kingdom with a view to handing these lists over to chief constables to keep an eye on them and report back any suspicious activity. In the event of war they will be rounded up and put in concentration camps – as you did with the women and children in South Africa.

"K" has no knowledge, no experience, no background in this sort of work, no brains, no imagination and a deeply prejudiced belief in the superiority of his class, his race and his sex. His aim is to increase police powers, increase surveillance, intercept the post, control any new science and technology that the boffins develop, find the spies, and make himself a top dog. You may have heard that there is now a way of transmitting the human voice over the telegraph, and from what I hear Kell has already started suggesting that his department should be uniquely responsible for controlling the process.

"But he can find no spies and so he has no choice but to make up his information. He does this in order to frighten people and so win the election for the Unionists who he believes will fund his department."

"So what is to be done?" I asked, stunned at this surge of secret information coming my way.

"I would not presume to say, Mr Jones," said Lord Cortney. "If you find this interesting you might like to expose MO(a) to (z) as a waste of public money, and their inventor as a man of dubious intellect."

Thursday 23rd June

I reported to work in the afternoon and wrote up my piece on Stonehenge. The social editor went to town with the red pen, and told me that the official line was that charging ordinary people an entrance fee to look at the national monuments and treasures of the country was exploitation. He also wanted more about these people who have time to swan about (as he put it) and less about how such journeys provide work for the hoteliers and the chemists' shops that sell petrol. We had a row, but with no other story on offer I re-wrote it as I was bid.

After that I went to Dorset Square where Mr Jenkinson told me that unfortunately his lordship was not at home, but agreed to give him a note. I wrote my apologies for what would appear in the paper.

Friday 24th June

After work Marie and I returned to the discussion of Captain Kell and the MO operations. As Marie said, "Bringing down one man who is a fraud is easy. But bringing down an idea is harder. And that's all MO5 is – a list of ideas from a to z."

Saturday 25th June

The Stonehenge article was published. I hated every word of it.

I went to see Mr Holloway and without giving him any details told him that I had discovered that Kell was about to be involved in postal intercepts, telephone monitoring, drawing up a list of all foreigners, and possibly the censorship of newspapers and the control of all new technologies including voice telegraphs.

Then I told him that I had no direct evidence that I could quote about the MO5 operations, but I'd got the information quite independently from two highly reliable sources. (I didn't say one was the daughter of the other).

He looked at me for a while. In the end he said, "You are either a total imbecile or a total idiot. I suspect the former. When I have found out what to do with your latest crazed idea, I will let you know. In the meanwhile people all over London are reporting the return of a man who kills young women and then gets away by jumping straight up from the street onto the rooftops. Look into that, will you?"

Sunday 26th June

At Marie's suggestion we went to see the Mayor of Fulham dressed up in his finest taking the salute at the Midsummer Pageant. It being a military occasion I wore my army togs if for no reason other than to annoy Norris if he happened to spot me (which I don't think he did). It rained cats and dogs, and we didn't last long in the open air.

There was one amusing moment when a major came by, and without even thinking I found my right arm saluting. He paused, looked at the regiment, and asked about my service. I told him and expected him to move on, but he persisted.

"Where yer working now, Sergeant?" he bellowed in a voice that had several dozen onlookers who were trying to hear a speech by the Bishop of London turning to shsh him. I told him.

"Journalist?" he shouted, ignoring the sounds being made all around. "Horsewhip the lot of you, that's what I'd do," he said. "Disgrace to the uniform." And with that he wandered off as the Bishop continued to tell us we were all going to hell – mostly because he didn't like the way we were treading on his flowerbeds.

Monday 27th June

With my Stonehenge piece having been poorly received (I would like to think because it had hardly been recognisable as my work by the time the social editor had finished with it) I was under orders to find a new story. Not Woolwich Arsenal, not the pictures, not toffs, not Leitch, not anarchists, and not Captain Kell and MO on which the jury was still having a natter.

Athletic News carried a short piece on Woolwich Arsenal suggesting that the takeover was floundering, there was no money to hire a team for next year and Norris was having difficulty coming up with funds because Fulham had made a loss the season before last. As Fulham's figures for the season just finished weren't yet out that looked like being a bit of a guess, but AN was not known for guessing wrong.

None of which helped me much as I read through every paper that came into the office looking for anything that would give me a new line, a new approach or, joy of joys, a new story. A note arrived from Lord Cortney saying that he fully understood that the article on the Stonehenge visit had been rewritten by my superiors, and he was glad I had enjoyed the venture. He also hoped he might have the pleasure of my company again sometime. Rather more surprising was a note from Alyson saying that she had enjoyed my company and hoped we could meet again.

Tuesday 28th June

I took to meandering around the office, looking as if I were deep in thought. It worked occasionally although Mr Holloway saw through the ruse within seconds.

In the late afternoon the story came through that a Zeppelin passenger airship had crashed. Most of us agreed that we'd sooner keep our feet on the ground. We ran the facts from the news agency, with a commentary from the leader writer.

I tried to talk to Marie after work but she was now deeply engaged in trying to write an article about a new book called **Principia Mathematica** which apparently covers all maths, from adding up to wherever it ends. Or it will do when the writers have finished the fourth volume.

"I thought you were an expert in English," I said.

"That's why they have given me this. I am working with Middleton – he's a mathematician and he has to explain to me what this is all about so I can write it up in a version of English that our readers can understand. I've only got as far as the fact that everything in maths comes from axioms, inference and symbolic logic, but since I don't know what they are in mathematical terms, I am getting nowhere."

"And is this important?" I asked.

She told me it was vital. I let it pass. We sat in silence. "Why don't you read more?" she said at last.

"I read papers and the occasional political document," I countered, (although the truth was that I hadn't read anything much since my earlier work on the Parliament Act and the anarchist pamphlet.) "And I read *Spies of the Kaiser*," I added.

"I'll bring you a book tomorrow. I reviewed it for the Times before this mathematical nonsense. It should be of interest to you – it is about the war between the social classes."

Wednesday 29th June

Marie brought me *Howard's End* by EM Forster and told me to read it to understand the difference between the classes more clearly. According to Marie's review, *Howard's End* is about two different families, one intellectual and one materialistic. The question is: what is the relation between the world of business and the world of intellect? How can they connect?

Meanwhile, back in the real world, the Chron is full of the Dickman trial – the man accused of murdering John Nisbet for the money he was carrying. I don't normally have any interest in such cases, but this one had an element that really fascinated me.

Dickman had worked in the family firm near Durham but then moved on through several employers in different industries, and, as far as I could tell, each time he managed to lose his job. He married the local schoolmistress, and eventually ended up as a clerk at a nearby coal mine.

All that was quite straightforward, but then in 1906 Dickman set things up so that the Morpeth Colliery Company was sold, and that sale forced him out of his job – which was the first odd thing. Why would anyone do a deal that means they lose their employment?

The answer turned out to be that Dickman received a huge commission apparently equal to four years' wages. Now I can well imagine that the owner of some backstreet coal mine might want to say thank you to a lowly clerk for fixing up a deal that perhaps made them lots of money, but I can't see them handing over this much. For the clerk to get four years' money he must have been central to the deal – but he was only a clerk. Exactly as he was in each previous job. What's more, he'd lost each previous job, probably because he got the empty (although that's not confirmed).

How could a man who changes jobs every few years suddenly have all the power and knowledge that would make him worth four years' salary in one deal? And how could he ever have written up the contract in such a way that the mine owners would honour it? They would have solicitors crawling all over the place during a sale like this – and a lowly clerk like Dickman would surely have settled for less.

Unless there was something odd going on behind the scenes.

Even odder still, Dickman then seems to have become a professional gambler. Yet there was nothing in his earlier life to suggest he gambled. None of the papers have interviewed the bookie that he used. There's no sign that he did the football pools. Why suddenly change direction like this? Surely his better bet would have been to go to other mine owners and show how much he got for the Morpeth mine and offer to do it again. After all, with a big sale like that he would have been well known in the local mining community.

Nisbet was supposedly carrying wages of around £400 to pay the men at another colliery. Dickman was accused of shooting Nisbet after they travelled on a train together in March – but there is still no sign of the money or the gun.

Thursday 30th June

I was summoned to the fifth floor and quizzed on the MO5 operation and the arch-twerp Captain Kell. I went through the story again, giving every detail save a certain bit of information concerning a break-in at the War Office. To avoid that topic, I particularly focussed on my work in what we now call the Union of South Africa and how we set up the process of reading the mail under Lieutenant Colonel Edmonds. That they liked. They were putting two and two together and getting twenty-two – and if that was in favour of me, I had no objection.

"So your source, Jones," said Mr Donald, "is your work in the Cape, and your association then and now with a prominent cabinet minister. Do you have other modern sources?"

"Can't ask Jones to reveal sources," said Frank Brangwyn who was there as the most senior reporter in the building for the day. Frank is the man we all look up to – a top ranking journalist who really gave the Chronicle some style and class. I'd never spoken to him save to return his greetings and call him sir. I also stepped aside for him at the front door once.

"But you are a man with sources," said Mr Donald.

"I have two separate sources for this story, sir," I replied. "They tell me Kell is in charge of the SSB and has drawn up a long list of what the SSB should do. He has the ear of government since he reports directly to a secret subcommittee of the cabinet."

"And Jones' sources have not let us down so far," said Mr Brangwyn, giving me more support than I could have dreamed of. "I can't see what we have to lose. The whole press is full of German spy stories. If we are saying that the government has set up a secret department to check up on spies, what can be wrong with that? If they deny it, they are denying that they are taking the safety of the realm seriously, and they won't do that."

"But if we say they are reading the letters we post…" said Mr Donald, hitting the key issue. "Would a British government really do this?

He paused, but then answered his own question. "We go. Confidence in you, Jones," he said. "Don't let me down." And with that the meeting was over.

On the way out Mr Brangwyn smiled at me and said, "Get it right and they take the credit for nurturing your wayward talent and seeing the truth of your story. Get it wrong and you are out of a job."

He was probably right. I used his telephone to ask for an appointment with Captain Kell and, to my surprise, I got one.

Friday 1st July

I arranged with George Barrett to meet up at the Rising Sun. He wanted to know who I was attacking in the King of London story. I said I was just playing it for laughs. So he then asked me if I had a theory, and I said probably not (on the grounds that I didn't know what he meant), which set him off.

His view is that life is not just what you see – there is always an underlying cause, an underlying tension. Only if you understand what drives the forces of society and have an ideal beyond the here and now to which you aspire can you then draw up plans for reform. I said that all sounded a bit too intellectual for the Chron.

"You don't have plans or theories or anything," he said, "but you could have – and you are wasting your talent as a writer without them. You could be making men aware of what is going on in the world – maybe through your humour. But as it is you just make fun of everyone."

Saturday 2nd July

At his trial yesterday Dickman claimed that although he knew John Nisbet he did not travel with him on the train on 18th March, his point being that he was on the same train as Nisbet but not in the same carriage. He said he had pointed out that he had bought a ticket to Stannington Station and intended to visit someone called William Hogg at Dovecot Colliery. However, he missed his station and got out at Morpeth instead. The prosecution made the point that the bag that Nisbet had used to carry the £370 was found at the bottom of Isabella Pit, a disused mine shaft near Morpeth – a possible link but a flimsy bit of circumstantial in my view. There is still nothing to show Dickman did it, nor to explain his bizarre lifestyle. Something is wrong here.

Although it wasn't due yet I worked on my next King of London piece – perhaps as a way of getting the whole business with Barrett out of my head. I made the point that the Cubs are the most powerful secret society in the world after the triads in China and Sinn Fein – except we know about Sinn Fein so they are not secret. I got a runner to look up the meaning of Sinn Fein – apparently it is "ourselves alone". Now I know.

I started to bring the King of London more and more to the forefront of the story as the invaders are tied up in knots arguing about who should have the lead role and star billing each evening. The King of London is marching around demanding the allegiance of everyone, but everyone is now so excited by the music hall that no one takes any notice. Several of the music halls acts are threatening to go on strike for more money. We watch the acts, we watch their argument, we will watch the strike. It's what we do.

At which point the footballers also go on strike for the end of the maximum wage – stating that if they don't win their case they will move their art to the music hall.

In the evening another first: what is known as a "dinner party" at Lord Cortney's house. Apart from his lordship and lady wife, Marie and me, there was

Lord and Lady Hangmorton and Mr Morecomb and his wife and (rather curiously I felt) Alyson. It was polite, but intense, and fortunately for me Marie carried a lot of the conversation. She had come up with the notion, prior to the guests arriving, that just as I might find myself out of place on occasion so would all these people if they were suddenly asked to work in a newspaper office. In such circumstances, she said, because I am a nice young man not especially given to hurting people, I would try and help them and explain what should be done – but I would also expect them to be sensible and ask questions, rather than just go blundering on. So it should be in her house.

All present were Liberals and there was much plotting and debating as to what the Lords will do at each turn.

What fascinated me was an argument from Mr Morecomb who apparently owns several printing works. "Do you know many enemies of society?" he asked me at one point. I said I'd met a few anarchists in my time and spent a while in a prison cell with one. "All very childish people," he said although I got the impression he'd not met one. "They torment themselves and through that torment other people," he continued. "Can tell them a mile off. Sad, depressed – have to watch them to make sure they have the knife turned away from their chests while eating a meal."

"Are you saying they are all of a certain type?" I asked.

"Absolutely," he said, "they are how they are born. See it in their faces. This is where there is a lot of wrong thinking going on – and you should put this in your paper, Mr Jones." I was about to say that what went in the paper was more the editor's line than mine, but he pushed ahead. "There's a number of types of personality, and these types lead us to be what we are. There's your victim type, your criminal type, your sad tormented type – those are your anarchists – your leaders and your led... but the worst of all are those who believe they can create an alternative society in place of ours. Against them, the anarchists are nothing. Not a thing."

"And you think we are born with this type – we can't change it?" I asked.

"Can't change it at all. You come out of the mother's womb, and there you are, fixed for life. That's what makes the world so varied – all these different types. And we are all dependent on each other. The victim needs the criminal to be able to fulfil his role in life. The sad anarchist needs a society to be sad about. Elsewhere there are the silent types who take in information and your communicators – journalists, people like you – who pass it on. Leaders and led – everything in balance. Conspirators and those conspired against – always the same. Without all this the world would be both exceptionally boring and would not work in the social sense.

Sunday 3rd July

Marie and I search for deeper understandings as to what is going on regarding Kell and his secret MO department. We needed to know a) what he will do next and b) what we should do about it (if anything) and c) when it would be safe to use some of the information we now had. Our general feeling was that what we knew came from such sensitive sources (the break-in and her father's revelations) that we needed to discover something else in order to hide the other two sources.

Having exhausted the subject of what Kell might do next we drifted into the question of ourselves and where we will be next year. And naturally it took us into a request again from Marie to meet my family, questions about where we see ourselves going, my lack of ease with her family and their friends (despite their undeniable courtesy towards me at all times), and so forth. I tried to throw in Woolwich Arsenal, but to no avail.

I said that I could cope with the manners and habits of the aristocracy, but what I couldn't do was see where our relationship could go with me earning just a regular scribbler's wage. She said that this was the problem of science fiction – tomorrow as a repeat of today only bigger. I said that wasn't true of HG Wells' *Time Machine* and we got off the subject.

Monday 4th July

With a day off and nothing booked in I went to the Old Bailey, waved my press pass, found a copper on the door who supported Woolwich Arsenal, and got into the Dickman trial. Cicely Nisbet, "the murdered man's wife" as they say, identified Dickman as the man sitting in the same carriage as her husband at Heaton Station – so that goes against Dickman's own testimony. Then they came up with the ticket collector who had been on duty at Morpeth that night, and he confirmed that Dickman had got off the 10.27 at his station. His ticket was for Stannington (exactly as he claimed) and so paid the ticket collector the excess fare – which is what the old boy remembers.

It was not as exciting as I had hoped – probably because I hadn't been following the trial from the start – and I was thinking of leaving when what I had hoped for happened. A really eccentric character, one Professor Robert Boland of Durham University, was called to give evidence as a "medical expert."

Boland had examined Dickman's clothing and he said that he had found blood on a glove and on a pair of trousers that Dickman had worn on the day of the murder. The trouble was that every time the Prof was asked a question he would lean back, stroke his chin and survey the court with one eye closed, as if we were a bunch of naughty school boys. Then he'd speak in this strange high squeaky voice, full of phrases like, "let me see," and "of course it is not so simple that a layman can understand it". Everyone looked to the judge to see if he would tell the Prof to hurry up, but he didn't.

Boland said that Dickman's Burberry overcoat showed signs of being covered in paraffin and in his learned opinion this was because someone wanted to remove the blood stains.

Then one of the barristers rose in his wig and gown and said that he was sure the Professor would want to remove the word "learned" since in court only the barristers were "learned" and there was much guffawing.

The AGM of Fulham FC was down for the evening, but there was no point my even hanging around the place since Norris would have his troopers out waiting for me, and as I am not a season ticket holder or a shareholder there is no way in. Rupert Disgborough who has a brother who is a shareholder went along for the paper and agreed to write everything down and prepare a readable copy for the morning.

I continued to write sketches for the future of the King of London's adventures. All attention is now turned to the music halls where the invaders are considered star turns. Although in effect all they do is wear their native costumes and talk in their native tongues, this is considered hilariously amusing by the music hall aficionados. No one goes to football any more. The King of London has backed the wrong sport, and his uprising has failed. He has invested his fortune and is broke.

But the sport re-emerges as Digby starts up a side for the Boy Scouts, and within weeks has a league going, and crowds are starting to appear at matches.

Tuesday 5th July

According to the report from Rupert at Fulham Town Hall, Norris said that he wanted to continue with his great work and take Fulham into the First Division, while the independent shareholders suggested he should leave before they sank into the Southern League "from which Norris had fiddled their election".

William Hall was given a very hard time over the running of the club, the players, the tactics, the money given to charities in the parts of London where Norris was building and, of course, Woolwich Arsenal. "What do you want two clubs for? You can't run one," was the call. They didn't realise he had three, and was casting his eye over Reading as well. I wished I'd been there to tell them. Apparently Norris was furious.

There was one other new theme: John Dean resigned as a director. No one knew why.

Wednesday 6th July

The paper is full of the trial of Dickman. John Badcock gave evidence on behalf of the National Provincial Bank saying that Dickman was overdrawn at the time of Nisbet's murder. Robert Sedcole popped up for Lloyds Bank and said the same. James Paisley of the Co-operative Society then toddled along and said that in October 1907 Annie Dickman had £73 in her account but that by March 1910, she was down to her last £4. So everyone got the picture that they were broke.

But... how did Dickman get overdrawn? Why did the bank let him get overdrawn? No one asks.

Superintendent John Weddell stated that when Dickman was searched after the murder he had tickets that showed he had several items with local pawnbrokers.

Dickman was the only witness for his own case. He admitted travelling on the 10.27 train on 18th March. However, he still denied sitting in the same carriage as Nisbet and said he was so engrossed in his newspaper (the Chron – one up to us) he couldn't say who else was in the carriage with him – or even if there was anyone at all. He said he knew Nisbet but didn't know about the collection of wages on Friday. Mind you, everyone gets paid on Friday so, in my opinion, if he knew Nisbet held that sort of position and Nisbet was stupid enough to show that he was carrying a bag, it would be totally obvious there was money in it.

But here's a funny thing. No one asked him what was so interesting in the paper of that day. It must have been a great story for him to have been that engrossed. Maybe it was one of mine. I left the court as the jury went out.

Meanwhile here's a coincidence: John Dean runs Dean's, the canvas bag company. And we used Dean's canvas bags in the Transvaal as water carriers during the War. Just a useless piece of information – except that it puts Dean in context. He is a local businessman with a successful business.

Norris is the power broker – the man who wants total control. Dean is a local businessman – a bit like Leavey. Norris seems to walk all over these men – and that's my guess with Dean. He didn't need the problems, so got up and walked out.

Another snippet. Chelsea FC made a profit of £1945 in its last financial year. How much would they have made if they had repaired their ground?

Thursday 7th July

The jury found Dickman guilty of the murder of Nisbet yesterday and he was sentenced to death. I am left feeling very bad about this case. Obviously it was nothing to do with me, and I wrote nothing on it – but none of it fits. Why and how did Dickman get all that money originally? Why did he turn to gambling rather than carry on in the mining business. Why was none of this background ever mentioned in court? Why did no one ask questions like this?

I was so engrossed in my thoughts that I hardly had time to think about the War Office – but I got myself to Horse Guards Avenue in time. Marie told me the building is neo-Baroque and gave me a lecture on what that meant, but I didn't take that in either. It is certainly modern – just a few years old and certainly an improvement. They were building the new place while I was working in Winchester House. My main memory there was the fact that we all used to get sore throats, apparently because the place was built on a cesspit.

Now our wars are fought from a magnificent new building with over 1000 rooms. It seems that while it is easy to stroll into at night it has an efficient reception in the day – I was greeted on the ground floor, directed to the third floor, met and directed along two corridors, met, directed along another corridor, met and told to wait.

After ten minutes or so Captain Kell sent for me, and as I entered his office he shook me by the hand and asked me to sit. Within his room there was none of the grandeur of the building outside. Just him and a lady who brought us tea and cake. There was his famous filing cabinet and his desk, chair and phone. Nothing else in his room – exactly as Marie had found.

I gave him my prepared pitch taking me from South Africa through to my present job and how as a reporter it was my task to put stories together. I had started to wonder if the work we had done in Section H was now being carried on here, and if there was a story concerning the catching of the German spies that so filled the press.

"Section H was an inspiration to us all," said the Captain, forgetting that it was I who had told him all about it. "And so I have to say it is an honour to meet a veteran of such a campaign. On the other hand I am told that one of the childish comic characters in your newspaper's stories is supposed to be me, so I am surprised you feel it is appropriate that we meet or that I tell you anything."

One relief: he wasn't even well enough informed to guess that it was me who wrote the King of London story.

"What's more," he continued, "I asked you point blank for your source of information about the torpedo factory in the Home Secretary's office and you refused to give. Treason I call that, even though the Home Secretary disagreed. Not sure we have much to say to each other, Mr Jones."

"I would have thought, Captain," I said, "that if your department had some publicity in the newspaper it would help you in your fight against the spies. You could pick up some useful information."

"How's that?" he asked, unable to see where I was going.

"I mean that if we say that there is a section in the War Office that is gathering information on spies, people would write to you with all their information – and that would make life easier for your network of men who are, I am guessing, out there, spying on the spies, as it were."

He sat for a moment, and then went on to tell me about the Germans, their invasion, the fact that even though *Spies of the Kaiser* was fiction it was based on fact, and that the author was clearly working for the Germans. "Do you realise", he asked, "that Le Q had copies of his books published in German, and that in the German edition the German army invades Britain and wins the war – while in the English edition, we win the war?" Another report of mine thrown back at me.

There was a pause, and then suddenly he started again. "You have inside information, Mr Jones?"

I told him that as a journalist I always dealt in information, and any journalist who didn't wasn't a journalist.

"I mean, details of where the German spies are meeting, what they are doing, who they are seeing."

"I thought that is what you did in the Directorate of Military Operations," I said. "Finding out where the spies are meeting."

"How do you know it is called the Directorate of Military Operations?" he demanded giving me a strange kind of sideways look which seemed to signify that he had just landed a telling punch.

"I think the word is out, Captain," I said. It would have been kinder to tell him that it was the name we worked under for Colonel Edmunds, but with someone like Kell who needs to be kind?

There was a long silence before I threw him a line. "I can't tell you about the torpedo factory, but I can give you our information on the spies." He perked up. "To the best of our knowledge the public places are where the meetings happen – and fortunately for the enemy our capital city is awash with very public places. They can meet in a restaurant, in Hyde Park, at a football match…" And in what he took to be that one unguarded sentence his world was set, his imagination took flight.

"A football match – of course," he said, as his slow mind clicked into recognition that a) I was a football reporter and b) the King of London story centred on the notion that the foreign armies were attempting to steal our football grounds. "In the crowd, no one would notice two men – a dozen men – exchanging information. They stand in a ground, the crowd is taken by the game, the exchange of notes, the subtle conversation, all open and yet all hidden… Why didn't you tell me before?"

"I…"

"Of course, of course, I appreciate your position here. You are no longer under command. Can't call you sergeant, eh? But it is excellent that you have brought this to my attention. Mr Jones, your information could be invaluable. Do you have names, dates, contacts…"

I gathered my thoughts. "Captain, in the journalist world we are noticing occasional events, but not pursuing. We don't have the resources of your department with your network of counter-espionage agents. But if you are interested I can certainly check through our records and see if I can find a few patterns that would be of interest. But you understand, as journalists we just observe what is going on."

"Of course, of course," he said. "But at the same time you can provide some insight to this department."

"My brief, sir, is to write about what the government is doing about the German spy menace. And, since it is related, to report on this department and how it is looking after the well-being of our citizens. What I am here to do is to ask you to give me some information about your department – how many men you have in the field, the details of one or two high profile spies you have caught, the way the networks work, anything like that. Anything you can tell me. In return I'll certainly be checking our records."

"Quite impossible," he said. "As you yourself pointed out, you cannot tell me how you got the torpedo information. I certainly cannot tell you about our networks."

"How many men have you in the Directorate, sir?" I thought the "sir" might sweeten him up.

"You understand that we are new and just starting, and at the moment there is just a small team. We get reports from the public; reports full of interesting leads and possibilities. My team sorts them, and then we go into the field to examine them. Not every one is a lead, but some are useful. If you care to give me a few leads I am sure we might be able to ensure that your paper is the first one to get the story about any arrests that result. Anyway, you'll know all this sort of thing – much like Section H, I imagine."

"Section H got most of its information by intercepting the mail," I said.

He looked shocked. "Did you by gad?" the booby said. "Not sure we can do that. Englishman's private correspondence is sacrosanct. Besides there is too much of it to read it all."

I pointed out that we only read the mail to and from known suspects, following up on the work of the men in the field, and after that the conversation dried up. I asked again about numbers, operations, activities, successes, but he wouldn't say anything other than "hush-hush."

In the end I had to leave before I started laughing.

Friday 8th July

A campaign has begun to get the Dickman verdict overturned – and I am not at all surprised. We carried an advertisement from the fellow's supporters saying that the execution of Dickman would be on purely circumstantial evidence. The advertisers wanted everyone to protest by postcard to the Home Secretary. I was distracted by the news from a junior that he had something on the insurance company for the Croydon Common stands. National Buildings was the insurer, and Central Croydon and Coulsdon did the investigation.

After work Marie and I went with a crowd from the Times to the Lamb and Flag and I told her about National Buildings and Central Croydon. She said she knew someone in Central and that they might be able to throw some light on it. She asked me to wait for a few days. I agreed. What else would I do?

Quite a vibrant discussion broke out in the pub about what a newspaper should be – and the difference between the Times with its attempt to be a record of the nation's activities and the Chronicle which reflects life from our own point of view.

"You must find us amazingly dull," said Duxborough, who was leading the discussion from the Times side. "We don't love, we don't hate, we hardly have opinions, unless it is about the arts. We might think that the world is going to ruin, that you can't walk down the street without tripping over a policeman, that you can't go out and get drunk without being arrested, but we can't say it. But you, my dear fellow, you can say it all. We reflect society, but you can lift the lid off it and watch all the maggots come crawling out. You can look at the latest fashions and laugh at them or approve of them. If you wanted to, in that comic sketch of yours you could be in favour of free love or against it. You could encourage women to go to football matches or urge the Home Secretary to pass a law prohibiting them."

"Not quite," I said although I loved the image. "The only reason my social pieces crept in was because an advertiser pulled out and we had a space. The only reason they kept going was because readers wrote in and said they liked my work. I can get the chop, but you will always have your facts – your record of society."

"I think we should take up a cause," said Charlotte who as far as I knew was the only woman reporter at the Times other than Marie. "Create a society in favour or something or against something. A society for the end of football."

"Don't you like football?"

"I don't know – it doesn't have to be football. A society for the end of the navy. A society for the abolition of hills. A society for the abandonment of the rank of captain in the army."

"I'm in favour of that," I said, and I told them about Kell.

"Put him on the stage in your comedy story," said Charlotte. "He could be a song and dance man."

"No, Jacko is the song and dance man," said Duxborough. I said I was surprised to hear that.

"Like I said," he replied, "we are boring – reporting life. The Marxists are boring too – they have their fixed vision of history. The anarchists blame society – yawn, yawn, heard it all. But Jacko Jones is new each day – one day football, one day the comic cuts, one day society updates from Stonehenge, one day breaking the Parliament Act story. Each day you sing a different song, Jacko, each day you dance a new dance. Whatever that measly paper of yours is paying you, it isn't enough." He raised his glass. "The song and dance man."

"Maybe that means I don't need a theory," I said – and explained what Barrett had said about me.

"God save us from men with theories," said Duxborough. "The song and dance man is the true Edwardian – he sings and dances through life and is never dull. Now we have George, and that means we no longer have a king who goes to bed with every woman he passes in the palace. We have the dullest most boring man in the world on the throne. So, Jacko, we rely on you even more. What's the new story – tell us all what the latest song is going to be that we will all be dancing to tomorrow. Is it the Nisbet trial? Should we protest to the government? Or is there a bigger story you are about to break?"

I told them Nisbet had been framed. Everyone looked impressed and I was bought another drink.

Saturday 9ᵗʰ July

The news has broken that George Hardy who has been at Newcastle has been appointed trainer at Woolwich, although as far as I can see there still isn't actually a new Woolwich Arsenal company that is taking over the debts of the old club – and without that they can't actually play next season and can't hire a trainer. Meanwhile the campaign against Dickman's conviction is gathering momentum and although we aren't officially supporting it we are giving it a lot of space. I am sure there is something wrong, but I can't find the key.

Marie and I spent another Saturday evening in the pub with a mix of writers from up and down the Street, playing one of those silly games that happens after a few rounds – everyone saying how they "look at things" – do you start by thinking everyone is a criminal, or that there are only a few crooks, or no crooks at all, or that thieves are born, or that saints are made by heaven. Of course, the arguments go round and round and get noisier as the night goes on, but they are no less fun for that. Marie is a real participant in these, and she caught me out once remembering that at around eight o'clock I had said that we needed some order and discipline in society and then saying at ten o'clock that everyone should be free to express themselves and make their own decisions. I said, "But I didn't ever say I was consistent in my views," and everyone returned to calling me the song and dance man. "One minute he makes you cry, one minute he makes you laugh out loud."

Monday 11th July

I wrote up a story about Vernon Kell and the Directorate. (I know it is called the Secret Service Bureau, but I am keeping that under my cap.)

I said that spying was a song and dance routine. Smoke and mirrors. Catch-as-catch-can. There were spies, but they had their mirror agents who did nothing but put us off. Just when you thought you were following a spy you find it is all a decoy and that you are on the wrong trail. The Directorate had to watch every public park, every bandstand, every political speech, every bookshop. Spies might even exchange notes after a Sunday morning church service.

I wrote that the spies and their compatriots – the double-bluff agents – are growing ever more sophisticated. A series of communications might be centred around the football ground, like the tic-tac men at race meetings, so that while a game is going on, members of the crowd are able to pass information around without even standing next to each other.

Then, with a dig at Chelsea, I suggested that I had heard of plans to invent a new club – called The Thames – which currently had no players and no history, and indeed no ground. But it was being set up so that the club could be a venue for spies.

The idea was likely to be taken up all over the country, and soon there would be new clubs appearing from Penzance to Wick, all existing as part of the spy and counter spy operation. In fact I had it on authority that it had happened already.

Tuesday 12th July

A phone call from Mr Churchill. He said that he had heard that I had been to see Vernon Kell and wanted to know what I was going to write. I told him with as straight a voice as I could manage that we were going to give information about where the spies met and how they communicated, and would point out that we were supporting the Directorate and its leader, Captain Kell.

"But if you want my opinion, sir, there's nothing there at all," I continued. "It appears to me that no spies have yet been caught – which means either there are none to catch or Kell is not very good at his job. But I am holding back for the moment – after all, to publish something that reveals either view would make the government look foolish. I could be much more positive, but at the moment the positive story doesn't sing an honest tune. If I suggest there are spies out there, all that will happen is that a lot of innocent Germans, Italians, Danes and goodness knows who else will get harassed for coming to live here."

"Trouble is, Jacko," he said, "this is a democracy, and there are things you can and can't do in a democracy. Worst sort of government there is, of course, apart from all the other forms of government."

I started to ask about Dickman, but he'd hung up.

Wednesday 13th July

Woolwich Arsenal Football and Athletic Co Ltd issued a statement to the effect that it was already £700 in debt – it seems they are about to have their official meeting of shareholders on Monday 25th. As a serious shareholder, I shall be there.

This is interesting to compare with Chelsea's apparent profit and the losses made at Fulham. Big grounds, it seems, are everything.

Which sent me scurrying back to my notes. The official line about Woolwich Arsenal's downturn was the smallness of the crowd. Some teams got more, that's true. Chelsea against Woolwich got 40,000 and Tottenham against Woolwich was watched by 38,000. The corresponding games at Woolwich got only 20,000. But leaving those special occasions aside, most teams were getting the same as Woolwich. Nottingham Forest and Everton both only got about 6000 when Woolwich played there.

Thursday 14th July

I met Marie for lunch and she dropped onto my plate three pieces of paper containing the assessment of the two claims for damage by Croydon Common. Both were on behalf of National Buildings. Both marked the events as suspicious. The third document was a confidential review of Norris by the assessors.

I looked at Marie and at the papers. "Two questions," I said. "One, how did you get them. The other, if they were suspicious why did they pay up – assuming they did pay up."

"One don't ask. Two go and ask."

There was a long pause.

"You broke into their offices." I said flatly.

She said nothing.

"Why?"

She said nothing.

"Is it because you wanted to do something that would help my career, or because you hate Norris, or because you like breaking into places?"

She said nothing.

Back in the office the story was emerging that the body of a woman had been discovered in a house in Hilldrop Crescent in Camden Town, and the police had started a murder investigation.

The woman is thought to be Cora Crippen, a music hall girl known on the stage as Belle Elmore. She had been hidden in the cellar and there were stories about the condition of the body.

Friday 15th July

I paid a visit to Central Croydon and asked to see one of the directors. I gave my card, but it obviously meant nothing to the lady on the desk. It meant something to Reginald Cox, who came out to see me.

"Chronicle is becoming quite the paper of investigations – especially where Norris is concerned," he said. We shook hands. He told me he was the director in charge of investigations. He was probably the only director in the shabby little company, but I let it pass.

I went for the full-on attack. "You were asked to look at two insurance claims for Croydon Common football club. Both concerned the grandstands, both were slightly suspicious. The insurance company thought there was enough in it to call you in. What did you find?"

"One thing wrong with your analysis," said Cox. "In about half the claims they get insurance companies call investigators in. If you have claimed twice you get investigated. In this case we found nothing untoward so we suggested they pay."

"Not quite," I pointed out. "You suggested they were suspicious, and you wrote a review of Norris which, if I summarise it correctly, said do not touch this man further than you can throw him. Which, given the Mayor's size, I would suggest is not far."

"How do you know that?" Cox was annoyed.

"I am a journalist. I follow Norris and it would be more surprising if I didn't know. So why did a report like that turn into one which suggested that the insurance company should pay up?"

"That," Cox said, becoming very imperious and rising up to his full five feet six inches, "is not a matter of public discussion."

"Which can only mean," I said, "that I have to make it public discussion. And if that happens insurance companies will be wondering what the point is of using you as an investigator, when they get reports that are not 100 percent to the point."

There was a pointed silence.

Then he said, "Can we do a deal?" I said maybe, and he spilled the beans. Norris had got wind of the investigation – in fact being a man of the world he must have anticipated it. The investigating team (i.e. Cox) had been approached by Norris who asked for a copy of the report in advance. Cox had refused, and Norris and Cox had come to an arrangement.

"So what did you find?"

"Nothing that pointed to a fraud. The stands were not very well built, and there was wind on the night of the second collapse. We were just a bit suspicious. Put it this way, either he used a very bad roofer on each occasion or he is a bit unlucky."

Saturday 16th July

After work Marie and I avoided the usual Fleet Street drinking places and went to
the Nag's Head at the Angel. I wanted to talk with Marie about the break-ins and
her life. To my surprise she was perfectly open about it. She enjoyed it. In the
course of the discussion I discovered she was a bit jealous of me and my success,
which shows just how much I understand of anything.

We went to Nightingales in Mayfair. Marie gave her name and was
admitted – it seems the place runs on having the right name and look and accent. I
got a dubious look on entering, but kept quiet and no one noticed me.

We had cocktails at the bar – Marie selected and paid as the price (as well
as any knowledge of cocktails) was out of my league. I watched the preening
peacocks gradually arrive and display an endless air of boredom and discontent.

There was a trio playing – actually not too bad, and every now and then one
of the swanky young men would ostensibly give the pianist-leader a sovereign,
and they played whatever he had asked. We would be stuck if we had to play like
that – we had our repertoire, but these guys seemed to be able to play anything
and everything.

The music was fascinating – and the few pieces I knew seemed to have a lilt
to them that made them quite different. The bass and drums had a way of playing
slightly off the beat that I hadn't heard before. It was, I thought, time to invest in
a gramophone.

Eventually Marie brought me back to the present. I apologised for my
inattention, but she would have none of my apology. "That's the whole point.
You have interests – you engage with society, Jack. You engage with music. You
engage with football. You are involved. Just as my father is involved working for
what he believes in. Just as Sophia is with the Suffragettes. Edward has his
photography. And George Barrett has his anarchists. We might not believe what
they believe but they are doing something, they are alive. These people," she
indicated those around us, "are the ghostwalkers. They slide through the world,
sneering at it, and spending money that others have worked for. And I don't want
to be like them."

"So why don't you write about it?" I said.

"In the Times? They wouldn't have it. And, as you know, the Chronicle
does not employ women. In fact hardly anyone employs women unless they are to
be domestics or cooks. Look at this club – the band is all men, the bars are run by
men… where are the women? They are the hat check girls. That's all they are
thought to be fit for."

She would have continued but we were approached by a couple. The
woman, in her 40s I guess, was introduced as Lady ("call me Sandra")
Lattingbourne. Her "partner" must have been half her age, cutting a dash in his
white tie and scarf. He was (he said) Charles Wilberforce – and if he had called
himself the Exceedingly Honourable Charles Wilberforce I would not have been
surprised. They looked as if they had never done a day's work in their lives.

There was talk of some artist called Rupert Browningrow of whom I'd
never heard and how he was so so good, with his use of light and colours, and a

concert they had been to that was so so dull, but all of it was so so meaningless. Neither asked me to contribute, and both seemed more inclined to talk at Marie than to her. She didn't look too inclined to contribute.

We were then joined by a second couple, this time of similar ages, and the conversation continued about... nothing. Some art, some theatre, some music, someone's dinner party, someone else's breakfast party. At one stage Lady Lattingbourne asked Marie how her father was and if he was still plotting in the Lords. Marie made a sensible reply, but Lady Lattingbourne seemed not to hear, but just went on saying that he was "Such a dear man, but he'll have us in the workhouse before long," and then asked about Marie's mother and "That dear friend of hers... what's her name...?" but then moved off to dance with another man while Charles Wilberforce looked angry and drank two cocktails in quick succession, shouting at the waitress to bring them over more quickly.

A fellow called Michael Ducant, a later arrival, did deign to talk to me at one point, asking who I knew and what brought me there, and it struck me that "who I knew" was the equivalent to talking about what job one had in my world. It defined who you were. I told him I worked for the Chron, and he clapped his hands and said to anyone who happened to be looking, "My dears, we are all going to be in the papers come Sunday!" No one took any notice.

We left around one o'clock, with those who bothered to notice us at all saying that we couldn't go now, the party was just starting, and leaving was just too too tiring.

As we waited for a cab, Marie asked if I was going to write it up. I said it would be more amusing if we could plonk them down on the terraces at Chelsea on a very cold January afternoon to see what they made of that.

"They'd giggle and point and walk away to find a hot whisky," she said. "It doesn't matter what you do to them, they don't know how to engage, how to create, how to anything."

Monday 18th July

Mr Churchill's man phoned and asked if I could go and see the Home Secretary. I said of course, and the car appeared ten minutes later. Mr Holloway scowled and asked if I could do something on the five-year-old child who had just taken control of China. The runner said, "Your car awaits, my Lord," and I went to box his ears and missed by a mile, which caused much guffawing.

Mr Churchill was in a highly relaxed mood, puffing on a cigar. He wanted to take up the conversation about Captain Kell, explaining that this was a delicate matter for the government. If it became thought that the spy-catching department was a fiasco and a waste of money, then that would not play well with the public, who were liable to think this a rum do, given that the government is currently proposing such a huge rise in taxation. It could give encouragement to the Lords in their attempt to stop the budget.

"You are not asking me to spike another story?" I said, trying to sound incredulous, rather than not surprised.

"Would that be such a bad thing?" he asked.

"On the one hand I would need a story of as much importance as I had before, to stop me running this. On the other hand the answer is the same. I am under instruction to find a story."

There was a long pause. "How about the chance to investigate the spy story from the inside?" he said at last.

I looked at him blankly.

"Become part of the team. Do some good for your country, and get to write up the insider's story on catching spies. No other paper would have it. Make you the journalist everyone knows."

"Two problems," I announced. "One, there are no spies."

"Oh I expect there are," said Churchill affably. "I haven't seen any myself, but you tend not to know them anyway, and if there are any in the Home Office they probably won't come up and introduce themselves."

"The other is Kell. He wouldn't welcome me in his little empire."

"He wouldn't know. If, as you say, there is nothing going on in Military Operations then there is nothing to be part of. You set it up and run it on your own. One man, taking on the entire spy empire."

"And officially?"

"Officially you are another government department investigating spies from a new angle. Only you are utterly secret."

I expressed concern, uncertainty, unwillingness to get too wrapped up into a secret mission, while all the time trying to be a reporter who was interviewing the Home Secretary.

"There would be some payment," said the Home Secretary. "After all you will be back on active service for your country."

"What rank?" I asked. It was the cheekiest question – but it just came out.

"Captain." And my mouth dropped open. It probably hit the floor.

"Come now, Jacko, I can hardly make you a major," said Churchill. "You would be a temporary Captain attached to the Home Office, reporting directly to me on a mission that no one would know about other than a small group in this building. You'd be appointed under Section 163 (d) of the Army Act. Your work with the newspaper is perfect cover. Until you discover your spies you stay quiet. When you do find them, you have the story. And if there really are none at all, then you have proven it and been well paid for so doing. You can also use that as a story if you want."

I hesitated, and he didn't like that. "Damn it, man, I need to know if there really are spies out there, and I need someone who is going to tell me the truth either by bringing in a spy or by telling me there aren't any. Cortney speaks highly of you, and you have kept your word totally on the little matter in Woolwich, and there was a certain matter in South Africa for which I am much obliged. You are the man – in fact the only man for this. Besides if you show up Kell to be the idiot you think he is, then you'll enjoy that too.

"You are also the only man who is left from Section H. You have the perfect cover: if you turn up anywhere everyone thinks you are covering a football match or hunting Norris. I'm a politician, Jacko, not a Bishop. God's officers might believe in the beauty of mankind, but I don't. If Kell or the Germans are making a monkey out of all of us, I want to know."

I thought about it – or at least I made out I was thinking about it. My mind was racing. I was being asked to catch a spy, on my own, without any intercepting, resources… except Marie.

Churchill was speaking again. "I can't offer you much – there is no official salary for a temporary captain. How would £400 a year do?"

I gulped. That was double my income.

"Do I get a uniform?" I asked.

For a dreadful second I thought he was going to take me seriously. Then he laughed and offered me a drink. I got down to the serious business.

"You need a report from me which tells you if there are spies or not. You would also like me to protect your public position by catching you a spy. You need me to do this on my own, but at the end of it all I can use it as a story."

"That story would have to be cleared by me, personally," he said.

"What happens if you lose the next election? The political pages are saying there will be a second election this year."

"I lose my job and you discover the exact nature of the word "temporary" in the phrase "temporary captain". In the meanwhile don't tell me anything – just do it. You will get a pass to show to the police if they catch you up to something nasty. But nothing more. Keep it to yourself, reveal nothing. Use the card only if there are three guns pointing at you and they are about to fire."

I got a cab back to Fleet Street, and dropped a note back into the Times asking Marie to meet me for lunch – where I proceeded to break the "don't tell anyone" rule by telling her everything.

"If there really are spies," I told her, "there genuinely must be a system of communication – which is exactly the thinking Colonel Edmunds introduced to Section H. Each spy will always move information on to another, either by letter or maybe through a bribed seaman going out of London or one of the other ports. There is no chance that a spy will be writing directly to Germany since that is too obvious – which means there must be some sort of command here, and so by finding one spy we get through to the centre."

"So how are we going to do this?" she asked.

"For want of anywhere else we can try Woolwich. Clearly there is something odd going on, otherwise they wouldn't have started moving the torpedo factory. Would they actually move a whole factory just because they found secrets going missing? Perhaps – perhaps not – but it is the only lead I can think of. Besides, every pub in the neighbourhood knows I am a football reporter for the Chronicle so no one is ever likely to challenge me."

We kissed. "Congratulations, Captain," she said. "You are going to need a good thief. Unless, of course, this is just a ploy by Churchill to get you off Kell's back."

"If so, I might just have to bring down the government," I said with a smirk.

"Don't do that," she said.

Tuesday 19th July

I have a problem with the paper. If I start following a long road which leads me nowhere Mr Holloway is going to get edgy. If I do tell him, he might have to tell others and the moment the story gets out around Fleet Street, I'm done for.

Marie, however, was convinced that telling the paper was the best thing to do. "For the paper you can promise the complete write-up once you have caught your spy – and if you don't catch anyone you can do the inside story on how the Daily Mail has whipped up everyone into a spy frenzy when the spies don't exist. Just because it could take a while to come to anything, doesn't mean they won't like it. 'Our man inside the department of military operations' – the Chron will love it, and keep utterly quiet to ensure no one else has it."

"But if moving the work at Woolwich to the Clyde was just a genuine concern from the government over the Erskine Childers vision of the Germans coming in across the North Sea – there's no story. No spies, no torpedo scandal – not much of a story. And if there is a big story Churchill may not give me permission to run the story – if I let it out, I could be locked up for treason."

"Then run a cover. Cover the Crippen story. And the protests against Dickman's conviction."

"I'll buy that," I said, "but it would be nice to tell mum and dad that I am a temporary Captain."

"And isn't it strange that my family won't give a damn? They believe in you, whether you are a temporary officer or an ex-sergeant. From what you've said, if you tell your mother it is hush-hush that will be like advertising it on the front page of the Wood Green Gazette."

I caught her tone. "You think I am foolish to want to accept being made an officer."

"It means nothing to me," she said off-handedly.

"But don't you see how I feel in front of you and your family – with the titles, your degree and everything else? I feel so…"

"Inferior," she finished for me, which was quite right. "But don't you see that the reason I choose to spend time with you is quite simply because of what you are, and the way you think, and the things you do. The smoke and drums of a temporary rank are irrelevant. Go and ask my father what he thinks of you some time."

Wednesday 20th July

I took the matter to Mr Holloway, impressed on him there was something special going on, and we got to visit the fifth floor in the afternoon. I said the two murders were considered unusual on high and that I would investigate, but also go back to Woolwich, leaning on my guise as the football reporter who was out to get the dirt on Norris, to make it look as if I was following the new lead.

They accepted the arrangement perfectly. I omitted to tell them I also got a pay rise.

Thursday 21st July

Thus to Woolwich, and a meander around the pubs where I was greeted kindly by the old faces I knew. They asked for the latest on the Gunners, and of course I had nothing new to tell them save that Norris would be in charge next season and the club would be staying in Woolwich, at least for a year or two. After that who knew?

I made a show of asking everyone what they thought of the situation, latching onto the men at the Woolwich factory gates as they came out for the lunch break. I got nothing.

In the afternoon I went into the Number 2 factory and asked if I could see any of the management. I got a Mr Hardcastle, who had heard of Woolwich Arsenal FC but clearly didn't approve of newspapers and didn't approve of football. I told him I was doing a background piece for the start of next season, focussing on the club and the men's lives. I asked if things had changed, if there was assured work for the future, if everyone was happy, if people here were worried about the spies that other papers talked about (I just threw it in as one question among many) and on and on. I got little back and retired to the pub.

By the evening I was back in Fleet Street in time to meet Marie – who bought me a drink and gave me a good lesson in keeping my morale up.

"You need an assistant, just like Holmes has his Watson," she said.

"What do you know about Dickman and Crippen?" I asked.

Friday 22nd July

Factory to factory, pub to pub. And nothing and nothing. After just two days I think I have proved that there is no story.

Saturday 23rd July

I am not sure how long I can keep this up. I am also amazed how many places there are where no one knows anything about anything.

It struck me mid-afternoon that Edward had once said that you could never prove that something did not exist, because you could always find it around the next corner.

Sunday 24th July

At least tomorrow there is a meeting of the football company. Meanwhile I need something on Dickman and Crippen to make it look as if I am doing some work.

Played with the band. Light relief.

Monday 25th July

Back to Woolwich and back in the pubs, plus sorties in and out of the factories. It was a fruitless day ending up at the Hen and Basket, complaining that I was trying to write a story about nothing. "Nothing ever happens," I told Evie. "How am I supposed to be your big time journalist when nothing happens? Give me a story, Evie. Something exciting. Something different."

"I'm a pub landlady," she said. "I don't have different. I do Monday, then I do Tuesday, then after that I do Wednesday, and if I don't forget I do Thursday..."

I told her I got the picture.

"I do get the letters," she said, "that's a bit different." I looked at her over my beer.

"For Mrs Smith. Letters from all over."

"What do they say?" I said rather stupidly, realising at once how dumb it was to ask.

"How do I know?" she said, "I don't read them. I just keep them and hand them over."

"Must be from her family overseas," I said. *"Glad you got a job making the beds at the Hen. Evie sounds a lovely lady. Send more money, mother is dying.* That sort of thing."

"Don't be daft. Mrs Smith isn't a foreigner."

"Do they arrive often?" I asked. "These letters, I mean, and why are they using you and not the Post Office?"

"They arrive two or three times a week or so," she said. "And they use me because Mrs Smith comes and goes on business. She's an important lady, and she picks up mail when she's passing through. She's not a RESIDENT." She emphasised the word as if doing so signified something.

"So what does Mrs Smith who is not a resident here actually do?"

"I don't know – there is no Mr Smith – not that I see anyway. Just swanky Mrs Smith."

"So you put the letters in a box?"

"I do indeed, Mr Nosey Parker Jacko Jones. I'd ask you why you were asking all these questions as if I didn't know."

"And then you just hand them over?"

"For the money she pays I just hands them over."

"And are there some waiting now?"

"One or two."

"Can I look?"

She dug out a box with three envelopes. One from Glasgow, one from London, and one from Plymouth, all for Mrs Smith c/o the Hen and Basket.

I gave them back to her, mumbled something about it being odd, and maybe I could make a story out of it. "Don't you mess this up, Jacko," she said sternly. "I get a shilling a week for acting as a letter box. You mess this up and I'll make sure you can't show your face in Plumstead again."

I gave her assurances, and sat down with my beer.

Five minutes later I was back at the bar, ordering another. "These letters, Evie," I said.

"Knew you'd be interested," she replied, pulling the pint. She gave a look that suggested that whatever I was up to she would win hands down.

"What did the one say that you opened?"

"I told you I never…"

"Evie, I just want you to tell me what was in the letter you opened." I slapped a shilling on the bar, and then slammed my hand over it, before she could take it. "I move my hand when you tell me what was in the letter, and because I don't want to be decapitated by you, I also give you my word that the information won't be used."

"Is decapitated rude?" she said, giving me a sly look.

"Not in the way you think, Evie," I said.

She sniffed. "Load of boring nonsense about boats," she said. "It is like a boys club – have you seen one of these, how far does it go, how many of them, what numbers, no I haven't seen one of those, but have seen one of these…"

"Just boats," I said, releasing the shilling. "How many letters did you open?"

"That and one other a week or two later. It was just the same. Boats. What have you seen? I've seen this and that. It's a ruddy club – cubs and scouts – that's what it is. She's running a little secret society for the lads, make them feel good, keep them off the street. Or else she fancies little boys."

"You have a terrible mind," I told her, and forced myself to finish my beer quietly and calmly, suggesting as I did so that this would be the easiest shilling Evie would ever earn in her entire life.

At three o'clock I went over to the meeting of the new "Woolwich Arsenal Football and Athletic Company". New company, new venue. This time we are in the Mortar Hotel in Woolwich. This wasn't all crowded and shouting like the past meetings – there were about twenty of us there, and it started off sombre and dignified – proper business being done by proper businessmen.

Norris got into a huge row with Dr Clarke. Seems Clarke still blamed Norris for scuppering the last attempt to rescue Woolwich Arsenal. Norris thumped the table, shook his fist, shouted and almost screamed. Clarke handled it perfectly, standing there looking at Norris, not trying to interrupt, just waiting and waiting, knowing that in the end Norris would have to stop, and then in a much quieter and calmer voice he answered. Norris, of course, could not stand this so started shouting again, and the doctor just waited. Then he repeated the episode, and again Norris took the bait. Third time around Clarke just turned to Leavey and asked if he was going to be allowed to speak – because if not, then the rules of normal procedure were not being followed and the meeting was invalid and void. Of course, it made no odds to the outcome but it gave Norris a bloody nose and was the first time I had seen Norris beaten.

Clarke's point was simple: was the club going to stay in Woolwich or was it moving to Fulham? Eventually the chair ruled in Norris' favour by saying that such a question was not the purpose of the meeting, but he did add that the club would have at least two years in Woolwich to show that it could pay its way.

Which pretty much reveals Norris' tactic – he would ride the losses for two years and then present everyone with the ultimatum – move the club to Fulham or else it closes for good. It was a gamble, but then I suppose that when you own as much as Norris does, a gamble is all there is left to keep the spice of life rolling along. (If spice can roll!)

In the end Norris looked red in the face but shut up long enough to allow Leavey to propose a change to the original plans. The new company (called the Newco apparently in business talk) agreed to pay Oldco £800 less than previously agreed to reduce their financial pressures. But Newco has to pay off all of Oldco's debts. This is where I perked up because, although Leavey got £1800, Leitch was back to zero. Now what on earth had happened to make that eventuality come to pass?

Eventually we got what we knew we would get: a company run by Norris and Hall, with Leavey as the local figurehead. Norris was the man who would go and see the liquidator, which means, in effect, it is Norris' club. I talked to the men from the West London and the Kentish. We all agreed – from the club's point of view this was a disaster. None of us was going to give Norris a good write up.

It was strange to jump from my Woolwich-football-reporter guise into my spy-for-Churchill guise, but by the time I got back to Fleet Street to meet Marie I had a plan worked out. Marie and I could break into the pub within the next couple of nights and take the letters. We'd need to cover our tracks to make sure it wasn't just the letters that were taken so we'd also raid the till. Naturally I didn't want Evie to suffer, so we'd then get the Chron to pay for the damage and losses, to thank them for all their support to our writers (i.e. me) during the Woolwich story.

I told Marie as soon as we got into Lyons. And she laughed. It was, she said, the most preposterous escapade she had ever heard – far too involved to pull off. If I wanted to do the job (she was now calling thieving "the job") then simplicity was always the key. All we needed was to find a time when Evie was not taking note of what was going on in the pub, open the letters, read them, and re-seal them.

"Evie is the pub," I said, "she watches over the place, morning noon and night."

"That shows what you know of a working woman's life. There will be a time," said Marie, "when life is slow – probably after she has finished breakfast. The guests will be back in their rooms or out, the working men will be at work, it will be too early even for journalists. That's when your friend Evie will go and sort out the laundry, check the bedrooms, and maybe even get an hour's rest. Someone else will be in charge – and Evie will feel safe because there is nothing happening. Go back and check, Captain."

Tuesday 26th July

I arrived at the Hen and Basket for breakfast. Evie was pleased to see me – thinking there might be another shilling in it for her. I finished the food and asked if she minded if I stayed on for a while arranging my notes. She shrugged. "It's a public house," she said, as she cleared away.

Ten minutes later Marie's insight was proven correct – Evie's father took over front-of-house duties, which basically meant he sat in the porch with one of his old-timer friends, smoking pipes, discussing the old days or whatever gentlemen of his age discuss, leaving me on my own inside. The letters were in the box next to the till, same as yesterday, very handily placed next to the kettle.

I checked my pocket watch, noted the time and nipped out to the doorway, told the old man I was getting myself a coffee, no need for him to disturb himself, and carried on. The sound of the kettle made no difference to Evie – whatever she was up to was not affected by sounds from below.

I boiled the kettle, checked again, ground the beans, let them stew, all the while standing right by the letters. Eventually I moved away – I'd had ten minutes on the spot, and watching the clock hands move slowly around it was another ten minutes before Evie appeared. I told her about the coffee, and said I'd checked with the old boy. She shrugged and told me the price. I asked for a discount because I had made it myself. She raised her hand to me, and I slipped her the coins. "Bloody journalists," she said. I blew her a kiss.

I told her she looked lovely when she played rough and asked if she had thought of the musical hall. She raised her hand again and I ducked out of the way, but as she turned back to the bar I could see her eyes looking at herself in the mirror. "The musical hall," she was thinking. I could have done that…"

Back in town I told Marie the result and she was triumphant. "We'll do it," she said, "complete with a shorthand transcription." There was no point my arguing with her. If I didn't agree to her coming, she'd just do a break in by herself.

Overall Marie was more animated than ever. Apparently a telegraph sent from the S.S. Montrose in the Atlantic had resulted in the identification of Doctor Crippen on the boat! They would be waiting for him when the ship entered Canadian waters. Now that was a story – much more fun than mucking around with spies in Woolwich. She added that not everyone thought that Crippen was guilty. I said that I doubted that would make much difference – not after the last trial I had watched.

We'd run the story of the grisly murder at Crippen's house ourselves – much more than the Times had, in fact, but the Times were taken with the first ever use of the telegraph in this way. That made it an item of record, rather than criminal tittle-tattle. According to popular opinion Crippen had undoubtedly murdered his wife (there was the technical issue of a trial, of course, but no one seriously doubted his guilt). Bits of the body were found under his kitchen floor, and he'd then done a bunk with his secretary. What more evidence was needed?

But Dickman was different. In that case I think half the country has doubts by now, and appeals to the Home Secretary continue daily. The Chron had lost interest in Dickman however, and we now ran the grisly bits of the Crippen murder leaving the Times to its international co-operation headlines, trumpeting the value of our link with the dominions plus the advances of the new age of wireless telegraphy. They'd probably interview the inventor of the system – whoever that was. We'd interview his missus and ask what it was like living with an inventor.

Wednesday 27th July

We were both anxious about the letters being picked up from the Hen and Basket before we could do our spy-catching deed, so decided to get straight back to Greenwich today and get the business done. I introduced Evie to Marie and Marie to Evie, and told her that Marie was a colleague, and Evie then went off on her routine while the old man carried on with his. I made two coffees while Marie steamed open the envelopes, and between us we wrote a shorthand transcription. Marie had even managed to bring some gum to reseal the envelopes. We had all five done and back in their places and were sitting enjoying the last sips of our coffee by the time Evie came back down. Grandfather on the porch was still reminiscing about the Empire in the days of the Queen.

The hardest part, looking back, was getting the coffee down. Marie was calmness itself.

The letters, as Evie had said, spoke about boats and ships with an enthusiasm that was indeed schoolboy-like, and invited the recipient to say what was going on her end. I found them lighthearted, interested, and dull, with their details of shipping in Plymouth, the Clyde, Bristol, Newcastle and Southampton. Three of them contained rather fine drawings of the ships that had been spotted.

It wasn't proof of a nationwide conspiracy of spies, but it was certainly a case of five people writing to another with information that could be of use to the enemy. But then, as Marie said afterwards, virtually anything could be construed as being of use to the enemy – and I suspect much of this information would be widely available in a journal of shipping. Besides which, if I went to Plymouth, looked at the ships and wrote a letter, I'd be classified as a spy on this basis.

Back in Fleet Street Marie and I debated ourselves round and round in circles but found nowhere to go. I gave Marie an update on the Dickman case. There were now allegations being made by a certain Mr C H Norman that the trial was warped, with the judge being bent. Norman – whoever he is – had now brought in cabinet minister John Burns to talk to Mr Churchill.

"I think I'd like to get into crime writing," said Marie. "I'd have to change papers, but it is much more interesting. A woman writing about gruesome murders and hangings – that must be worth a few more sales."

"What about spies?" I said.

Thursday 28th July

Another Woolwich day. Either we have just made a complete breakthrough in the spy story, or we have discovered that the spies are nothing but people who like boats.

I went wandering around the dockyards again, talking to anyone who would talk to me without getting any further – although that was hardly surprising. After all, what was I supposed to say? "I'm really fascinated with shipping. I don't suppose there's a local club where I can share my enthusiasm with other fellows of a like mind?" I didn't really think I could pull that off.

At noon I went to the river and looked across the incoming tide. The day was as clear as a bell and, as befits such a scene, there was a gaggle of men already there watching the water, minding their own business. I went and introduced myself as Jones of the Chron, the man who covered the Woolwich Arsenal story.

When I asked them if they'd be going to the games at Plumstead next season they laughed. "Why do you think we're out here?" asked one. He had a thick accent and clearly wasn't English. "They're laying us off – they need more people in the engine room, the ammo house and the fuse factory, but if you have a name they say is not English they turn us out of a job. The torpedo men who don't want to go to Scotland are getting the spare jobs."

I agreed this was tough – and stupid given the longevity of some of these workers. But it was the first side-effect of the torpedo policy that I had come across, so I tried for more news. "So what will you do?" I asked.

"People pay for information," said one. The others didn't look too excited to have this line of talk explored, but the speaker, the oldest man and perhaps the most bitter in the group, didn't seem minded to be shut up.

"I am as English as you, Mr Jones," he says, "but because my name isn't Jones or Smith or Brown, but is Schmidt, they throw me out after twenty years. My grandfather came here from Germany before it was even called Germany – my parents were born here and so was I and if I was young enough I'd fight for the Empire, but no – wrong name, no job. And you know what happens as a result – there are newspaper reporters like you who pay money for stories as to what's going on."

"I'm just a football man," I lied, "But I could take a message back to Fleet Street if you have a story. Might get you a few more shillings. So, what sorts of stories?"

"Stories about what's happening in the yards. You're all right, Mr Jones. You give that Norris a run, and that's good work. But most of those silly buggers at the Mail and the Post, they don't want to get their feet dirty talking to the likes of us, so they ask those as can write or draw to send in reports, and they pay pennies for them. A shilling would be an improvement."

"And you post them in?"

"No, drop them in at the King's Head or the George, or the Hen come to that – saves on the post. Write a good story or draw a picture or two and then they drop you some pennies if it's a good one." The others were all remaining quiet, but there was agreement in their faces.

"What sort of information are they buying?" I persisted. "There's nothing much left in the football story – at least until next season."

"It's anything really," said the old fellow. "The ships going up and down the river, that sort of thing." And I thought, that's odd. Because I'd never seen a hand drawing of a ship at Greenwich appear in any Fleet Street paper. Nor any details of the shipping traffic. There was a Lloyds paper that covered that – but not the nationals.

Friday 29th July

I couldn't take another day in Woolwich so I sat in the office reading the papers, but there was nothing much going apart from a piece in the West London saying that Fulham was in dispute with some of its players over the wages to be paid. How very Norris. Cut costs, cut costs, cut costs. Their goalkeeper, Dickie Skene, who I never thought to be much good anyway, had said he wouldn't play unless he got a living wage.

And then, lo and behold, in strolls George Allison, the only other man on the Street who covers Woolwich regularly in the nationals. George writes half a dozen columns under different names and in different styles so it looks like each paper has its own reporter, but in effect it is just George Allison. We shook hands and I told him how very much I had always admired his work. And he was nice as pie about me, saying he'd admired my tenacity and liked my cheeky style. Lots of slapping of the back.

Anyway, turns out Mr Allison has been given the job of editing the Woolwich Arsenal programme next season – which makes him an insider and a man to keep friendly. I bought him a drink.

Mr Allison's view is that the debts of the old Woolwich Arsenal are now more or less sorted, and no one is going to raise a fuss any more. I asked if he knew why Leitch had given up his claim, and he didn't know. "But Norris is in it somewhere – you can be sure of that," he said.

He had heard talk of "simplifying" the accounts – of there being one bank account, with one bank loan that is repaid slowly, so everyone gets their money back in drip feed from the profit of the company.

He also announced that John Humble and George Davis, another Norris nominee, have also joined the board as shareholding directors – another bit of news to stick away for later use.

After work Marie was full of excitement about the Nisbet and Dickman case, which surprised me as I thought she was now totally focussed on Dr Crippen. Seems that on Wednesday another person, Mr Mildoning, claimed that he had travelled with Nisbet on the train, shot him and then jumped out of the train with the money before it got to the station where Dickman was seen. Now why would he say that (unless it were true)?

Saturday 30th July

I reported the results of the Woolwich expedition to Edward. "I can't draw for love nor money," I said, "but if someone could do me a drawing, we could slip it into one of the pubs and offer it up and see if we get a bite. Otherwise all we can do is sit and wait for the person behind this to turn up at one of the pubs and then follow him.

Edward then announced that the honourable Sophia had two abilities. One was dressing up as anyone from any walk of life, and the other was an astonishing ability to draw anything at full speed. "She can draw anyone and it looks right –

and she works at an amazing speed. She's done a few drawings for the papers to keep the Suffragettes in the news when there's no action."

Monday 1st August

Sophia and I went to Greenwich – as far away from the out-of-work brigade as I could find while still within site of the factories. We'd not really hit things off before – she always seemed too involved in her campaigns to have time for anything else. But Edward has turned into a very good pal, and I owe it to him to try and get on with her – and I need an artist on this job.

Her costume was perfect, and as soon as we arrived she started drawing the torpedo works building and the tugs outside which in the past would carry the finished cases upstream. I doubt this site has any value to a spy, but it seems a good place to start.

Sophia amazed me: she was fast and accurate. We were within minutes of packing up and setting off to the Hen and B with four pictures completed when another woman approached. Good looking, refined dress and that positive step that marked her out for me as one of the Bloomsbury women. She looked at Sophia's work, and said it was an unusual thing to draw.

Sophia looked up with an extraordinarily helpless look. "I heard that some of these newspapers pay for drawings of the yards – showing how prepared we are to take on the Germans. I've just lost my job here so I said to Jones, 'You come and I'll draw some pictures of where I worked in the office as a secretary, and maybe someone will want to buy it'."

"Well," she says imperiously, "I wish you success in your joint venture."

Sophia mimicked her as the woman turned on her heels and walked away. I took Sophia's pictures and asked her to stay and do a couple more before getting back to town. Then I set off after the woman in spy-mode.

Tracking is tracking. The slow simple movement, using the eyes not the head to look in all directions, the careless change of direction, walking into the crowd if there is one, watching not where the target is, but where he (or in this case she) will be in 15 seconds.

She was not very good at covering tracks, largely I suppose because she had no thought of being followed, and after ten minutes I got her back to a terrace in Gatehouse Road – certainly not a place where she would live – at least not with those clothes and accent. In she went and I perched myself downwind a little, able to see the windows but very unlikely to be seen, and stayed there to nightfall, which was around nine o'clock. There was a gas light inside and maybe a candle or two, but no movement. Either she had got a way out the back, or she was packed up inside for the night.

Tuesday 2nd August

What I need is a team to keep an eye on the house. I am unlikely to get it from Mr Churchill so I have had to use my own resources. The paper let me take Edward – I told him we were watching a suspected bank robber woman and gave him the back entrance to cover. I had Sophia there to draw the girl, if she came out, and I got Marie to come to do what I had asked her not to do.

I also took four items of equipment: four police whistles. Edward approached the house, knocked, and we watched from across the road. There was no reply, so Marie went in.

She was, I had to admit, superb. Ten minutes later she was out, with her notebook, totally unflustered and walking in that relaxed manner of hers.

"There were two letters in there, both describing the coming and going of the shipping. No drawings. She must have picked them up last night or this morning before we arrived. There's also an address book, with a handful of addresses, each with the person's first name only. I copied them – plus addresses in France, Holland and Spain."

"Which makes sense. If the state does start looking at mail it will be the mail to Germany. So she avoids that."

"But," said Marie, "it is all like the items we found in the pub – all very low level. These are not the secret command orders of the War Office.

"That information tells the invading navy what they are up against," I said, rather obviously.

"Is it a crime?" asked Edward, "To get people around the country to tell you what everyone can observe with his own eyes? What's wrong with that?"

"If it aids the enemy, then it probably is a crime," I said, but it does seem rather ludicrous. When most people talk of spies, they think about stealing secrets from the War Office, not just looking at the boats on the river.

The discussion made us all less certain, and we meandered over to the Corner House in town for a spot of lunch.

It was the usual scene, waitresses running orders in and out, crowded tables, and moderately warm food. We were eating the pudding when the elegant lady of Woolwich turned up.

"So, my friend the artist," she said to Sophia, standing by our table. I cursed myself for dropping my guard. We'd been doing too well, the territory felt too much like home. "What have you drawn today?"

Sophia looked at me, and I took the pad from her basket and handed it over. Marie and Edward were suitably quiet – if the spy woman heard either of them speak we'd be scuppered.

The woman handed the pictures back. "I might be able to find you a home for these," she said. "A shilling for all four."

"They're worth more than that," I said quickly. "Took her all morning."

The woman looked ready to move on. "Besides, a guy we met at the Rabbit told us he'd pay one and six a picture."

"Well if you can get that money," she said haughtily, "you take it. You're doing well. Good luck to you and," she looked at all four of us, "good day to you."

Edward was about to speak, but I put my finger to my lips. I didn't want any of us saying a word until the woman was gone and we too were out of the eating house.

Ten minutes later, arranged around a table in a corner of the Hen in such a way that no one had their back to the door, I told them of my mistake. "Out of practice," I explained. "There was no telling who was listening to us in the Corner

House. I didn't see the woman come in, and I have no idea if she had accomplices."

"Perhaps they use the Swiss navy?" said Edward.

"Or the Vatican Guards?" asked Marie.

"What are you talking about?" said Sophia.

Wednesday 3rd August

Mr Churchill had asked me to report my news back to him personally, and I made the call asking for a meeting. I was told to present myself at the office of the Committee of Imperial Defence in Whitehall. It sounded impressive, but inside the building it seemed to be just another set of rooms. Mr Churchill, however, when I found him, was full of the place. "This is government" he said. "Not parliament. This is where we work out what we're doing, why we're doing it and how we are going to keep doing it." He waved at the books, "We even have our own historians keeping records for us, working on official histories, so if I die tomorrow, someone will have a record of what I was doing. The Historical Branch it is called. Set up two years ago and already running out of archive space. 'Compiling the naval and military history of the nation' they tell me."

"Then they have a rival," I said, and I told him what we had found. "If the woman from Gatehouse Road is the spy we assume she is (and she is certainly out of place otherwise) then she's compiling details of our naval capacity now, while your people are compiling it for yesteryear."

"So what are you going to do?" he demanded.

"We need to keep a watch on the woman, on the pub, on her house and on her mail. Which means a rotating team of 12 to cover the three locations, and another two in the postal sorting office."

Churchill made it clear there was no chance. "You've got four – which is far too many for my likings, but I can't change that. Stay with your four and work at it."

But it was easier said than done. Marie was now heavily engaged in trying to get the Times to cover the approaches to the Home Secretary over the Dickman case and the claims that the judge had been nobbled. Sophia seemed happy to join the chase, but Edward was needed elsewhere by the Chron to take pictures.

It was easy to see how the German spies got away with it, when our official counter operation was sitting with a filing cabinet and a sandwich in the War Office, and Sophia was the only one of my crack team who could be relied on to show up for the daily counter-espionage operation. As for the British public, Dickman and Crippen were all that mattered.

Thursday 4th August

I took Sophia with me to Woolwich, found her the location to draw, and told her to get a couple of drawings done quickly and then take her time. If she was approached, she had to tell the woman that "Jones" was round the football ground trying to get work, and that she'd been told not to sell any pictures until he got back. But, if the woman insisted, to agree to a sale at whatever price she offered, and let it go.

I went off to the Woolwich Arsenal to see if there was any football story to be made out of the fact that training for the new season had started. I watched and generally found myself overwhelmingly unimpressed. Eventually I walked back to Sophia. She'd got through six pages of brilliantly detailed work and was getting bored. No one had approached her. I called a halt.

Sunday 7th August

I was invited for lunch at Dorset Square, and after a quick update with Marie on the failure of my brain to come up with any new tactic or explanation for what we had found we moved on to her current enthusiasm.

Yesterday the Daily News ran a story by C H Norman about whether Dickman should be hanged. Norman who was part of the Society for Abolition of Capital Punishment and the Penal Reform League said that Dickman was innocent of the murder of Nisbet and that Mr Churchill must consider the case again. But his cause was not helped by the fact that Dickman's brother had suggested in the press in the north that Dickman was very much guilty and should die as soon as possible because of the stain he had left on the family's good name.

"Can you imagine anyone saying that about their own brother or sister?" asked Marie. "'You've stained the family honour so must die'. It's rather 19th century."

Meanwhile Churchill had ordered further investigations as to who was at the station and got another expert to give evidence on the blood on the coat, but as matters stood Dickman was due to be hanged on the 10th.

Monday 8th August

Norris' solicitors have fixed up to see the Chron's solicitors and so a meeting was held to gather evidence. We had the fact that Norris had the election papers in his house – a very minor infringement of the law and one that most politicians were probably guilty of. We knew that he had then removed the evidence and taken it to the club – something we had yet to reveal. And now we had the fact that the insurance investigator had a slight concern over the Croydon football stands issue.

"None of this is earth-shattering," said our lawyer, "and, without witnesses, none of it is going to stand up anywhere. Your evidence of the papers in the house comes from a break-in, and thieves do not normally turn up to court if they can help it. The removal of the papers later is better, as is the finding of them in Fulham's ground, and if those street urchins will testify that should be enough. We have one item which is enough to get a deal – especially when we hint that we have documentary proof of one of the other infringements. But I would not advise going to court."

Tuesday 9th August

Unexpectedly I received a note from Mr Churchill asking me to attend on one of his secretaries – Mr William Williamson in Whitehall. Once there I was told in hushed tones that the Home Secretary had ordered that mail to the house of the "Woolwich Woman" would be intercepted for two weeks. In order to avoid alerting possible criminals I was ordered by the Home Secretary personally to stay away from the area.

Wednesday 10th August

Dickman was hanged in Newcastle. Marie was furious – not so much about the lack of reprieve – although she like me was sure that there was far more to the case than we knew – but because the Times had refused her piece on the case. She had walked the length of the Street seeking another publisher. I told her she could lose her job for that, but she said she didn't mind. The story was good and needed telling.

Thursday 11th August

Marie reports that the Express will run her story tomorrow. She fully expects to be given the empty when she goes into the Times in the morning.

I went to Whitehall and met Mr Williamson, who showed me transcripts of the letters delivered by post to the Woolwich house. It was all very ordinary – a letter from an aunt and one from a friend called Roland. Both were writing from Rutland – about as inland as you could get, so no mention of shipping.

Overall this spy business has taken an unexpected turn. I think I've found a spy, but can't understand what on earth she is doing. And without that understanding I might as well not have found her.

Friday 12th August

Marie was, as expected, asked to remove herself from the Times once they saw her piece getting a major splash in the Express. She went across the road to ask the Express for a job, but was told that they were full, although if she had any other pieces of a similar nature they would be sure to look.

"I am," she said to me, "at your disposal."

I gave her the details on the intercept letters and how utterly ordinary they are. "But that is not an ordinary woman," said Marie. "The clothes, the manner, the accent… The only women who wander around the waterfront talking to men are the cheapest prostitutes. Every other woman is either working or doing the washing and ironing or preparing the household's food and looking after the nippers or sleeping after a hard night at the night-club. She is wrong in every regard."

"You're the criminal detective," I said. "You tell me what."

"You found the hole in the Dickman case," she replied. "You tell me." We sat in silence.

"Unless it is in code," Marie said eventually.

"But the letters all made sense," I protested. "Codes never make sense – they are jumbles of letters and numbers, words like XKJRS, not proper sentences. If anything was in code it was those letters at the pub, not the mail from Rutland."

"Unless most of the letter is totally invented, and the code is tucked away within it," she said. "Supposing the fact that the writer is in Rutland means the writer is in Plymouth. Supposing the fact that Aunt Mary has had a cold is a code for the fact that the production of ships is on the increase. If you only need to say a handful of things, you could use complete phrases for each message."

We sat and thought.

"We should go to Plymouth," said Marie at last. "Sort out what is really going on."

I couldn't see the paper allowing me another period off work without getting something back on the story.

Saturday 13th August

Marie asked me over to Dorset Square after another pointless day at work and stunned me with the fact that she was openly suggesting to her parents that we go on holiday together. When I asked where, she said, "Oh I don't know, somewhere by the sea, somewhere like Plymouth, where there are lots of boats. And maybe up to Bristol – lots of water there – and after that perhaps to Newcastle…"

The plan was to be flexible – to take the car and drive around the coastal areas, being a holiday couple. She showed me a ring she had which would be enough to help us pass ourselves off as honeymooners. "Honeymooners do all sorts of silly things," she said, "like sit around dockyards watching the workmen. So in love they notice not the world."

I wondered if her parents knew the whole plan – but I supposed they must, otherwise Marie would not have been able to get the car. I didn't really fancy telling my mother – having mum hold Marie in awe had advantages.

Just as I was recovering from Marie's suggestion, she hit me with a second. "Last night, after you had gone, I wrote a new piece about Dickman and hawked it up and down Fleet Street. The People took it and are running it tomorrow."

She was thoroughly excited, and so she should be, and to cap it off Lord Cortney came in with his ever faithful butler carrying a bottle of champagne with the appropriate bucket and glasses, and we toasted his daughter's latest success. It was only as I was drinking down the fizzy that it struck me that the timing was a little opportune – had he been listening in? If so he'd know exactly what the holiday entailed. But surely a man of his position and experience would never just "listen in".

I asked to see the article, but Marie insisted I read it first in the paper.

Sunday 14th August

And there it was. "Was Dickman a Double Murderer?"

Marie was arguing that there was more to Dickman than met the eye. She used the oddity of the £500 to suggest that here was a most devious man, a man who was of high intelligence and cunning.

That, she argued, cut two ways. Firstly, it meant that the evidence against him in terms of the stains on his coat (the stains that Churchill had had investigated a second time, and which the second witness had suggested were not as clear cut as the first witness had said) might have been planted. For would such an accomplished man make such an error?

Secondly, he might well have murdered another time. This was new, and it was clear that Marie had done a lot of digging in the archives. According to Marie, the police were now looking into the fact that Dickman had a connection with Herman Cohen, a German-Jewish moneylender from Sunderland, who had been murdered in March last year.

There was nothing particular for me at work, so I called Dorset Square, found Marie was in and arranged to go over.

We had more celebrations, and I was invited to stay for luncheon. When I hesitated Lord Cortney took me to one side and was rather interesting (as I admit he generally is). "In some houses," he said, "an unexpected guest would be an embarrassment, because quite reasonably the lady of the house would have bought just the right amount of food for the household for that day. One more person would mean everyone going short and therefore it would be rude to accept an invitation to lunch. But in this house we have the extreme good fortune to have extra provisions laid by and the ability to go and purchase more. Our butcher's shop might be closed, but for a double fee he will open if we need him."

And so we moved to lunch where, after examining Marie's handiwork for the People one more time, I asked where Marie had been doing her research. "A bonus of being a Peer," said Lord Cortney. "We have a most excellent library."

After that we moved on to Marie's next project: Florence Nightingale. Probably the most famous woman in the country, she had died yesterday. "I think the murderers are more fun," said Lady Cortney, and Alyson agreed more vigorously that I thought was necessary.

Monday 15th August

Marie and I went to Whitehall and after a lot of using Mr Churchill's and Lord Cortney's name, plus the waving of my temporary captain's card, we had a second look at the letters that had been copied before being delivered on to the house in Woolwich. Each one was as mundane as the last, and it looked as if we were never going to know what anything meant.

Lord Cortney had agreed to show me the House of Lords at lunchtime, and after food Marie and I took the tour, ending in a tea room – having agreed between us that given that we had no progress on our spy hunting we would give her father all the facts.

He listened carefully and politely as he always does. And then he said, "I think you should see a friend of mine in the Admiralty." He went to a phone, made the call, and returned to us with a sheet of paper giving an address.

"He's there now. Dilly Knox. Room 40. Top man from Oxford – just drops in occasionally during the summer. Knows more about codes than anyone else."

And so we went to the Admiralty building on the Thames, found our man, showed him the copies of the letters and told him the problem. He looked for all of three seconds before giving an opinion.

"This is not code," he said, "it's nothing. "If there is a message here it is behind the words. Have you had the original paper checked?"

We said we hadn't. "Come on then," he said, grabbed his hat, and led us out of the door. We were in the street before he turned back and said, "Where are the originals?" We told him they were delivered on to the recipient – but one or two new ones come in each day and are copied in Mr Churchill's office.

"Waste of time," he said. "You're copying the wrong thing. Lead on – we're going to see today's letter."

We got into Williamsons' office. "Dr Dilwyn Knox, Fellow of Kings College Cambridge," he said, introducing himself. I explained that Dr Knox wanted to see an original of the Woolwich bound letters. One had come in through the final delivery of the day and had just been copied.

Dr Knox looked at the letter carefully, holding it to the gas lamp, turning it back and forth. "Invisible ink" he said. Marie and I looked at each other; this was new to both of us. "You can see the signs if you know where to look. See here – and here – scratches on the page. The paper here, and here" – he pointed as he talked, "the colour changes – this bit is shiny, this bit is different. Thank you."

He handed the letter back and walked towards the door. "Wait," I called, "what does the letter say?"

"I've no idea," he said, "to find that out we'd have to use chemicals – and that would destroy the letter. If this is going to be delivered tomorrow it needs to be kept intact."

"So what do we do?"

Dr Knox turned and looked at us with surprise. "First level," he said, "you've proved you have a spy. No one but spies and over-excitable boy scouts writes in secret codes. Second level, when you are ready to read a message, we can do that, but you also need to be ready to move in on your spy the day you do it because the letter will be undeliverable." We went to ask for a meeting urgently with Mr Churchill.

It took four hours before Mr Churchill could be found. We gave him the details from Dr Knox.

There was a long silence. Eventually he said, "We'll move the next time two letters come in on one day. If she knows when each letter is due to arrive she will know a letter has not arrived. Either she'll assume it has just been delayed, or she'll run. But there is a chance, given that one arrives, she'll assume the other letter has been lost somewhere. Either way we have her followed. How many people do you have?"

I reminded him that there was only Marie, Sophia, Edward and I – exactly as I had said last time when I asked for a whole team.

He snorted. "Proves you didn't need it. And with £500 a year you are achieving more than Kell with £7000. That is what being British is about, Jacko." And he slapped me on the back so hard and so unexpectedly tha I fell over.

Tuesday 16th August

Marie was full of excitement – her Nightingale piece had come on well and she'd submitted it, and now she was on the tail of another woman, Mary Anderson, who apparently held the patent for a window cleaning device for a car. It would clean snow, rain and sleet from a windscreen at the front of the car by using a handle turned from inside.

There was no special reason to celebrate Mrs Anderson just now, except that cars on the streets of London were starting to get the devices, and so it was interesting background. And here was a triumph of a woman in the industrial world.

At this rate Marie will have overtaken me with scoops and special reports by the start of the new football season.

Mr Holloway called me in and asked if I was actually still working at the Chronicle. I told him we were getting near to the top of the biggest story ever to hit Britain. He looked singularly unimpressed, which is his normal look. "Have you got anything on this story about a woman in Dulwich who has a tame leopard in her back garden that eats raw meat from her hand?" he asked. I told him it was a hoax and I'd given it to the People.

Thursday 18th August

At last – a little something for Mr Holloway. Alf Common has signed for Woolwich Arsenal from Middlesbrough for £250. Some years ago (I sent a junior running to find out exactly when) Alf had signed for Middlesbrough for £1000 – so maybe a quarter of that price was worth it. Except that Woolwich were never going to be able to sell him on.

On the positive side he has always scored goals, and that was certainly what Woolwich have been missing, so maybe Norris does know more about football than me. (Scrub that – that can't be true).

The runner came back and said Alf had played for local teams in the north until he joined Sunderland in 1900 – and they did well that year, coming second. But he hadn't stayed – he'd gone to Sheffield United for £325 – and Sunderland went on to win the league without him. An omen? I made a note and wondered if I could get away with a "Written in the stars" article to keep Mr Holloway happy. But Sheffield had won the Cup that year and Alf had scored in the final.

I asked the runner for his name, and he said, "David Walsh, sir," very respectful. I told him he had done very well, and perhaps he could get me a coffee while I decided how to write the story. No one had ever told me I'd done well when I'd first joined, and this kid was probably only 15. I'd spent most of my life being treated like a piece of dirt. His smile and the speed he took the stairs down to the basement made my heart move. I am going soft.

The full story emerged. Alf became an England international, but demanded to go back to Sunderland to look after his business (this was something I had heard of a few times – some of the more intelligent footballers setting up a business like a corner shop or even a local magazine that traded on their names). Sunderland paid the record fee of £520 plus a goalkeeper. But by the following February he went to Middlesbrough for £1000 – Middlesbrough buying him as part of their effort to avoid going down that year. The report ended with the note: 168 games for Middlesbrough, 58 goals.

David Walsh came back with my coffee. "Where's Middlesbrough?" I said.

"In the north," he said.

"Near Sunderland?" I asked.

"Newcastle, Sunderland, Middlesbrough, Darlington – the towns near the coast. All got teams, sir." This kid was good.

So that's why Alf Common wanted to stay in one or other of those clubs. Whatever his business was, he had it in the north. I wondered what he would make of London. And what had happened to the shop.

Friday 19th August

Marie raised a point at lunch: we are finding out lots of "what" but no "why". Why would Norris be involved in an insurance scam when he is so rich? Why would people write bland reports on shipping from around the country and send them by a personal courier to a pub in London, when others are sending secret messages through the post.

I asked about Florence Nightingale. "Problems with her family, never married, no men-friends, probably preferred the company of women, which is not actually a crime, became very ill and spent the last ten years of her life in bed. Largely regarded as a saint, saved a lot of lives."

"She didn't make any difference in South Africa," I said. "I was shot twice, and both times the care I got was non-existent."

Marie asked for the details, and I gave her a sketched outline. "You are a genius," she said. I told her I knew that, but in what particular aspect of my intellectual glory was she bathing this time? She said that the story was not that Nightingale was anything other than a saint, but rather that the War Office, once shot of her, had backtracked on her reforms and our troops were now as badly off as they were in the Crimea.

Apparently the military hospital in Woolwich which opened last century was also down to her. I asked if Marie had ever heard of Alf Common, but she hadn't.

Saturday 20th August

Marie told me that Sophia has said that she and Edward are going to announce their engagement and want us to be at the party.

I told her that was ok and that I was getting used to this toff stuff, and I could wear my uniform so I didn't have to worry about clothes.

And she said, "Can you dance?" And I told her that in South Africa there was little call for formal dancing skills amidst the ranks, but since being in the band I've shaken a leg or three following the current styles. I could even manage a rudimentary waltz, but needed further tuition.

"What current styles?" asked Marie, puzzled.

"Ragtime dances, animal tangos," I said. "You must have noticed some people dancing when Harry's Men play."

"That was dancing?" she asked. "I thought the people had had too much to drink and were holding each other up."

We decided to do an exchange deal. I would teach her the Cake Walk, the Grizzly Bear and the Turkey Trot, and she would beef up my waltz and teach me the two-step.

They had now established a gramophone in the small library in Dorset Square along with a growing collection of discs and we went out and bought a few more for the lessons. I selected "Everybody's Doin' It Now," and "Mississippi Rag" while Marie chose "Scented Roses" for my first waltz lesson.

Teaching Marie the Jitterbug over the weekend proved to be a hilarious, glorious, eternally memorable experience, not least because the butler and the cook came in to watch us and were later joined by Lord and Lady Cortney plus Alyson Fairbright who asked questions about the dance and unnervingly took notes. We used the Rag for the Turkey Trot which also caused considerable amusement. When Lord Cortney said he had work to do the party continued with Alyson and Lady Cortney forming a partnership.

Sunday 21st August

With no movement on any newspaper story that I could cover, I carried on learning to dance, bringing Edward and Sophia into the game. I was given a rundown of the Redowa, and I returned the compliment with the Bunny Hug and the Camel Walk. How much fun we got out of a gramophone – and I started to think about an article on gramophones and discs.

Monday 22nd August

The big legal day concerning the Chron and Norris didn't go as planned. The meeting was at Norris' solicitors' offices in Fulham around two tables pushed together. On one side his law man and Norris, one our side me and our law men.

There was a formal introduction where their side thanked our side for turning up and hoped that all could be resolved. No need to waste the court's time and so on. They said the accusation was serious and that Mr Norris denied any wrongdoing at all. I was under strict orders not to say anything but to write down my thoughts in clear plain English and slip them across to the solicitor if I thought they might help.

We replied courteously that there was evidence that the electoral pages were in Mr Norris' house that fateful night.

There was silence, and then our man said, "We also have evidence that Mr Norris then did not attend a meeting he had been booked into that night, but instead stayed in his house after the break-in and removed the documents in question, taking them to Fulham Football Club, wherein they were stored."

There was a silence. Norris said words to his man with his hand in front of his face, and the solicitor said, "Our client strongly denies such action."

Our man then says, "We have three witnesses, all of whom not only saw your client remove the documents from his house but also saw him leave them in the club. What's more, your client made the journey twice because of the weight of the bundle."

Norris said one word to his solicitor, and he said, "We deny all of this."

Our man then continued, "Unfortunately, upon his first visit to the club house your client simply put the documents down, failed to lock the door, and then returned to his house for the second collection. Upon reaching the club house for a second time he gathered up all the documents and put them in a safe."

There was a pause.

"We deny that such an incident took place, and even if it had, there is no chance of these witnesses coming forward since to do so they would have to admit to breaking and entering – a serious felony."

"These witnesses will come forward in the court case, for there was no breaking or entering. Your client left the door of the club unlocked, and they, not knowing who he was at the time and fearing that a theft was in progress, entered the building to see what was going on. They then called the police, who felt that they could not act because, as I have noted, there was no breaking and entering. However, the witnesses were quite certain to make sure that proper police records were kept of the event and to keep a few sample pages."

Mr Norris stood and started to speak in an extremely loud voice. His solicitor stood, and with more nerve than I would have credited, squeezed himself between Norris and the table and spoke to him just inches from his face, suggesting we had a brief interlude and actually saying at one point, "Mr Norris, you will conduct yourself in a civil manner!"

The interlude took some ten minutes. I was ordered into strict silence, so we sat and waited, before returning to the meeting room to find Norris and his lawman both looking red in the face.

"My client denies that these alleged incidents took place, and believes that these so-called witnesses have been set up by an unscrupulous newspaper with the aim of gaining publicity and sales for itself and denigrating himself. However, although he will be cleared of all charges, he is not happy to give the newspaper the coverage it craves and therefore proposes that he will drop his claim of libel and in return the newspaper will drop its story. Furthermore, the newspaper will give a written undertaking not to mention my client in any way, either directly, or through a reference in a sketch or similar article, or allude to a fictional character who readers might reasonably interpret as being my client."

There was another pause.

"Such an offer, over a period of time, would effectively mean that the newspaper would be barred from covering important events," said our man with exceeding calmness which merely emphasised the agitation on the other side, "and that is not conducive to the freedom of the press which is an inherent part of our unwritten constitution. Your client is a man about the city, and he has courted publicity by seeking public office as Mayor of Fulham, and is the owner of several football clubs. He may also become a Member of Parliament. It would be wholly intolerable if my client could not write about your client at moments of great political import."

Sharp words behind hands across the table.

"Our proposal is not negotiable," came the response.

"Then," said our solicitor, "out of courtesy and so there is no suggestion that we have not been giving you the fullest set of information, I have to inform you that our client has been investigating the issue of the destruction of two stands belonging to Croydon Common football club which my client understands is owned by your client. My client has reason to believe that there was something..." he paused looking at his notes to find the appropriate word, "unusual in both cases, and an article on this has been prepared."

Norris rose to his full six feet two. Before his solicitor could stop him, he was out round the table and almost on top of me. I was about to stand and punch him when a word in my ear said, "Stay," so I stayed, which left Norris shouting down at the top of my head.

There was no stopping him. He called me an evil bastard, a guttersnipe, a louse, not fit even to attend a football match, that I was banned from his grounds... I thought at one stage he was going to hit me which would have been most aggravating. But in the end he turned and thumped the table. He must have misjudged it slightly for he hit the edge of the table and the bruise came up on his hand almost immediately and there was blood under the surface of the skin, but still he didn't stop, until eventually our man said very calmly, "I think it might be helpful if your client withdrew in order to regain his composure."

Each side retreated again to its ante-chamber, and we sat in quiet contemplation. "I think it is going rather well," said our man at last.

Eventually we resumed. Norris sat there plunging imaginary daggers into my heart, but it was agreed that the Chronicle had had their day with the story, that they really had no desire to take this particular story any further – it was a most minor transgression – but there was no chance of the paper giving up further stories. Mr Norris, a busy man with numerous personal engagements in the political and business world, had no desire to waste valuable time on such matters, and therefore if the Chronicle would agree not to reprint or in any way mention these allegations (which Mr Norris still denied) again, then Mr Norris would not proceed with the case.

It was agreed. Oh, and I was personally banned from attending any matches at Fulham, Woolwich Arsenal and Croydon Common.

Back in Fleet Street Mr Holloway was enthralled by the report. "Right, Jones," he said. "First Woolwich Arsenal home match of the season – you will be there."

I said I would be delighted.

"And in the meanwhile do me something on the Stonehenge story."

Despite myself I asked what story that might be.

"The one about the London property developer who has been removing the stones and breaking them up to use in house building in the south west of the capital."

I said it sounded like Norris and I'd do my best.

Tuesday 23rd August

There were practice matches at Craven Cottage and Woolwich, and I was debating which to meander towards when the call came in from the War Office. Two letters had arrived today, and one was being looked at now. Our spy would be expecting them by the late afternoon delivery – but only one would go in. We had to be there, watch the Woolwich Woman and take whatever action we considered necessary.

I called Marie at her house. She said she would collect Sophia and Edward, and I met them at the Hen and Basket.

Armed with nothing more than whistles, blank journalist notebooks and pencils, we moved in. I watched the back door, Edward had the front, Marie was 150 yards up the main street from the place where the back lane met the main street. By walking back and forth continuously she could see Edward and me every 20 seconds. Sophia was two hundred yards down the road, watching to see which way the Woman went if she came out at speed. The signal system was simplicity – if either Edward or I saw an arrival we would raise our right arm and Marie would rush back to the other and repeat the gesture. A departure was the left arm.

At twenty minutes past the hour I got the signal: a left hand – she was leaving by the back door. Marie immediately ran along two alleys in order to get ahead of the Woman as the alleyways met Hescott Street further away from the river. Sophia, having spotted the move, did as I had commanded: she became a front tail. Meanwhile I had to make it from the other side to be able to watch from a distance. After 200 yards I realised just how out of condition I was compared with the army days. The drink was having its effect. After 300 yards I vowed to cut back. After 400 yards I vowed never to touch a drop again in my life.

Somehow I made it and found my companions in their spy-catching positions, Marie with hands on hips and head to one side, showing her mock contempt for the time it had taken me. At least I hoped it was mock. Gasping for air I sauntered along the road, trying to look the part of an out-of-work Woolwich man whose one hope of money – the girl who could draw – was meandering ahead of me. Edward disappeared into another back alley several hundred yards ahead. Marie was moving slowly on her tail, keeping to around 100 yards distance.

We continued the ducking and diving for four streets, before we approached the General Abercrombie Tavern – a dim and dingy place, and certainly not one where a woman of substance or class would be seen. The Woman ventured in, and Marie walked by and on down the road to where Sophia was observing. I saw them talk briefly before Marie moved on to cover the back of the pub. There was no chance of the Woolwich Woman getting out unnoticed from such a place but there was also no chance of Edward or the ladies getting in unnoticed either.

I wandered in. It was a grim place with a few drinkers and dim lights despite the brightness of the day. The woman was gone – upstairs to a room I guessed – and my total lack of planning for such an eventuality hit me.

I went back out and walked towards Edward, suggesting with a flick of the arm that we'd come around to Sophia and Marie via the alleys. When we got together neither reported any sign of movement.

"Who uses that pub?" asked Edward.

"Drinkers. It's the cheapest beer."

"So who goes there?" he persisted.

"People who just want to drink, and don't care about their surroundings," said Marie.

"Boatmen?" said Edward. "I'm thinking the twenty minutes between receiving the letter and leaving the house was about enough to decode it and then write a new one, which could be brought here and given to a sailor headed for Germany or any other foreign port. He'd be paid on delivery and would possibly have something to bring back – for another payment."

"She must have twenty or more contacts," said Marie, "and a list of every ship that sails."

"So the only way to catch her at her game," I added, "is to pick her up between the house and the pub and search her."

"It certainly reveals her as a spy," said Marie. "And tells Germany she has been caught. But you told me that in South Africa…"

"…we tried to keep the supply line running, only with false information. True, but we were dealing with amateurs. Their codes were simple to break."

"Do you know yet what was in the letter Churchill and Dr Knox decoded?" asked Sophia. She did not like Mr Churchill, and was always ready to suggest that he was holding information back.

I acknowledged that I didn't have that information and that such information would help, but that even without it we should hold on and see what happened. I reckoned a spy would leave the General Abercrombie and head back home, probably carrying new letters picked up in this pub. But she surprised us again. She certainly left – but not for her home (if that is what it was). She headed for the train station, bought her ticket and waited for a train on the London side. Marie and Sophia followed her, while Edward and I went back to the river and took the ferry to the north bank.

Back in London, we headed to Whitehall to report to Mr Churchill's assistant. Halfway through the debrief Marie arrived, reporting that she had lost the woman in the West End. Sophia had kept looking (although I suspect she simply didn't want to meet Mr Churchill – should he be there).

We gathered the information together. The withheld letter, we were told, had revealed in invisible ink some details of ship building and the comings and goings in Plymouth in the south west. "Not very exciting details," said the ministry man, "and quite probably information that was in the local paper, but still details."

"So the house in Woolwich is nothing more than a drop," I said. "She travels out from whichever fine hotel she is using in the West End, picks up whatever turns up by the post in Woolwich, delivers a new message, and sends it out on the next tide to her masters in Germany."

"Jack was thinking we could feed her false information," said Marie. "I presume Dr Knox can show us how. All we need to do is take out the spy in Plymouth and replace his news with information that is quite wrong."

I looked at her in horror. It wasn't so much what she was proposing, but the fact that she probably intended to do it – with or without government support. The civil servant said that it was an interesting proposition, and he would convey it to his masters.

Wednesday 24th August

Marie called the office and asked if I could come to Dorset Square for the evening, mentioning that she was inviting Edward and Sophia too. A change of clothes was not required.

I joined in the opening round of drinks – my resolve to cut down deferred by the notion that it would have been rude to stop at this point. Edward and Sophia arrived twenty minutes later, Edward having clearly changed after work and Sophia looking as she always does, immaculately turned out. My clothes now looked so out-of-place that when Lady Cortney came in to greet us I tried to explain that no insult was intended, that I had come from work, and she hit me lightly round the face with her open hand. I stood there with my mouth open.

"Mr Jones, I will slap you again if you do not close your mouth on the grounds that to hold your mouth open this long signifies an illness of some kind." I wondered if Lady Cortney might be related to Mr Holloway. "Apologise any more and I will have Jenkinson throw you onto the street." The butler who was standing discreetly in the door coughed politely but otherwise stood in his usual fashion.

She turned to the butler. "Can you talk sense into him?" she asked.

"I fear not, ma'am," he said discreetly. She said she had guessed not and instructed him to feed me more alcohol on the off chance it might help. As she left Edward fell into a chair, expelling all the laughter he had bottled up. I pointed out that I might not need a cameraman any more, but it didn't stop him.

And then the final guest of the evening turned up, announced by Mr Jenkinson as "Dilwyn Knox, Fellow of Kings College, Cambridge".

We all expressed surprise. Lord Cortney entered and shook him by the hand, and explained that he and Dr Knox had known each other some time, Dr Knox being a strong supporter of the Liberals and keen on reform of the university of which apparently the party was in favour.

And of course we fell to talking about secret messages for all of thirty seconds until Dr Knox said to Lord Cortney, "And what is so extraordinary is that it wasn't about spies at all!"

There was a silence around the table as Lord Cortney innocently said, "Oh I hadn't heard that... what was it about?"

And I am sure that Dr Knox was within an inch of telling us, but I guess you have to be bright to be a Fellow of Cambridge, and he caught on. He got about as far as "Why it..." and then looked at the table, and the intensity of our looks gave the game away.

He coughed and said, "I think this has become dashed difficult," and made to rise from the table. Lord Cortney put a hand on his shoulder. "Dilly, if there is any difficulty it is mine. My daughter and her young friends are very discreet in what they do and don't say. We'll say no more of this."

Somehow we got through the meal without more talk of spies and at 10 o'clock Dr Knox left for his town house, leaving the rest of us looking at each other in a mixture of disbelief and dismay.

"You didn't know," said Lord Cortney as we stayed for a final drink of the evening. We agreed we didn't – and that if the letter decoded by Dr Knox was not about spies and shipping, then we had not got a clue what it was about.

"Were we running around Woolwich on a hoax?" said Marie.

None of us knew.

Friday 26th August

Henry Norris had an article in the West London summarising the quiet close season and saying that he felt the Fulham squad were ready to challenge for promotion (despite a singular lack of signings). Woolwich Arsenal did not exist, at least according to his piece, but there was a mention of the "parlous state of the Chelsea ground" and a warning to supporters to be careful of the roped-off areas. He forgot to mention that the ground had been designed and overseen by the same person who had developed the stand at Fulham five years back.

Norris also announced a practice match at Craven Cottage tomorrow afternoon at 3pm which would be open to all supporters for a fee of 1d each.

Saturday 27th August

Marie, through some mechanism I do not understand, has made peace of a kind with her ex-employer and is now busily writing about William James of whom I have never heard: an American psychologist and philosopher. It seems he died yesterday.

I decided to venture to Fulham for the first team against reserves at 3 o'clock.

Sitting in the stands was going to be likely to bring me into contact with Norris, so I paid my penny and stood on a terrace near the halfway line.

The crowd was small – hardly a thousand, I guessed – and the match was poor. At times it was hard to work out which was the first team. Just before the changeover I made the mistake of slipping my notebook and pencil out of my pocket and started to make a few notes in usual journalist fashion. Within a minute two burly coppers appeared from nowhere and suggested that I was "persona non grata" and invited me to leave the ground at once. When I showed a certain reluctance to comply they grabbed me by the scruff and escorted me out the way I had come, to a certain degree of ribald laughter from those around me and gusty applause from George Allison sitting in the stand.

I went back to the office and wrote up the story, focussing mostly on the police, what they looked like, their numbers, and what they said and did. I reported that the game was so utterly atrociously awful that I thought at first that the police were a half-time entertainment put on to try to cover the terrible truth about the quality of Fulham's play. I added that in the course of helping the police to find the nearest exit I noticed an orderly queue forming behind us of other souls who were asking if they too could leave the ground in order to avoid the torture of having to watch the second half.

I ended by asking if every journalist is to be banned from Fulham? And if so, what of Mr Norris' other clubs – Woolwich Arsenal, Croydon Common... and the other clubs that he is expected to buy in and around the capital in the coming months.

Norris won't like that, I thought. Mr Holloway said much the same as he read it, and I swear to God he almost smiled although he also asked if I knew anything about hedgehog spines being proven to be a cure for the common cold and demanded that I find such an animal and perform some experiments. On myself.

In the evening I met up with Marie who had written her piece on William James and the notion of functionalism, which if I now recall correctly means that we adapt ourselves to the world we live in. Which I thought fairly obvious, but apparently it isn't. I tried to suggest that I adapt by paying 1d to go into a ground that Norris says I must not enter, but apparently that isn't the sort of functionalism that James had in mind. It doesn't seem much of a theory if the first example of it that I come up with doesn't apply.

I spoke briefly of my somewhat less intellectual day, showed Marie my piece on Norris and the game, and she dutifully laughed, and then we were back to the issue raised by Dr Knox.

"We can say," said Marie, "that Woolwich Woman is clearly beyond the norm. The house, her looks, her clothes, her actions, the secret letters, the General Abercrombie. None of it is normal and all of that put together gives us a person acting beyond the law. If she is not running a spy ring, she sure is running something else."

"A brothel?" I asked, clutching at straws. Marie hit me on the nose.

"We only have two locations to work on," she observed, "her house and the General Abercrombie. I think I'll do the house again and then try the General Abercrombie." She wasn't asking for permission; she was just saying what she would do.

"I think there is one other issue," I said. "Mr Churchill's refusal to tell us we were on the wrong track. Why would he do that?"

"Because he has no desire to suggest to us that it is something else."

"Martians?" I said.

Marie shrugged. "What was it Mr Churchill said in that speech the other day about reforming the Lords? 'Never run away from anything'." We'll just have to follow his instructions."

I continued to ponder this for some time. "Part of something else." It rang a bell. A very dim and distant bell. But there was a definite ting-a-ling none the less.

Saturday 28th August

With Marie threatening to take the Abercrombie apart I gave the place a quick once over before going to a practice game at Plumstead. Both the pub and the game were appalling.

Monday 29th August

And thus we went once more to Woolwich. I had a feeling that using Edward and Sophia would simply advertise our presence even more than we had done before. At least with the two of us I could pass myself off as doing a Woolwich Arsenal story and bringing a fellow journalist along.

The General Abercrombie was empty at 10 o'clock as we came in, and after a few seconds an old woman appeared at the bar. She looked at Marie and said, "No women".

"But you are a woman," Marie said patiently.

"Women disturb the sailors," she said.

"There aren't any sailors," Marie replied, and I slipped a sixpence across the bar for the woman.

"You have a woman in here sometimes," I said. "Tall, blonde, elegant – looks like she's a toff."

"So does this one," said the woman, sniffing, and looking at Marie.

"Taller," I said. "And blonder."

"Mrs Clegghorn," she said. "She owns the shipping line."

"Which one?" I asked, hopefully hiding my interest.

"Dunno," said the woman. I gave her another sixpence.

"Silver Mast," she said.

"What do they ship?" Marie asked.

"Dunno."

A threepenny bit this time. It was getting very expensive.

The old crow laughed again. "I really dunno," she said, and set about polishing the bar top. She looked up again. "Are you going to drink?"

"I thought you didn't serve women," I said, and we went out.

Tuesday 30th August

Marie's father knew someone at Lloyds who was more than happy to tell us about the Silver Mast. Half a dozen ships sailing to and from Germany carrying machinery. Apparently there are machines that the Germans make better than us and machines that we make better than them – and so there's a two-way traffic. All sounded very odd to me, but Marie said it was true. Apparently they also brought in rice, although I couldn't see how that got to Germany in the first place.

In the evening, as a practice run, we went to a night club and waltzed and two-stepped. I was complimented on having remembered it all and I pointed out, a little sourly perhaps, that as a musician I am supposed to have a sense of time and an ability to remember a rhythm.

Wednesday 31st August

I met George Allison at the Fleet Passage. He wanted the update on how I came to be thrown out of a practice match at Fulham. I gave him the latest and told him about the way I had written up the piece. He laughed.

"A twin attack," he said. "You and me."

I protested that he was writing the programme at Woolwich, something that Mr Norris kept firmly under his control at Fulham. So surely he had specific instructions. "He'll have a surprise then," said Mr Allison, and we fell into using first names. We drank to it. And then we drank to it.

I gave him the background on Norris, much of which George already knew of course, and an outline of my battles. George had met both Norris and William Hall, and his guess was that neither had much intent on getting deeply involved in Woolwich. "Too bloody far for the likes of Fulham Man," he said. "Norris," he said, "remains Fulham through and through, and Hall is just his yes man. He wants Woolwich to sink and sink fast, and then he'll do the amalgamation job. He has asked me to report back to him on each match – full report on what the locals think – he's judging the best moment to close the Woolwich down, and I'm to be his mouthpiece."

"Don't you mind?" I asked.

"Course I bloody mind," he said, "so I won't play his game. I'll find my own way – and we'll have a laugh along the journey, you and I, Jacko. I'm from the north east – we don't mess around with words up there." We drank to that.

We exchanged notes on what else we did. To my surprise he'd come across my non-football work – and to my double surprise, he was a writer beyond football as well. Seems he is what he calls "London correspondent for the New York Herald" – which means he writes a weekly piece on London life and posts it across the sea each week – more often if there is a big story.

So I am not the first writer to move in and out of football. We drank to the football writer who writes politics.

We ended the night very late on with protestations that we would share everything. I don't think I mentioned spies. At least I hope not.

Thursday 1st September

To Woolwich for the first match of the season: Manchester United.

After the fun at Fulham I thought I would try my luck further and presented my press card at the press gate. I lasted about two minutes – long enough to see that Norris was indeed present but not quite long enough to avoid two rather large men who came by and "invited" me to leave. As I was being removed I saw Gunner's Mate who was laughing all over his face.

"Afternoon, George," I said, as I was dragged along the narrow gangway. "Afternoon, Jacko" says he, and there was much merriment among those in the know.

I paid my sixpence and stood as inconspicuously as I could in the crowd watching Woolwich get beaten 1 goal to 2. The programme announced the opposition as Manchester Untidy which I rather liked.

There were 15000 present, but I had to stand in front of a commentator.

After a few seconds he said "Too short, Woolwich." I assumed he was speaking to his mate and let it pass – certainly he was not shouting loud enough to be heard by the players, even if they ever took any notice. A moment later it was, "Where's the movement?" Then another "Too short," followed by, "Second ball, Woolwich, second ball!"

After the third "second ball" I turned and glanced at the man. Judging by the looks on the faces of those either side of him, neither were his friends – he was talking to himself. I turned back to the game.

"Movement!" came the little shout from behind. "Too short, Woolwich, too short!" A pause. "Second ball. Where's the second ball?"

"They only play with one ball, mate!" came the comment from one of the men behind, clearly getting as irritated as I was. There was no riposte from the commentator save another, "Too short, too short!" a few seconds later.

And so it went on. For a while, with nothing else to occupy me (for in truth the match was uninspiring), I kept a tally: eight "too shorts", six "second balls" and four shouts for more movement. That meant we were short on a movement call, and I gave it. There were some chuckles from behind, and one of the lads behind gave a call of "Too short, Woolwich!" to more laughter.

Within seconds another had taken it up, and we had worked out a little chant – "Too short, Woolwich, second ball". It passed the time.

After the game I met up with George in the Hen. We both agreed you couldn't judge too much by this game, and Manchester looked a well-organised side – which Woolwich certainly did not. On the other hand one could also say the ref was, well, minded to help the northern team. I wondered who was paying him.

I congratulated George on the new-look programme (failing to point out the spelling issue) which contained a piece by him full of high promise for the coming season, and a piece by Norris saying he had great confidence in the squad.

"Why don't you write a piece for the programme?" he said.

I told him Norris would never stand for it.

George suggested I work under a pen name, and I said I had enough difficulty finding things to write for the Chronicle, although if he was paying really top wages I might consider it.

He wasn't, as I knew he couldn't be, so we left it – but not before I had a chance to ask him how he was going to cover the fact that the first game of the bright new era was lost, and he said, "I shall tell them what I think. Especially about Gray" (the right back, and responsible for both Manchester goals).

I wrote the headline "Too Short Woolwich lose the Second Ball" and suggested that the commentary taken up by "several thousand in the crowd" was a secret message to the Swiss Navy who were even now gathering at the mouth of the Thames.

Dined with Marie at Dorset Square and was asked by Marie's parents to write a piece for the Chron about the need for political reform. They told me an election is on its way, probably at the end of the year, and Marie suggested that I could write about blowing up the Lords, Guy Fawkes style, which her father dismissed as a joke but her mother took rather more seriously.

I said I would think about it.

Friday 2nd September

Marie asked me about *The Man Who Was Thursday* which she hasn't read. I told her that Chesterton raises the point that we don't have to worry about the thief because the thief believes in personal property – all he wants to do is move it around a bit. Likewise the bigamist is no problem to society for he believes in marriage. No, the big threat comes from the anarchists who reject property, marriage, love, religion and the rest.

Meanwhile the dear old West London and Fulham Times ran a story reporting that Fulham supporters were very unhappy with the deals done with players during the summer break. It seems some of the lads have been talking to the press complaining about their money for the coming year.

In his own column Norris also complained – this time about press reviews of the forthcoming season (the West London writers were really flexing the muscles and claiming that Fulham's squad was very weak – probably because Mr Norris was notoriously poor at paying good salaries).

There was also talk in the paper that the merger of Fulham and Woolwich to form Fulham Arsenal was just a matter of time, and that it was possible that Norris would buy not one but two clubs "to the west of London" and merge them. I guessed Reading and Brentford – two Southern League clubs that he could take upwards.

I wondered how far Norris might go – if he saw himself as Mr Merger he could maybe combine Tottenham and Clapton Orient as well. This could be fun. Clapton Hotspur? Tottenham Orient. The Orient boys in the office always called the Spurs the Tiny Totts, which I rather liked.

I wrote a piece about club mergers being the way forward, putting together Birmingham City and Aston Villa, Nottingham Forest and Notts County. Manchester City and Manchester United and of course the Norris teams.

I also hinted that financial problems seem to be overtaking clubs and that some clubs would go to any length to secure their future – including match fixing – although I hastened to add that I had no evidence, save that things had gone very strangely at Woolwich this week.

Then, in the Jerusalem Cross after work, just doodling in my note book, contemplating the world, a woman came up to me in the bar and started talking. I hardly looked at her at first, but suddenly realised to my utter astonishment that she was Alyson Fairbright. She suggested I write another story, this time on the issue of the vortex. She suggested calling it the Slayer of Souls.

"Pretty one that," said Robert behind the bar. I just nodded.

Saturday 3rd September

And so, with far more nervousness than I ever had going into battle, I went to my first society ball.

Marie drove us in the Rolls – all very smart and toff-like. We took the Great North Road which is supposed to be the main route to Scotland, but is in fact little more than a mud and dust track. "The dust issue" said Marie. It is going to be a central plank of the Liberal Party election manifesto. The villagers turned out to look, wave, and in some cases throw things at us. I tried to look pleased and smiled dutifully, not wishing to reveal I felt sick with worry. I'd dealt with the Cortney family, true, but I've always felt that they dealt with me more than I dealt with them. But Sophia's?

It took us five hours to reach Rutland. The dust was appalling. Marie took us right up to the front of the mansion where there was a bevy of butlers and footmen taking our bags. We were about to enter when a jolly fellow came puffing down the steps and clasped each of us by the hands and introduced himself as Mr Rolls of CS Rolls and Co – the maker of our (well, not my, but Marie's father's) car. "CS Rolls of Conduit Street," he said over and over in between puffs, checking all the while that the car had not been damaged since he had sold it to his lordship.

I told him I thought it a wonderful machine and, inspection complete, he linked arms and led us up the steps and into the house. "How was the speed?" he asked. "You didn't keep to this wretched 20 miles per hour affair did you?" Marie admitted we had gone somewhat faster where the road permitted. "Good, good" he said and then for effect repeated himself twice.

"Every year they keep saying they are going to have a new Act to replace the 1904 law. But they never do. It was temporary, but they won't repeal the Act. Disgrace, disgrace. It is hardly appropriate to have a law that no one follows, but there it is, there it is, there it is. I don't suppose you could speak to your father ma'am…"

Marie said she would consider it.

"I was told there would be a bill allowing up to 25 miles per hour, but now with another election coming and the thing about the House of Lords I can't see that, can't see it, so they'll just renew the act year upon year upon year, year upon year. It is holding us back, keeping British industry at bay, not what made the

Empire you know, not at all. You agree? Good, good." He then clearly thought we hadn't quite got it, because he ran through the last piece again before adding, "They don't have any of this nonsense on the Continent. Holland is speed restriction free, you know, and France will go that way next year. Next year! What we need is no speed restriction – no speed restriction - but suitable punishment for anyone who causes an accident.

"And of course we need roads – just like the Americans have. Roads! We need a motor road from London to York, and just think what that would have done for your journey here today! Done it in a tenth of the time and with no dust problem at all! No dust! The cost of building the roads from tar will soon sort all this out. Soon sort it."

"What about racing? I asked. "I heard people are racing cars now."

"No – a passing fad. In fact it has just about stopped. We'll keep the race on the Isle of Man, but that's about it. There simply isn't enough fuel for racing. No fuel. None at all. None!

"We've got nearly 30,000 cars on the road, and I think that is about it now. Too many cars and not enough buyers eh? But your family is very kind to have a Rolls. Want another one? Another?"

Eventually we escaped and were shown our rooms. Sophia's parents had not bought the story of Marie and I being married, so I had to wallow in the overwhelming luxury on my own for a few moments.

Back downstairs we met the engaged couple and exchanged many handshakes, kisses and good wishes, and Edward and Sophia treated us as particularly special guests. Edward went out of his way to introduce me as "his boss" which, given the way I still quaked in front of Mr Holloway, was hilarious. But it confirmed that Edward's life in Fleet Street was as much an adventure for him as being here was for me. And it did occur to me that he felt I had looked after him in the strange world of Fleet Street. Good for me.

Before the grand meal of the evening we were introduced to various aunts and uncles and the singularly opinionated and obnoxious brother of Sophia called Justin who actually said to me, "Come on then, let's hear some cockney – that's what you Fleet Street wallahs do, what?" Marie grabbed my right hand and held it behind my back.

Then we were presented to Sir Richard, father of Sophia who looked hard at Marie and said, "Your father Lord Cortney?" very abruptly.

She said that was the case, and looking sideways I caught a dark look in Edward's eyes. The temperature in the room dropped to around minus 20.

"Liberal, isn't he? Supports that Churchill?"

Sophia's mother was in quickly, ordering Sir Richard to stop, but he was on a roll now. "Man's a traitor to his class!" he shouted. "Hear me? A traitor. And if your father supports him, he's a traitor too. Sorry to say it, young lady, but it has to be said."

Justin then saw his chance. "And 'Jack – oh' didn't you write that article supporting Churchill in that newspaper of yours?" And turning to the watching throng he added, "He did you know!"

There was a dreadful silence. I had no idea what the correct thing to do was, so I did what I always do. I reverted to my army training. An officer insults you, so you insult him back – but in a way that he doesn't quite get.

"Sir, I must apologise. I didn't realize Mr. Churchill was a Liberal."

"Not a Liberal?" said Justin rolling his eyes. "What the devil did yer take him for?" Sophia looked very unsure, but the smile was back on Marie's face and on Edward's too. They'd seen the game.

"A gentleman, sir. My error. Now I've met you I know how a gentleman behaves, sir."

"What the devil," began Sir Richard, but Sophia thought it was time to call it a day. "Father, these are my guests," she said with calm dignity. "You cannot speak like this."

"Well!" he said, and then said it again several times. "It's my house!" Then he turned back to me. "What d'you say your name was, boy?" he asked me.

"Henry Rousseau, sir," I said, and we backed off.

"How do you know about Rousseau?" asked Marie.

"Obituary in the Times today," I said. "I am trying to keep up."

The meal was formal, I kept my head down, Marie guided me through the formalities, the speeches were made, we toasted the King and the happy couple, and everyone seemed to have forgotten the contretemps. And then came the dancing. My abilities at the waltz, the redowa and two step were hardly exceptional, but my desire was to get by unnoticed and in that I succeeded.

And then, and then, oh and then, prompted by Edward, and having had a few drinks and a few more, I approached the band leader and asked for a rag. He gave me a look of pure disgust, and I thought that was that, but Edward said in that wonderful loud voice he can put on, "I say, lads, don't none of you know the Cake Walk?"

It was clear that while the leader didn't want to indulge in such commonplace merriment, the ensemble did, and Edward was one of the nobs, a guest of honour, so we got it. Cake Walk Rag.

The stiff in charge turned to the audience and said, in the plummiest voice in the history of fruit in the mouth, that he had had a "Err... herumph... a request... which, err, several herumph... members of the band will acknowledge..."

And I was not going to let this moment pass. I put my hand out flat to one side, and Marie put hers on top. Edward and Sophia spotting the game followed, and slowly and with utter grace, me in my uniform and Edward in his formal attire, with the girls as pretty as can be imagined, we processed onto the pitch. There was a shuffling backwards as space was made. God knows what they thought they were going to get, but whatever it was, it wasn't the Cake Walk. The band started up, I closed all thoughts of the audience out of my head, and we did it. At the end I just turned to the band and said, "Turkey Trot" and blow me over that's what we got, and after ten seconds another young couple who had obviously spent time in the night clubs joined us, and that gave us the victory. By the time we hit the Bunny Hop there were six couples and, always knowing when to quit, I then led the walk off the floor.

To their credit a fair number of the old timers gave us a round of applause and there was much goodwill and good humour there. Good on them, I thought. Next time it's the Grizzly Bear.

Sunday 4th September

We survived the overnight stay and that strange affair of breakfast in which one serves oneself while the servants stand and watch. Sophia tried to apologise again for the initial difficulties with her father and brother, and we all said there was no problem. "A suffragette, an anarchist, a photographer and a football reporter – who could ever make anything of us?" I said. We laughed a little and Marie threw a bread roll at me, claiming she was not an anarchist.

We stopped for tea at the pleasant town of Watford which seemed to be owned mostly by the Earl of Essex. Marie showed me Cassiobury Park where his house was and where she had been once or twice. We kept a low profile and in a newsagent nearby bought the Sunday papers and started reading them over tea and cake in a local shop, and everything was nice and cheerful until I dropped my cup. In the Popular Press Norris was accusing me of being an anarchist – or maybe a Labour supporter – or both – and saying I was dangerous. I had run the story of the Parliament Act in order to undermine Parliament, I was a known friend of anarchist leaders like Barrett with whom I had been imprisoned, I had been working football grounds and mixing with known criminals, and was a renegade from the Army, a deserter and known subversive. My behaviour was so disruptive, he said, I had been refused permission to report at a number of football grounds and had oft been seen sneaking in. The army's own intelligence officers knew of me and were alerted to my activities after I had spent much time hanging around the War Office looking for work.

"Bloody wolfshead," I said.

Marie and I sat there looking at the article. I was frustrated and angry – but had to acknowledge that Norris was merely fighting back in our battle against him. Although I felt I had never got quite that dirty.

In the end we decided that the key questions were: what would be the Chronicle's view of this; and did it give us any new insight into the issue of the spies, Mr Churchill's behaviour in not revealing what was in the secret messages, Woolwich Woman… or come to that anything at all.

I was so taken up with the story about me in the paper that I forgot to look at the football results from yesterday in the paper and had to ask Marie to stop two miles after the tea shop so I could dig them out of the dicky. Woolwich Arsenal had drawn one goal to one with Bury.

Monday 5th September

Marie has found herself a new story, and it seems this time the Times is really interested. The Roman Catholic Church has insisted that every priest in the church takes an oath denouncing the idea that the Church and its beliefs were created by people and not by God. God tells the pope and the pope tells the church. It is called the battle between the church and the modernists.

I apologised to Marie and said I could not quite follow the details, and wished I could.

We stopped at a chemist shop for petrol, and went for a drink. "We are the same," she said. "I have no idea what the pope is trying to do. You have no idea about the spies. Would you like to read something else I'm working on?" When I agreed she gave me a poem. It began, "Full ninety autumns bath this ancient beech helped with its myriad leafy tongues to swell,"

I read it. I didn't understand it, and Marie started to explain but I interrupted. "That's not it," I said. "That's not it at all. I just said I don't understand, but actually the meaning is not important. It is the sound of the words. That is what makes the piece. 'The dirges of the deep-toned western gale, and ninety times hath all its power of speech Been stricken dumb, at sound of winter's yell'. It is the sounds. Of course there is more, and you can understand more, and Edward and Sophia will understand it too. But there is also the sound."

It was called "Written in a Wood". I have no idea if it is any good or not, but the sounds haunted me. I know each word's meaning, but not the implication of the whole. Just like Woolwich.

"We need to put a stop to this, and find out what is going once and for all," Marie said suddenly. "We go back to Woolwich, go to the General Abercrombie, and if necessary wait there for days, if necessary take it apart bit by bit," I said. "We make the pub talk to us, and we listen to what it has to say."

We arrived at the General Abercrombie at half past eight. It was packed to the edge and into the street with hard drinking men. "Good time for anything to happen," I said. "One man in a desert stands out to the horizon. One man in a crowded pub goes unnoticed."

I went to the pie stall by the docks and bought food for us both – which was not necessarily good for our health, but we needed something. We moved into the shadows and camped down, watching the front and back entrance between us as the men poured in and then, from around midnight until around three in the morning, poured out. Of the Woolwich Woman (or anyone else who stood out like a sore thumb) there was no sign.

As is the habit of such pubs they threw the last few men out, locked the doors, and left the place in the early hours, knowing that they had the morning to clear it up, ready for the drinking to start again at around 10 o'clock. Anyone needing a drink before ten would not mind the mess. Such souls don't mind anything.

We gave them an hour after the last man was pushed through the doors and into the gutter. Marie wanted to move earlier, but I knew my territory. Every gas light, every candle, dead for an hour. Then you move. "Half an hour is long enough for everyone to fall asleep, but not long enough for any drunks by the roadside to wake up to be sick and see us. You sleep your most solid sleep between one and three hours after you close your eyes – that's when we move in."

"Boer trick?" she asked. I agreed it was and from that there was no arguing. Marie had the knack of knowing when I was speaking from knowledge, as opposed to most of the time when I was making it up as I went along.

At four o'clock, well before the first slight sign that against all the odds the earth might have managed to spin round once more and give us another day, we moved in. I did the door, and Marie watched the technique. She nodded – at least I hadn't lost that ability – although she could probably have done it faster.

Together we searched for two hours covering every inch of the two bars and checking everything from the back of the till to the disgustingly dirty back of the sink. We didn't find anything – that is if you don't count two identical packages, tucked under the now empty till, each done up with yellow string. It seemed a good idea to take them outside to investigate later when there was enough light and no chance of being caught in the act. So that's what we did.

Sitting with those packages on the first bus of the morning, then the tram, and then the hansom, all the way back to Dorset Square, was nerve wracking, although perhaps not as nerve wracking as the fact that at half past six Jenkinson opened the door before Marie had her key half in the lock and looked as fresh and organised as if it were six in the evening.

Without even being bid he directed us to separate bathrooms to wash, found fresh clothes for me which were not my style but did actually fit (now where did they come from?) and by the time we were back in the smoking room he had supplied us with wonderfully and amazingly refreshing hot coffee. No question, no quizzical raised eyebrow. The man was a marvel. If I ever make some money I resolved to give him something as a sign of either class solidarity or gratitude. One or the other.

We said nothing but both gulped our coffee greedily (I was amused to see that even at this point Marie was unable to take hers without cream and sugar). Then, using a knife Marie had purloined from the kitchen, we prized the parcels open.

We knew from the feel that the envelopes were packed and that each package bore the single word "Saviours". What we didn't know was that the envelopes were packed with crisp £5 notes. How many I could not work out at first although Marie, perhaps more used to seeing large sums of money, was more readily able to get down to the main task of counting. I just gawped. We had something in the order of £10,000. Enough to pay an entire football team for six years (more if it was a Norris team) in each envelope. Not that anyone was thinking of paying a team for six years. It's just that my mind works that way.

"Not enough to buy the government," said Marie, "but enough to buy a lot of voters."

We looked at it and poured more coffee. I asked Marie if I might find a whisky, and she just nodded, indicating that she'd have one herself. Talk about people who need a drink before ten in the morning.

I was just pouring the whisky into the coffees when Lord Cortney entered. "I was informed we had guests," he said, in that lilting voice he had. "'Looking as if they might have been in an adventure', was the exact report that reached my room. I was not told," he paused as he took in the piles of money, "that you had robbed the Bank of England."

"We think it is about £10,000, father," Marie told him.

"And where did you get this?" he asked.

"Sir," I interjected, "I have put you in a bad position. When we brought the packages in we had no idea what they contained. I also apologise for helping myself to your alcohol."

"Oh for God's sake shut up, Jacko," said Marie.

"For once I seem to concur with my daughter, Mr Jones," he replied, "I don't know what gives me more pleasure. The action you bring to this house or the apologies you continue to issue in my direction. Incidentally, I hear that you defended the honour and beliefs not only of my daughter, but also my family, in front of that oaf, Cranbourne-Rickley, the father of your good friend, Sophia. I think I owe you, sir." He placed the accent on the final word, and that smile once more played on his face before giving a mock bow. "Besides if you have the right to any of that money, you can treat me to breakfast at the Ritz. While you tell me what is going on."

Marie told him.

As she finished Lord Cortney decided that maybe the Ritz wasn't right. He decided to join us in a whisky.

Tuesday 6th September

I got some sleep at Dorset Square before going into work so late that I couldn't even think of an excuse. Mr Holloway and Mr Symmonds wanted to know what I was working on, and I told both that I was following a lead for the Home Secretary and that it would result in the biggest story ever.

We then had the inevitable conference to review Norris' attack on me in the Sunday papers. The general feeling was that we should hold our fire, I would be given some more time to get something extraordinary on the "old devil" as Mr Symmonds liked to call him, and that we would not reveal our hand until we had it.

Mr Holloway was not particularly impressed with the approach, although he was keen for more on the notion that had been put to him that Queen Victoria was still alive and living on the Isle of Wight. After pottering around for a while I went to meet Marie at the Lyons.

"What do we conclude?" she asked at once, referring back to the discovery of the envelopes.

"That the notes are not part of the business process of the General Abercrombie. Spies – at least the spies I have known – are paid tiny amounts – you don't pay them enough to live on for a couple of years, because then you lose them. You give them enough for beer and fags for a week, maybe two if they have done well, and then they come running back for more. On the scale that I have seen we have enough here for fifty spies. But if you were the paymaster of an army you wouldn't leave your entire financial stash for the troops in a pub."

We looked at each other. Eventually I had a doughnut.

"First option, go back and try to track Woolwich Woman. Second option, we hand the money over to Mr Churchill and demand an explanation. Third option, we go back to the General Abercrombie and see who is hitting whom. Fourth option, we go to Woolwich woman and tell her we have her money," said Marie.

"Fifth option," I took over, "we hand the money over to the police and wait and see what happens. Sixth option, we spend the money. Seventh option, I write a note in the Chron saying that a huge sum of money was found in Woolwich, and the police are waiting to find out who it belonged to."

"And meanwhile…"

"We hide the money somewhere no one will find it."

"Where?" she asked.

"Not Dorset Square, not Wood Green, not Fleet Street."

"Sophia's room at the house in Burley-on-the-Hill," Marie suggested. "Right in the homeland of our enemies. That is a possibility. If she'll take the train she can be there and back in a day. She's got her own private room and an arrangement with the staff not to touch certain things in it."

We agreed that would be safest. Marie said she would contact Sophia at once. I told her not to use the phone – which sounded melodramatic, but… Marie also said, in relation to nothing I could think of, that she wanted all four of us to go on holiday in the car together. She had the date when she could borrow the car, and we were going. All right? I said it was all right.

I went to the office and started typing

Huge stash of money found in public house.

Mysterious Woolwich Woman sought.

Secret society of the Saviours thought to be behind plot.

Mr Holloway took it straight into news and gave it to the duty editor. The duty editor turned back to me. "Where did you get this?" he asked.

"I was there," I said.

"What is it with you and Woolwich?" said Mr Holloway. "There is a man in Totnes who claims he is the rightful heir to the Kingship of London. Go and talk to him."

I shrugged and they took the story to the editor. It was a sure fire thing for publication; mystery woman, money, secret society, dim and distant part of the country (Woolwich). What else could a story have?

I headed home and went to play with the band. Three negro guys came in with two rough guitars and a beaten up bass and asked if they could play. The publican said they could do something while the band took a rest, so they played. They played as I have never heard before in my life. Their accent was so thick I couldn't understand a word of the song, and not much of what they said. But I got the title of "Rich Man's Blues." The music was The Blues. It was American. I felt my life move to another level.

Wednesday 7th September

I was due to arrive at work at half past eight. The police picked me off the street as I left the underground station at twenty minutes past and seemed content to bypass the mere technicality of a warrant for my arrest. That I could deal with. The fact that they had a warrant to search my parents' house was much more worrying. I pleaded to be able to go back home, but there was no giving way. I was taken to Bow Street Police Station and awaited the pleasure of the company of whoever it was who might feel like talking to me.

Eventually Inspector Build invited me to sit in a whitewashed room and face him across a desk.

"Jacko Jones!" he said.

There didn't seem much to say by way of reply.

"Tell me about the money," he said as a starter. I asked which money that might be.

"A substantial amount of money that you were seen removing from a public house in Woolwich – a part of the country that I am told you often frequent."

I asked if I shouldn't be interrogated by the Woolwich police, but this got me nowhere. There was a question about whether I was in the company on the night in question of the Honourable Marie Cortney, whether I was in Woolwich last night, and if not where was I. I told him I was in Wood Green. When asked for witnesses I gave the name and addresses of the band, the publican, and the names of a dozen or so regulars that I knew. I apologised for not giving their addresses. I also started talking about the negro trio. The Inspector had stopped writing after the list of my fellow band members. I told him I had heard the most extraordinary new music I had ever known. He wasn't impressed.

"Three negroes in the White Hart in Wood Green?" he said.

"Playing The Blues. It's a new form of music. Unlike any other. The length of the bars changes…"

"I don't care about the bleeding length of bleeding bars," shouted the officer. "The only bleeding bars you are going to care about…"

"Are the ones in the prison," I completed. "Yes, I know."

He calmed himself. "What do you know of the General Abercrombie?"

My story was that I knew the pub and suspected it to be the centre of a spy ring based around the docks, and that I have been doing my job as a reporter in trying to track the story down. The inspector having read *Spies of the Kaiser* could see some logic in where I was heading. I said I thought the nation's security was under threat, although not as much as the nation's music. Or my security.

Then I added that whoever it was who had reported me to the police as having stolen some money was clearly either himself a criminal or working for the enemy, and that by taking up my time and his own time on this matter the police inspector was himself doing the enemy's work. I suspected the secret society of the Saviours.

"What about the woman you have been chasing?" he asked.

I tried to give a look that suggested that this was old news. "I've seen her around the area. She's smart, well-dressed and totally out of place for a district like Woolwich. Once I saw her going into the General Abercrombie, and that's why I snooped around there."

"So you admit you were snooping!" came the smart reply.

"It's what journalists do," came the smarter retort.

"And what about this anarchist that you mix with?"

"Norris?"

"George Barrett!"

"He and I have known each other since I started writing," I said. "Yes, he goes around talking about anarchism, but if that is a crime, you know who he is and where he hangs out so arrest him again. But, for what it is worth, I have never seen Barrett anywhere near the Woolwich Woman nor anywhere near the General Abercrombie."

He didn't like it, but there was not enough in my story to allow him to charge me with anything, so instead he decided to hold me on the charge of manipulating the king's English.

After four hours Mr Beckwith turned up and demanded a meeting with the inspector. In the end Mr Beckwith, the inspector and I sat down for a chat and Mr Beckwith made several abstruse legal points that the inspector listened to in silence.

Finally he said, "The newspaper will vouch for Mr Jones and ensure that he does not leave the capital. If you let him go now and stop harassing him, I can guarantee that this incident will not be mentioned in the paper. If you do not, I can give no such guarantee."

The inspector gave up, and we left.

On the way back I asked how the paper had found out where I was. Apparently, the moment the police had finished turning over my house my father had taken a cab to the newspaper and told them, and they had swung into action. An hour or two later.

I phoned Marie. As I guessed, the police had not thought of bringing her into a police station – that would be too demeaning – but they had asked her some polite questions in Dorset Square. Her father had been at the House of Lords; the police had gone there and been refused entry, so Lord Cortney had not been questioned.

I asked Mr Holloway why it had taken the solicitor quite so long to get to me, following my arrest, and was told that they wanted to give the police a good experience of what it was like working with me.

"Four hours," he said. "That should teach them. I told them that once you started talking they would need a nerve specialist." He laughed.

Thursday 8th September

I set the juniors to search for references anywhere to the Saviours. It was a measure of my esteem among the kids that they did what they were bid without any raised eyebrows. With nothing particular to do I asked if I should write up the story of my arrest and was told that the word from the solicitor was to hold. The word from the fifth floor was to go on exploring, and that they might be able to get me out of whatever I got myself into if I let them know where I was going.

"Might" didn't seem quite the level of security that I was hoping for.

I went to see Marie. We agreed that unless she had any particular locations she wanted to rob we would lie low for a day or two.

Edward and Sophia turned up, and I told them about The Blues. To pass the time and to throw the police who were following me off the scent, we went touring the music shops looking for a guitar. And a book of instructions.

Friday 9th September

The juniors reported that the Saviours were a very secret society also known as the Slayers of Souls.

Norris had a piece in the West London about his Fulham side going to West Bromwich tomorrow and how he was now, as promised, giving more time to Fulham's affairs. Therefore he would be travelling with the team to give them his support.

I thought that was jolly good and took that as an invitation to go and watch Woolwich Arsenal. Marie was doing some research in the Lords' library. Sophia was out demonstrating. I asked Edward to come with me.

Saturday 10th September

Woolwich Arsenal 0 Sheffield United 0 will hardly live long in the memory of football fans, but it will live forever in my mind.

Edward and I approached the press entrance carefully, and seeing Norris' henchmen on the gate we edged backwards into the crowd – which was certainly smaller than for the Manchester United match.

I took up a place on the terrace near the halfway line opposite the stand, and Edward set himself up just in front of me. We watched an endless succession of off-sides as two inept teams kicked the ball around a bit. Mr "Too Short" was not around, so I started the call myself. "Too short Arsenal!" I shouted, as loud as I could half a dozen times, before a huge gent with a Scots accent demanded what my game was, and I shut up.

Wondering what on earth I could find to write about the event which I hadn't covered in a previous column, I suddenly became aware of a certain amount of shuffling and moving behind me and to my right.

It was hard to turn away from the game without being too obvious but I did the only thing I could. I complained loudly at yet another Woolwich offside and drew attention to myself turning my back on the pitch. No one is ignored as much as a man drawing attention to himself. As I turned I whistled to Edward, and he turned too. I pointed to my left.

About ten steps back and to my left a little group of men were pushing their way through the crowd, causing much annoyance. "You're going the wrong way," I shouted, "the way out's behind you," and there was some laughter.

The moving men ignored me and kept coming. Eight of them, almost in formation, pushing through the thin crowd, letting no one stand in the way. Keeping up my commentary I watched them while waving to Edward indicating exactly who I wanted photographed. They were edging along, leaving a trail of annoyed men who were not happy at the treatment – although curiously after a few moments several of them seemed calmer than I would have expected.

I kept looking back, and there was no doubt. As the men approached there were reproaches. I heard one man shout, "Stupid dunt," but then afterwards everyone was looking inwards, and down. The noisy protests had gone, the match was ignored, and there was quiet talk – quiet talk!!! – and nervous looks back along the terrace at the group as they edged further along. This was not exactly what you normally find on the terraces at Woolwich or any other football match. They make more noise at Wood Green Town.

I took action, moving diagonally away from the pitch, putting myself in line for an intersection with the advancing group, waving to Edward as I did so. He got the message, hopped over the barrier, and ran along the touch line with his gear, much to the amusement of those in the crowd who had not understood what was happening.

I got there just in time, and turned back to the game as the shouts of protest got closer and closer. Then they were there, and all around me, pushing and courting no interference in their route. One moved next to me while another was on the terrace above and one below.

They could not be pickpockets. Pickpockets in the grounds work in pairs, one to knock you off balance and one to take your pocket watch and money. They work in crowds on the streets, stopping the peelers from pushing their way through, but never ever do they work in crowds in the confined space of the football ground.

I turned to get closer to the action. One old boy was holding a sovereign – which seemed a lot of money to bring with you into a football match.

I asked what had happened. There was muttering, but eventually one of the lads broke ranks and told. The group had pushed past, and then done exactly the opposite of what I had thought. They had pushed a pound into the old boy's pocket.

I turned and started to follow the gang which was still pushing its way through the crowd. Every few places along I found another little group where, suspecting a pickpocket, someone had found instead a gold oncer in his pocket.

After moving along for several minutes I stopped. It was clear that this practice was continuing. After a pause for thought I pushed forwards, grabbed Edward, and we left the game. This was crazier than the King of London story.

Back in the office I told Mr Holloway who checked my breath and told Mr Symmonds who checked my breath. Edward shut himself away in his dark room. There was editorial annoyance that I had not managed to get one of the coins myself and a feeling that without that the story was simply unbelievable. As such it was spiked.

They checked my breath again. Edward came out with pictures of the men in three different places in the crowd. Mr Holloway looked as if he wanted to check Edward's breath, but held back.

The news came in that West Bromwich Albion had beaten Fulham 2 to 1.

Sunday 11th September

"To be honest I don't believe it either," I said. "It must have been my imagination."

"And George Allison won't have seen it," Edward added, "because he was in the press area."

There was a long silence and we looked at Edward's pictures.

"Unbelievable sums of money being left in envelopes in a disreputable pub. Now men putting pounds in pockets. It is insane," I said.

"Unless, of course, someone wants to do a bit of redistribution."

"A modern Robin Hood?"

"It's an explanation."

"Which means we have to work backwards and try to find out where the money came from in order to be redistributed."

"The amount of money you found in the Abercrombie would have had to come from the sale of part of one of the shire estates," Edward added knowingly.

"But you can hardly expect one of the landed gentry to turn into a Labour supporter." I said.

"If it is anyone it is Lloyd George," Marie replied – and I have to agree. "Set the dogs on us," she quoted.

"Or what about an anarchist device to overthrow the state by undermining its currency?" said Edward. He was quite interested in conspiracies.

It was possible, but it seemed just, well, odd.

"If this is a result of the money that we found before, then someone is going to a lot of trouble to turn £5 notes into sovereigns," I said. "What are they doing – buying their wives dresses and using the change?"

"Maybe there is an earlier link in the chain," Marie said. "Not something as odd as buying dresses, but something that we don't know about which transforms the money into coins."

"But why?" said Edward, and there was no arguing with that.

Monday 12th September

A simple day: Edward, Sophia, Marie and I in conference at Edward's family home in Park Lane. We ruminated. And got nowhere.

In between I was learning to play the guitar and trying to remember exactly how The Blues went.

It was Sophia who had the greatest imagination. She suggested that Germans were bringing in fake fivers in boats that unloaded in Woolwich under the supervision of Woolwich Woman. The money would soon cause people to panic because they were not used to being given money (a weak point in the tale I thought). Meanwhile, the Saviours, a secret society, had found out what was going on and was trying to stop the problem.

"Just supposing any of that is true," I said, "how do we find out if the fivers are forged without giving ourselves away?" I asked.

None of us had any idea. We decided to work on Lloyd George before anything else. It was, after all, easiest.

I went home and left notes in every pub between my house and White Hart Lane promising that, if negroes who played The Blues should turn up, anyone who let me know in time to hear them would get a pound's reward. I couldn't quite remember how they played *Rich Man's Blues* and it was driving me insane.

Or rather, more insane.

"Do not let go," Marie told me. "Jacko Jones does not let go."

Edward and I (permission grudgingly given by Mr Holloway) assigned every junior available to check for any sign of the men pictured at Woolwich Arsenal handing out sovereigns in any picture anywhere. Marie and Sophia called in every favour possible and worked the Times archives.

We all drew a blank. In the afternoon we decamped to the Lords and gained tickets to their lordships' Library as "research assistants" for Lord Cortney. Our task: to search for clues in the life of Lloyd George. At six o'clock we went back to Lord Cortney's house, shared an exquisite meal, as always, and brought our notes together.

Lloyd George. Born in Liverpool, but brought up in a Welsh village. He is now the ultimate hero of his country – a liberator against the English oppressors. (One possibility: he was undermining the English currency as a step towards Welsh independence. Sophia as a Suffragette was anti-Liberal, and she was the only one who gave credence to this).

We found talk of "avenging the crimes of generations", and got the impression that our neighbours in the Kingdom had as much desire for independence as those in Ireland – although Wales is standing up against Rome as well.

What Lloyd George is alleging, and no one was really gainsaying, is that there had been voting corruption since the 1832 reform. "Vote as I tell you or you lose your farm," was the word of the day, he says. Even the church seemed to be the enemy of the people in Wales. The Welsh go to chapels to worship in their own way, while the state gives money to sustain a church which seemingly no one wants.

Marie had found in her father's personal library a picture of Lloyd George's home near Snowdon, and we spent much time just looking at it, trying to understand how life would appear from that perspective rather than from the streets of London or the countryside of Rutland. His village of Criccieth seemed as alien to us as the plains of Africa had seemed to me upon my first arrival. And as unpronounceable.

Mr George is also totally committed to free trade and totally against armaments. In fact he says both are connected – tariff war leads to a munitions war. Marie and Sophia nodded profoundly. I didn't quite follow.

So we moved on to Mr Lloyd George as Chancellor of the Exchequer, raising his extra £25 million for social reform, pensions, the Labour Exchange, sickness insurance, unemployment insurance. And he is on record as complaining that he only gets half of the money for his social programme with the other half going on weapons – which quite possibly makes him the enemy of Mr Churchill who supports expansion of the military. Mr George on the other hand is a supporter of the idea of the International World State.

Could it be, we debated, that the second most senior man in government might actually be redistributing wealth in a way that we couldn't actually bring ourselves to understand? Is he moving this money around to get more people to spend more money, so that there is more "free trade" and then more money raised in tax?

"I don't think it works like that," said Sophia, and I took her word for it. She had, after all, done economics at London University.

Wednesday 14th September

For the first time in weeks I played with the band. It was a relief. George Barrett was in the audience, a long way from home. In a way I wished he hadn't been, but still for old times sake I went and asked if he had come across any sort of anarchist scheme involving fake currency.

"It's a theory in a lot of the books," he said, "but no one has done it that I know of. We want to get rid of money. Not have more of it."

"But making thousands of pounds could undermine the economy," I said, not being quite sure what that meant, but having heard the girls say something along these lines.

"How?" he said.

"I don't know," I admitted, feeling silly. "I thought you might tell me."

"Is this what is going on?" he asked.

"Not on a big scale," I half lied. "We have seen one attempt at this, but it was small scale stuff. You'd need an army to make an impact."

At that moment an old timer came rushing up to me shouting that the negroes were playing at the Rovers four streets down. I grabbed George, told him this he had to see, and we rushed through the Monkey Parade. The negroes were just finishing as we got there.

I grabbed them, and they looked scared. The old timer was shouting for his money. Everyone started making a fuss. I persuaded the old boy I would give him his money tomorrow, and begged the band to play *Rich Man's Blues* again. But the publican didn't want more music, so in the end I dragged them into the street, emptied my pockets of change and handed it over and they played for me. Four times. I made notes as they played.

Thursday 15th September

It was Edward who said it first. "Maybe football is more important in this than we imagine. We've been thinking that the men were placing the sovereigns at

211

Woolwich as incidental – the key was the money, the football just happened to be the place. But supposing it was the other way around. Supposing Norris is trying to build support for his team by giving people money in the ground?"

"Wouldn't it be cheaper to let everyone in for free?" I asked.

"The word gets around that some people hit the jackpot, so next match they all turn up, and the next one," he replied. "Then maybe five games on he gives out money again, and so they all keep coming."

"Is this real money or fake?" I asked.

I played him *Rich Man's Blues* on my guitar which I had taken to carrying around with me.

Friday 16th September

I had to write up a football story and quickly. It was all very well my being on the track of what appeared to be the biggest tale of all time, but if I couldn't actually tell anyone about it – and I certainly felt I couldn't at this moment – then I didn't actually have a story. We still had no connection between the five pound notes and the sovereigns, and the individual stories made no sense. And without sense I could hardly accuse Mr Lloyd George of being Robin Hood. Nor could I blow the whole show wide open to reveal that I had been given the job of undermining the position of the man in charge of our secret police if the real story was that I had been given a meaningless job to keep me out of the way.

And here was another thing: did any of this go all the way back to the original story of the torpedo factory?

As I contemplated the muddle it struck me that Mr Churchill was quite probably playing all sides off against the other. He was part of a government that was paying Captain Kell £7000 a year, while at the same time telling me to get the evidence against Kell, while not telling me what was in the letter that the Woolwich Woman received. Maybe he was also engaged in forging bank notes or sovereigns in order to....what? Undermine the government?

On reflection football seemed easier, although I had nothing new on Norris and had been told that without something very new it was time to let that drop. Croydon Common were certainly not national news, and nothing seemed to have happened about Reading.

I went back to my other stand-by: Leitch. He was never charged with any offence over Ibrox, but clearly he was implicated. He had worked at Woolwich Arsenal ten years ago and had never been paid. Just when it looked as if he would be paid, suddenly he wasn't. He had worked at Fulham and Chelsea at the same time and put through plans which said their grandstands were going to be the same, when in fact they were not. A minor offence, but still... And the Chelsea ground had significant problems five years on. He'd also been the architect for Manchester United's ground (no crime in that, of course, but I had decided I didn't like Manchester United).

I telephoned the Manchester Guardian and asked for the football desk.

"Well, well, the famous Jacko Jones," came the response when I got through. James Williamson. We'd never met, but he'd heard of me. That made life a little easier.

"I am chasing a story, and need your help," I said.

"And in it for me?" he asked.

"I'll share what I've got. In fact," I said, using the Reading ploy once again, "In fact, I'll tell you something, straight up, to show you how honest I am."

"An honest journalist! Jacko, there are no honest journalists."

I agreed, but as I had nothing else I could do, I continued. I reminded him of Ibrox, told him that Leitch had never faced an enquiry or a trial, that he had tried to hide some evidence, and that he had never been paid for the job by Rangers. But he had then gone on and built elsewhere.

"So you are looking for what exactly?" he asked.

"Another ground with problems, or other cases of him not being paid, or anything unusual. Or failing that something you can make up. He built Old Trafford. Did it work – is it good?"

"Sad to say, Jacko, it is ok. Nothing has fallen down. No terrace problems. But I'll enquire. If he was not paid a proper fee I'll tell you."

I went back to the typewriter.

The piece started, "If you notice a crack in the concrete where you are standing, the chances are you are in a ground designed by Archibald Leitch."

It was a hatchet job. I didn't really like it, but as far as I could see all the facts were right, and even if he was nothing worse than a sloppy workman, he deserved some exposure for that.

I had just finished when the telephone rang. James Williamson. "I'll tell you straight off that Manchester United has problems in the terracing. Tell me something else you know, and I'll give you a bit more."

"Chelsea has terrace problems. There hasn't been a week for the past five years where there hasn't been part of the terracing that is not roped off. I think they used the wrong concrete mix."

"Ditto Old Trafford. To be fair it is minor, but there are rumblings. Anything else I should look for?"

"You could check planning permissions," I said. "If there is an offence it will be small, but it can all add up."

We said our farewells, and I re-wrote my piece with Manchester's concrete added to the mix and handed it in. I had expected a grilling on the facts, but to my surprise the story went through almost untouched. My reputation seemed to be doing me some good.

In the evening I played *Rich Man's Blues* on the guitar to the band. They had no idea what I was playing and couldn't follow it at all.

Saturday 17th September

Continuing my "taunt Norris" line I went to Craven Cottage. Fulham lost by one goal to nothing against Hull City. 16,000 in the crowd, which meant that Fulham and Woolwich were existing on a similar sort of income – although Woolwich were trying to do this in the First Division. I tried the chant of "Too short Fulham," and this time, instead of menaces from a large gent from the far north, I found that, for a reason I could not possibly explain, the lad on my left took up the call. "Too short Fulham," he shouted. "Too right, mate," I replied. "Too short Fulham!"

"Who's too short?" said the man on my right.

"Fulham," I replied. "Too short Fulham! No movement! No second ball!"

The youngster on the left agreed. "Too short. No movement, no second ball."

"You're right there," said the man on the right. "No second ball." And then louder, "No bloody second ball Fulham".

It spread. Not like wildfire but it spread. Ah, Mr Norris, I thought, make of this what you can. I turned to the man behind, and on the pretext of instructing him in the finer art of the famous "second ball" tactic, I scanned the ground for unusual movement. There was none. But he nodded appreciatively and accepted my judgement. "No second ball," he said to the fellow on his right.

"No!" I said. I thought that covered most of it.

"Fulham catch the Second Ball disease," my headline said. I made no attempt to explain what I meant, largely because I hadn't the slightest idea. I did however add that I heard a man nearby sing *Rich Man's Blues* to his mate at half time.

Woolwich Arsenal lost at Aston Villa by three goals to nil, and so far this season they have not won a match. As I typed up my report, *Rich Man's Blues* continued in my head. It is as if I have been tricked into thinking that everything I have ever heard or played was music, when in fact music is something else, something far more powerful… I can play the song now on the guitar and maybe in another 200 years I might be able to sing it like those negroes.

I finished off my piece with a review of the police marching band at half time.

After that I went home, packed my case and took the bus back to Dorset Square, for an overnight stay and then…

Sunday 18th September

My first ever Holiday: Marie, Sophia, Edward and I in the Rolls, with as much luggage as we could pack in. I insisted on bringing the guitar, even though I can only play one song. There was much commentary, but as I said, if I can't be eccentric in their company what can I be?

There was much giggling as the girls put on their fake wedding rings (Marie doing so while driving which caused much hilarity as we missed a giant ditch near Acton). We headed south west.

I argued that the issue of the money had thrown us all off track – we were no longer seeing spies who wanted to know about ships in the dockyards, but something far harder to understand. Everyone we passed by could be carrying some of the sovereigns or even the fives. No one disagreed, largely because it is impossible to hear yourself talk in a car let alone have a conversation.

It had been clear to me from the start that our original plan of driving to Plymouth was not on, at least not if we actually wanted any time out of the car during the week. It was interesting to see that the others had no idea of the need for any sort of planning. They were just saying, "Yes, we'll do it", and "It will be fine, you'll see" without even looking at the map. I suppose it was the army again; towards the end when we were running out of officers – or at least officers who were not dead drunk or dead scared – those of us who could think, did.

So I had drawn up a new plan, and the rest of the holiday party giggled and said "Yes, Captain".

If I had got my calculations right (and we would know on that first day) we should be able to stay in Poole for a day halfway through the trip. If not, we had a day spare and could change the route to catch up. I had even thought of bringing a map. The others had brought hampers of food and champagne and fine glasses and cutlery. I think they believed that there was no civilisation beyond Reading. Probably expected to find Romans and Celts.

While I had been searching the parliamentary records when writing up the Parliament Act piece I had found the Farnham Gas and Electricity Bill going through the Commons – which meant they had power – which is why I had chosen the town for our first stop. The rest of the party had just assumed gas and electricity were everywhere, so were not surprised.

Marie told us that she intended to commit a crime in each place we visited. I closed my eyes and prayed to a God I did not believe in. We made better time than I had imagined and got to Farnham in time for afternoon tea.

We went to the best hotel in town (of course), the Queen Anne, and then went for a wander. There was much interest in the pottery kilns they had discovered, showing that ancient industry existed there.

And a Roman settlement, which interested Edward. He took photographs in the gathering gloom. "It was a Saxon village," he said, and I tried not to show my ignorance of who or what the Saxons were. But either I wasn't very good or he was going to tell me anyway. "King Alfred the Great brought the Saxons together and fought the Danes," he said.

"Why were we fighting the Danes?"

"Because they occupied most of England."

"When was that?" I asked.

"Around the eighth century."

"That's all right then."

In the hotel bar the barman told us that this was where the road to the west met the road from the east – or something like that – I rather lost touch with the conversation as it drifted between past and present.

There was apparently a castle too, and there was much talk of seeing it tomorrow, along with a 1000 year old church. How these people could not read a map and yet could debate the ancient history of the country that I had no idea had ever existed was quite beyond me. This town had had the plague, I was told.

They also talked about people travelling to work from here to London by train each day – which took me by surprise. And then we went off to find a pub and discovered the William Cobbett – another historical landmark – and

215

something perhaps closer to our current area of interest. Cobbett was a political radical and he was born here. Not just here in the town apparently but in this pub.

We dined well and went for a walk, Marie disappeared for a while and came back with a silver ring on her finger. We said nothing.

Monday 19th September

My confidence has been rising following a successful first day, and I relaxed more, worrying less about the route and judging that if we did take the wrong mud track we were all having too much fun and no one was going to blame me.

Poole on the map had looked interesting – a huge harbour stretching for miles inland and a port. We might not be going to Plymouth, but we could at least see some shipping.

It was a big town. 20,000 people according to the reference book – which of course was the size of Woolwich Arsenal's ground – but for a port that struck me as huge.

There were potteries and several signs to Bournemouth which I plan to visit tomorrow. It has a sandy beach according to the map – and it will be my first look at such a place. I tried not to let my excitement show and asked if the Danes had occupied Poole. Apparently they had got as far as Cornwall.

On the harbour front we dutifully admired the Customs House and Harbour Office and the swing bridge across the harbour entrance and sat in a quayside pub surveying the scene. The ships carried grain and fish.

I was frustrated that we had not taken the matter of spies and fake money further forward, which only led Edward to say that since we were paying for each hotel with the mysterious five pound notes we were doing all we could to bring the criminals to us. I hadn't realised that this was how the trip was being funded.

We found a suitable hotel. It had a ballroom. We danced, not quite till dawn, but close. The Monkey Shrug had not reached this part of the Empire, it seems, and by midnight a crowd had gathered.

"They think we are clowns," said Sophia.

"Just don't let go," I said, as I did the double twister.

Tuesday 20th September

A further look at Poole – we were told by the hotelier that we had to see the Park and note the cinema that had opened in the town centre the previous month. And then on towards Bournemouth. All very gentle – everyone seemed much older than us, and life proceeded at one tenth of the speed of London.

We walked on the sand in our naked feet and splashed in the sea. Afterwards in a pub we agreed there was nothing to suggest that the notes we had found in Woolwich at the General Abercrombie were not the business.

I announced that I was happier than ever I had been in my entire life, sitting in a pub opposite a beach in the late summer sun with my best friends and the woman I loved. There was much cheering and raising of glasses, but Marie wanted to explore musical issues and wouldn't be swayed. "It must be like you seeing a painting or a sculpture which I can't fully see," I suggested. "I can explain elements of the music, but all of it is more than an individual line, and the words are not adequate. When I explain it, it falls apart."

I sang *Rich Man's Blues* again, and Sophia accompanied me with the spoons. I wasn't sure it added anything to the musical experience.

Edward lifted his glass. "To music," he said. "You are the maestro on that score, and we bow to your knowledge," and the glasses all came up again, and my happiness reached a new level brought down only by the theft of a motor car by Marie that night. She had the grace to return it to the place from which she took it, after a little ride, but deliberately left it pointing the other way.

We persuaded her not to return in the morning to see if the owner noticed.

Wednesday 21st September

Bristol was more alive than anything else we had seen on the trip; everyone told us to see the famous suspension bridge and the electric trains, the ship building, and the chocolate making. Poole was a little town; this was a city. It was noted by Edward that there was a university, and by the ladies that it took women.

We sat for the evening meal, two "married" couples, travelling, and thoroughly enjoying life. Whether I could actually get used to not thinking about every penny we spent I doubted – even though we had no idea of the source of the money.

We were more boisterous than we had been at previous evening meals – perhaps more certain of our position, more creative, more inventive. Sophia brought a paper to the table and we read it between us, deriding comments, condemning the lack of insight, the lack of good football coverage, the lack of coverage of the Suffragettes, the lack of insightful analysis of the two murder stories. And we ended with a very loud toast to "The Chron."

"All the words," I said, rising to my feet, "I toast all the words."

No one knew what I meant, but they raised their glasses, and Edward patted me on the back as if I had just spoken an eternal truth.

A young man from a table near by, who looked like he was staying with his parents, approached. "I say," he said. "You don't work for the Chronicle do you?" he said. I said that Edward and I did, and that Marie was with the Times, and started to apologise for disturbing his and everyone else's dinner with our noise.

He ignored the apology. "Do you remember that story, The King of London?"

I told him I did – by and large – remember the gist.

"I just thought it was the best thing I had ever read in a paper. My parents," he nodded across the room, "they don't like it, of course. Say it is dangerous and revolutionary, so I have to read it privately. I think they," he indicated the parents again, "are going to complain to the management."

"Yes, most rude of us," I concurred.

"Jacko – why do you feel the need to apologise to everyone?" interrupted Marie. "We were raising our glasses to toast the venerable Chronicle. That is not a matter for apology."

"Because these people," I waved my hand towards the young man's parents, "have as much right to be here as we do. They are not interrupting or disturbing us, so why should we disturb them? It is not good manners."

"Jacko Jones!" said Sophia. "I do believe you are being very middle class."

I was about to reply, but the young man interrupted. "You are Jacko Jones?" he said peering at me. "I mean you are Jacko Jones! Are you?"

I admitted that by and large and all things considered, taking the long and short, I was he.

He then screamed, put his hand to his mouth, and then proceeded to tell me that I was the funniest man he had ever read, funnier than that Mr Wodehouse, and how he would like to have my autograph – and how he had the whole King of London series pasted in his scrapbook. And when was it going to be published as a complete book, and when were there going to be more, and why weren't the stories twice as long… and "Where do you get all your ideas from?"

I told him I had no idea where the ideas came from. I have never had any idea where the ideas come from, but that didn't seem to be the right answer. The others were looking at me, so I changed tack and said, "They were left to me by my father." The young man looked serious, and then laughed. "Doesn't your father give you any ideas?" I continued. The young man, who gave me a card proclaiming that he was Gerald Smithson-Blythe, said that his father was bereft of all ideas except the need to rid the country of Mr Churchill, whom he described as a traitor to his class and a menace to society.

"It must be difficult," I said, "not being left any ideas by your ancestors. That must mean you have to think for yourself."

Picking up the idea he laughed and said that, yes, that was his problem. I asked him to join us at our table.

"Jacko is an expert on The Blues," said Sophia. "It is a new kind of music. From America. If you are extremely rude to him he will sing you a Blues song, just to annoy."

That evening, after Gerald Smithson-Blythe had left us to our port, I asked the rest of the ensemble why everything had to make sense. They looked at me curiously, but were hesitant to come straight back in with an answer.

"I can't make sense of the fact that when I look at a globe of the world, I can see South Africa, and it looks like everyone there is upside down. But I have been there and they were not upside down and didn't fall off. I can't explain why *Rich Man's Blues* is the most important piece of music in the world, so why should I be able to explain what the Saviours are and why some idiot left two bundles of notes at the Abercrombie? What makes sense of the fact that young Gerald thinks The King of London is the funniest thing in the world and his parents want Mr Churchill strung up from the nearest tree with photos of the hanging appearing in every morning paper?"

"A world without meaning?" asked Marie.

"Just as long as it is not a world without photographs," said Edward.

"Or Jacko Jones," said Marie.

Thursday 22nd September

No university in Reading. The girls called the town backwards. I offered to show everyone the football ground, but there were no takers. The Royal was a fine hotel, another jeweller's provided Marie with some late night entertainment, and once again we paid our bills with Woolwich money.

Sophia told us about her feelings for the Movement, as she called the Suffragettes, and argued that even if nothing else had meaning the Movement certainly did. Edward looked on occasion slightly ill-at-ease which was interesting.

"Talk to me," said Marie when we were alone. "Make sense of the world with your words."

"The world is made of clowns," I said.

"Just hold on to it all," she said.

"Talking to yourself is cheating," I said.

Friday 23rd September

My schedule held up, the car survived, our friendships have deepened, and my life has changed once again. I lived for five days without any concern for work or money. People brought us food and drink at our command, we did as we pleased, and others did as we said. It isn't the real world, which is why the conversations without meaning fit well.

Tomorrow I shall be back in the land I know, which is unsettling. But Edward is in that real world with me – although he doesn't have to be. Marie is in my world too, also completely by choice. And Sophia is in the world of a full time politician – except working outside of the boundaries of being elected. A bit like someone in the Lords, I suppose.

Saturday 24th September

I suggested that since I had been the guest in my friend's adventure, they should be in my adventure: I took them to Woolwich Arsenal.

As she drove the car into Kent Marie announced more firmly than before that she wanted to meet my parents. I caught an exchange of glances between Edward and Sophia, which made it plain that they had known this was coming up.

We watched Woolwich Arsenal 0 Sunderland 0, a travesty of football. The gang sympathised with my plight but proved to be very good at joining in the "Too short Woolwich," commentary. Then Sophia and Edward started an argument, Edward saying that Woolwich were "Too short" while Sophia suggested that it was a question of the "Second ball". Within moments others in the crowd, driven to distraction by the poverty of the game, joined in, taking sides at random between the arguing couple. I tried to suggest that "Movement" was the issue, but was fiercely shouted down.

I also did my best to give the ladies some news of interest. The game saw the return of the outside left, David Neave, playing his first game of the season at right half. David had been at the club since I'd returned from Africa, and had even managed somehow to wangle his brother Andrew into the club (although Andrew had never actually played).

"But shouldn't you be right-footed to play on the right?" asked Marie, watching Neave intently. I told her she was dead right and ought to apply for the post as manager.

After that we turned to the programme. Gunner's Mate had gone berserk, tearing into the team with a style of criticism that went beyond anything even I said in the newspaper. This was a story worth following up.

After the game we returned to Dorset Square where several scratches were noticed on the car by those who are paid to note such things, but it didn't take the edge off our safe return – and I was rather pleased to note there were expressions of admiration for my navigational skills. In fact I got more praise for working out how to reach Poole than I ever had for a somewhat more taxing journey from Bloemfontein to Colesberg in 1901.

On the home front there was no news about Woolwich Woman, the money, Mr Churchill, spies, the Saviours, or indeed anything I was working on.

Monday 26th September

Edward and I presented ourselves at the offices and were greeted by Mr Holloway with the inevitable, "What have you got for us then?"

We told him we had been on holiday, and had not been paid for the adventure. "Don't think that doesn't mean you don't have to work," Mr Holloway replied. I thought there were too many negatives in that sentence but let it pass.

Edward protested that he had taken some interesting shots of the towns we visited, and that by publishing them the newspaper would move away from being so London-centred.

Mr Holloway would have none of this. "Of course we are London-centred," he said. "The world is London-centred."

He then instructed us to go and watch a charity match between Fulham and Woolwich Arsenal at Craven Cottage, to annoy Norris, and take pictures. He also said that there were reports that the Martian canals were showing signs of shipping activity, and he wanted pictures of that too.

Edward started talking about fixing his camera to a telescope, but I kicked him from behind and took him to Fulham. And I am so glad I did because we got our break.

The gang were hard to miss because the crowd was so small. They were working more openly this time, placing coins into people's hands or pockets and walking on.

We walked round and placed ourselves in their path, and each of us duly got a sovereign. Edward suggested he would spend it, but I was adamant this was evidence. For what I don't know.

We watched the men move around the ground, and I walked behind them at a suitable distance as Edward did his best to get a photograph. When they got to the grandstand they walked across to the gates which were, of course, locked to stop non-payers entering, and demanded an exit. Looking at them from close up it was clear these were people who normally got what they wanted.

We followed them at a safe distance up Harvard Street to the bustle of Fulham Palace Road and across the avenues as they headed north eventually turning into Aintree Street where, without bothering to look behind them, they entered one of the tenement blocks. We noted the number and waited.

"Looks like a job for Marie," said Edward, and I cuffed him.

"What was the score?"

He looked at me blankly.

"Mr Holloway is going to want the score of the match. We were sent to cover the football."

At half past five we gave up and walked back to the football ground and found a groundsman. Woolwich had won by three goals to two he said, but it was a poor game. I wrote it in my notebook.

Tuesday 27th September

For lunch I met George Allison in the Retreat and quizzed him about his programme notes. Apparently Norris is very happy with the attacks on the players. "Calls them a load of good-for-nothings," said George, "tells me I can say anything I like. You and I are alike."

I asked him how so.

"I tear into players, and you tear into the men at the top – Norris, Leitch, anyone else you can lay your hands on."

"Is that what football reporting has come to?" I asked.

"You've seen them play," said George. "What do you think?"

I agreed. They were rubbish.

Wednesday 28th September

Edward came up with another idea: the money is used to fix football matches. I found it hard to see what distributing it within the ground was about in that case, and we lapsed into silence.

"Even if the money was fake," I said. "it doesn't work as a theory – the money gets spotted sooner or later and the person who has been given the money gets rather annoyed with the person who gave it to him. Which is why real money is a better bet, but I still can't explain anything."

We looked at each other.

"Unless…

"You don't know who gave you the money."

"Because that person just stuffed it in your pocket."

"But that still doesn't solve anything."

"No,"

Thursday 29th September

"Mum, dad, would you like to meet Marie?" I asked over breakfast.

"And about time too," said mum. "Turning me into the laughing stock of the street, not having met her." Mum was resplendent in her mumness.

"Mum, I want you to meet Marie, because she is my girlfriend, and the truth is I love her...."

"Have you told her?" mum interrupted.

I said I had but in a roundabout way, and asked her to let me finish. She told me off for lecturing her, and then we argued about what a lecture was, before mum realised she had been successfully sidetracked. So she started up again, and I just stood there and waited.

"Mum, I would like you to meet Marie, but on my terms, not on yours." I said at last.

"You are trying to tell me what to do in my own house?" she shouted. "Well I never. My son..."

And then dad, the quietest, calmest, warmest of men, stepped in. He laid a hand gently on mum's shoulder. "Annie," he said calmly, "the lad is offering to do what you have wanted him to do all year. Don't spoil it. Let him tell you what he plans."

There was silence in the house. A rare thing.

"I want you to meet Marie, because she is my ladyfriend. I don't want it to be a street thing, with everyone leaning out of their windows to catch a glimpse of her, and you telling everyone about it. I want you to meet her, as if she was Doris from number 45."

"Well, you can't keep things like this quiet," said mum, her waterfall of words pouring over me. "Mrs Clarkson from next door will have to know, otherwise she'll be upset thinking I'm hiding things from her, and she is my oldest friend. I am not having her upset because of your new hoity toity ideas. People will talk, and what am I to tell them? A laughing stock, that is what I am. There's already talk of you talking to black men from Africa in the streets of Wood Green. Much more of this and we'll have to move out. Me! Forced out of my own home because my son can't think of anything but himself! Black men, indeed. You know what people will say round here. I don't mind them, of course, but the neighbours talk."

"Any minute now and you'll tell me I can't go to Tottenham Hotspur because the ground is full of Jews," I retorted, raising my voice to about 1 percent of mum's current level.

"Now son," said dad, but it had gone beyond that. Mum was on a high, and I was not backing down. Mum was complaining about Edward's fiancé being a suffragette and how she was becoming the laughing stock.

I went out to play with the band. As I left mum said, "So when shall I say she's coming round, this ladyfriend of yours? When shall we meet all your hoity toity friends, or are we not good enough?" I said I'd let her know but we'd need to speak about it some more because I was not happy with her attitude.

It wasn't a good thing to say, but then, coming back home after a week away had been tough.

Friday 30th September

I suggested to Marie that the only way to introduce her to my parents was to turn up with no warning. They are always in from five o'clock onwards so we just do it. Then mum won't have a chance to sell tickets. After that we could invite them round the next night to Dorsct Square.

I told her of Julian, who had died in the War. Marie had a brother who was in India with the army and a sister who was married and living in Shropshire with an arch-Unionist. It was so strange. We had known each other eight months and never asked these questions before. "At the moment there are only dots," said Marie. "Only when they connect do we see the picture."

At work, it appears that Leitch is suing the paper. He's probably taken legal advice from Norris. With nothing else to do I started to write a story about the Slayer of Souls.

In the Winchester Bar stands a lady. She is past the first flush of youth, but attractive with an oval face and long flowing hair. Men have been known to fight duels over the chance to lead her in a waltz. Yet there is something in her face, something that says, there are depths are so hidden you don't even know they are there...

...The job of the slayer of souls is to unravel the meanings that are forced into your brain. You see the world as others invent it, not as it really is. She wants to change the world and destroy the vortex but she doesn't explain exactly how...

Tony Attwood

Saturday 1st October

"But what the devil is it?" said Mr Holloway. He took his glasses off, and inspected them, suspicious that they were carrying messages of their own.

"The opening of a story," I said. "For the Review."

"The Review," he repeated, pretending he was the one person in the Street who hadn't heard that the Chron was launching its own weekly magazine. I wasn't in the mood.

"We're worried about the rising sales of The Sphere, so we have to fight back," I said more slowly than was strictly necessary. The Sphere is the Suffragettes' magazine.

"But it doesn't have a start or an end," he said, looking at my *Slayer of Souls* piece again, as if was a slice of a dog just dragged out of the Houndsditch.

"It has a start," I protested, "and it will end later. I'm offering it through you to the Review."

"And you don't have anything on the discovery of the highest mountain in the world in the north of Scotland?"

"No. If you don't want it I'll take it to The Popular Magazine. They are doing Rider Haggard, so why not me?"

"Because he can write. So can Zane Grey." (Thus revealing that he did read the weeklies.)

"The last copy had 194 pages," I said, which proved nothing but sounded important. "I could write for them, and if my work is as bad as you say it might close them down if they publish me. I'd be doing the Chron a favour."

He scowled, and I left for Woolwich Arsenal 0 Oldham 0, in front of a miserable crowd of 12,000. Three 0-0 draws in a row, meaning the Gunners have played six, drawn four and lost two.

I found George, and put it to him that he was going to get shot soon, either by a player or a supporter or by Norris. In the programme notes he was now describing the team as pathetic and playing like children, the training methods as old-fashioned, and the management as dangerously outmoded.

"But you are a fan, George, you are always here," I said. "You can't do this to your own team."

"I can if it will make them better. I can't print pieces that say, 'Norris is trying to bring Woolwich down so that he can merge them quickly and then build houses on the land', but I can write pieces that make people think."

Then I added, "One other thing... have you seen those men who walk through the ground – a group of about six or eight of them."

"The pickpockets? Yes, you get them at other grounds too."

"In such numbers?" I asked, trying to find the key question without giving myself away.

"Saw them at Chelsea, Tottenham, Clapton, Fulham. Regular thing."

"But I thought they worked in two's."

"Change of the times. We are no longer Edwardians – George is on the throne and even the pickpockets have changed their tactics."

We had a laugh, and I went off, making my notes on the bus across town.

I had taken the precaution of leaving some clothes at Dorset Square and, despite my protests that I was perfectly capable of looking after my own kit, I found them neatly pressed and laid out for me in what was now becoming "Mr Jones' room".

Several friends of Lord Cortney dined with us, and there was talk of "taking on the Lords" (meaning the House, not my host) and "changing the constitution once and for all". I even heard the word 'Revolution' mentioned – although perhaps without the capitalisation.

One immoderate guest, Sir Richard Guverns, stated that he felt the Liberals had to "destroy the Lords by any means." He once even turned to me saying, "Can't you write something, Jones, to make sure that everyone knows what asses the Lords are being."

I pointed out that I was a journalist not an editor, and while I could write something, there was no certainty that I could get it published. Unless, of course, they gave me some news that turned it into a insightful story rather than just my opinion. Something along the lines that there was a secret gathering of Liberals, including some peers, at a rendezvous in west London on Saturday night where the talk was of nothing short of Revolution (with the capitalisation). The discussion was not over whether something should be done about the Upper House, but of ways and means. That, I suggested, might persuade the fifth floor.

Of course, at that they backed away, yet Lord Cortney's eyes twinkled. I have to admit I do like the old boy. I think we share a sense of mischief.

Sunday 2nd October

The article written upon my return from holiday has not seen the light of day and has evidently been spiked. No one seemed to know where in the building the start of the Slayer story had gone, so I decided to give Mr Holloway something else to think about.

I wrote a piece about "Gunners' Mate" with his outrageous attacks on the club in the programme and suggested that Norris allows this to continue because he doesn't want the club to succeed – and also that there is discontent on the terraces.

But not as much discontent as might be imagined, I added, because of the new London phenomenon – of the Put-pocket. "We all know the Pick-Pocket", I wrote, "who will happily relieve you of your lunch money or that threepence put by for a pint in the pub. But now the football grounds of London are witness to a new spectacle. The Put-pocket. The men who put money into your pocket." I listed the clubs where the gang had been spotted, and said you'd think that the supporters would be queuing at the gate when they had a chance to come out of the Manor Ground with more money than when they went in. But only 12,000 turned up for the last game.

What is the matter with London? I asked. "Doesn't anyone want something for nothing any more?"

I then suggested that the police could do nothing because the money was being given not taken, and the clubs could do nothing because the gangs broke no law. They even paid to get into the grounds.

Finally, I invited the readership to write to the paper and tell us why this was happening – and if they had seen it at other football grounds. If not, would they welcome the put-pockets at their ground?

Mr Holloway kept me in his room, standing in front of his desk, while he read the piece. He slapped it down on the table and shouted, "Is this true?"

"Of course it's true," I said quietly. "Do you think I make all this up?"

"'Of course it's true'," he mimicked. "Of course you make it up, you're a journalist. You're also an idiot," he said. "What are you?"

"A reporter," I said.

He stumped out the room, came back ten minutes later and told me to get out of his sight.

I asked who was handling my submission for the Review. He told me to look into the problem on the Great Western where three locomotives had disappeared in the tunnels in the past ten days.

Monday 3rd October

My story made the front page. "Sovereigns being given away at London football matches – Exclusive". Apparently the intrepid Jacko Jones had been on the trail since the start of the season, and was now able to present his findings from the grounds around the capital.

Woolwich Arsenal and Gunners' Mate were dropped – this was entirely about the Put-pockets – and they kept my phrase. They also kept the invite to readers to suggest what was going on, and whether it was happening in their neck of the woods. I hoped the old ladies in the letters' office wouldn't mind too much.

And, oh yes, they also announced that a new serial by Jacko Jones would be appearing in the next edition of the Review. Strangely no one thought to tell Jacko Jones.

There being nothing for me to do in the office, I took my day off, and spent it with Marie and decided today was going to be the day. Marie would meet mum and dad (not to mention vice versa). We strolled into my parents' house at just after six o'clock. We were as ready as we could ever be.

These Edwardian semi-detached houses have a little private alley at the side of the house which leads round to the back door. That door leads directly into the kitchen. It is the route into the house used by all scruffy urchins not given a front door key and had been my route into the house since I moved in after the war. It was how I led Marie in.

Mum was cooking. The kitchen was in its usual well-organised well-disciplined state. Any plate or fork out of position would have been severely disciplined and reprimanded by mum at breakfast and was unlikely to see our house again. We take these matters seriously in Wood Green.

"Hello, mum," I called in as normal a voice as I could manage. Mum didn't turn. "'Lo, Jack," she replied. "Take your boots off before you walk through my kitchen."

"Mum, this is Marie. Marie, this is my mother."

Mum turned round, looked, dropped the cup and saucer she was holding, and screamed. Quite loudly. And quite a lot.

Dad came in from the sitting room at a double trot, took note of the situation, helped me pick the broken crockery off the floor and led mum to a chair.

"No," my mum kept saying. "No, you wouldn't do this to me, Jack. Not like this. I'm sorry, miss, but you don't know my Jack. He's a naughty lad, and he shouldn't scare me like this."

She hadn't actually fainted, merely tottered a little in surprise, so we just took her through into the parlour and sat her down. Dad made her a cup of tea as we re-established that this was Marie.

"I'm sorry, your ladyship," mum began, and gave me a look of utter dismay when I laughed.

"I have the same problem with Marie's father," I said, and Marie came to the rescue saying that she would like to be called Marie.

Mum then went into a long piece about how the place was such a mess, and how if only I'd said, she would have made something special, and how, no we couldn't possibly have tea out of those old cups that dad had brought in, they were all chipped (which of course was untrue. Anyway I always reckoned that if a cup got damaged next door, mum would know and suggest that the neighbours should move because they were bringing down the tone of the neighbourhood).

I told mum that Marie and I often had lunch in Lyons Cornershop, and that our everyday crockery was way above their standard, and mum said, "And so I should hope – whatever will Marie think with you comparing your home to a corner shop," and so it went on.

And on.

Eventually the storm around the house calmed a little and we talked and established that it was better that mum should meet Marie like this, because Marie could see where I lived in a normal state without anything artificial going on, and it would be unfair on Marie if she couldn't get the true picture, because my home is a reflection myself, and stuff like that.

Dad was wonderful. He was calm, asked simple questions about Marie, her work, why she'd left the Times, what she wanted to do, what stories she worked on, which ones she enjoyed, if she knew Edward of whom I had spoken, and whether she had met the difficult Mr Holloway (she confirmed she had not). In fact he was perfect. He focussed totally on Marie. Not a word about her father and his politics. Not a word about our house. He was sincere, kind and helpful. I loved him more at that moment than I ever had before.

And as it was all going so well I then dropped the second bombshell. Mum and dad were invited to Dorset Square tomorrow evening. That we reckoned would not stop mum going out and buying new clothes, but would make life easier for dad – he'd only have to put up with a day of preparations – and mum would have to choose between a day shopping or a day telling the neighbours.

Mum made to faint, but we told her not to, and Marie laughed, and so mum laughed, and Marie told mum that Lady Cortney was just the same and how they'd get on like a house on fire.

Then we got ready to leave, and of course mum wanted to know where we were going. I told her we were going to the White Hart where the band was playing, and mum was horrified that Marie – a lady – should be going to such a rough public house. Or indeed any public house.

And Marie said it was fine, she'd been before and everyone was very nice.

Tuesday 4th October

A curious note was on my desk. Someone had called (no name of course) and left a message for me on Monday. They said that I ought to look into the issue of St Michael's Church in Fulham.

I had no idea where the church was, but apparently we had a reference book on churches and one of the juniors looked it up. With nothing else to do and with every desire not to have to face the ladies in the letters' room, I took the bus to St Michael's. It was a traditional church with all the trimmings and a vicarage next door. I knocked up the vicar, told him who I was, and said I was doing a piece about the churches, the number of parishioners who attend, and how the vicar sees the future.

The vicar, the Reverend Cuthbertson, was kind, polite and vicarly, telling me that his numbers were fairly solid, although the congregation was aging a little, but they had no worry.

And that was it. No story. Someone had been pulling my leg.

I left it at that and went back to Dorset Square for an afternoon with Marie before mum and dad arrived. We'd given Lord and Lady Cortney the rundown of how things had gone at my house, and they knew that my mum would be on tenterhooks, on the edge, half way over the edge, falling into the pit, hitting the bottom of the pit, bouncing back up, and occasionally somewhat muddled. The meal was to be kept simple, the wine was to be kept simple, the rituals were to be kept simple.

Best of all, Lord Cortney greeted my parents himself at the door, made every effort to talk my parents through the meal, explaining the oddities of etiquette just as their little ways, and explaining firmly to mum that just as her name was Mrs Jones, his name was Lord Cortney – and that was that. There were no other formalities to be done.

It was simple, it was kindly thought through, and I was pleased. Marie was too. At the end of the evening I took mum and dad back home in a cab, and it took mum all of, oh, I don't know, six or seven seconds before she announced what she was going to tell the rest of the street.

It took thirteen seconds for mum to ask me when we were getting engaged, and it took me one minute after that before I interrupted her tirade to say that she'd wanted to meet Marie's parents, and Marie had wanted to meet them. It would, I said, be a shame to spoil the two occasions by making demands.

There was a brief discussion on the topic of modern youngsters, their insolence, how I hadn't been the same since joining that wretched paper, and how there had been no telling me since I had appeared on the front page, and the subject was dropped.

It was, overall, a success.

Wednesday 5th October

The situation with the men at Aintree Street is simple, and our only course of action was clear. Edward, Marie, Sophia and I decamped to the street and took in the scenery. The houses had no rear exit, which made it easier, but as with Woolwich Woman we had no notion of whether the men were in the house or not.

After an hour of no movement during which time I gave the assembled troupe half a dozen unaccompanied versions of *Rich Man's Blues*, it was clear we needed "phase 2" (as Sophia had taken to calling it), as the alternative was that she would procure a shotgun from a friend in Fulham Palace Road and put a premature end to the Blues as a form of music performed by a white man. She also spoke of "plan B" but none of us had any idea of what that was although it too probably involved violence.

Edward went to the door, holding the sovereign that he had been given, and knocked, with the plan that if the door were opened he would hand it over as if returning found property. The story was thin, but sometimes so is ice, and Edward with his upper class voice could probably convince water to support his weight even as the temperature soared into the 60s. To the incumbents he would just appear to be another toff slightly off his rocker.

But no one came. Which meant we had no alternative but to allow Marie to do a bit more breaking and entering. Worryingly, she was actually getting faster each time she did it.

I stayed by the door, Edward down below, Sophia further up the street, whistles at the ready. Marie took six minutes, came out carrying a parcel and said, "let's move away quickly." We did as told. No calls of, "Why, what have you found?" as they do in the boys' adventure comics. We just moved. Once away we took it at a normal speed, two couples strolling along together, back into the bustle of Fulham Palace Road, and onto an omnibus, and then a tram. I sang *Rich Man's Blues* again which made sure no one approached us.

We went eventually to Dorset Square and then, in the library, with no one near by, Marie talked.

Two large boxes each filled with sovereigns. Plus a set of letters. The letters were of the type that Woolwich Woman had received – from various centres around the country and full of everyday chitchat most certainly with nothing about anything to do with spies. They were not the sort of letters that the men we had followed to the Aintree Street flat would be receiving. Indeed I wondered about their ability to read.

Oh, and a stash of guns. Marie had removed one of each type.

We sat there and tried to draw some conclusions or, failing that, a plan of action or, failing that, 'Plan B'. Failing that, I said I would sing the Blues again.

First, we agreed, this was irrefutable evidence that the bundles of money and the everyday letters were linked. We'd assumed this, and now we knew. Second, it showed that Woolwich Woman was not isolated. George had said the put-pockets were elsewhere – this was more proof of how widespread their activity was.

Third, the link could be Norris, since he was involved centrally with both clubs – but that didn't fit easily. A few visits to Chelsea or Tottenham – or, come to that, Clapton or the smaller clubs like Brentford – would indicate if the game were being played beyond Norris' boundary of influence. We guessed it was.

Fourth, we needed to know what the secret message was behind the letters Marie had picked up. And that was a significant problem since the only person we knew who could do this was Dr Knox, and he had realised that we were not in Mr Churchill's inner circle of confidence. That led to the idea that we might bring in Lord Cortney except that, as Marie said, he was an active member of the political party that had Mr Churchill as one of its prize spokesmen.

She put speaking to her father down as a last resort which meant trying to find another decoder. Dr Knox was at the Admiralty who were hardly going to take lightly to a journalist, a photographer, and their lady friends walking in and asking for help, no matter how high born three of the party turned out to be. Access to government secrets was probably not on.

Fifth, we agreed that without seeing what was in the secret code behind the letters we had no idea of what the underlying issue was. Nor who was running the show. We could try following the people carrying money, but on this point I was cautious. "Breaking and entering is one thing," I argued, "and I suspect I am the only one here who really knows the consequences, having spent some time at His Majesty's pleasure. But coming face to face with this gang, or whatever they are, is not going to be a picnic. Just because we are unscathed so far does not mean that round the next corner there is not a knife waiting to be pushed into the stomach."

And that brought us to the guns. Marie had picked up a Dreyse pistol and a Mauser C96. "The best and the latest," I said, checking six times to make sure the safety catches were on. "I doubt anyone in the country has access to these."

So we looked at the guns and considered. Do we carry on alone, three toffs and a journalist taking on either the criminal underworld or the entire German military might (depending on who was behind all this), or do we find someone in authority who is not going to cut us out of the picture as Mr Churchill has done?

Thursday 6th October

I continued with the Slayer story.

"I will be your servant," say the men who fall under her spell. "Command and I will obey. Take my soul – I give it willingly. And give me orders, for all I ask is to serve you. Angel or devil, Alyson, I take you as you are. I take all that

you represent, all that you will become. In return take me from this world and do not force me to worry or think ever again...."

She turned to me, and looked me straight in the eyes. "Trust yourself, and you are free. These souls..." she gestured to the pathetic line following her, "they cannot be free, because they cannot trust themselves. They are so set in their way. The ghost walkers."

Friday 7th October

If there is a cardinal rule to being a successful criminal, I imagine it must be not to return to the scene of a crime. Marie does not believe in rules.

Tonight the Lord Mayor of London held a ball at the Mansion House for the district and borough mayors, people such as Norris. Tonight Marie decided to do his house once more.

At least this time she allowed me to stand guard, whistle at the ready, but there was no disturbance. She was in and out so fast that I doubted that she had been in at all – or I would have doubted her had I not seen the way her work was speeding up.

We walked from the scene calmly, using the back streets until well away from the area.

"Nothing," she said. Another dead end.

Saturday 8th October

Mr Philpott, blond hair rakishly combed from the centre and flopping over his ears, had taken rooms on the fourth. On the door it said, "The Weekly Review." I didn't bother to knock.

"Jones?"

I concurred.

"Mr Holloway says you write football reports!"

"From time to time," I said.

"And you wrote the King of London story that appeared in the Chronicle itself?"

I agreed that this was a reasonable summary of events this year.

"Your story about the Slayer of Souls got a lot of letters," he said.

"It gives the dear ladies who answer them something to do," I replied.

"Who is this Slayer of Souls?" he asked.

"I have no idea." I said.

"Is she a ghost?"

"I doubt it," I said.

He thumped the table, the effect only slightly reduced by the fact that it clearly hurt his hand. "Damn it, man – what happens? How does the story end?"

"I don't know," I said, "I haven't got to the end yet."

"This is intolerable," he said. "You can't write a story without knowing how it ends. Supposing you can't think of an ending? Then where would we be?"

"In the middle," I suggested.

"This is not how the Review works," he shouted.

"It's how Mr Holloway likes it," I said, and went back down to sports.

Mr Holloway made it clear (again) that he wanted regular football stories from me no matter what game I was playing with the literati, and with Woolwich Arsenal playing away at Bradford I had the option of nominating a game. Just to annoy him I chose Chelsea reserves against Tottenham reserves in the South East Counties League. It gave me the opportunity to go and look at the potholes while getting Edward to take some photographs for the lawyers in the Leitch case.

After ten minutes play we also found four large men doing the tour of the terracing, placing the money in welcoming hands.

I stayed out of sight as Edward took up a position and accepted a pound as the men passed by. They were around the ground and out again within half an hour, and after that we had little to do other than watch the match which ended with a Chelsea victory by four goals to two.

One point of interest was a gaggle of Tottenham men standing behind one goal. Edward got a couple of photographs of them, and we wondered if this trend would spread. "Why do it?" I asked. "Tottenham are playing at White Hart Lane today. Why not go there – why come here to watch the reserves?"

"Maybe they don't give out money at Tottenham games?" he asked. I chuckled – it gave me my story. The crowds are starting to follow the money. Good idea Edward.

We meandered back to Fleet Street and caught up with the results. Bradford City had beaten Woolwich 3 goals to nil in front of 26,000. Tottenham had drawn with Preston NE one goal each. Neither club was doing London proud.

"And now?" asked Edward as we headed back to the West End after filing the report and handing in the pictures for developing. We had shown that this practice of giving away money had grown – but it now looked like it was not a Norris plot – which cut my neat circle into shreds. And we didn't even dare to contemplate what they were doing with an arsenal of the most modern guns on the market.

We went to the Goring by Buckingham Palace. The doorman had Edward in fits by refusing to let me in because of my dress – I not having changed since the game. Eventually I got out my security card showing me to be a captain working directly for the Home Office and told the doorman that Edward was a dangerous lunatic-lord who meandered the streets in fancy dress to gain admittance to new nightclubs and who could only be kept under control by regular doses of gin. If we didn't get some soon, I suggested, we would all be in trouble.

The girls were already there, deep in yet another discussion about Suffragettes and why Marie would have nothing to do with them. I got dirty looks from the rest of the clientele, which got dirtier as I pushed Edward in front of me calling out, "Warder coming through. Dangerous lunatic, take care". Somehow our behaviour as a gang was getting out of control. And notorious, I noted, seeing a photographer from the Star close by.

We reflected. We had four incidents of passing money around inside three stadia and two major stashes of funds found in ludicrous places. We could go on following the people with money, we could go on breaking in, we could go on tracking football matches, we could go on taking packages and letters – but for what? Nothing was leading us closer to the solution. And there were the weapons.

"Part one," said Sophia (ignoring my interruption of "You mean it is not plan C?"), "is we need the Aintree Road letter decoded. And since even Cambridge University will have started up again by now, there is every chance that Dilly Knox has left town. Which means, Jacko, that you could stroll into the Admiralty, explain that Dr Knox did the last decoding, flash your government card and ask who can do this one, urgent. Hand it over, get the job done, and incidentally ask what chemicals they use so we can do it ourselves next time. Oh, and ask them when the next police assault on the Suffragettes is going to happen."

It sounded perfectly reasonable – apart from the last bit. I agreed to go on Monday.

"In the meanwhile," said Marie, "I think we should push the operation forward."

"What does that mean?" asked Edward, not unreasonably. It sounded horribly to me like Plan D.

"Think of the Suffragettes – as Sophia does day and night."

"How do you put up with that?" I interrupted, with a dig at Edward.

Marie would not be put off. "The Suffragettes are doing – they are not sitting around waiting or watching. They stand up and do."

"Marie and Sophia: women of action," said Edward.

"Jacko, you said in one of your articles that we are just people who watch," said Sophia.

"I didn't know you read my work in such detail," I joked. It was that kind of conversation – no one was letting anyone complete an idea. "But I have never claimed to be a person who is either logical or consistent – least of all in what I write."

"The Suffragettes do act – we are always acting, we are not sitting around. The miners act by going on strike. Mr Lloyd George is getting ready to act with his 'Set the dogs on us' speech. Even Norris acts – he wants to get control of Woolwich Arsenal so he does it. And someone is acting in this mystery – someone who has us running around in circles trying to catch him. We are the ones walking behind, watching."

"And what would you have us do?" I asked, "remembering that the enemy is armed, and we, most certainly, are not."

"Become a song and dance man," said Marie.

We all looked at her incredulously. "You can sit and watch the world from the outside, or you can get involved. What do you do with Woolwich Arsenal? You get involved – you taunt Norris by going to the ground when he says you can't. Edward takes pictures, and that very taking of pictures changes the world, because the people in the ground turn to look at Edward in his eccentric costume (sorry Edward!). We are doing the same chasing around Woolwich and with me going into the War Office. We are acting – and we need to do more of it. So much, in fact, that we become equal players on the stage with whoever is running the show. We stop being shadows, and become the leading man and lady."

And as I looked at her an idea dawned. "Cheat the Prophet," I said. Marie got it, of course, because she'd gone to Charing Cross Road and bought the book, but the others had not heard the tale.

"The one book found by Marie in Kell's office was *Napoleon of Notting Hill*," I said. "It has always puzzled me. Why that book? In the prologue Chesterton puts forward a game that is played by the rustics of Shropshire. They go to lectures and listen to the greatest men of the day talk about the future, and note down what they predict. Then these Shropshire rustics go and do the opposite. They defeat the future. Hence 'Cheat the Prophet'."

"And what exactly does that have to do with Woolwich Woman or anything else?" asked Sophia.

"We don't always have to act logically and obviously. If the enemy is at the gate we can reinforce the gate, build new barriers, throw boiling oil on his head, get bigger guns. Or we can open the gate and let him in, and charge him double rent for the rooms."

"Or," said Edward with a grin, "leave the city to the enemy because his city is nicer and is now undefended – so you march in and take his place, while he takes yours.

"Insinuate. Flit around. Be glimpsed in the shadows."

"Yes," shouted Sophia, suddenly getting an enthusiasm for the game. "Just make it up."

At the end we tipped the waitress well, and shot the doorman with make-believe Mauser C96's.

Sunday 9th October

I went into work and polished up the piece on the virtues of reserve games. I then added that since we were almost certainly going to have another election at the end of the year we could expect to be given some money any time now to get us to vote one way or another.

Mr Holloway snorted when he read it. "Got anything about the ducks being abducted from the Serpentine?" he asked.

Monday 10th October

To the Admiralty, with one of our Aintree code letters to hand over and a second in my satchel in case the first one contained no code. I went through the ritual, and, as Sophia had predicted, Dr Knox had gone back to his chalky minaret. I didn't even have to show my officer card; the fact that I knew the names of everyone there seemed to be enough. I went past Nelson's Staircase, which I gather has particular importance, and was let in to Room 40, where I was introduced to Mr Reginald Hall who told me that everyone called him Blinker. I said everyone called me Jacko, and from that point we got on famously.

Blinker knew exactly what one did with cryptic literature, examined the paper, showed me the giveaway pen marks and took me into the laboratory. As he worked I asked what he was doing.

He talked of ammonia solution which could hide the scratches made with the pen (which was why I couldn't see them). Apparently the ink was made of cobalt oxide in nitric acid, which then disappears if you blow on it. He also talked about some of the messages turning up under the hallmark (he meant stamp) and not on the letter at all – the letter is a complete blind. I made a few notes, excusing myself by saying that as it was an official government project I was charged with the responsibility for keeping records of the whole liaison.

But (rather annoyingly I felt), each time he came up with something, he then told me that it didn't apply in this case.

He then suggested to me that tincture iodine vapours should detect what we had there. But they didn't   He didn't seem the slightest bit embarrassed – I began to like the man. He was following a set of links and working his way towards an answer. "So our writer has ironed the paper and the spies wet the paper after writing. They are professionals – we keep going… Are you all right to wait, while I do this? Would you care for a sandwich?"

I said it was fine, and I was fine. He plodded along, working through one then another analysis, always using one tiny part of the page so as not to damage too much text as he worked, rising to each challenge. Eventually he gave a shout and said "lead nitrate – unlock it with sodium iodide."

He gave me the page, and before my eyes was revealed the hidden message, written between the lines of the bland text (in this case about winter in the highlands).

I gave him the second letter I had with me, and he used the same approach with instant success. Which was a relief as I would have been most unhappy if we had been hunting someone who changed their furtiveness every time.

I was careful not to suggest that there was anything definitive in these messages, giving the impression that this was all routine, confirming what we already knew, just part of the general day-to-day plod of your average military operations secret agent.

We ended the session with a trip to the Crooked Compass just along the way.

I like Blinker. Good taste in beer.

Tuesday 11th October

Missive one said: October 4, the Lamb and Flag, Rose Street
   Missive two: October 12, Cittie of York, High Holborn.
   That was it. No more. Two public houses. They looked like drops.
   Marie was working on the story that President Roosevelt had ridden in an aeroplane, and was distracted from my earthbound concerns by the question of how to present it. Was this showing the President as a man in touch with the latest developments in this exciting world, or a man who still lived the life of the aristocrat, far removed from the ordinary people, unaware of what it was like to live in the vortex?
   As for me, I had to decide, do I now follow up my article and act like a song and dance man (however that might be in these circumstances) or simply go to

see Mr Churchill and say, "Look, Home Secretary, we have discovered this rather interesting snippet which you didn't tell me about even though I am supposed to be your man, and well, that is to say, what's going on?"

Wednesday 12th October

Marie, having written up and sold the President and the Airplane, was now working on H.H. Farzand-i-Khas-i-Daulat-i-Inglishia, Shrimant Maharaja Sir Sayajirao III Gaekwad, Sena Khas Khel Shamsher Bahadur, Maharaja of Baroda, (I copied all that from her notes, but may have made a few spelling mistakes on the way) on the occasion of his visit to England, which had started on 19th July and was continuing until 23rd November. He was doing a world tour.

Marie had managed to interview the king (if that is what he is) while he was being painted wearing his Baroda uniform and Maratha-style turban.

Playing in a different league I went to the Cittie of York in High Holborn and sipped my drink very slowly while reading first the daily press and then *Clayhanger* by Arnold Bennett, which Marie had just reviewed for the Manchester Guardian. Like so much of the literature that Marie thought important, I found it frustrating and retarded – why didn't Clayhanger break free from his old man's restrictions? Answer me that!

I had been in the pub for three hours reading and observing (as one does) before Edward entered, much to my relief. After I had stretched myself we eyed everyone, and then, after we'd finished every conversation we could think of, Edward started on the papers, and I returned to the Five Towns.

When the event hit the pub I have to admit we almost missed it. Enter Woolwich Woman while Jacko and Edward read. She waited for the mistress of the house to appear and quite openly handed over an envelope of the type we had now seen several times before. As she turned, her transaction complete, she looked at us, and quick as a flash – literally as it turned out – Edward had his camera up and took her picture.

It was pure panto, and as our eyes cleared from the light and smoke we saw the woman coming straight at us, and just like Jack in a Box I jumped in front of Edward and met her, face to face, giving my pal time to gather his equipment and the precious photograph.

"I would be much obliged, sir, if you could give that photographic equipment to me," she said in a gentle and charming voice. Where I had expected menace, she beguiled. I protested, gave out the general air of one who knows nothing (a part the major of my platoon had once said required no preparation on my part whatsoever). She was pushing straight at me by then, I with arms akimbo looking for her accomplice. Alarmingly there didn't seem to be one. Either the backup's ability to blend into the background was at the highest level or else Woolwich Woman was so certain of her position and strength, she hadn't brought one.

"Madam," I said, "you have me at a disadvantage."

"No, sir, it is you that has me at the disadvantage. Please do allow me to at least inspect your intriguing photographic equipment," she replied, giving my shin a vigorous kick.

"These are things of which I know nothing, dear madam," I lied, living my life through the imagined world of the stage. "I am but a humble drinker sitting here enjoying a moment of rest from the weary hours of the day, taking in as you can see the latest papers with my friend, and contrasting our lives with that of Mr Clayhanger. We are but simple folk…"

"You are, sir, a simple fraud," she said with a calmness that was not shown in her eyes. "A snoop, a sneak, a thief. You trace your world from Woolwich to Fulham. This is not the work of simple folk or indeed gentlemen. You shall not have my photograph, sir, so please kindly hand it over before the police are called, and called they shall be forthwith unless we reach an understanding."

Edward nudged me to show he was packed and ready to move. With my arms wide open I stepped as close to the lady as I dared without risking a charge of assault, and let Edward move behind me to the door. I then turned and backed after him. Edward was in the street heading towards the underground as I blocked the door. Inside, the pub was still in stunned silence.

I looked at her more calmly. She was elegantly, perhaps beautifully, dressed and she looked like a beauty in herself, and yet, and yet… "I think perhaps madam, it is you who should do some explaining to me," I said.

The blow, when it came was stronger and harder than I expected. Not a lady's flat of the hand on the cheek, but a fist at my nose. The reaction she expected was of both my hands removed from their blocking duty and raised to my nose – a natural human reaction. Not making it was one of the first fighting routines that we were taught when facing the Boer in street fighting. My hands stayed in place, and she walked straight into them. Blood dripped onto her fine coat. "There is a station used by policemen, as I recall, just along the way in Lambs Conduit Street," I said.

"Do you read poetry, sir?" she asked. "Beside the contemporary novel, I mean." Her eyes were dancing, looking for her backup. I was pleased. At least I knew he was there.

"A little poetry, madam, I hear Owen is up and coming. Yet I am more inclined towards the adventurous and the humorous. Exaggerated spy stories are my style."

"Then you should try Mr Wells and Mr Wodehouse," she said, and we gave each other to understand that both knew far, far, more than either of us would ever say.

"But madam," I retorted, "we are here not to discuss the finer points of the writer, but rather the finer points of the punch in the nose and significant amounts of blood which I can see dripping onto you. I have a public house full of witnesses to this criminal act. This is us – the police station is out there. Shall we?"

Edward would be in the underground and on a train, but I was trying for an even more emphatic win. I forced her out of the pub and walked her, both hands on one wrist, careful to match her step.

"And Lord Byron," she said, attempting the continuity of the literary distraction, "you have not entered his realm?"

"Madam, I believe him to be a poet, although I usually have to take guidance on such matters." She tried to duck away, but this was not her skill. Nerves of iron, maybe. One hell of a punch, indeed. But escape from Jones with a ducking trick – I think not.

After a dance of some ten minutes during which our exchanges meandered through EM Forster, William Shakespeare and (from me) GK Chesterton, she stopped. "Will we do this all day and night?" she asked.

"If you wish, madam," I replied. "It is your tune."

"I will walk up to the next police officer and accuse you of molesting me and attempting to steal my purse."

"And I will show him an identity which will have him calling me sir, and carting you away to the nearest nick – irrespective of whether it has facilities for a lady."

This got her attention. "Who are you?" she asked.

"I have been hoping to ask you much the same," I said.

"Eloise Birmingham," she said, which seemed unlikely, but I accepted it for the moment.

"And your occupation?" I asked.

"Occupation?" There was almost a sneer on her face despite the manners. "I do not have an occupation. But your occupation, the one that makes policemen call you sir…"

I shrugged. "Please, tell me your connection with these packages of money. With attempts to overthrow the state. With a stash of weapons…"

"Very well," she said. And with that she made a complete turn, despite giving her wrists a severe Chinese burn. Two men, both over six feet, stepped in front of me and hit me hard in the stomach before I had a chance to continue in pursuit. She was into the crowd, with the men coming at me again. Jacko Jones, I said to myself, as I tried to get some breath into my lungs, you have lost your touch.

I went back to the office to give my superiors a report on the latest episode of an increasingly odd story.

Thursday 13th October

Edward's picture was blurred but not so much that it couldn't be used on the front page. Edward was thrilled and I was deeply pleased for my friend. He'd done his job better than I had done mine.

"Have you seen this woman?" was the banner, along with an Exclusive! flash beside it – and exclusive it was. None of the other papers had any idea who she was or where we were going with this story.

Eloise Birmingham was, I said in my commentary, central to the operation of the gang that was attempting to undermine the economy of the Empire, and the police would very much like to talk to her.

The article spoke about anarchists, socialists, Welsh independence revolutionaries, Germans... I threw in the lot. Political parties trying to buy votes, football clubs trying to fix games, South Africans seeking revenge for the Boer War, Italian barrel organists, you name them, I went for them. I felt it was necessary. The doc said my nose was broken.

Mr Symmonds did his bit with the fifth floor. By the time they'd finished with the piece, there was a reward of £50 for anyone with information that would help us find the Woolwich Woman and bring her to justice.

Friday 14th October

Despite not having a clue what we were talking about several papers had picked up on our piece. The West London and the Kentish both had the story for the locals, and the Express and Mirror were running it, upping the reward just for spite. They used the woman's name, used my phrase "put-pockets" but with "so-called" in front, and interviewed the regulars in the Cittie of York who reported a mass brawl and the presence of several people of German origin.

As I'd expected, we had the biggest post bag since the relief of Mafeking, which was, of course, before my time as a journalist. With much glee Mr Holloway dumped three postbags on my desk which he said the ladies on the third floor couldn't handle, even with all their extra staff, and with even more merriment I reported that Mr Churchill had sent a car for me and was expecting me immediately. "Get something on the statue in St James that weeps ice cream will you?" the boss cried as I hurried down the stairs.

* * * * * * *

"Jacko Jones!" the Home Secretary announced (in case I had forgotten my name) as I was ushered into his office, "you've broken your nose." I peered into the corners of his room in case Vernon Kell was hiding under a cushion.

"Where do you find these adventures, Jacko?" he asked simply once I had sat down. "What's it all about?"

"I was hoping you would tell me, sir," I said.

"I don't know! I want the information from you, Jacko. That's why I made you a captain and pay you a salary. You want me to tell you, you'll have to make me a knight."

I'd half expected this, and had a story ready. I told him we had 'come across' a couple letters of the type that had been found in Woolwich while we were tracking the put-pockets in Fulham. "I naturally took them to Dr Knox for translation, but since he had returned to Cambridge another member of the Room 40 team took them and revealed the secret writing. It led to the Cittie of York, and the meeting with Miss Birmingham." I paused and then threw in the over-arm ball. "I presume that the earlier letters that Dr Knox decoded did not reveal similar leads, because I felt sure you would have informed me."

"You, Captain Jones, are far too clever for your own good."

"I am sure you are right, Home Secretary," I replied.

"Shouting state secrets from the rooftops by putting it on the front page of the Chronicle is not necessarily the best approach for a secret officer."

"Then why the hell don't you tell me what is going on, sir?" I asked.

"Officially, Jacko, because it should not be revealed to anyone below the inner cabinet or Field Marshall. Unofficially – and this is completely confidential, and I shall have you shot if you reveal a word of it – it is because I have not got the faintest idea."

"You don't know who is distributing the money?"

"No."

We sat in silence. Eventually I said, "Is there something you would like me to do?"

"Find out who is behind this of course," he snapped. "What do you think I am paying you for?"

Back in Dorset Square Lord Cortney said that the key issue that divided the main parties was not just taxation but also the vortex.

"A man loses his job, slips into poverty, there is no escape. He becomes a non-person, nowhere to live, no way back. His wife and children don't eat. They scavenge. They are all so invisible that journalists like you, decent men like you, don't even write about them. You heard David Lloyd George, didn't you?"

"The 'Turn the dogs on us' speech? Yes I heard that."

"'Our Waifs and Strays' is helpful but ultimately it is a bandage and not a solution. We need a solution – but there are grave disagreements as to what the solution is."

Saturday 15th October

All the popular papers are now running the put-pocket stories. I pleaded to be allowed out of working on the post-room overflow on the wholly untrue grounds that Mr Churchill had given me a new lead to follow which I was under oath to keep quiet but which could give us an even bigger lead. Elsewhere there were stories of unrest in the coal fields. Marie tried to link the two themes together.

"If you were a mine owner who didn't want a strike," she said, "you might put the wages up. But the mine owners argue that if they do that it will just cause another strike and another. But if you wanted to break the mine unions you might use put-pockets to keep the strike going – before you suddenly withdraw them."

"But is there any evidence of the sovereigns reaching coal towns?"

"No," said Marie, "but then the same was true in London before you spotted it. If you had not been banned from the stand by Norris, you wouldn't have been on the terraces, and you probably wouldn't have noticed what is going on. If you were an ordinary working man standing on a terrace and someone slipped a pound in your pocket you are hardly going to write to the press to complain."

"But the coalfields are in chaos. Every time we mention them in the Chron it is because of a riot or because the owners have locked out the workers or because the workers are staying underground refusing to come out until their voices are heard. They even had a hunger march last week. Would all that be going on if someone was handing out sovereigns all over the place?"

"I think we should go to Wales and see for ourselves," she said.

"We?"

"We! Get on a train at Paddington and we get off at Tonypandy. Change at Cardiff." She had looked it all up.

"Is there a station in Tonypandy?"

"Taff Valley Railways."

Tonypandy was the place where, at least according to Fleet Street, the main action was taking place in the confrontation between miners and owners, although I retained some doubts as to the accuracy of the reports. (After all, I knew how some of my reports are invented.) I agreed to go tomorrow. At least it gives me a story to work on.

"Today!" said Marie.

"I am booked in to watch Woolwich Arsenal," I said. Apart from anything else I wanted to know if the crowd was up and if Miss Birmingham's gang was still in operation. We agreed to hold for a day.

In fact the crowd was not up – only 11,500 turned up according to the figures released by the club. But that only told half the story. The number of people milling around outside the ground was about five times what I would normally expect, and among all the pushing and shoving it was clear there were at least three gangs of put-pockets working.

Three! I'd had an effect on events.

Woolwich Arsenal amazingly beat Blackburn by four goals to one – largely because Blackburn had two players sent off for fighting. It was Woolwich's first win of the season. Gunners' Mate was as outrageous as ever. Goodness knows what the players were making of it. Goodness knows what he would say for the next match. I wondered if George had noticed the crowds outside.

Sunday 16th October

We took the train to Cardiff and then on to Tonypandy where we booked into the Queen Victoria Hotel as Mr and Mrs Jones – Marie having remembered her gold ring. That, of course, made the whole trip worthwhile. But it was also a revelation to see her at work on a story.

We had four and a half hours on the train – travelling first class (Marie having bought the tickets without consultation) – and I used the time to pick up the background.

Apparently there is a change going on in terms of the way wages are calculated in the mines with the money the miners get now linked to the amount of coal they produce – hardly a fair system since that depends on the depth of the mine, the time it takes to walk to the seam, and the ease of working the seam. If Mr Holloway ever hears of this he'd implement it with my work at once.

There was a growing dispute at "Cambrian Combine" where there was either a lock out or a strike going on – we couldn't work out which, not least because the London papers (apart from the Chron) were biased in favour of the owners and against anything that they claimed smacked of being anarchist or socialist activity. The talk seemed to be that if a settlement was not reached soon all hell would break loose.

Marie had bought every London paper and around 20 weekly magazines, and in between talking we searched each one for news about the strike.

At the Severn Tunnel I took out my notebook and pencil and wrote more of the Slayer story.

She is the ultimate politician, the ultimate entertainer, whose meaning is unclear, drifting around our world, sliding effortlessly between the dark of the vortex and the scientific future of the Empire. She has the aura of knowing something that none of us should ever know. She knows about the vortex. But more. She knows how to end its horror...

Her promise is that without the poor there is no crime. Without the poor there is no fear. Without the fear we are liberated to build an even greater and better Empire. A 20th century Empire that will make our efforts in the last century seem puny and childish. And we can do this, if we don't have to worry about the poor...

There were a lot of strange looks for us at the hotel, and considerable difficulty in understanding our accents just as we had difficulty in understanding theirs. But money is the same anywhere in the Kingdom, and we secured the best room, a good meal, drinks in the bar, and a gentle walk around town in the twilight (where we were followed by a herd of grubby boys in raggy short trousers).

I was a journalist again, doing what I knew best, but my head was still with the Slayer.

Monday 17th October

First to the Post Office where I posted my Alyson piece to the Review. Then to the Ely Pit in Penygraig where we asked to meet the managers' representative to have their side of the story, all the while looking for any sign of put-pockets. At the offices of the Naval Colliery Company we were welcomed and given a warm treatment – complete with drinks and some very curious looks for Marie, with comments about "Ladies working as journalists."

The story that we pieced together was that the management were opening a new seam at "Upper Five Foot" and they had been doing some test mining from which they had come up with their price per ton for the miners. That price had been agreed last year – but now the management claimed they had evidence (although no one told us what it was) that the miners had been fixing the system by working at half speed on the test mines in order to get higher wages. The price of 2/9 per ton had come down to 1/9, and the workers were not happy.

For the management in their quality clothes and top hats it was a matter of principle, a feeling that if they gave way to "blackmail" that would lead to a breakdown in production because the men themselves were not able to organise anything.

So in August the owners had shut down the whole mine "because it is a matter of principle". 800 men had been locked out since 1st September, so the other Naval pits came out on strike in support. Apparently the workers saw it as a matter of principle as well.

"Damned illegal if you ask me," said Mr Ferrington, the manager, although I wasn't too sure what his argument was. "Fortunately the local MP showed a bit of sense for once and got them back to work – but then told us that we had to increase our pay offer. Damned cheek of the man – as if it was any business of his how much we pay."

"And did you – increase the offer?" asked Marie.

"Took it up to 2/1. And they were still not satisfied," said the indignant owner. "Still talking about a strike."

"But won't a strike hurt you?"

"Not that much. The Coal Owners' Association will support us – and when it comes down to it, so will the government. If we give in it will be one step from anarchy. No, we've already agreed that no man who goes on strike will ever be employed again in the South Wales Mines." He said the capital letters. You could feel it – even if he hadn't been banging his fist on the table as he spoke.

That seemed to be that, so we wandered out. Back in the town we asked questions and were directed to the office of the South Wales Miners Federation, the local trade union. Derek Frayne, the senior officer in the surprisingly spacious offices, was more than happy to talk. "'Bout time the London papers took an interest," he said.

"The Executive Council of the Federation held a special conference," he told us, "and on September 16th it was recommended that the conference agree that the all the workmen employed at the Cambrian Combine should go on strike. They would be supported financially by a levy on the earnings of every other miner in south Wales. This was going to be organised through the Democratic Club Distress Committee.

"We had 250 delegates here, representing 150,000 men," he told us with pride, and seemingly they voted in favour. "It was totally democratic and proper. How many owners are there? One family. One family against 150,000 men. Which is the most democratic?"

I had to admit he had a point, although it probably wouldn't put food on the table.

"Gave them a week's notice, we did, which is all proper."

"So you are going on strike?" Marie asked.

"I hope not, ma'am," said Mr Frayne, "but if that's what it takes, that is what the men will do."

"But the owners have said that anyone who strikes will never be employed in a mine again."

"Words, ma'am, just words. You'll be surprised at their threats and intimidation. They are threatening to bring in the army to shoot strikers, but army men would never shoot on their own kind."

I wasn't sure. In South Africa we put the women and children in concentration camps and they died of cholera.

I tried to bring the subject round to our particular issue. "Do you have any support groups here?" I asked. "People who argue your cause, who maybe can help with a spot of money in case the strike goes ahead."

He looked at me curiously. "We have the strike support committee. They organise the money and look after our people with shortages."

I tried again. "You see, Mr Frayne, there have been stories in London that you are going to win this fight because a mysterious organization is providing money for the miners. An organisation outside the mining community."

"I don't know of this," he said, but his eyes said something different.

And then Marie came through like a train. "We have them in London – and they are transforming the political landscape. They are giving out money to workers in the dockyards, and we thought they might be working here as well."

"If there were such people, I'd know about it," he said, "but no we don't have that." He was not a good liar.

We thanked him and left, with the usual accompaniment of children. "He's lying," I said.

"Shock, horror, hold the front page. Mr Jones states the obvious," Marie replied with a smile. "Actually that could be a title for a column of yours." I pulled a face. "If Frayne had never heard about put-pockets he would have said, 'But if you can persuade them to come up here, that would be great.' And he would have said that because he would believe that his committees could control the distribution of the money, which would give him power. The fact that he didn't say that makes it obvious that it is happening, and it is by-passing him. No one in power likes being by-passed."

"It is always about power, isn't it?" I said. "It is almost as if a working wage is incidental to who can pull the strings."

"And that," said Marie, "is almost certainly the key to the put-pockets. And incidentally it is what Lenin said." I told her I had heard that from Mr Churchill.

We walked back to the hotel where we tried our questioning again, but there was nothing going. If we were going to get news it would be in the pubs, and they were totally men only.

For once Marie accepted my call, and she settled down in the lounge of the Queen Victoria while I took in the hostelries and partook of the beer.

I visited five pubs, consumed five pints, and saw the game in two of them. They weren't using the put-pocket approach; the money was simply slipped across the counter with the drink. You pay tuppence for a drink, and receive a pint and £1 in change. Everyone took the money quietly, slipping it into their pockets and carrying on drinking. No one gave me anything other than the beer.

I went back to Marie, and gave my report. "Someone wants the fight to carry on for a long time."

Tuesday 18th October

We travelled back to London and reported to Sophia and Edward – with none of us quite sure what we had found out.

At work Mr Holloway found me in the canteen, and told me to go and interview Rev. Richard Free (Vicar of St. Clements, Fulham) who has apparently just received a substantial gift from a Mr Norris also of Fulham which will allow him to rebuild his vicarage. I said, "That's very nice, but is it important?" And he said, "It will be if the rumour that Norris is then going to offer to do renovations on Fulham Palace is also true."

Turned out it wasn't so he asked me to check on the arrest of a singing quail in Tottenham Court Road.

Wednesday 19th October

The miners are our lead story. Having read my piece ten times and secreted away a dozen copies of the Chron to give to Mum, Dad and the neighbours, plus another half dozen of the Review, I sat looking out of the window, wondering what on earth I was going to do next.

George Barrett rescued me with a request for a meeting as soon as possible. At the Lamb and Flag. "Who is doing this?" he asked, having kindly bought me a pint. He tapped a picture of Woolwich Woman with his cigarette. I told him that I genuinely had no idea of anything other than that which was printed. He looked disbelieving.

"George, believe me, if I knew, I'd be splashing it on the paper. Don't you know what's going on?"

He told me he didn't have a clue. He'd been asking around the anarchist groups, but not got anywhere.

"How did you know she was going to be at the Citte?"

"That was a tip-off," I said, adding before he could ask, "don't ask me where it came from – I absolutely can't tell you. Can't you give me any leads?"

"I genuinely can't trace it. No one in any of the groups knows about the woman or the money going to Tonypandy. The miners' unions don't like us because we challenge their power and control over the workers, but we've got some supporters in the mining communities, and they don't know either. I'll swear to you that if this is an anarchist plot, it comes from completely outside the normal circles."

We sat and looked at our beers. "It's the second great mystery, Jacko," he said at last. I asked him what the other was.

"Closing the torpedo factory. You dropped that story a little too quick for my liking – and we never found out why the factory was being moved to Scotland."

"I can tell you I never found out," I told him, "and I had no way of pushing the story further. It was my first big story, and the blocks came down. The source was in government, and when he said stop, I had to. I didn't have a way of reaching around it."

More silence.

"But Churchill is your big pal," he said. "You were in Africa with him."

"One to you for getting your research done," I said, "but 'with him' is not quite right. I was a sergeant, he a journalist toff, and we spent a couple of days together with me as his guard after he screwed up an operation. That's how we met, and let me say before this gets difficult, I cannot tell you anything of what has been said between us since I met him again earlier this year. But you tell me something – do the anarchists have any contact with the socialists?"

"Only through insiders. We have one or two people who attend their meetings and report back, and I've no doubt they have the same in reverse."

"So could any of this money business be a socialist plot?"

"Same answer: if it is, it is the most secret plan we've ever seen. I'd say it is more likely to be the Germans preparing for invasion."

"That's a good answer," I said, "but there's no evidence. Just because authors write invasion novels doesn't mean we are about to be invaded."

He looked straight at me. "You really are telling me the truth, Jacko, aren't you?"

I threw him a scrap. "I can tell you there are weapons involved – and not just any old weapons. The most advanced guns available. And you'll know that I have not used that fact in a story, so if it gets out, George, it tells me you are the source."

"Who has guns?"

"The put-pockets – which is why finding out who they are is becoming more important. If they start using that weaponry on the streets we are all in trouble. Are your groups armed with Mauser C96s?"

After we finished I took a bus to Dorset Square only to find Marie was out. I was invited by Jenkinson to take an afternoon sherry in the library, something I am not sure I have ever done before in my life, and I woke up an hour and a half later when Marie dropped a book on my head.

I apologised and said, "Ow" at the same time, followed by a kiss and, in response to her request, details of my day thus far. I gave her a copy of the Chron and the Review but she said she'd already bought six copies for the house while on her way back from Fulham Palace.

"Don't worry, I didn't steal the bishop's mitre," she said. "I just had a stroll around the place looking for signs of Norris-type activity."

"And…"

"Nothing. It is unguarded and unprotected – anyone could walk off with anything, but no sign of changes. No gangs of workmen knocking the old place down. After that I went to see the Reverend Richard Free and asked him if I could do a piece about the modern church in relation to the advent of business as the new religion."

"That's good," I said, but Marie, as honest as ever except when she is stealing things or pretending to be my wife, admitted it was an idea that had been explored in several philosophical books. "We talked, got onto Norris, and he said Norris was helping repair the nave and the west window by having his workmen do the job for nothing."

Thursday 20th October

Another phone call, another request to meet, this time at the Lamb and Flag.

Woolwich Woman entered within seconds of my arrival. She must have been waiting outside, and in that case her signalling and her camouflage were very good. I hadn't had an inkling that she was there. God, I am going soft.

I offered to buy her a drink, but she declined. I collected my beer and led us to a seat near the door. She was, in her fur coat, so utterly out of place that she looked like a cartoon from Punch. Everyone in the pub was looking at her – as well as several people who peered in from outside.

"Have you finished your Matthew Arnold book?" she asked. I told her that I had stopped reading it yesterday when I had fallen asleep.

"You are clearly a man of action – and imagination, Mr Jones," she replied. "Your visit to South Wales must have been exhilarating. The Severn Tunnel is a most marvellous work of engineering I am told, although I've not been through it myself."

"Rather like the Northern Line," I replied.

"Mr Jones, you are becoming a most famous – even notorious – writer. Such contacts, such leads, such information. Where do you get it all from?"

"The fairies talk to me," I said. I was damned if I would play her games. George I could work with. He had a view. Not a view that I share but still a view which was honestly held. I doubt he would ever knowingly hurt anyone. Alyson I could turn into a story. But this woman…

"Mr Jones, Mr Jones," she said, "we really do have to get to know each other better. Of course, I'd invite you out for a weekend in the country, but I gather you already have such experiences with the delightful Marie Cortney. I wouldn't be surprised if Marie had a secret in her life. A little extra activity that her father doesn't know about…"

I did my level best to keep my face composed, but it was hard. Was she aware that Marie and I had travelled as husband and wife? Or was she speaking of one of Marie's nocturnal activities… Or the discovery of the weapons? "We need to reach an understanding, Mr Jones," she said.

"Won't you tell me your real name?" I asked.

"For what purpose? You would not know if it were my real name or just an invention, so where would that take you. Besides I quite like Woolwich Woman. No, let us talk about you leaving the story of the mysterious money alone, shall we? Shall we say that if you do, a sizeable sum of money, which is perfectly legitimate, will come your way. Enough to live on for the rest of your life. Enough to marry your dear Marie. And, in return, my friends and I will not do anything about that dear, dear lady."

I said nothing.

"You have five seconds, Mr Jones."

"OK, I accept," I said.

"Not quite the answer I was expecting, Mr Jones, but I will take your word as an officer."

That one really did hit me.

She showed no sign of recognising my discomfort, save one slightly raised eyebrow.

I turned and left the building. And walked straight into a police sergeant and two constables. "Jack Jones," said the sergeant, "you are under arrest."

Friday 21st October

It was Edward who came to see me first. I'd had something like six hours questioning from five different people, all out of uniform, all coming at me from different angles, all suggesting that they knew a lot more than I thought they could know.

I was still furious with myself at letting my face slip in front of the woman, especially when she was quite possibly only fishing. "As an officer," she had said. The possible explanations were that she had just used it fortuitously as a phrase, or that Marie had told someone else about my temporary captaincy, or that Churchill had let slip. Of the three possibilities I only liked the first. The others gave me nightmares.

Because there was a chance that I had only been found out by guesswork, I just told Edward that Woolwich Woman had threatened to get Marie and that she had to avoid going out alone and take absolutely no risks – especially at night. In fact, in an ideal world she should stay at home. "She'll not like that," he said, and I agreed. "But please tell her, her life and her future are both in severe danger in equal measures. All it needs is a couple of days of patience."

"What about getting you out of here?" he asked. "What are you being charged with?"

"Exceeding the speed limit, treason, entering Wales without a permit, playing the piano badly, and writing articles that people read."

"But you don't have a car," Edward said, rather amusingly I thought.

"Whoever is behind this either wants me off the streets or is absolutely out to get me, or both. Tell the Chron, and see if they might get a solicitor onto the case. Again."

A police officer came in and told Edward his time was up, although quite how they determined that I didn't know. I went back for another questioning session. I was extremely thirsty but my requests for water were rejected.

The solicitor didn't arrive, which was annoying – probably Mr Holloway's doing. At eight o'clock I settled down to another night in the cell.

At eleven I was woken by a hand on mine. I jerked up quickly, hitting my head on the empty bunk above mine and only just managing to stifle a shout. Marie's voice said, "Very good, Jacko. Clearly a man trained for such occasions." I reckoned that Marie's voice might have Marie behind it, and so it proved to be. "You were trying to warn me," she said, "But Edward was somewhat vague as to the details."

"I was trying to warn you to keep your head down, and most particularly not to go on any jaunts that might end up with you possessing something for which you do not have the rights. I did not warn you not to break into my cell, because I never imagined you could do that."

"There's gratitude," she said, "and for your information I did not break in. I spoke nicely to the duty constable."

I looked at her uncomfortably, not specially liking the sound of "spoke nicely". She saw the look. "Don't be daft, Jacko. I gave him a single kiss and slipped him five pounds from the stash that Sophia is looking after. Now will you tell me the problem?"

I told her about Woolwich Woman's threats and her possible knowledge about my being an officer. To my annoyance, she smiled. "Anyone interested will know you are an officer," she said. "It appeared in the London Gazette. All official appointments do – it is the publication of record."

"So she could have looked it up in the paper?"

"Quite so – it is the origin of the phrase 'Gazetted'." I duly reprimanded myself as I'd heard the phrase a hundred times in the army, but had just accepted it as meaning, "to be raised in rank".

"Don't worry about me, I'll go home now. Sophia is in the entrance with our friendly bobby, and we'll get a cab."

"Keep your head down," I urged, and in response she lowered her face and gave me a far more exciting kiss than I hoped she had given the policeman.

Saturday 22nd October

The solicitor finally arrived at nine o'clock in the morning, and given that they were not going to charge me the forces of law and order let me out. The solicitor told me I was ordered to attend my masters in Fleet Street and put me in his cab.

I gave them the full story (except the bit that revealed me to be a captain who didn't know the meaning of 'gazetting') and moved on to the simple fact that we still didn't know who was behind all of this.

Eventually their nibs said, "Thank you, Mr Jones, you may go," and I went. It was only as I started to leave the building, thinking a clean up would not go amiss, that Mr Holloway did his "Where do you think you're going?" imitation of a sergeant (which he can't do as well as me) and told me that I was on an assignment.

Apparently Dick had been on the lash again – first time in nine months, and Mr Holloway was covering for him – which meant he simply gave me the job. Millwall's new ground at New Cross was opening today, and tired and hungry though I was, I was to go and see a Southern League game. The President of the Football Association, Lord Kinnaird, was to be there to open up. "Your last pieces have been a bit political," said Mr Holloway, "and you are supposed to be in my department, so something about football perhaps. And nothing too serious. A little humour maybe, unless your pals in the Upper House have got some dirt on Kinnaird in which case we'll go with that."

I turned back to him. "You are asking me to be funny?" I said incredulously.

"I don't ask for miracles – but the superior being on the fifth feels that while it is good to cover the big news of the moment, not all of our readers know where Tonypany actually is, if you follow my meaning."

"There's a meaning?" I said, and I wished I hadn't.

Getting to New Cross turned out to be slightly easier than I feared – someone had decided to build an underground station near by, so I got to the Den early enough to buy a disgusting pie and an almost drinkable pint.

I also managed to get hold of Tom Thorne, the director of the club who had overseen the move, and did a quick interview. "Do you always dress like this for you work, Mr Jones?" he said, and I apologised, saying I had been working on a report for the paper all night and was here now because my colleague who should have covered it had been taken ill. I doubt he believed me.

We moved on to football. Joy of joys, the ground had been designed by Archibald Leitch. I decided not to tell him that I suspected the terracing would collapse. The ground cost £10,000, and it struck me that if Woolwich Woman kept up her activities for much longer, every club in the land would be able to buy a new stadium with faked money. Maybe her aim was to get work for Archie.

So I took my place in the (still upright) stand, ready to admire the activities of Brighton and Hove Albion who had won the league last year. I had no particular idea what I was going to write about when the word got about that Lord Kinnaird was actually in the ground at the Canterbury Road section rather than up with the toffs.

As if that weren't enough, he was identified by the crowd, and we all watched in stunned amazement as police tried unsuccessfully to get him out of the terracing. Of course the toughs were not going to have it, and there was shouting and pushing as he was jostled around and eventually hoisted up above the mob, like they do with little boys who get stuck and can't get out. It was the most wonderful sight, and totally reinvigorated my spirits. Eventually he was propelled to the front, and then dropped six feet over the fence onto the ground, as policemen rushed in to rescue the old blighter. Where was Edward when I needed him?

Then they walked him in front of a delirious crowd to the Cold Blow Lane end with the crowd singing "For he's a jolly good fellow".

So at last the players came out onto the pitch, and a big brass lion was unveiled with an inscription in a language I couldn't understand. (Eventually I was told it was Gaelic for "We'll Never Turn Our Backs On The Enemy". I never knew this part of London was in Wales. Or Ireland.)

Millwall lost one goal to nil, and I went straight home, happier than I had been for a couple of days.

The evening paper told me that Woolwich had beaten Nottingham Forest in Nottingham by three goals to two. Things were looking up.

Sunday 23rd October

Never has there been an easier piece to write, and I swear that half a smile found its way onto Mr Holloway's lips although his brain quickly realised that such an expression was wholly unacceptable to his general demeanour and hid the signs.

"I suppose it will have to do," he said. He huffed and puffed. "Is it true?"

"Every single solitary word, Mr Holloway. Every syllable. Every verb. Every comma. Every,…

"No passing of money through your put-pockets?"

"I was laughing so much I didn't notice," I said, and went off to write the next Slayer episode.

One more generation of the rich will play God.

Tuesday 25th October

Having kept my head down with Marie yesterday I ventured back to work only to be asked to see Mr Churchill.

"Read your piece on Tonypandy," he said. "Difficult matter."

I nodded gravely. That seemed to be the thing to do.

"Didn't know you were interested in that sort of politics," he said, fishing.

I shrugged.

"Problem is, country needs coal, and country needs law and order. Can't have the anarchists taking over," he said, watching me keenly.

I told him I had seen no evidence of anarchists, just a trade union.

"It's a threat to the good running of the state. A threat to law and order," he said.

I said I doubted it. "See here, Jacko, you don't have the full picture, the full implication. It is a threat, and we need people to see that. Your piece – very interesting, very amusing, of course – but it didn't really cover the basic facts. The miners are getting violent, challenging the very fundamentals of this country. We need to sort out the mess with the Lords over the budget, not be distracted by violent demonstrations."

I said I didn't quite know how a miners strike was related to the Parliament Act, but Mr Churchill just nodded and said it was, and that seemed to imply that I ought to believe him.

"What I would like, Jacko, would be for you to write a piece saying that the miners are wrong and should go back to work. They've got their pay rise, and all they are doing now is trying to challenge the natural order of things. They can't win – tell them they can't win."

I tried another approach. "Do you know where this money is coming from – the money I wrote about in my piece about Tonypandy?"

"Anarchists," he said without a pause. "Or socialists."

I told him I didn't think so, and that while the miners' strike was important, I was particularly concerned with the money. I wanted to know who was behind it. Mr Churchill insisted he did not know.

Wednesday 26th October

Lord Cortney announced that knowing my interest in ecclesiastical matters in Fulham he had invited the Bishop of London to dinner that evening. It would be formal dress, he was sorry to say, because of the nature of his guest, but they had a suit that would fit me, if that was all right.

It was not a productive occasion. Marie, Lord Cortney and I conspired to lead the Bishop into Norris-land by the main course, but he genuinely knew little, and what he did know confirmed the vicar's view. Norris was doing some good work on the buildings of Fulham at his own expense. There had been a little talk that after the church had been fixed he might have a look at the Palace, but nothing had been agreed.

Just as we were drawing to a close the Bishop raised the issue of the Review, as if seeking to confirm that I was the Jacko Jones who had written the story. I confessed. He nodded and fingered his cross. "Excellent work, Mr Jones," he said. "If there is anything I can do for you… the notion of abortion is an abomination."

"It's not about abortion, your Grace," I said, "it's eugenics."

Thursday 27th October

I called the office, told Mr Holloway that I was feeling unwell, and stayed in Dorset Square. And it was true, in a sense. I was feeling unwell, because Marie started to tell me that Sophia was planning an attack on Parliament with her Suffragette friends. I asked Marie if she approved, and she said, "did you approve of violence in Africa?"

The Chron called back to Dorset Square. Apparently Mr Holloway was extremely discreet and deferential when he got on to Lord Cortney, explaining how dreadfully sorry he was to break into the working day of his lordship, but it was a matter of some importance and if his lordship would not mind the intrusion could Mr Holloway have just a few seconds on the telephone with Mr Jones whom he had been told was staying at the house, if his lordship didn't mind.

"Your boss wants to shout at you," said Lord Cortney as he gave me the phone.

And he was quite right.

I got to Fleet Street to find all hell had broken loose. I went straight to the fifth floor. "I have half of the Unionist party on the phone," said Mr Symmonds. "The issue is simple. If we don't tell them within half an hour your source for the Slayer of Souls story, they are planning to put through an emergency bill shutting down the Chronicle for suggesting that 'some people' want to sterilise the poor."

"It's just a story," I said. "It's fiction." I looked at them hard as an idea wormed its way into my head. "Are you telling me that forced sterilisation of the poor is going to be the policy of the Unionist party at the next election?"

"It is – and so is the closure of the Chronicle. In fact," said the editor, looking straight at me, "I think we are about to sell more copies of this journal than ever before. And apparently the Review has just reprinted. That's a first too."

"Am I being given a rollicking or what?" I said.

"Rollicking?" said the editor, rolling his eyes. He turned to Mr Holloway. "Get this man off the beer, sit him in front of a typewriter, and get him writing. The Review wants a new story out of him next week, and I want a lead article on eugenics."

Saturday 29th October

It was a relief to get away from everyone and return to Woolwich. I wasn't supposed to be there – the political department were demanding more details on anything and everything – but I just walked out. Got to the ground early and did the round of the public houses, talking, asking, listening. The put-pockets had not been around again but there were a lot of men hoping for another handout.

Gunners' Mate was much more positive in the programme, but I feared for the team in the next edition. Woolwich Arsenal were awful and lost to Manchester City nil to one. There was a man called Quaile playing at left back who was just about the worst footballer I have ever seen in my life. How could they ever play someone that bad? The answer had to be that the manager had never seen him before.

I met George Allison in the press room (amazingly no one threw me out). "Shall we sterilise the lot of them?" he asked. I told him what I thought of Quaile, and George told me that the organisation within the club had broken down. Quaile was "borrowed" from a local amateur side because they were short of players after Shaw reported in sick.

I wrote up my notes on the way back, typed them up and then got involved in a long conversation about the miners' strike with Mr Symmonds, and found myself instructed to return to south Wales to cover the start of the strike on 1st November.

As a result of that I was late arriving in Dorset Square for a dinner event with Marie's grandfather.

As Jenkinson opened the door for me I strolled in and virtually collided with the old fellow who was coming down the stairs. He took in my work clothes and said, "Mr Jones! I read your work – Marie writes and tells me all about you. A pleasure to meet you sir, a pleasure to meet you. Your piece on sterilisation – cat among the pigeons, what?" I hadn't had the foresight to find out whether he was another Lord, so I called him sir, and he immediately launched into a long and rambling story about the Wanderers, and how he played for them in 1872 in the first ever year of the FA Cup. "I played in the semi-final against Clapham Rovers," he said, "but got injured – hurt me knee, and so couldn't play for the rest of the season and missed the final. I was at the final though – beat the Royal Engineers one to nothing at the Oval. Grand match – champagne afterwards. We played in Battersea you know, on the park, grand place. Good mates all, not like now, of course, when they are all paid. Played in brown, orange and pink – what d'you think of that? Won the Cup five times, you know. Still got two winners' medals at home!"

I asked him what had happened to the Wanderers, and he said that it had folded, there had been trouble playing at Battersea, as the crowds had got bigger, and then when the professional game came along they couldn't find anyone to play with.

"Talked to a man – bit of a bigwig out that way – didn't like the fella myself, but he was interested in giving us a place to play in Fulham… Talked about London's oldest club, the proud tradition of the amateur game… Wouldn't trust the blighter as far as I could throw him."

"Norris?"

"That's the fella. Nothing came of it. Don't know why."

As he spoke we were ushered into the dining room, and there were cries of relief that both grandfather and the wayward visitor had finally entered the fray. "Just telling Mr Jones about the Wanderers," he announced. "Mr Jones writes about football – association you know, not the rugby game…"

The diners admitted they knew – diners whom I discovered included Marie's sister Dorothy – but I hardly got to talk to her. Marie's grandfather had me at his side and he was not going to let me go.

I love that sheer resolute enthusiasm – he doesn't care that the world is moving on – he's going to move at his speed and never give up on his world in the past. A lovely man. I promised to visit him and keep him up-to-date with footballing matters.

Monday 31st October

We packed, and once again went to south Wales. Fortunately, Marie phoned ahead to book a room. Fortunately, because on arrival we found the whole area awash with journalists.

The strike is due to start tomorrow, and there is serious tension in the air, not aided by some journalists trying to get interviews with men and women whose accents they barely understand – which of course resulted in a lot of journalistic invention en route.

From what I can work out, the owners have drawn up plans to bring in miners from outside the area. As we walked from the station we saw extra police arriving, and although they were under strict orders not to talk to us, we did find that some of them had been brought in from over 50 miles away. The families are very thick here and they clearly don't want to risk a constable coming up against his own uncle.

Tuesday 1st November

A stand off day in which nothing much happened save a number of journalists attempting to encourage action by throwing stones. Several were arrested.

I sent a cable to the office and told them there was nothing happening. The reply was, if it is calm tomorrow, come home.

Thank you for a total waste of time, Mr Symmonds.

Wednesday 2nd November

This is the strangest experience. All around me there is a story: Tonypandy, the money, Woolwich Woman, the unsolved torpedo factory issue, German spies, anarchists, but nothing is coming together. Nothing is moving. All I have resolved is that the Unionists are bringing in a policy of sterilisation for the poor. As Marie said, they needed an alternative to the Liberals who would deal with the vortex by giving old age pensions and unemployment pay. It is the starkest choice I've ever seen. Spend your money on the poor or leave it with the rich.

Not surprisingly, no one had a copy of the Review in south Wales. In fact there were precious few copies of the Chron to be had.

I sent a telegram and asked for a junior to phone Norris and get his appointments. Apparently tomorrow Mr Norris is going to a dinner for the mayors of London – his final duty as mayor before his term of office comes to an end. I thought I could live without that but nevertheless we took a train back to London.

Marie was getting excited about an attempt by one Ernest Willows to fly to Paris from London which is being covered in the Times (a copy reserved for her at treble price by the hotel). Marie had done an interview with him before he left, despite him saying he didn't want to talk to the press (must be her smile), and she has the story lodged with the News. Whether he makes it or dies, the story will be used. If he's delayed and we get back in time she plans to be at Croydon Aerodrome to watch him take off, and then wait for news from Paris. Or as I said rather gloomily, from the fish.

Friday 4th November

Three strange events to lighten my gloom. First of all, it seems that contrary to my predictions Willows made it to France and landed safely. Marie's story is promised a big spread in the News tomorrow.

Secondly, the first posters have gone up relating to the forthcoming election. They show Alyson (representing the intellectual elite presumably), a farmer, and three children from the vortex with their hands out begging. Underneath is the slogan, "This is us", a phrase I used in the Slayer story.

Thirdly, and much more oddly (if that is possible), was the case of the Hatton Garden diamond necklace. A month ago there was a jewel robbery in Hatton Garden – which although not commonplace is not utterly unheard of. The only people who covered the story were the local London papers and none of them gave it more than a column. Then a week ago the same shop had a second break-in, and during that event the diamonds were put back.

It was a story that was right up my street, and I had missed it. What took me back to it was that the owner was now saying in the Chron that the returned necklace was not the original necklace. In fact he was saying something even more odd: that the diamonds were not diamonds. They were make-believe.

The Chron had talked with the jeweller, who said he only realised there was something wrong with the necklace when he came to clean it. And, yes, he was quite sure that the original necklace was genuine. "What else would it be?" he said. Indeed.

And another thing: both break-ins were identical. They'd come in through the back door by breaking the lock.

I told Mr Holloway. He looked at me is disbelief. "So you can't solve any of the cases you are currently working on, and therefore you want to go off to Hatton Garden and get another one you won't be able to solve either. Brilliant. There's a story about the local authority putting meters on the benches in Cheyne Walk so you have to pay to sit down. Go and cover that."

Saturday 5th November

I decided to take in a new ground: West Ham United – the old Ironsides. They were playing Brighton, whom I'd seen at Millwall's first game at their new ground. It was a goalless draw. They really are going to have to change the rules to allow more goals.

Back in the office the news came in: Everton 2 Woolwich Arsenal 0 Crowd: 10,000. If Woolwich Arsenal go down to the Second Division, what would Norris have achieved? True, he can move Woolwich to Fulham, and have games on alternating weeks, but so what?

I wrote a simple report on the West Ham game, with something about Brighton being an up-and-coming club, and how we might see them in the Football League one day soon. I had no enthusiasm for the piece, and wasn't at all surprised when it was spiked.

Sunday 6th November

There is a motor fair on at Olympia, Marie had told me, and I proposed that I go and give the man-in-the-street's view of cars, having been in them a few times now, but naturally not owning one. I could build on the meeting I had with Mr Rolls and all that he had to say.

I was half way to persuading Mr Holloway that this was acceptable, when Mr Symmonds came in.

"It is about to happen in Tonypandy," he said. "Find your friend the photographer, get on a train, and get there."

So much for a gentle stroll around a bunch of cars.

I called Marie, told her, and asked if she wanted to come. She said certainly, and suggested that there was something to be said for an article on how the women cope with the strike.

I phoned the Queen Victoria and we got our room again, with Edward next door – all the previous crowd having left soon after us.

On the journey Marie gave us a run down on the law, courtesy of her father. There was an Act – the Trade Disputes Act of 1906 – that gave the miners the right to 'peaceful picketing'. Her view was that with the sort of activity that was being predicted, this was not going to be peaceful picketing. That was why they wanted Edward. Pictures of a riot please, and make it snappy.

Monday 7th November

Marie was right. The strikers had announced that the officials of the mining companies were not going to be allowed anywhere near the mines and the yards. We were awoken by the sound of a trumpet player walking through the streets bugling a call to work. It was too early for breakfast (which I found annoying) so we went out to find thousands of men facing off anyone who wanted to get near the mine. I went back in, kicked Edward awake, and we set him up in the window of the ballroom on the first floor, looking down on the scene. We could see up and down the street, and if there were any miners or workers coming in from any other working area there was no chance of them, or anyone else, getting through.

There were also police everywhere – and it soon became clear that our press passes were not worth anything. The miners didn't trust the London press, and the police treated everyone as the enemy. I was told that some of these coppers were known for aggression in Aberdare and elsewhere. There was talk of half of the miners of Wales being out on strike.

Marie disappeared to follow her woman's perspective story, and within minutes every road was blocked. All Edward and I could do was wait and watch.

What we saw was a united community – wives and children were out in the streets taking up their position on the pickets. It was hard to see anyone getting through. News (or maybe just rumour) filtered down that in the Cambrian colliery the ventilation fans had been put out of action – which meant no one could go down the mine.

It continued through the day, rumours and counter-rumours flowing back and forth. Marie came back unscathed and very excited with the interviews she had done (although many of the women were as suspicious of her as the men were of me), and along with Edward we managed to team up with a few other journalists – at least ones that we could understand. A couple from the nationals and some from Bristol. There was only one other photographer on the scene. If our luck held Edward was going to be a star.

By the evening the word was that all the pits were shut, save for the safety workers who were stopping the mine from flooding. But still the stories continued – mostly about the hated Leonard Llewellyn, the manager of the Glamorgan colliery, who was now accused of not just keeping the safety equipment running but sneaking in blackleg labour from Cardiff. Cardiff, we learned, was a foreign country.

By 10 o'clock the story had moved on. The men who were now in the mine were in fact the police. Will John was up on his soap box most of the time, appealing for everyone to stay calm and not to listen to the stories, but you could see at a glance that his moment was gone. Distrust was the order of the day.

The problem was beyond doubt the number of police – now perceived as an invading force from foreign lands. In fact, if they had been Germans the effect would have been the same. The women screamed at the lines of police, "Where's John, where's David, where's Bryn?" indicating the lack of their regular policemen drawn from the villages. Once a community loses respect in its police force, everything goes.

It was the power station just beyond the high street that was the key – and we moved with the crowd as people began to gather on the hill above, throwing stones onto the building.

Edward took a picture, but I couldn't see the story. "Throwing stones at a building that size… so what? Let them throw. They will run out of stones long before that building gets a single chip out of a single wall."

Which I still think was true, and it would have petered out had the police not moved in – a tactic which was seriously flawed. Some idiot sergeant had ordered his men forwards in a line, with no protection at their sides, and within moments the crowd had instinctively pushed around the edges of the line, trapping the police within.

The police then began to fight with their batons, and eventually moved themselves into a tight military square pushing their way back to the building.

From here it was easy to see what their next move would be: the baton charge against the unarmed civilians. "For God's sake get a picture of the charge showing the police and the fact that the miners don't have weapons," I shouted to Edward. "Get that, and your reputation is made."

Reinforced by police from other guard duties the forces of law pushed the miners and their families backwards towards the town, breaking heads until peace was more or less restored with the population in the town square. Edward got his shot.

I thought that would be it – leave the police on guard and let the people go back to their homes, but no, these policemen had tasted blood, and would have none of it.

With the crowds hemmed into the narrow streets of the town, we watched as the police charged again, catching the population in the corners of the square, and battering them until they were on the ground, and then some. This time we could find not a vantage point to take pictures, and no way through to the hotel. We just stood at the fringes, watched and tried to keep ourselves safe.

Tuesday 8th November

By the morning the talk everywhere was that the cavalry were on their way from Tidworth Barracks. We grabbed food and ate it (much to the management's utter disgust) in the doorway of the hotel as we waited for developments. There was tension in the air such as I had not known since the Transvaal. Rumour was the only currency of the day. Mr Churchill was sending in the mounted troops. Mr Churchill was sending in the Met Police. Mr Asquith was sending in the army.

Having dealt with (indeed having been imprisoned by) the Met in recent days, their possible arrival did not strike me as any worse than the situation we already had, but for the locals the "London Police" were an unknown. Mr Churchill might as well have said that he was sending in a division of Icelandic Sea Monsters.

The troops did not arrive in the morning – but extra police did. About 70 on horseback and 200 on foot, all with the Met's distinctive costume. The Cavalry were said to be hanging back just beyond the hills. Rumour, as always, won the day. It was no contest; the situation was out of control.

The news that all the workmen on strike were being paid off by their companies came as the police started to enter the town. They followed the first rule of the non-imaginative military planner. If a tactic works once, do it again. They pushed everyone into the narrowest streets.

But, to my surprise, the miners had learned something, for they moved out to the more open spaces of the Tonypandy Athletic Ground.

In one of those odd flashes of memory I was reminded of the way in which this diary started – recording the way in which Mr Leavey failed to gauge a meeting and so lost support that should have been his. Mr Leavey could be excused, of course, for he is a gentleman's outfitter. But in Tonypandy the error was made by a stipendiary magistrate, a state official, a formal keeper of the law called Lleufer Thomas (I checked the spelling), and he chose this moment, when rumour was rife and tension at its highest, to stand on a box and read a message from the Home Secretary.

The problem was exacerbated by the fact that Mr Thomas was not a good speaker, and there was much noise in the crowd. From what we could gather, Mr Churchill was saying that the soldiers were here to maintain the peace so that the majority of honest decent people could go about their lawful everyday business unharmed and unhindered.

There was much shouting, but the situation was rescued (at least for the moment) by Will John who repeated the message adding that he was being invited to meetings with the Board of Trade.

That carried the crowd, so we all trooped away back to the Glamorgan Colliery, hanging around just in case something happened. It didn't until it got dark and scuffles started to break out.

What was particularly clear was that the Mounties (as we had started to call them) were as disorganised as the police on foot were yesterday. Orders were shouted such as "C Division close up", but the policemen and mounties looked at each other, each quite unable to work out what they were supposed to do and assuming therefore that the message was meant for the other party. They might as well have said, "C Division, second ball."

At one point a London cop fell near us, blood pouring from his head. We dragged him away from the crowd and Marie tore part of her dress to act as a bandage. When he came round after a few seconds he assumed he was under attack again and tried to arrest both of us. I told him to listen to our accents and look at our clothes.

We stayed with the copper for nearly an hour, exchanging thoughts and ideas, and he confirmed what we had guessed. There was no plan, no one knew what they were coming into, there were no lines of communications.

Finally a sergeant came by, assumed we were attacking the man, and lashed out with his baton at Marie (he slipped and missed). Fortunately I was able to get behind him, lock his arms, and invite the man we had so gallantly helped to inform his superior what we were doing. Edward was completely bemused – I don't think he had ever been threatened by a bobby before.

By the time we left that situation the Mounties were fighting wildly on their own with the regulars on the ground trying to avoid the horses while finding Welshmen and women to hit. They weren't even very good at that.

Eventually the crowds were pushed back once again towards Tonypandy, leaving what looked like a battlefield with hundreds of injured lying out cold or crying in pain. There were no medical facilities within miles.

And so we had two sides, untrained, tired and maddened by the fight and the blood. And then, just for fun, the Swansea and Cardiff police joined forces with the London police (whose lingo they couldn't understand) as the local miners were joined by those from other fields. Unfortunately an argument broke out between miners about tactics, and that led to fighting between the working men, which the police were quite happy to leave alone. There was some looting, mostly by outsiders and a few of the police under the guise of protecting the shops. And in the midst there were a lot of shops that were just left alone.

We kept to the walls, used the side streets, and finally made it back to the Victoria. A number of windows were already smashed, but the residents and staff had formed a guard on the door (which we joined) and that seemed to be holding. After an hour's haggling over the price I managed to phone in a report to the Chron.

Wednesday 9th November

At 8 o'clock we looked out into the emerging dawn to find that the troops had arrived and were patrolling the streets with a fresh delivery of London constabulary.

We went out to talk with the constables, one of whom recognised me having done some duty in Woolwich while on loan to the Kent force. The thinking was around 200 police injured, but I guessed that was an exaggeration, as these numbers always are. The police were also putting out the story that the journalists were part of the conspiracy and we were being advised to get out quickly.

Marie was still keen to find more local women to talk to so she ventured out while I borrowed the hotel typewriter to write up a further report. Edward escorted Marie and took pictures of the wreckage of the town as far as he could.

Thursday 10th November

We returned by the early train. Back in the office I wrote up my commentary but it was clear that my work was being heavily cut and re-written. Criticising the police is not official Chron policy.

Mr Holloway brought me the jolly news that at a meeting of the councillors of Fulham Norris had yesterday been elected as mayor for a second year.

I put in a further request to cover the motor show, but was told some upstart young reporter had done it while I had been in Wales. There was, however, the case of the spontaneous combustion of a scout hut in Dorking which needed my urgent attention if I would care to venture south.

When I indicated that I didn't care so to do I was offered the Lord Mayor's Banquet which was being held that night but I turned that down too on the grounds that I couldn't face the sight of Norris preening himself. Instead I went to Wood Green to wash and change, and then on to Dorset Square where we were joined by Edward and Sophia.

Sophia listened with interest to our tales, for she was full of the demonstration being planned for Sunday at Parliament and was pumping us for every detail on police tactics, the troops and what the miners did right or wrong. I was sceptical that there would be any comparison – there were thousands of miners in Tonypandy, I reminded her. How many normally turned up at Suffragette demonstrations, I wondered. Fifty?

"Why are you always so against us?" she demanded, returning to an old theme that I thought we had buried months before.

"Because... because... because, I worked for years in an environment where following orders was everything, even when those orders were clearly stupid. I worked with officers who had not got a clue, but my oath and the regulations meant that I still called them 'sir' even when correcting their mistakes.

"Going against law and order is not what I have been brought up and trained to do. Now I find myself in a new world where the established order is challenged day by day, and questions are asked that I had never considered.

"If you ask me, should women have the vote in Parliamentary elections, I would say, yes, of course. But if you ask me, is this worth dying for, I would say no. If you ask me if the miners deserve better pay, I'd say yes. Should they have their heads bashed in for protesting for that right? No." She went to interrupt but Marie called for me to be heard. "So I have no idea what the solution is – but there is something extremely odd going on, something so odd that I can smell it and almost touch it. It swamps all concerns about Parliament and voting and strikers and everything. If the Unionists really seriously are putting forward mass sterilisation as a policy, then that is what we should be fighting. In that case Parliament is becoming irrelevant, and the Suffragette movement is helping make Parliament irrelevant. Then does "votes for women" matter? No, because Parliament does not matter.

"But I still can't figure out how this ties in with the money being circulated, not just at the football, but in Wales as well. Or a necklace being stolen in Hatton

Garden and then being replaced with something that looks the same but doesn't actually contain diamonds. Or why both Norris and Churchill, in their own ways, are utterly desperate for power.

"What odds would it make if women could vote for Parliament and then Germany invaded, or if Parliament was overthrown by the anarchists? Or the Unionists won?"

"So does that mean we should not even struggle?" Sophia was dismissive, and angry.

"No, it doesn't. But you are asking me why I am not as deeply involved with your movement as I am with Woolwich Arsenal, or why I seem so affected by what I saw in Wales, but not about your friends being force-fed in prison. The answer is partly because I have a job that five years ago I could never have dreamed I would have, and partly because I think I am being made a fool of – and I don't know who by, or why."

"It has to be Churchill!" said Marie. "He never told us what was in the original Woolwich Woman letter. And he sent the troops in against the miners. I wouldn't be surprised if he supported compulsory sterilisation of the poor. He certainly voted against the extension of public education to 14 year olds – and made a virulent speech about dirty little boys being only fit for the streets, and how they wouldn't be containable in a classroom."

"But I can't see the Home Secretary organising the entry of tens of thousands of pounds of false bank notes and sovereigns onto the streets of London, and then having them distributed to the working men in Wales that he next attacks with the troops," I replied.

Saturday 12th November

I am in high dudgeon. My work on Tonypandy has been rewritten in such a way that all criticism of the police is removed, although Marie has had more luck and is hoping for a significant piece on the women in the strike in tomorrow's paper. Even Edward's pictures which showed the baton-wielding police lines were cut, and the extent of the problem was starting to get home to him.

I was told that if I had nothing else to do I should do my usual tour of duty at Woolwich, which took me to a one goal to nil victory over Sheffield Wednesday. 10,000 were there. I found nothing to say, except that in the Hen and Basket after the game I was told that John Humble had become a director of the club again – although I had no idea if that was significant or not.

I went back to the office and wrote the piece up, arguing that if the off-side law was not reduced to one player, and the goalkeeper not restricted to an area near the goal, football would be dead within six months. I left for Dorset Square before anyone could say anything.

I asked Marie to give me a summary of the Suffragette position. "According to Father," she said, "virtually everyone in the Commons wants votes for women, and they keep passing bills. But the bills don't become law – they just go to committee, and I think this is Asquith's way of stopping anything happening.

"The issue keeps getting stuck on how many women should have the vote – some MPs say none, some say just a few, some say the same as men. However you do it, it doesn't work, because most women don't own property, and an electorate based on property ownership or rent paid (as with men) doesn't work equally for men and women. You have the vote don't you?"

I confirmed that I did. I paid Mum the requisite rent, presented my signed letter, and was on the register. I'd voted for the first time in the general election at the start of the year.

While I was speaking Lord Cortney joined us. "Sadly, many in my own party don't like the current proposals," he said, "because it just gives the vote to a bunch of rather rich women who will all vote Unionist, and that won't help the Liberal cause at all. We might be the party of Enlightenment, but we are not completely enlightened when it comes to taking ourselves out of office. Worse for the ladies, the Irish MPs will vote against anything to do with electoral reform, because they want debating time for Ireland and its independence." He turned to me. "Will you be at the demonstration, Mr Jones?"

"I shall be there as a journalist observing an event, I imagine," I said, "Looking for anyone passing sovereigns or diamond necklaces. Unless Mr Holloway sends me to find the Loch Ness Monster."

Sunday 13th November

I phoned the office from Dorset Square and said I was following up a story which would link to the Suffragette demonstration next Friday – unless they needed me for anything. They didn't, so Marie and I stayed and talked to Sophia and Edward who joined us.

Sophia gave us a lecture about the Women's Social and Political Union of which she was a member and the National Union of Women's Suffrage Societies which she despised. Sophia's group took the view they would do anything to achieve their ends – and in that I felt she had the support of Marie. Any means to reach the end. We had that in South Africa.

Christabel Pankhurst of the Women's Social had been let out of prison last week after being accused of hitting a copper at a Liberal Party meeting. Infiltrating such meetings is a prime tactic – they stand their ground and shout through megaphones to disrupt the situation. I did a piece about one last year, with a little skit about them trying to disrupt the noise of a football match happening next door. I doubt it got many letters, and fortunately Sophia did not know of it.

At one stage the girls got into a particularly intense debate about illegal actions and Sophia's annoyance at what she called "the pointlessness of pointless theft" which she compared with "organised disruption", after which the talk was of sexual equality which was getting Edward quite excited. "Deeds not words" seemed to be the slogan of the day, and Marie's thieving was left in abeyance.

I picked up what seemed to become my hobbyhorse of the day. "Surely if we support the Liberals, the Parliament Act will get through, and they will have the money to help the old and the sick. They will tackle the vortex of poverty."

"So you are with those who would talk out any bill," said Sophia, with real venom. "Let's help the old and the sick with Lloyd George's budget, so better not have votes for women just now."

"But you won't be poor in your old age, Sophia," I said.

"So are you going to tell us about your impoverished childhood, and how you were forced to pick up a gun at fourteen and fight for the empire?" she demanded.

"I was not brought up in the vortex," I said, "but I have seen those who are, and some of my fellow soldiers who were not able to adjust after coming back from Africa have fallen into it. If you want to know, my prime concern is the vortex – and, of course, the fact that there is a proposal to make matters worse by not treating the destitute as people any more. But that is not an argument about votes for women; it is just a reflection of where my life has taken me."

"We attack any party in power," proclaimed Sophia, and Marie told her to lower her voice. "It is the Liberals today but after the next election it could well be the Unionists. If Labour was in power we would attack them. We support no change that does not include votes for women. And if that includes your precious pensions and hospitals so be it."

"But don't you support help for the poor?" I asked. "Don't you support the removal of the wealth of the landed gentry? Don't you feel for the miners who can hardly live on their wages while the owners sit in their mansions. Aren't you moved by Mr George's speeches?"

"We are only doing what Campbell-Bannerman told us to do – you know who he was?"

"The Prime Minister," I replied with a sigh, trying to indicate that I was a little fed up with suggestions that I was stupid, just because I came from a different class.

"He told us to go on pestering," she said. "So that is what we do."

"But you don't support the Labour Party," I said, "which wants votes for all men and women. You just want votes for rich women."

"We are against all political parties," said Sophia. It sounded like a phrase from a manual. "Because we are outside of political parties we are outside of politics and the economy. No votes, no tax." It was another political phrase. I was surprised at Sophia. She was, I knew, much too intelligent to parrot such rubbish.

"This is press baiting," I said.

"I'm just telling you what we believe in the movement. I thought that was why we were debating."

"No," I said. "What you are describing is setting up events just to get publicity. Which is press baiting. Throw stones at MPs houses, get arrested, refuse to plead, refuse the fine, go to prison... get publicity. And it is dependent on the newspaper owners – who are all men – giving you that publicity."

"When Marion Wallace went on hunger strike last year it was not part of any officially organised campaign – she did it out of her feelings of disgust for the society in which she lived."

I let it go, and went home.

Monday 14th November

Having had Sunday off I felt obliged to go into work and found to my surprise a little something to take my mind off events.

There had been a robbery at a jewellery shop in Oxford Street. I went down with Edward to have a look. A diamond necklace had gone.

"About your quest," said Edward, in relation to nothing at all, "this whole thing with the false money and its meaning, the Woman from Woolwich, spies, the vortex, all of that…"

"I am fairly familiar with the subject," I said, and got a grin in return.

"Have you ever felt that this is, well, life?"

"What?" I turned away from the shop. "What?" I repeated.

"I think what I mean is that my life has become more like a dream than life. Sophia with the WSPU, Marie with her… The money, Norris and Churchill and the quest for power, Leitch, what you saw in Wales. And then all that you have told me about Africa."

"What?"

"I went to a Labour Party meeting last week…"

"What?"

"Just to see, and the speaker said that we kept on having wars in foreign countries so that it didn't mess up the estates of the landed gentry."

"Probably true," I said.

"And that lots of people think Mr Asquith and Mr Churchill conspired to kill the king."

"Why would they do that?"

"To revive the country, to make our blood flow like true Englishmen by giving us something to be passionate about. It is like a dream I have, where I have to run, but I am trying to run in every direction at once, and of course I can't and one minute I am going one way, and then another, and everything is confusion."

Tuesday 15th November

"Doesn't the WSPU have shops?" I asked Edward.

He confirmed that they did.

"Does Sophia ever work in them?"

"She's on a rota. They sell things to raise funds and get publicity."

"Do they ever receive gifts?"

"Not in the shops," he said, "but sometimes supporters give money to the Union."

"Wealthy women – they give money?"

"I guess so."

We looked at each other.

"You don't mean…" he said.

"Woolwich Woman as a Suffragette," I said. "It's an option. She gives the Union a load of sovereigns, and they pass it through the shops."

Wednesday 16th November

"Tell me something about the prime minister," I said to Marie, in relation to nothing in particular.

"Ignorant, stupid, lacking in imagination," she said. "Exactly like Captain Kell – except the story is Kell can administer. I am not sure Mr Asquith can. 'The poor are the poor and are always with us'."

"Was he against the Boer War?"

"I don't think so," she said. "That was Mr Campbell Bannerman."

Thursday 17th November

Three central London shops were broken into last night. Marie assured me she was responsible for only two of them, both belonging to the Women's Social Political Union. The Union said nothing was stolen which was slightly odd because according to the thief six pounds in sovereigns was removed from each.

The third shop was a jeweller's in Bond Street. It had been broken into at the start of the week but the story was only breaking today. I went to interview Mr Dangerfield, the shop keeper, and met Edward there. The old boy was rather bemused, because the real story was that the diamond necklace that had been stolen on Monday had returned to the shop last night.

"Are you sure it is exactly the same one?" I asked. Edward photographed the shopkeeper holding said necklace. "Not a different version?"

"Why would anyone give me a different version?" he asked.

"Why indeed!" I said. "Perhaps they are trying to run in every direction at once."

"I think he means it is always worth checking," said Edward helpfully.

We went to the Admiralty, where I used my Captain's card to get me into Room 40. Blinker Hall welcomed me like a long lost friend and instantly suggested a trip around the corner to the Malt Shovel.

"A bit of a tricky one this," I said, having procured the pints. Blinker was all ears. "How would you tell if a sovereign was a fake?"

"Three or four ways," he said without hesitation. "With a paper note you look at the paper, you feel it, you check the watermark – that's the start. If you want to go further you put a chemical on the corner. Sovereigns are much easier: you weigh them first and, assuming they match up, you scrape a little off and check the composition. They should have a gold content of just over seven grams. A fake would probably have a gold content of round about one gram – otherwise it is hardly were bothering with."

I gave him one of the coins lifted by Marie. He rubbed it between his fingers and then tossed it up and down in one hand with a coin from his pocket in the other. "It's very good," he said, "would fool the average shop keeper."

"Unless both are fakes," I said. He looked and laughed.

"What a wheeze!" he declared. "If we are all used to handling fakes every day, how would we know?"

I gave him another, and the result was the same. He held it near the gas light, and then away, drained his glass and marched us back to the Admiralty. "We do the specific gravity test – in simple terms you check the weight of the gold in two different mediums…" and then he went quiet as he carried it out. And he stayed quiet as he tested my two coins and the one from his pocket.

"Yours are both fake," he said quietly. "And so is mine."

"Don't tell anyone, Blinker," I said, and led him back to the pub for another round.

"But what's its all about?" he demanded, downing half the pint in one go and looking slightly shaken.

"I think it might be connected with a book by GK Chesterton – but when I know for sure," I said, "I'll tell you."

Friday 18th November

The demonstration by the Suffragettes was not due until the afternoon, so I dropped into Fleet Street, put up with a long moan from Mr Holloway about a total lack of work since Tonypandy, and told him the Big One was on its way. He asked if I had anything about the plans to place all carrot production in Shropshire while turning Northants over totally to cows. I said I thought the Mail had run that piece a week ago.

I picked up the Kentish and read an article by George Leavey saying that Woolwich were certainly not going to leave Manor Ground at the end of the season and he would personally guarantee they would still be playing in Woolwich next September. He didn't say what league they'd be in. Nor, come to that, what sport they'd be playing.

Mr Dangerfield at the jewellers in Bond Street called while I was still contemplating Woolwich. His message was simple. The diamonds that had been replaced were worth more than the originals.

I wrote up the story of an outbreak of thefts of necklaces – and their return – and suggested for the first time that there was a link with Woolwich Woman. I had no idea how to include the issue of fake sovereigns without causing a major panic or the arrest of half the people I knew. I shouted for Edward and we went to Parliament to watch events.

We took tea at the Lyons opposite Westminster Bridge, and Edward informed me at length that the current issue for Sophia was the failure of the latest consolidation bill which had gone to committee and disappeared.

As we watched, the Suffragettes approached Parliament. This was nothing like the situation in south Wales for the pushing and jostling was not coming from the police or the women on the march, but from working men. There were a few fruit sellers around who seemed to have brought along some old stock which was going at a farthing for three. It all began to look horribly organised.

Edward took his first picture, and we chatted amiably enough while we waited for developments. "Which do you fix first – the stomach or the politics?" I mused, reflecting on the row with Sophia.

"I'm with you," Edward said. "I run in all directions at once." I think he's getting the hang of this journalism lark.

We watched the demonstration as the first fruit was thrown followed by a lot of jostling. "The police are doing nothing," Edward protested. "I'd better help…"

I grabbed him. "Do that and you are no longer working for the paper. The police will act if the women get attacked, but they'll spot your background from the cut of your clothes and pull you in. Added to which, if Sophia ever finds you went into the fray at the first sign of fruit throwing, she'll never talk to you again. Forget the wedding, and probably most of your teeth."

So we watched, and Edward took the pictures.

And it became clear that my prognostication was wrong. Repeatedly the Suffragettes tried to make it across the square to Parliament and repeatedly as they reached the police line they were pushed back into the mob. I guess there were around 400 women there, far more than I had expected, and what I will say for them is that they were extremely well organised. The miners could have learned a lot from these women – and that I decided was going to be my theme.

I felt pleased to have got a story and slipped my notebook into my pocket, ready to tell Edward to take a last shot and then turn back for Fleet Street, when I paused. The mob was launching another surge and this time the women started to take a real beating. Two men dragged one of the women into the bushes by the square. I shouted at Edward to bring his camera, and we pushed into the fray.

As we got close I called to Edward to protect his camera, take pictures if he could, and to stay out of trouble, for I doubted his ability in a free-for-all. The dear fellow would probably expect no hitting below the belt and would lay off, just because his opponent went down.

I dragged the two men off the woman in the bushes while Edward took a flash picture of them. The light blinded them, and I used the moment to hit and kick each of them as hard as I could, which left them lying in agony. "Get up and run," I shouted to the woman who was looking bemused. I didn't dare put my hand down to help her up.

Instead I shouted to Edward, and we moved into the crowd in time to stop a second assault.

Then as we emerged from that one back into the roadway I realised that our little excursions had provided a diversion for some of the women enabling them to get out of trouble and, incidentally, closer to Parliament, from which point they were now being pushed back towards the rapists by the police. Meanwhile some of the mob was edging our way. They had seen the flash light and had guessed what we were up to. As with Tonypandy, so in Westminster, we were not loved by anyone.

But to my relief a couple of journalists whom I knew from the Star emerged, and they joined us with a shout of "With you, Jacko" as we pretended to face the mob down. Fortunately for us (for I fear we would have been badly mauled had it come to a fight against so many) a shout went up from the roadside as another group of Suffragettes surged forward, and the police, clearly fed up with not getting enough action, drew batons and moved in with full violence.

"Get a picture of the police," I screamed to Edward above the tumult. "If you get nothing else, I want the police hitting women," and from then on the event turned into a battle. The organization of the WSPU was such that they could have taught my commanders a thing or three ten years ago, and I watched in sheer admiration as they split into three groups at the sound of a police whistle that they had brought along (an incident which had the dear old bobbies quite confused for several seconds). Through this manoeuvre they were able to distance themselves from both police and the mob, and cleverly avoided getting stuck between their two sets of assailants.

Meanwhile my little band – which had gained an apprentice from the Times and a completely bemused political commentator from the Manchester Guardian – was looking to me for commands.

It was clear we were not going to have any effect at all in the general affray, but I reckoned we could pick off disorganised elements and give the women a chance of escape – if they chose to take it.

So that's what we did. With Edward circling the police lines waiting for his chance to take pictures I moved the team to one side where the mob and police were close together. "When I say 'run' head back to our last position," I shouted. "Don't wait, just move, otherwise you might get hurt." I turned and led our own charge against the mob.

As I had hoped, the police, seeing violence, turned on the event with vengeance. Within seconds I was shouting "Run", and most of the merry band heard me and followed, leaving the police and the mob to slog it out against each other. One of the three women's flanks spotted the opportunity and ran through the gap in police lines left by the attack on where we had been. That took the Union's front a further ten yards on and temporarily out of trouble.

No sooner were we back in our position than our ensemble were ready to repeat, but I held back. "Go too soon and even the dunderheads in the helmets will spot us. Hold back. Besides, the light's almost gone." Indeed the gas lamps were on, but they gave only a partial illumination, and that, I felt, might give us more grasp of the situation.

We stood and watched the three sections of the women's group. I saw one of the leaders watching me. I indicated with a raised arm a position where I was contemplating our next rally. The woman gave no indication of having seen or understood my signal, but I took that to be her problem, not mine. Man helping woman in Union punch up? They were not going to like that! Besides, she wouldn't have any instructions to cover such an event.

I used my police whistle left over from our break-ins in Woolwich as the signal for the second in and out, and we caused more havoc. When I looked back, the middle Union flank had taken advantage. I caught the eye of the leader of that section, and raised a hand to her indicating the direction of the next sortie. This time I got a short raised hand in return. They were getting the hang of the guerrilla campaign.

The battle raged until eleven o'clock – how long it would have taken without us there, I have no idea. Likewise I also don't know what ended it all, but suddenly one of the three women's groups was missing. I took that as the moment to get my band out. We worked hard right, found Edward, before taking the mob and police with us, and led them into each other, and my band and the Union sections moved out.

Edward and I rushed back to Fleet Street, shouting out the story to editors as we entered the building, with me bashing the keys of the typewriter before I was even sitting and Edward using every apprentice in the place to get his pictures developed. No one was going to edit this story out of existence.

Saturday 19th November

We named it Black Friday – the day the English bobby and English working man took it on themselves to fight unarmed women. The lowest point in the history of the Empire I called it. Even the Danes who fought Alfred the Great never got that low.

The piece came out as a personal tirade. I did not fight for an Empire in which women peacefully protesting their point at Parliament are attacked by an unholy alliance of rapists and coppers, I roared.

"You may not agree with the Women's Social and Political Union," the piece continued, "and you may be totally against votes for women. But this country has liberty, and I, and millions braver than me, have fought to protect that tradition of liberty.

"Liberty means the ability to protest your point of view – no matter how foul or alien others find it. Liberty means protecting the weaker sex, even if they adopt the stance of man and protest their position in front of Parliament.

"Every policeman involved in this disgraceful and despicable violence should be removed from the service at once," I bellowed.

Mr Holloway eventually came out and shouted, "Will someone get this maniac off that ruddy typewriter… and tell him we went to press an hour ago."

The fifth floor picked up most of my story, stopped the press, and ran a new edition. But it wasn't me, of course. I'd seen a chance, but Edward's pictures carried the day. There was discussion about which of the assault pictures we could run – and in the end they cut one in half to avoid showing the lady's legs, but that made the point even clearer. Policemen were implicated in both rape and assault.

Even the news that one group of women had broken away from the demonstration to attack Asquith's car as it was leaving Parliament didn't deflect from the power of the argument, and I wondered in passing what Mr Churchill would make of it. It does, after all, come under his department.

And as far as everyone in the office was concerned, it was a great story – and time for a drink. They noticed me still peering intently at two of Edward's photos, but everyone was so taken with the story that no one really cared – except Edward, of course, who brought a magnifying glass to help us both see better.

We didn't speak – which I suppose made it all a lot more dramatic – until finally I said, "It is, isn't it?" and Edward nodded. Two of the men who were leading the mob and who had been caught on camera by Edward, were part of the gang that we had seen at Fulham distributing coins. We'd followed them to their flat in Aintree Street.

Sunday 20th November

I cannot express my delight. The rest of the papers are with us on this. Even the Mail, which had until now has done nothing but pour scorn on the Suffragettes, expressed moral outrage at the action of the police – a first!

Of course, they all ignored the fact that the Chron (orchestrator: the song and dance man, Jacko Jones) had led the defence of the defenceless women. Of course, they didn't recognise the terrific work done by Edward either, but as I told him, that's what you get. We had the pictures, they did not.

I even forgot about Woolwich Arsenal until one of the runners told me they'd beaten Bristol City one goal to nil. Beyond every doubt, football, at this moment, did not matter. It will matter again tomorrow. But not today.

This was the first time that the Suffragettes had got the general reader on their side, and I feel I have done something rather important on my own initiative. At lunchtime the news came through that two women had died as a result of police violence. Over two hundred had been arrested. There was nothing on the subject of action against the police. My mood changed and I felt suddenly very angry and very sick. I still do as I write this.

Monday 21st November

A sombre day at Dorset Square. Lord Cortney asked for as truthful a report of events as we could give him, and we tried to oblige. He said that he expected statements from the government in Parliament today or tomorrow.

Sophia was particularly subdued, and after Lord Cortney had left she thanked me in front of Marie and Edward for what I had done in the square. I said it was nothing, although in truth that is not what I feel. But her thanks dispelled any remaining animosity from our earlier discussions.

Edward proposed a trip to the Empire in Leicester Square in the evening to take our minds off everything, and Marie sent out one of the household to get us tickets.

Some of the Ormiston Chant gang were outside the theatre campaigning against the moral standards of what was going on inside, and I wanted to tell them that if there were issues more important than football, there were issues more important than having women on the stage, but the others dragged me in. Gradually we cheered up.

Tuesday 22nd November

Today the government started to do something about Black Friday. The Prime Minister announced that if the Liberals win the forthcoming election they will introduce a bill to allow women to vote – which was a bit daft since as far as I can see they have been doing that and then failing to get it through the Commons for the last three years.

The WSPU would have none of that. They wanted a full enquiry into the police handling of the event and they wanted the police involved prosecuted for murder and attempted murder.

Mr Churchill made a speech criticising the police, which must be a first for a Home Secretary, arguing that as women are citizens they have rights including fair treatment by the police and protection under the law. The feeling throughout Dorset Square was that it was political opportunism: say something to calm the situation, and then walk on as if nothing had happened.

Sophia saw it differently. "The bastard was nearly two hundred miles away and he was able to organise the troops to clear the streets in south Wales," she said, "but he can't even restrain his own policemen when they are fighting opposite the House of Commons."

Wednesday 23rd November

Although I didn't realise it until half way through the day, this is the moment when the Parliament Bill started to take shape.

The bill was introduced by the Marquis of Lansdowne who couched it in that formal language that members of the Houses of Parliament use so that no one knows what they are talking about. "If a difference arises between the two Houses with regard to any Bill other than a Money Bill in two successive Sessions, and with an interval of not less than one year, and such difference cannot be adjusted by any other means, it shall be settled in a Joint Sitting composed of members of the two Houses…."

I suppose I would have given this more attention had it not been that we were still running Black Friday stories. I was calling for both the Commissioner of Police for London and the manager of Woolwich Arsenal to be arrested.

Marie was more taken with the fact that they hanged Doctor Hawley Harvey Crippen, and her pieces on him appeared in a couple of papers. She'd done a lot on Ethel Le Neve, Crippen's lover, and the use of the international telegraph, and of course the human remains buried under the floor of the coal cellar. Her view was that Crippen was clearly innocent. Why would he bury just tiny bits of the body and cart the rest away? How come only two policeman were in the house when the body parts were found? Why did the detective inspector resign the moment Crippen was found guilty? This was, she proclaimed, a second fixed trial in the course of one year.

(She also told me that her original copy then went on to implicate the Home Secretary in both murders, but no one would publish that bit.)

Thursday 24th November

Crippen, Suffragettes, Tonypandy, fake jewels, fake sovereigns, the police… I woke up and suddenly I thought: Mr Churchill had been so alarmed at my story of the torpedo factory leaving Woolwich that he had given me another story in its place, and a captain's salary…

Why?

Saturday 26th November

Woolwich Arsenal 1 Newcastle United 2

Nothing unusual in that – Woolwich are having an up and down season. But today we had Norris handing out prospectuses with a letter which stated that there was going to be a new, new share issue, as opposed to the last new share issue, which is different from the previous old new old share issue. Everyone who loved Woolwich Arsenal could buy back their club and keep it forever in Woolwich, he proclaimed. If they did not oblige, it was certain the club would eventually leave Woolwich. Sticks and carrots. Roll up, roll up, buy a share, or lose your club.

There were 14,000 at the game. Would they buy? I doubted it. In fact I think most of them were still turning up hoping to bump into a put-pocket. But there were none to be found. The number of women at the game was up though.

I watched the match from the press area. Norris seemed to have lost interest in taunting me, and besides he didn't want a spectacle on the day he was selling shares.

Back at the office I found that Wolverhampton Wanderers had beaten Fulham by five goals to one – and at least that would have annoyed Norris. It made me feel a little better.

Sunday 27th November

Sophia was still haranguing the rest of us on Churchill. Marie tried to cut through the rhetoric by making a list of what we knew for sure, rather than what we might believe.

"First of all, given the torpedo factory incident, we know he's secretive and will go to any lengths to keep certain actions quiet. Secondly, he was willing to use any resource to put down disorder as at Tonypandy, but quite happy to stand by and let the fighting continue – as on Black Friday.

"Thirdly, he can be devious (as when not telling Kell he was employing Jacko, and not revealing the truth about the Woolwich Woman's letters). Devious, ruthless, secretive." We all agreed that there was no other conclusion. I reminded the group that I'd also seen him behave in very unorthodox ways in South Africa – way outside the rules of engagement.

"Running in every direction at once," I said.

"Guilty of mass murder," said Sophia.

"Guilty of sending innocent men to the gallows," said Marie.

The Home Secretary's popularity seems to be in decline.

Tuesday 29th November

Three jewellery shops were broken into last weekend. The police have asked all the papers to hold back on the information because, they say, they fear this was the work of an organised spy ring (as opposed to a disorganised spy ring, I thought).

Edward and I went for a drink. "Do you think Churchill has organised the fake money and the jewellery thefts?" he asked.

I loved the idea, but couldn't work out why he might do it.

Wednesday 30th November

Marie and I agree: if we could find a way to unite the issue of the put-pockets and the jewel raids on the one hand, with the torpedo factory, Woolwich Woman, why Churchill lied about the spy messages, police violence and the two murder trials, we'd have the story of all time.

Lord Cortney joined us. "There is a bit more," he said, as we gave him a resumé. "Mr Churchill has said that in his opinion the Liberals should support the policy of mass sterilisation of the poor."

I got a cab back to Fleet Street and wrote a piece about the vortex, contrasting the notion of unemployment benefit and old age pensions with sterilisation. I added a note referring back to the Slayer of Souls story, making the point that the Chronicle had led the way, as normal.

Thursday 1st December

The Chronicle wouldn't run it but *Society* had a complete review of all I was thinking about, leading to the conclusion that our country is falling apart. They went through everything from the old spy stories to foreigners, then threw in fake money, striking miners, the Commons against the Lords, and the police attacking women.

Then just for fun they blamed in on Halley's Comet. The Earth passing through the tail had destabilised mankind, resulted in the death of the king, and caused the end of civilisation. I wish I'd thought of that.

Friday 2nd December

I am not the only person who is finding news hard to come by. The Kentish filled up space by re-running Norris' begging letter with its threat of movement of the club if local people don't buy it back. I toyed with an article about how, within a year, newspapers will be dead and replaced by gossip machines which randomly take two people and two items of news and put them together. But I tore it up. I didn't want to give Mr Holloway a heart attack. Not yet anyway.

Saturday 3rd December

Football is now something of a relief; at least I can go back to writing about the pubs, the fashions, the people in the ground, and occasionally even a match.

I started out at the White Hart (one has to start somewhere) meandered down the Lane and got to Tottenham Hotspur for their game against Woolwich Arsenal (three goals to one). For the fourth game running Chalmers (now permanently replacing Rippon) scored and is now the Woolwich top scorer despite having missed the first part of the season. Tottenham only managed 16,000 in their ground which I thought was poor for two London teams. But at least eight of them were put-pockets, which was interesting. Despite their defeat Woolwich were back to normality. The left-footed players were playing on the left.

Meanwhile Norris went to Fulham's one goal to nothing victory over Chelsea.

I wrote up a piece which says that the crowd proved once and for all that people don't move across the city – they go to watch their local team or a good team. I then added the fact that two women sitting a few rows in front of the press box offered Eddie Bateup, the Arsenal keeper, their hats as he came off at half time. I tried to introduce myself but their menfolk told me where I should disappear to.

Back in the office I discovered the general election had started without my noticing. I was wondering why they had so many of those "This is Us" posters up.

Sunday 4th December

At Dorset Square we had a fine afternoon and a grand Sunday evening meal, during which Lord Cortney said, "What will happen next, Mr Jones?"

"I normally ask you for political information, sir," I said.

"You are more in touch with the events than us politicians," he replied.

"Then if what I have is more than the politicians, God help the politicians – and the country," I said. "I have no idea what is going on, and there's no one out there who will tell me. It looks like the diamonds that are stolen are replaced overnight in the shops from which they were stolen – if that makes any sense at all."

We all agreed it did not.

Monday 5th December

"Go and watch a bleedin' football match for God's sake," said Mr Holloway, "you've got the look of a man who's walked into the morgue and seen himself on the slab."

I told him I did not quite understand his metaphor, and he suggested that after the game I could look into the case of the herd of swimming sheep seen off the coast at Deal.

I thought I might do a second game at White Hart Lane, simply because it is my nearest ground (apart from the amateurs at Wood Green Town, for whom I have always had a soft spot, even though they never win anything.) What I picked was the final of the London Challenge Cup: Tottenham Hotspur against Fulham. Unfortunately it was not being played at Tottenham as I expected, but at the neutral venue of Stamford Bridge, so I had to get a bus and, running late, a cab. At my own expense, no doubt. I couldn't see Mr Holloway paying for my mistakes.

Thus Tottenham Hotspur 2, Fulham 1. Norris was in the stand, and could do nothing (it not being his ground) when I tipped my cap to him and gave him a broad smile.

No money exchanging pockets; an ordinary game. I went to play with the band afterwards. Slightly more enjoyable.

Wednesday 7th December

A telephone call from Sophia to me in the office – that is a first.

"Jacko – I have a piece of information I don't quite understand. Can I talk to you without it going straight into the paper?"

"I am obviously not a Suffragette," I said with as much huff as I could manage, "but I thought I might have earned your respect a little by now." I had after all saved a couple of women from a fate worse than...

"I've been working with members of the Union who were arrested or hurt," she announced, "and quite independently of each other they are telling the same story: that people were mingling with the mob on Black Friday giving out money. Did you see that?"

"No," I said, "and I would have told you if I had. I would also have reported it in the paper. But once the fighting started I was trying to direct operations."

"So what does it mean?" Another first – Sophia asking me what something meant.

"It either means there is a huge conspiracy by people unknown to achieve an end unknown, or else we have moved from a world where cause and effect have broken down, and now we are all simply running in lots of different directions at once, without purpose, without rhyme and without reason."

"I'll take the conspiracy option," she said.

"Which is a problem – because we can see the effects, passing the money, the fake jewels... but for what purpose, and who is behind it? I don't know. Marie doesn't know. Her father doesn't know. Edward doesn't know, and he studies the photographs. Just ask yourself the question: what would anyone have to gain by passing money around the mob on Black Friday?"

"To fight the Union and discredit us," she said with a firmness that suggested she had said that many times.

"In that case it was a total failure, wasn't it? All the papers – even the Mail – were outraged at what happened. And why do the same in Tonypandy and at the football games? In Wales and at Westminster the people who got the money got bad publicity – remember the Chron was the only paper that even half-suggested the police might have been a trifle heavy-handed at Tonypandy.

"And what about the football matches? Or think of the jewellers shops. Ask yourself 'why?' and when you know come and tell me."

Saturday 10th December

It is not that I have been avoiding Marie, it is more that I am so puzzled and dispirited, I can't think of how to make anything of this, and I hate to talk with her when all I can do is either moan or just admit failure.

Out of habit I went to watch Woolwich Arsenal. Despite Norris and the problems of getting from London to Plumstead I have quite fallen for the club this year, maybe because of their hopelessness. Owned by a man who doesn't want them to survive, playing as a London club but outside London, finding their support being moved away to Glasgow, having money given to them....

Woolwich Arsenal 0 Middlesbrough 2. 10,000 people there, and the booing started long before the turn around. Same team as played against Tottenham, and it clearly isn't working. Maybe the left and right switch is worth trying again.

After the game, I wrote a derisory piece, saying it was all over for the Gunners and that even the crowd had given up being entertaining.

"Someone got out of the wrong side of the bed," said Mr Holloway, when he saw my proposed headline: "This is not football"

Sunday 11th December

How extraordinary. I might just have it. I called Marie from the office but she wasn't there. I came home and played with the band and that helped, but I must talk with her.

Monday 12th December

I took the underground and bus to Dorset Square but Marie had gone out for a drive with her father. Jenkinson was, of course, most accommodating as he always is, and we chatted for half an hour about football, but in the end I had to leave him to his work.

Tuesday 13th December

"Right," said Mr Holloway, "Go and annoy Norris. He's buying land; find out if he is moving out of football. Find out what he is doing with the church. Find out something and write it and if you can't, find someone wearing a stupid hat, round up twenty kids off the street and get them to throw stones at the man, and then write that up. I've checked the schedule and there are no more riots due for another two months, so start one. Or you can do me a story about the six monkeys in Cardiff that have escaped from the zoo and are now standing for Parliament."

Marie called and said she would be at home this evening. I went to Wood Green and voted Liberal. It would have seemed dishonourable to have voted anything else.

"Kell's office," I said to Marie as I walked through the door at Dorset Square. "You know the book you found in there?"

"Napoleon of Notting Hill," she said.

"Did you read it?" I asked, rather stupidly. Of course she read it.

"Of course I read it," she said.

"That's the key," I told her and swirled her around the room destroying several highly valuable sherry glasses placed rather ludicrously, I thought, on a small table on one side of the room.

Wednesday 14th December

To the offices of Fox, Housefield, Burnett and Baddeley. The auction was of two estates which had been carved out of the farm in Crabtree Lane at the edge of Fulham. I was feeling uninspired about the occasion, but to my surprise there were a couple of other journalists watching events, including Douglas Goode from the Times, whom I had met once or twice with Marie during her days there. To my surprise he had actually read my piece on Black Friday.

Norris was there, and I enjoyed myself once more by tipping my hat to him. Childish yes, but he was clearly annoyed, so it was worth it. Norris went off to have a loud conversation with either Fox or Housefield or Burnett or Baddeley about having me thrown out but they must have decided against it. Perhaps because the Times was there.

Norris with Allen sitting next to him bought the first lot for £20,000 and tried to get the second for £15,000, but apparently the sellers had wanted more so the whole thing stopped. Douglas kept up a running commentary on the finer points.

It was all over by half past four, and we sat there watching Norris in deep conversation with the rest of the crew. "What you writing?" said Douglas. I told him I had a whole series of stories and none of them led anywhere.

"Know what you mean," he said. "Still, you can always follow Norris. You and Norris – you haven't had a big set-to for days."

I looked at him. "Mr Holloway suggested that too," I said. "Shall we tail him? If he spots me, he'll call a copper. But with you and me, we stand a chance… But, really, does the Times do this?"

"Not much," he said, "but why should the Chron get all the fun?"

Norris headed north in a cab. I have never in my life said, "Follow that cab," in the style of Sherlock Holmes, so doing it was fun. The cabbie gave us a very strange look, as if to say, "You're taking the Micky", but still he did it. The Times even paid the fare.

We got to Piccadilly, and Norris hopped out into the Criterion bar. His guest for the drink was already there: it was none other Charlie Crisp. We took seats by the door out of the main light.

I told Douglas about Crisp and Football Chat. "A magazine might change its name once every ten years or so but the Chat changed every other week. It did a couple of issues as Athletic Chat then Athletic and Sporting Chat, then Football Chat, Football Chat and Athletic World, then it would stop publication for a bit, and then emerge again as Athletic World and Football Chat… Think of any combination of "Athletic', 'Football', 'Sport', 'Chat', and World' and keep re-working them. As far as I recall they threw in Cycling once or twice as well.

"But what was the point?" he asked, not unreasonably.

"They had few readers and fewer advertisers. It was basically Charlie Crisp and a bent accountant who kept his head down. The funny thing is that Norris, supposedly the big know-it-all businessman of the era, bought Football Chat or whatever it was called at that time a couple of years back as a way of increasing the chances he had of getting published on the state of football. Then he discovered that it was a dud and closed it down last year."

"Norris bought it from Crisp?" He was staggered and his voice rose – I had to hush him. "You would expect Norris, with his temper and his desire to sue honourable citizens…"

"… would make him more than willing to sue Charlie Crisp. But he didn't, and here they are having a drink. Now why is that?"

"If we think of Norris and his history," said Douglas, "then they are here because Charlie Crisp has something that is of benefit to Norris. What is it?"

I didn't know, and we had no option but to sit and watch. As time passed by the group around Norris grew, and within the hour there were half a dozen.

Suddenly Douglas hit his fist into his palm. "I know that one… fellow with the white hair and thin moustache. Name of Forrester. He's big in the Masons."

"Norris is – or at least was – a Mason. He was a member of one of the lodges, and then left suddenly. I haven't dug around to find out why – I always assumed that it would be secret. But when I followed him to Reading…"

"What was he doing in Reading?"

"As far as I could see, looking to buy a southern league football club from another Mason…"

"It's strange that – because Forrester is a Reading man too."

We watched them as a couple more men arrived. Then Douglas said, "It's a Masonic meeting – they'll be off to dinner in a moment. Someone is getting initiated I imagine. It will be ring-a-ring-a-roses and a glass of champagne."

We decided to get out before Norris saw us.

Thursday 15th December

The researchers dug out the background on Charlie Crisp. He's now (and has been for quite a few years) a referee working the Southern League and Division 2 of the Football League. I knew I had seen him – he ran the Millwall against Brighton game.

I have never understood referees, and have always suspected that they were simply not good enough to be players but liked to show off in front of 10,000 people. To the best of my knowledge they are unpaid and just pick up a few shillings to cover the cost of getting to the game. According to Athletic News there is a referees' association which fixes who takes what game (which I suppose is handy).

So Charlie Crisp ran a bent magazine that he sold to Norris. And Charlie Crisp was a referee who like as not was quite often refereeing Croydon Common and Fulham games. And Charlie Crisp had not been made bankrupt by Norris, which was a bit odd, given Norris' background in not showing restraint. True they were both Masons, or so it appeared from last night, but even so, that wasn't normally enough for Norris.

A thought: could it be that Fulham and Croydon won more matches when Charlie Crisp was in control? I decided to kick the juniors out and do the research myself.

Friday 16th December

Oh yes indeed! In the past year Charlie Crisp had refereed four Fulham games, and they had won all four.

It was harder to check on Croydon, because the Southern League yearbook doesn't contain referees details, but the one game I could find notes on was the local derby against Clapham Rovers, and Croydon had won, which was a bit of a surprise, Clapham being a Cup Final team and highly rated.

Of course it wasn't enough to prove anything, but it fits, and it makes me itchy, and anyway, who in Fleet Street ever cared about facts?

I called across the road and told Douglas. He stood me a drink.

Saturday 17th December

George Barrett turned up in the office. "I think I have something for you," he said, "but I'd like something in return."

"Tell me what it's about," I said pompously, leaning back in my chair and still contemplating referees, "and I'll try my best to meet your needs."

We had a little chuckle at the formal language. "You've written a couple of bits about jewellers, diamonds going missing, diamonds coming back." I agreed that was a fair summary of one of my recent trips into fantasy land.

"Why fantasy?"

"Because it can't be real. Who would do such a thing and why?"

"There is a word around that a group are going to do a jewellery job somewhere around Liverpool Street."

"That's a bit vague, George," I told him.

"The big point is that these guys will pass themselves off as anarchists, and what's odder is that the news is leaking out through the wrong sources. It looks like an event which will give the police and Fleet Street the chance to declare war on the anarchist movement and round us all up."

"I don't think it's the police who declare war," I told him.

"And you can say that after Tonypandy and Black Friday!"

I could see his point. "What I want you to do," he persisted, "is watch out for it, and if you can, make sure you cover the story but tell it like it really happens, making the point that these aren't anarchists."

"Always presuming these are not anarchists, George," I said. "Not everyone is as honourable as you."

"But you know everyone is blaming the anarchist movement for the fake sovereigns," he said. "And the jewels are part of it. Maybe it is the factory where they make them?"

"So how am I going to know that people committing a jewel robbery are not anarchists? You don't have a secret handshake like the Masons, do you?"

We paused for a moment, both of us trying to take in the insanity in which we now seemed to be living.

"Did you ever unearth anything about the torpedo factory?" I asked.

"It's a money scam, like it always is. A building firm wanted it on the Clyde, and there was an architect who designed the whole housing and factory project for nothing."

I was so surprised I had to ask him to repeat the story. "So a firm of house builders and an architect pay an official in the War Office to get a whole factory moved to the Clyde, so they can build on the place – and presumably make a profit on the houses?" I asked.

"That's what I said," said George, frustrated that he was not seeing this as such a big deal, "except the way I heard it, it was not an official. It was one of the ministers. And anyway what architect would work for nothing?"

"I know one," I said.

"They had a code name for the scheme," he added.

"What?" Code names were always good – even if you didn't know what was going on, the use of the correct codeword in a meeting could suggest you did and get someone involved to panic you more information.

"Making the arsenal."

"What?"

"Will you stop saying 'what'?"

"What has Woolwich Arsenal to do with making anything – they closed the torpedo factory down."

"No: it's the code for the whole torpedo factory scam. It is called 'Making the arsenal'."

"And are the sovereigns and diamonds linked to the torpedo factory?"

"That's about it."

"Why?"

He shrugged, which was no help at all.

We talked some more, I told him I sympathised with the tough life of the anti-political activist, thanked him for the story, and then left him to do whatever anarchists do when not overthrowing the state, as he reminded me that my side of the deal was to make it clear that the people in the Liverpool Street job would not be anarchists. I took the bus back home and then wandered along to see dear old Wood Green Town (formed 1894 as it said on the gate) against Tufnell Park in the London League. Six goals to three. I wondered why I ever bothered with Woolwich.

Trouble was that I missed two of the goals – not because I wasn't watching, but because I wasn't looking.

Sunday 18th December

Proud Preston, the Invincibles of old, had beaten Woolwich Arsenal by four goals to one, but in front of a little Lancashire crowd of 6000. Question: how can they survive on 6000 when Woolwich struggle on twice as many?

I was about to go to Dorset Square when the news came in. Big jewel robbery in the City – not too far from Liverpool Street. Apparently the robbers were armed and there was a siege going on. This wasn't my province at all, but there was nothing to stop me wandering along – and so I did, armed with my Captain's pass and my Press Card. One of them ought to work, I thought.

It was all happening just by the Monument. By the time I got there, we had ambulances, lots of shouting, and the police rushing around and colliding with each other – the usual disorganised emergency force activity. I got talking to a Clive Blackmore and his friends from the News. Usual banter, ("Jacko – you have to learn – they don't play football in the City any more. Football – open spaces, mud and grass, back page news. Armed bank robbery, City of London, front page news. Tell him someone..." Ha ha.)

I took it all and told them a thing or two about their own work, and then they gave me the benefit of their insights – which were few. Half a dozen men had broken into a jewellery shop at closing time, and forced the owner to open the safe and hand over what he had. A bobby, who as it turned out regularly stopped by for an end of day cup of cocoa with the owner, walks into the shop and promptly gets shot. Someone near by recognises a shot as a shot, calls another constable and he goes inside to investigate and he gets shot.

"They're not very good at this, are they?" I said.

"The police or the burglars? asked Clive. And then he added, "This isn't one of your steal-it-and-replace-it scams is it?"

"If it is," I said, "it's the first time it's been worth killing for."

I stayed for a few moments, but it looked as if the action was over. The police had got their reinforcements and finally burst into the shop, only to find the crew had got out through a cellar and up into the alleyway at the back. The jeweller's body was not there. Looked like he hadn't been shot after all and they had taken him with them.

Monday 19th December

The last day of what seems to have been rather a long and uneventful general election. I can understand why we had elections lasting over a couple of weeks in the old days before the Royal Mail, the train and the telephone, but now it seemed rather pointless.

Went shopping for Christmas presents. Marie and I had discussed what the upper class give and receive at Christmas, and she had been very practical. If I ask mum she says, "Oh I don't want anything" and she would go berserk if I didn't somehow find out what she really wanted and get it. Dad was easier: a new pipe and some tobacco and a new copy of the complete piano sonatas of Beethoven – his old edition having fallen to pieces.

Dorset Square was harder. Chocolates and books for the seniors of the family, and a non-diamond necklace for Marie. I also got three of the fake sovereigns put into little glass displays – one for each of my companions as a reminder of 1910.

I dropped into the office and told Mr Holloway I had been at the jewel robbery and did not believe they were anarchists, but since I had no proof or further insight he was, not unnaturally, not interested. "There's a story coming in that Norfolk has declared independence," he said. "Could you cover that?" I said I'd look into it.

Wednesday 21st December

The polls closed on Monday at lunchtime, and by the time we closed the press on Tuesday the results were more or less in, leaving aside the bits of kingdom still ruled by the ancient Britons, the Picts, the Celts, the Danes…

No one is ever quite sure who is on whose side when it comes to the middle, but Mr Symmonds' department put up a big chart on the second floor where they added together the Liberal Unionists and the Conservative Unionists on one side, with the Liberals under Mr Asquith on the other side, and the results came out pretty much neck and neck. Outside of the main grouping Labour were going to stay in the 40s and the Irish Nationalists in the 80s. No one would ever do a formal deal with Labour, and the Nationalists won't deal on anything without a total promise of home rule, so it is another tie. Which is a shame. I had hoped my "This is Us" idea on the poster would sway the day. But at least the Unionists' policy of mass sterilisation has been put on hold.

The guess in the political rooms is that this means the Liberals will bring back their budget and force the end of Unionist power in the Lords (which Labour will support as a route to their ultimate aims). There was very little chance of votes for women but it would mean the arrival of the pensions for the old folk plus some new hospitals.

Back in Dorset Square I met Alyson who said, "Colonel Edmunds sends you his very best regards, and says he always knew that someone whose daily reconnoitre reports were as fictional as yours would come good, and he says he would be delighted to see you at his estate in Norfolk if you would care to join him in the new year. He also wonders if you have kept any souvenirs from the time when, apparently against his most explicit orders, you ventured into the house of Jan Smuts, in particular a collection of gold coins that he had..."

I was stunned. Stunned that he remembered me, stunned that he would find anything to say about me, stunned that he had known all the time about the way we manipulated the reports, and double stunned that he knew about the raid on Smuts' house.

Thursday 22nd December

It turns out that three bobbies had died in the shootings at Monument, and the City was shut down for the funeral. They did it in the grand style with a procession from Liverpool Street all the way to St Pauls. All the nobs were there and absolutely no levity of any kind is to be allowed in tomorrow's paper.

I didn't go to the parade, but Edward was there taking some photos on the ground that we would have to put something in the paper tomorrow and suitably solemn pictures would be permissible.

Friday 23rd December

With nothing much to do, I admired Edward's handiwork. He had pictures of the crowds, the police, the coffins, the grieving widows...   The grieving widows, you couldn't see their faces clearly, but there was one picture where...

I didn't know what, but still with nothing else to do, I looked up the names of the three deceased and called over one of the juniors, telling him that somewhere there must be a reference book of policemen. Seems there is. It is called the Police Officer Registry. We didn't have one, but there was one in the News of the World. I told the junior I didn't know anyone there, and he said it didn't matter because he'd just been down the street and nicked theirs.

None of the deceased is listed in the official record of who is a copper.

In the evening there was a party in Dorset Square to celebrate the return to power of the Liberal Party. Marie was expected to attend, so I tagged along.

Despite the presence of a considerable number of top brass, Lord Cortney had time for a chat with me. I told him of the suggestion that was brewing in my head that there was a much larger scandal going on linking everything together. Even the Monument jewel robbery.

"All I can say, Mr Jones," he said, "is that I would not be surprised at anything people get up to in general, nor government or opposition in particular. And if you are thinking of turning again to Mr Churchill, take care. He is by and large a man without friends. His old party hate him as a turncoat, and my party distrust him now more than ever."

Eventually we left the throng, and as we did Marie demanded to know the significance of the Chesterton book.

"You remember that it's 1984 and the King of the United Kingdom is selected randomly. When Auberon Quin takes power he institutes a government of jest."

"The 'sublime victory of the joke'," said Marie, quoting directly from the novel. "He divides London into walled boroughs, and disputes and minor wars break out between these little states, while everyone in each borough has to wear ludicrous municipal costume. Everyone just does as they are told, no matter how crazy it becomes. I remember it well, but what's your point?"

"That someone might read that book and think that even when their class is outnumbered and outvoted it might be possible to take over a society by making it face the incomprehensible."

"Like taking jewels from a jewellers and then replacing them with fakes?"

"Indeed. As a result of the king's policies – all of which are based on humour – people die, which the king in the story never intended. But he doesn't relent – he keeps creating ever greater chaos, and because he is the king, no one stops him. People suffer, but they respect his power and authority."

"But Chesterton doesn't believe that," argued Marie. "In '*The Man Who Was Thursday*' he makes the point that the wholesale belief in a single idea, no matter what, is stupid."

"I agree," I told her, "but just because Chesterton wrote these books as a warning against totalitarian states, it doesn't mean that a bunch of idiots utterly removed from the real world and with so much money that they can do anything, can't mistake the warning for a blueprint."

"You are speaking of the landed gentry," she said with a smile. "You think that the Unionists would deliberately make Britain chaotic?"

"If faced with the prospect of massive taxation on land which has never been taxed since the kingdom was founded. They know they can't win an election and so instead they choose another route."

"And three policemen who don't exist die in the jewellers' shop," she said slowly. "Fake fivers turn up in the pubs, fake sovereigns are given to football fans, miners and the Suffragettes, fake jewels… It is the opposite of cold, clearly argued anarchism – it is chaos in which everyone loses faith in everything and eventually turns to the old families, the very people who caused the chaos, and begs them to sort it out – even if it means sterilising the poor as part of the final solution."

I said I couldn't have put it better myself.

Saturday 24th December

Life at home has become impossible. With mum and dad invited for evening drinks at Dorset Square tomorrow, mum is in a state of total permanent panic. I can't even come to breakfast unshaved without getting told what for.

I went to see my old chums Woolwich play Notts County and win by two goals to one, although only in front of 8000 which is the lowest crowd for quite a few years – and nearly as bad as Proud Preston. But then it is Christmas Eve, and that means everyone is off shopping with the wife. Woolwich introduced a new left winger, Thomas Winship, who looked quite remarkable. I am going to get this wrong I know, but I think this guy could make the difference.

Norris put out a document with the programme (which itself contained another attack on the players and the club from Gunners' Mate) saying that they had only sold 50 of their £1 shares. I'd bet Norris had no intention of selling more: he has gone through the motion of offering 5000 shares which he knew perfectly well he would never sell, and can now say, "I have done everything. I have put my own money up. I have rescued this club. I have then asked the local people to buy 5000 shares and only 1% of those shares were sold. I own 99% of the club, and I am taking it to Fulham."

Aside from Winship it was an ordinary game – and I made notes on a piece that says Wood Green Town play better football, and that Kent is too cold for the sensible supporter.

But Woolwich avoid being in the bottom two for Christmas, although still looking down the wrong end of the gun (to coin a phrase). That was win number five out of eighteen, and that's relegation talk. How amusing if Woolwich were to go down, leaving Norris with two Second Division teams. Extended my piece into one about how the ice age is returning, but how it only affects south of the river. The ice, I suggested, will be Woolwich's secret weapon for the rest of the season.

And so, home to my parents, with mum getting flustered, and dad raising his eyebrows. It's Christmas.

Sunday 25th December

Dad gave me a most wonderful pocket watch, which must have cost the earth, and then we did the Christmas thing in which my parents stood in front of the mantle piece together and said they were so proud of me. I had shown bravery in war and determination in peace and given them more joy than they could have thought. It was very formal, as Christmas morning always is. I told them how wonderful they were to me as parents, and how they had always supported me no matter what I had done, and how lucky I was to have them.

Then the formality declined a little and they said they wouldn't mind if I stopped playing with the band, and they had heard that this Sophia was a Suffragette, and really I should not be associating with such people, and I should be careful not to upset Lord and Lady Cortney, because Marie was so charming and this was my great opportunity in life and I must be careful not to blow it away, and they were worried I was drinking too much, and Mrs McCafferty from across the road said that there were stories that my newspaper pieces were secret code informing the German High Command where to attack, and Doris three doors down had been told by her brother that I was consorting with anarchists...

We put out the decorations and lit the candles and gave the cards, and dad had arranged for the firm to give donations to the charities for injured workmen which mum carefully recorded so that we knew we had been Christian. We had a tree and we had a turkey and all we were short of was a maid. I started to make a joke about that, but thought better of it. Dad would never forgive me. There was that look in mum's eye. A maid...

To church, and a sermon on how the speed of life was not what the Lord intended, and that the 20th century was the devil's century, and we had to return to our peaceful, better days...

I have so little time to talk to dad week by week, but today we talked about the growth of the cities, about the general election, about Home Rule, about the People's Budget, about the vortex and sterilisation, about how all the shops were exploiting vulnerable people with the promise of Christmas. And goodness, we even talked about Woolwich Arsenal, and why I had drifted over to them instead of Tottenham.

Dad had also heard about how all the Christmas presents sent to the troops still in South Africa as part of the transition force had got lost. I told him to ask Lord Cortney tonight, and he said he couldn't do that – so I tried to persuade him to talk about his work in Stoke Newington. It is after all what my dad is. My grandfather (a wonderful old guy whom I remember with terrific beard and whiskers) built the factory. This is us, our family, and it is something to be so proud of.

Then we washed up lunch, cleaned the house in case burglars turned up and were scandalised by the dirt, and then dressed, compared our clothes, changed, dressed again, and then our pre-booked cabbie turned up (double rates, but I paid so Mum would not know and not make a fuss) and we went for our evening with Marie, her parents, her brother and her sister.

It was fine – it worked well – mum was more in control of herself, and dad and Lord Cortney did get into deep conversation during the evening concerning the baby grand in the smoking room.

I can't find it in myself to believe in the Lord, after what my country did in Africa, but if I did, I would thank him for today.

Monday 26th December

The usual Boxing Day in the office – there was no news, and Mr Holloway was moaning about the poor sods like him who had come in on Christmas Day to produce today's paper, and people like me who thought it was ok to take a day off. "Where's the news?" he shouted over and over while to me he said, "Where's this 'Making the arsenal' story?" I said I just needed a couple more days, and wondered how on earth he had heard that phrase. I certainly hadn't told him.

I made the tedious slog across the city to Woolwich where, according to the programme from the last match, the reserves were playing Chelsea in the South East Counties League. The first team were in Manchester.

In the Hen, Evie was in moaning mood. "What is going to become of us?" she said, alternating it with the variant, "I don't know what we shall do."

The cause of her worries was simple to see: if Woolwich Arsenal football club moved out as the story was suggesting (and I must admit, it was my story that had suggested this so I couldn't tell her I made it up) and the factories closed, then she'd be left as a pub on the edge of town with no bonus match days. It was no good telling her to do something else. The Hen was her life.

"But you must have had lots more drinkers in here when that story about the sovereigns broke," I said, and she had the grace to admit that was true, but then complained that they had all drifted away again now the put-pockets had stopped attending games.

Boxing Day is always the same. The toffs go off killing, and the footballers set out to prove that it is possible to play while drunk. The one thing you can be sure of is that they won't do much running around. But the humour of the crowd of 8000 was good, and it was a bright sunny day, with Woolwich Arsenal beating Chelsea by four goals to nil. It being a reserve game, and it being Boxing Day, there was no sign of Norris, so I sat in the press enclosure along with Stallybrass from the Kentish who gave me an orange. After the game I bought him a pint.

But despite my generosity there was nothing he could add. He had heard the phrase "Making the arsenal". "I think it is your friend Mr Norris," he said. "He's trying to recover some lost ground."

"You don't mean he seriously thought he would sell five thousand shares at one pound each?"

"No," said Stallybrass, "but he thought he might sell fifteen hundred. Fifty was a total slap in the face. I suspect he'll start doing property development in Woolwich and Plumstead – do here what he did in Fulham. Or maybe he might try another city altogether. Birmingham, Manchester, Glasgow…"

Back at the office the news was Manchester United 5 goals Woolwich Arsenal nil, in front of a crowd of 35,000. I had had more fun in Woolwich.

Tuesday 27th December

There were rumblings and mumblings, mostly suggesting that Ireland was going to be made a separate state. Mr Asquith's proposals for votes for women has gone quiet and a suggestion from me that I might interview a veteran of Black Friday for the paper did not go down well. "They don't buy our paper so we are certainly not going to write nice things about them," is the official line.

Instead we ran the story that the police were getting bonus money (also known as "danger money") for their work on Black Friday, as well as overtime payments. The people who needed sorting out were the men who control the force and who let them (or maybe ordered them) to run riot. And ultimately Mr

Churchill who had singularly failed to walk across the road from Parliament to take control. Goodness knows what our police would do if we get the sort of football rioting they seem to get in Scotland.

Norris has gone to ground, Leitch is untouchable because his court case is technically still on the table (although looking more and more moribund by the day) and I sit at my desk looking down into Fleet Street, trying to find that word or phrase that might describe anything that seems relevant.

Wednesday 28th December

"Is anything at home inside the brain of this supposed reporter?" Mr Holloway shouted, and several of the old hacks chuckled. The apprentices, junior and runners looked on in horror and fascination. The boss walked round my desk and trod on my foot.

When he released the pressure I turned to the onlookers. "An old Fleet Street tradition," I said. "When the sports editor stands on your foot, you know you have fully arrived at the top of the tree."

"Get in here," Mr Holloway growled, and we went into his room.

"Merry Christmas to you, sir," I said, and he mimicked my voice in a way that used to annoy, but which I now view with some affection.

"And so, what is your story?" he demanded. "You've been staring out of the window for days – even your addled brain must have come up with something."

"Turn the Norris story upside down, and say that he is going to keep Woolwich Arsenal at Woolwich and is planning to develop property in the area. It will be the making of the Arsenal – and we call it: "Making the Arsenal." A great tribute to the hard working men and women in the armaments factories. Proper decent housing for those people on whom the defence of our nation depends. What's more, Norris is going to build this whole community despite the fact that they have turned their backs on him by not buying his shares. What a wonderful man Mr Norris is."

"And when he doesn't build this new community?"

"There is always a chance he will – because I still don't see the real benefit of having Woolwich Arsenal playing in Fulham on the same day that Chelsea is playing just across the road. But if he doesn't bite we'll just accuse him of betraying the working man in the armaments factory who is just as important as…"

"Yes, yes, yes," said Mr Holloway, and I smiled, because irritating Mr Holloway had throughout this year of change been one of my constant pleasures. "If you could perhaps try and write it in English, and maybe avoid mentioning the Hen and Basket in every other line. And top floor says, no more on policemen or Suffragettes. That story is played out. Yesterday's news. But get something on Norris building houses in Glasgow."

An hour later I had written "Making the Arsenal" exactly as described, and given it to the runner. It was mildly amusing to anyone who had followed the tale, but didn't make everything fit together. In my notebook I had the sketch of a totally different story.

I played with the band again and was introduced by the publican as the leader of the Suffragette movement and given a flowery hat to wear. It got lots of laughs. I remembered a phrase of Churchill's from South Africa. "Let them loose and they just reproduce."

Thursday 29th December

Dad's birthday. Coming so soon after Christmas I always feel sorry for him – mum is always saying she's had so much to do that she can't be expected to make a cake as well, but then she does, and we are all happy.

I gave dad the first book of Bach's "48" and a tie and a fountain pen with his name inscribed, and we had a hug, which mum always thinks is unmanly between father and son, but since Julian died has been part of how it is with dad.

In Fleet Street it was still quiet. Trafalgar Square was getting ready for the drunks, and there was a lot of suggestion that this was going to be particularly bad because New Year's Eve was a Saturday, making the first day of the new year a holiday, so no one had to think about going to work the next morning. There was talk of calling the troops in.

My fulsome piece in praise of Norris got a fair splash in the features section, and I wondered what Norris could do. If he denied it, we could run "Norris jeopardises future of Woolwich" and he wouldn't dare look in at the club for the rest of the season. If he didn't then he could keep playing the local lord and master, but each time he did everyone would ask when the building work was starting.

In the afternoon, George Barrett dropped in. Apparently he had been in Scotland. I asked him how the revolution was going and he scowled as he does when he thinks I am being flippant, but admitted that he liked my stance on the stupidity of police commanders both in Tonypandy and Westminster Square.

"I wouldn't rely on it to last," I warned him, as we strolled across the road to the Wig and Pen. "You are my one faithful fan. I shall ask Mr Holloway for a rise in recognition of your readership."

But he would not be diverted. "This bit about "making the arsenal". That is what I kept hearing in Glasgow."

"Do they have a team called Arsenal? I thought it was all Rangers, Aberdeen and Partick Thistle.

"They do have a new torpedo factory," he said, "and that's where I have been recruiting support for the cause. "What they say is that they are 'Making an arsenal.' Not making the arsenal, but making an arsenal."

"Maybe it is just the way they speak up there," I said.

Saturday 31st December

If yesterday was a non-day, apart from my confusing information from George, today was… an end of year to remember.

I was getting ready to go to watch Woolwich Arsenal against Bury and chatting with Edward about our trip to Sophia's country estate for a New Year's party when every telephone in the building seemed to start ringing. There was something happening in the Exchange Buildings in the Houndsditch and talk of jewels, anarchists and... I grabbed Edward, shouted at Mr Holloway (I shall regret that in due course) and said this was "the big one". This was the moment that George had spoken of. That first burglary must have been a trial run; Houndsditch bumps into Liverpool Street.

Edward grabbed his gear, we called a cab and urged full speed. As we approached the 'ditch, police tried to usher us back but we ducked into Cutler Street where we joined a crew from the Standard and another from the Mail. The anarchists – or so everyone was calling them (it has become the slang for criminals) – were in the jewellers' opposite, and the police were preparing to go in.

Edward prepared his camera with a larger lens than I had seen before. Probably a Christmas present. The word was the army had been called. The word was Mr Churchill was here. The word was the police were armed. "This will be chaos," I predicted to anyone who wanted to listen.

As we watched I made the point that this was not an anarchists' gang, although I only said it because George said so and I didn't want my piece rejected at the Chron because it was out of step with every other paper. Several hacks behind the barricade made a note.

A bobby came by. He turned out to be a Fulham supporter who hated Norris, and gave us the story. A group of anarchists had been found digging a tunnel from their rented accommodation into the jeweller's shop next door.

"Couldn't they be German?" I suggested, a little lamely.

We waited. We watched, my eyes dancing around the buildings looking for snipers, vantage points, sudden movements, the twitch of the curtain. And then the show began. Talk of song and dance man, this was the music hall stage in the middle of the street. The police openly went up to the house and politely knocked on the door. "An Englishman does not enter without being invited," said the man from the Star, and I wrote it down. I'm not proud.

"Jesus Christ," said Edward, and by and large most of us agreed.

Getting no reply, the coppers looked around to see what to do next and scuttled off to the side of the building and down the alley. At which point, beyond all sense and rationality two other policemen approached the front door and knocked. I couldn't work it out. Had they not known that the first two had already done knocked? Or was this a game? A code? A subterfuge? Three coppers had supposedly died a few days back in a jewel raid, and this bunch were dedicated to knocking at the front door!

And the world turned even stranger as one of the "anarchists" opened up.

We couldn't hear, of course, but it looked as if the coppers started asking the man questions. It also looked like the anarchist was not saying anything by way of reply. Next (and I swear this is the truth, unbelievable at it must seem) the police pointed into the house, as if they were telling the anarchist to go back inside and get his mum or his mate or his pet rabbit or maybe someone who might speak English.

I should not make fun of this, but it was insane. Every instinct in my bones was telling me to scream at those men to get out and take cover. This is not how you approach the house of the enemy. And above everything you do not send the enemy AT YOUR COMMAND back into his lair so he can go and get the weaponry. You take cover, you tell him to come out, arms up, and suggest that if he doesn't you'll open fire.

But send the man back into his house is what they did, and (what a surprise!) he did not come back. The two police at the door started looking up and down the street, and I swear to God one of them was laughing at the impossibility of his situation.

Orders were barked across the road by whatever idiot was running the show, and then the policeman carefully pushed the door open and went into the house after the man. I put my hands over my eyes and bowed my head.

I think the others were watching me, and I heard Edward say, "Jacko? Are you all right?" and then the shooting started.

Despite myself I looked up. This was the moment when every single constable should have been ordered to take cover. If there was such an order I did not hear it, and as Edward shot his pictures, policemen from all sides broke cover and rushed the house. "No matter how much you love your comrade," I said to Edward, "you secure the area before attending to a wounded man – even an officer. Otherwise you walk into the simplest ambush in the book."

We heard the shooting again, as more men went down. They were being picked off one after the other.

Ultimately it calmed, we sneaked out of the hideout and back the way we had come. The police were now doing house-to-house searches of a sort. We headed up Cutler Street and through the back roads until we could get a cab to Fleet Street.

In the office I typed it up, comparing the incompetence here with the incompetence in Tonypandy and the incompetence of Westminster.

Edward's pictures were brilliant. I don't think the story even went by Mr Holloway. They just ran it.

Sunday 1ˢᵗ January 1911

We took the early train from St Pancras to Oakham, Edward and Sophia, Marie and I. Our mood was… hard to describe.

The Chron had rushed out a Sunday special edition to cover the fiasco, and Edward and I were the heroes of the hour in terms of our reporting, but it was hard to take any pleasure.

Sophia had a theory that the anarchists had been running a replica of the Sherlock Holmes story, the *Red Headed League*. I was the only one who had not read it, so after suitable period of hitting me about the head with a copy of *The Napoleon of Notting Hill* that Marie was now re-reading, my lover and my friends told me the story of how the League took over a shop in order to be able to tunnel into a bank.

Cars were waiting for us at the station and they drove us to Sophia's country house, where for the second time I marvelled at how a family could take up such space.

There was the champagne, the delicate little items of food, the hoorays, the shouting, the butlers, servants and footmen doing the bidding, calling everyone sir, and I felt I wanted my head to disengage from my body.

I was just achieving a successful divorce from reality when Alyson arrived on the scene. She approached me, put her hands to her lips, and said, "The Colonel sends his regards once again and says you might like to know that it was Churchill who persuaded Norris to buy Woolwich Arsenal."

"What?" I screamed, and every head turned to look at me. Very clever, Jacko. Alyson slipped away, that infernal smile playing on her lips.

"I'm surprised she's here," said Marie with an element of suspicion.

But we had no chance to take this further, because my shout had brought into our orbit a fopp, a dandy, a tall overweight lordship of a fellow with piercing brown eyes who looked like he spent more time on his hair each day than I had spent in writing the whole Parliament Act piece.

He approached Sophia, and bowed deep. "My lady," he said, "my honour to be here at your father's splendid house…" He kept his head down, and then rose, knowing that he held us in his aura. "And these must be your… ah yes… your friends."

Sophia, through gritted teeth, did the honours. "Lord Willoughby de Broke," she announced. "My fiancée, Edward, ("Sir" said his lordship,) "Marie Cortney", ("Madam," says he, "your father and I have crossed swords in the House many times,") "and my good friend, Jack Jones."

And he sneered, the sort of sneer that only the aristocracy have time to perfect, a sneer reserved for the beater who gets in the way at a hunt, the sneer of the mineowners about to set their dogs on Mr Lloyd George and Mr Asquith, the sneer of the Colonel who has never once worked with the ranks.

"Mr Jones," said Lord Willoughby. "The Battling Reporter. The man who promoted the Parliament Act and betrayed his country for, what would it be Mr Jones, three pounds a week? What say you, Mr Jones?"

I felt all three of my dearest friends move forward in my defence, but I put out my hands very gently. "My Lord, I am not sure of my betrayal…"

"Promoting that wretched Bill," he said. "Whipping up the masses for a Bill that aims to destroy the very heritage of our kingdom while aiding those who contribute nothing but beg and steal on the street corner. What say you, sir?"

His mouth was contemptuous, his voice drawled, taking more time over each word than was ever necessary for the whole sentence. Had he had a whip with him, I felt he would have used it on me there and then. Watching him I wasn't sure how fast my reflexes were any more, and for the fourth time in a year I vowed to lay off the drink.

"I say, my lord, that all I have done is my job."

"But what a story, Mr Warrior Writer!" He moved in closer and pushed a forefinger into my chest. I stood dead still, and his finger bent a little. I let a fraction of a smile pass my face. "How long have you been at this, Mr Writer? A year? A year of trying to find out what is going on? A year of wandering around where… Woolwich, is it?" A waiter passed by with more champagne. He seized two and knocked the glasses back one after another, before grabbing a third by dropping the first two on the floor, forcing the waiter to grovel at his feet.

"A year! To find out what? A year in which the Gutter Press has found nothing. You have no idea."

"No idea of what, my lord?" I asked as evenly as I could.

"'No idea of what, my lord?'" he mimicked. He wasn't as good as Mr Holloway. "No idea of how snivelling little upstarts like you are dealt with. Make the most of it, Jones, because you have not long!"

"Lord Willoughby!" protested Sophia, "You exceed yourself, sir."

"My lady, I mean no disrespect to you or your family," he said, "but your father, good friend though he is, cannot expect me to remain silent when he invites a man like Jones here."

"I invited Mr Jones, Lord Willoughby. Insult him, and you insult me."

"Then I shall not insult him, my lady," he replied, "I shall tell him, in simple words, how wrong he has been. And in the morning I shall enjoy the Chronicle giving him the empties, as I believe it is called."

"Empty," I said with the air of one bored by having to correct an ignorant child yet again. "When a working man loses his job, he has been given the empty. Not that you would know my lord, never having had a job."

"But while you know the lingo of the guttersnipe, Jones, we have been building an arsenal. You go and watch your trivial football nonsense, and we build a new world. Isn't that rich? You didn't even know where to look." And he laughed. We looked at him in bemusement.

"The Napoleon of Notting Hill," I said taking a wild guess. "The foundations of your arsenal. Move out the work, sterilise the poor, keep the miners' strikes moving along by giving them fake sovereigns, promote the Suffragettes, the rich lose faith in everything – even their own jewels, there's a run on the banks, and the new arsenal becomes your fortress from which to launch your attack on the nation." I shrugged. "Not bad, but we didn't feel it really warranted coverage in a national paper. Not until you use your new arsenal to attack the government. All that power and you couldn't even win an election."

"It is like talking to a rather dim pig," announced his lordship. "The Woolwich workers hardly bother to go to work now they have their sovereigns, and why should they? Half the country believes in German spies, and the other half in anarchists. And you, my lady Sophia, you and your chums do our precious work for us, turning the people against their police. Indeed, Warrior Writer, I hear you've been at it again today, criticising the bobby on the beat, eh?

"Jacko Jones – you are the toast of the Party at every meeting. Never has a man done such a job for us without being paid a penny of our money. You four – you should be knighted – no, you should be Lords, except of course you will all shortly be in prison for treason. But I shall miss you."

He saw another waiter and arrogantly called him, again taking several glasses and stumbling slightly as he did so.

"Clever idea though," I said, "to do the jewellers' shops and get more violent each time."

But he would not pick that bait. He turned to Marie. "Your father, Miss Cortney, your father thinks we will surrender our lands and our heritage to his Liberal values. But it is he who will surrender. And what will your mother say, dear Marie, when she finds that the necklace she wears is not worth one hundred and fifty pounds, but is in fact worth no more than a half sovereign. And quite probably a faked half sovereign at that! And her dear – what shall I call her? Her "ladyfriend", Alyson. Such a 'progressive' family you have. So modern and liberated. But will she stand by your father when she finds that the family is, oh what's the word?.... A yes. 'Poor'."

Marie was clearly ready to slap him, but I held her tight. At last we were getting clues. And in a big way he was right. We hadn't worked it out. Or at least we had not put it all together.

"With the working men striking or drunk – or both – and the wives of the liberal peers in revolt at being sold pups, and the personal 'ladyfriend' vanished up country with an old booby colonel, what then? What then as our navy sails up the Thames armed with its new torpedoes and parks itself outside Parliament and says, "Come, come, dear friends, it is time to visit the Tower."

He took another glass and drained it, before dropping it on the floor and went to walk unsteadily past us. I checked all four compass points, and finding the ground clear, brought my knee up between his legs. As he went down I called a waiter. "Can't take the drink," I said, and we stepped across the prone figure, each taking care to crunch our feet onto his hands, each breaking bones that would probably never be properly reset or repaired. The glass on the ground didn't help.

Monday 2nd January

We needed to take the details back to the government, but that proved to be more complex than I had assumed. When we returned to Dorset Square Lord Cortney noted the story, but did not, as I had expected, leap up ready to rush off and tell his colleagues.

"The money is out there," he said, "and there is not too much we can do about that. If we try to take the fake sovereigns and fivers out of circulation we will just cause resentment among the people who have them, which is what the Unionists want. Willoughby's concept of the jewels of the wealthy is right – the ladies would not be happy to find their prize possessions are in effect valueless."

I was about to bring up the torpedo factory when the butler entered telling me that there was a telephone call – not for Lord Cortney, but for me. Mr Symmonds requested my presence in the office, when I could make it. There were more developments in the Houndsditch story.

Edward and I made our apologies and left to gather the news in Fleet Street. Which was that the police had found the members of the anarchist gang hiding out in Sidney Street. The Met were preparing for a siege. And this time they were armed.

"God help us all," said Edward. And I knew exactly what he meant.

We got to the scene at half past seven. It was dark, peaceful and cold. Police were taking up positions, and we could see their arms, which they carried unnaturally and uncertainly. It looked to me as if none of them had been trained to hold the guns and rifles, let alone shoot them.

I did the usual trick of ingratiating myself by talking football to a copper or two. When I got a good look at the weaponry I nearly cried in dismay. The police were carrying bulldog revolvers, shotguns and in some cases rifles fitted with .22 Morris-tube barrels – all of which had been around in the Boer War. None of these were going to be any good for firing across the road, which was all that was going to be possible, given a terrain of three storey houses either side of a street. I pondered the possibility of pointing this out, but the stupidity of the idea struck me. This was the police. No one of any sanity would be in charge.

Edward and I looked for a house from which we could observe the proceedings, working our way along, offering money for a room overlooking the road. Naturally the locals knew when they were on to a good thing, and the price was rising by the minute. Eventually we settled on a house opposite the action, seven or eight doors down, two along from the pub. Edward set up his equipment while I made supper arrangements with our hostess.

A camp bed was found which looked like ex-army issue, and Edward and I arranged to take the night in turns, both of us laughing at the change from the exquisite linen sheets and views across the valley last night.

Tuesday 3rd January

By the morning we could see well over two hundred soldiers plus double that number in coppers. The word was that there were three "anarchists" holed up on the far side in number 100, a flat owned by one Mrs Betsy Gershon. "How to become famous," I wrote, sketching a headline.

At half past eight Mrs G came out the door, minus skirt and shoes, which was rather odd and almost stage-managed, but she raised a cheer from the onlookers before she was quickly whisked away by the boys in blue. I saw a face at a window for a second looking to see what the noise was. Clearly whatever nationality they were, they hadn't expected that this would turn into joke. GK Chesterton – how did you know?

And then the real fun started. Having lost several of their own men in the Houndsditch a few days before by knocking on the front door in the polite English fashion, Inspector F. P. Wensley of the H Division went and – I can still hardly believe it as I write it – knocked on the front door.

"There's no one in," shouted one of the reporters, and there was much laughter. "Tell him you're the milkman," said another.

I watched, Edward photographed as the said Inspector bent down into the grimy Whitechapel Road, picked up some stones, and threw them at the window.

"He's throwing stones at the…" I said to Edward, and was cut off because someone inside had started firing at the police.

Whatever weapons the gang had inside they could deliver rapid fire. And yet what was very odd was how inaccurate it was. Only one man down, and he looked as if he was still alive as they removed him. But it was now quite clear that any police within shooting distance might be picked off easily. If we just looked at numbers the police and military would win hands down. But take the weapons into account and a stalemate was more likely.

It was nearly noon when there was the sound of a couple of revolvers being fired. A copper came into our hideout just to check who we were. "A man was shot there this morning," he told us, in case I didn't know.

From time to time there were further shots, then there would be silence. It was quite impossible to tell who was shooting whom. "I wouldn't be surprised if the police start shooting each other," Edward told me. He was getting the hang of this.

I decided to go for an exploration, left our hideout, and edged down the street to the next corner and into the Rising Sun. To my surprise the bar was full of life – everyone was drinking, shouting and laughing, while boys and girls made pop sounds and pointed make-believe guns and rifles.

The landlord was completely occupied and didn't notice as I edged to the back room, found the stairs and headed to the attic. A score or so of scribblers had beaten me to it and were looking down, even though it was clear that if the gang had fancied putting a head over the parapet of number 100 they could have picked off the journalists very easily.

There was another flurry of shots, and I hit the deck, much to the amusement of several journalists. But a couple of them who knew my background suddenly looked concerned. "Can they get us here?" said a fellow from the Telegraph, and I told him about the weaponry. The younger troop sneered. The older fellows took cover.

The bullets from the hideout were ricocheting off from the walls a little way up the street, which showed just how high a velocity their weaponry was (and how badly aimed). From the new vantage point we could see the house clearly; the soldiers were lying behind makeshift barricades and staying put while the shooting continued.

We had another period of silence and waited – the stupid standing and looking out the windows, the experienced staying on the floor. On the roof of a brewery opposite there was another crowd. Every window in every house was occupied. Someone was going to get killed, I thought.

All we needed was the song and dance man. And Death in a black cloak.

I plucked up my courage and looked out, and when the next round of shooting happened I stayed fixed watching the house.

"Jesus wept," I said, "We've got this wrong." And I was about to continue when a Bentley arrived at the end of the street, and out popped a fellow in a tall hat and black coat. I went down the steps ten at a time, back up the street, retracing my route and finally back to Edward, shouting at him as I got into the room to take pictures. "It's bloody Churchill," I screamed, and within seconds Edward was on the case.

The troopers stopped firing as Churchill started giving orders. Don't shoot while your commanding officer is speaking. First rule of war.

"Pity he couldn't have got to Westminster Green as quickly," said Edward.

I gave him a new instruction: when the firing starts up again from the house, try somehow to get a picture of the moment the guns go off. He started to tell me how impossible that would be, but I just asked him to try. For me. Then I went for another walk, this time south, turning left and then left again back up Damien Street which runs in parallel with Sidney Street. The houses were back to back. I counted up the lean-tos and worked out which one backed onto number 100, opened the backyard door and walked up to the house and knocked on the door. There was no reply, so I pushed. The door swung open.

Inside there was a man waiting. He was not in uniform, but had all the bearing of an army sergeant. It does, after all, take one to know one. "How are we?" I asked, using my best captain's voice.

"On time, sir," he said, and then, "have to ask for identity, sir, most particular orders." And so I took out the captain's card that Churchill had given me, and the sergeant, overwhelmed by the fact I had a warrant card personally signed by the Home Secretary, took a step back and saluted.

I returned the protocol, told him to be at ease and said I was just "Doing the walk" to make sure all was in order.

"Just waiting for the signal, sir," he replied. "We'll be down the alley way" (he indicated the narrow passage between the houses which I had just negotiated) "the moment the smoke blows."

I told him he was a good man, pushed myself hard not to chance my luck, and turned ready to go out the way I had come. Then I turned back. "Who's the officer of the day, sergeant?" I said.

He gave me a curious look. "Captain Kell, sir," he said, "but…"

"Don't worry, Sergeant, I'll tell him you were cautious to the last," and as I turned down the path I saw a second figure with a face so familiar I nearly choked. Without a word and without any decorum I took the wall in one leap and ran as fast as I could.

I was shouting at Edward as I went back up the stairs. "Get to 16 Damien Street – it is just round the corner, wait for someone you recognise and take the picture. Most important, don't be seen – it's the military, and if they spot you with a camera you'll be locked up for the rest of your life. Hide in a pile of rubbish, disguise yourself as a rat, anything, just get the picture. Absolutely do not move until the place is empty, then get back to Fleet Street and get the pictures developed and take them to the fifth. Do not come looking for me, no matter what."

Edward to his credit didn't ask, and he was out of the house and on his way fully laden within a minute.

I stayed and watched the scene below.

Churchill was still there directing events, and was checking his pocket watch regularly. By his side was a much larger group, and a little way back two fire engines had crept up to join in.

Churchill turned, spoke to a major, and then retreated a few steps. The order was clearly expected because there was no relaying of the message, no "tell the captain to tell the sergeant to tell the men" stuff. Without a word four men carrying torches ran up to the house and threw them in through the broken ground floor windows.

As soon as the men were clear four ranks of troops moved forward and emptied every round they had into the house. With half of my mind blanketed by a red mist and the other half reaching clarity for the first time, I carefully put my notebook in my pocket, took the stairs six at a time, pushed open the front door, and charged across the street.

By the time I had got to number 100 the fire was starting to take hold. It was a perfect diversion.

Churchill took the impact of my eleven stone full in the face. It drove him flat onto the ground, with me on top – and I got the better of the landing. He looked at me, focussed, but his words were lost in a sudden burst of firing from number 100. When it finished he laughed and said, "Jacko Jones!"

"It's you!" I replied.

"I know," he said, and that was about as far as we got because by then there were half a dozen policemen and soldiers grabbing me, clicking off the safety catches and getting very ready to shoot me in the head.

"Gentleman," said Churchill, getting to his feet, "please stand down. This is Captain Jones, an officer in Military Intelligence."

Behind me the fire was racing up the stairs inside the house and the upper windows were gushing smoke. The men from the fire engine were ready with their hoses, but clearly had been told not to move until Churchill gave the order.

"Serving in Military Operations," I said in a loud voice for anyone still thinking of shooting me, "along with Captain Kell, who ought to be around here somewhere." The flames were now coming out of the windows. Still no one moved. "I hope he got out ok."

"I don't think we'll have too many injuries here," said Churchill. "A successful operation in fact."

"But to what end?" I shouted. The stood-down soldiers and police were watching us curiously. Not every safety-catch had gone back on. "No one is going to come rushing out, are they?" I said. "No anarchists, no Latvians, no jewel thieves, no forgers!"

"A successful day," Churchill said, and started to walk away, knowing that I would stay at his side. The posse moved with us.

"Unless someone points out that maybe, with this many soldiers and coppers there ought to have been some bodies found inside. Unless someone asks how we just managed to bury three brave non-existent policemen who took the house in Houndsditch." He didn't flinch, although I think I saw a slight frown. "Unless someone goes looking for their families and finds that their wives are actresses," I added. "Unless someone notices just how many anarchist guns were fired at once. Unless someone asks why guns that can fire at that speed can be so utterly inaccurate that no one is hurt."

"An interesting supposition," said Churchill, "but just in case you are thinking of taking that step, I do have a friend or two on what I believe in your newspaper is known as the 'fifth floor'. Every newspaper has a fifth, Jacko, and there is a line that no owner will transgress. Not if he wants to stay in profit."

"No bodies," I said. "No bodies at the siege of Houndsditch, no bodies in Sidney Street, no bodies in the coffins…"

"There are sometimes matters of state…" and he put an arm round me, and we continued to walk away from the fire and from the watching troops.

"This is your own cause," I surmised.

"A cause you should understand Jacko – a newspaper cause. A publicity cause."

"No!" I shouted. "This is not some matter of high politics. This is money and power. But you don't need money so much that you are prepared to become the most hated aristocrat since…" I stopped. My history lessons had vanished.

"Castlereagh?" he suggested.

I was willing to accept it as a suggestion. "So for what? What is it you want money for?"

"For the war, Jacko – the war."

"You surely don't believe there is a spy on every corner?"

"Of course not – Kell may be a fool but he has his uses, and proving there are no spies is one of them."

"But your party is about to push through a budget that will raise unprecedented sums in tax. I helped the publicity to get the Parliament Bill through for goodness sake. The "This is Us" slogan: I wrote that. You have retained power, so you have the money."

"No – Mr Lloyd George has the money. You are right, of course, it is the sort of budget only the Liberals could pass – the Unionists could never raise a tenth of this budget. But look at what Lloyd George will do with the money. It goes on pensions and unemployment pay – but we need that for defence. We have a German king for goodness sake – which is why the first thing we have to make sure we do is fight the battle in Europe and not here in England. Which means I need to let Germany know they can't invade us by sea. I need ships, I need cannons, I need weaponry. This is not war against the farmers of Africa, Jones, this is a war between the two greatest industrial powers the world has seen. It is a war about power. Our empire, or their empire, which is it to be?"

"And so setting fire to a house in Sidney Street gives you that money?" I knew where he was going, but I wanted him to spit it out. He was cleverer than that, though, and the silence and looks hung between us.

"So what am I? Your little pet puppy dog?"

"You, Mr Jones, are providing an invaluable service for the state. You were the one person who bothered to sneak around Woolwich, of all god-forsaken places, and you had connections within the Liberal Party. If anyone was going to catch a whiff of what was going on you would – and you did with the torpedoes."

"Which you put in Scotland, so that no one from Westminster is going to tumble to just how many weapons you are making. Which means you can continue to plead poverty and the need for more arms. You get your friends Norris and Leitch to build you lots of new houses for the men, and in return Norris closes down the football club to emphasise the point that Woolwich becomes a ghost town, because, you say, we haven't got any money to build any more weapons. The poverty cry – we have no money! No one would ever think that the home secretary who closed the Woolwich Arsenal was actually making a new arsenal in Scotland.

"And all that money will come from the higher taxes that no longer have to go on unemployment pay and pensions. It is so clever – you can support unemployment pay and pensions because... because there won't be any poor unemployed or old people because this generation is going to be sterilised. Oh and I suspect that the sterilisation is going to be a bit dangerous and could go wrong, but no one will notice because they are just the people from the vortex. They can't vote, they aren't counted, and actually it will make London smell a bit better when they are gone.

"It is clever. Home Secretary – you get the Liberals to destroy the landed gentry in Parliament, you get the Liberals to pass the biggest budget ever, and then shortly after it is all done and dusted, you pass the sterilisation bill on a free vote, and suddenly all that money that Lloyd George had isn't needed. Still, never mind, because we can now fight the war. And all the time the boobies in the Unionist party think they are about to take control by sailing their ships down the Thames and pointing the guns at Westminster. Which means, I guess, if anything goes wrong, you can blame them and send Lord Willoughby de Broke and his friends to the Tower."

"Don't make it sound like a solo crusade, Jacko," he replied. "HG Wells, Shaw... these are the people supporting this notion of sorting out the vortex."

"Oh no," I said, "I know about Wells. He wants sterilisation for the feeble minded. I don't like that either, but you are talking about the whole of the vortex of poverty and just in case anyone asks, let's blame the crisis on the anarchists and jewel thieves."

We fell quiet, and looked back to number 100. The fire was ripping through the building now, and the fire engine was creeping closer with the soldiers sheltering in its cover. Eventually they put a ladder up to the top floor window, and, with covering rifle shots, a fireman crept up with a hosepipe, pushed it towards the window, and the water came on. Troopers were facing the burned out front door as if they truly expected the desperadoes to emerge.

"Perhaps I should tell them to take a peek around the back," I said.

"Best not, Mr Jones," he said. "You've got no evidence of anything, and it is you against the office of state. Accept the world as it is, even if you don't like it."

"So you cause disruption and chaos on an ever increasing scale in order to blame the desperate people without jobs, in order to get opinion formed towards the idea of sterilising them, in order to reduce the number in the vortex in order to avoid spending the budget on the poor, in order to have more weapons to fight Germany. The only good bit in all this is that Norris was an unsuspecting pawn in the game."

Suddenly he became very brisk. "I need your help. A story in the paper – a Chronicle exclusive, I think. Two bodies in the kitchen. That would mean some have escaped, we don't know how, so we can keep the story going through the year…"

"I think I would sooner have a story from a policeman or ten saying, 'Actually now you mention it Jacko, we never did see anyone who was in the house, and we never did find a body…'"

Churchill shrugged. He had nothing to fear from me. "Tell me," he said, "what gave you the final clue?"

"Everyone makes a mistake," I said, grateful to take him away from thoughts of Kell's office. "I learned in Africa: all you have to do is wait long enough. Yours was to use the same men several times. Man at Fulham who was handing out sovereigns – we followed him to Aintree Street. Man trying to rape a woman at the Suffragettes meeting – probably won't be troubling women for some time to come – same man. Man in the back of number 100, not walking very well, I was pleased to see – same man."

He pulled away from me suddenly. "You have been around the back?" For the first time that smug look of self-satisfaction came off his face.

I shrugged. We finally had the measure of each other. He would assume that I had not acted totally alone and that simply removing me from the scene – a tragic victim of a sniper's bullet – would merely alert whomever I had told, not to mention Lord Cortney. The fact that I had instructed Edward to take some pictures would remain my little secret.

There was a noise in the street behind us, and we turned to see the Scots Guards all in their fancy dress come straight from the Tower of London (the same Tower, I reflected, that Mr Churchill might well fancy putting me inside if he thought he could get away with it.)

The crowd cheered, in that half appreciative, half sarcastic way that London crowds have, and we continued to watch as the firemen moved onto the roofs of neighbouring houses the better to direct water onto the devastated number 100.

Within seconds the roof of the siege house gave way, the flames roared up again, and then firemen set about their business in earnest. I heard my name.

Marie was running across the street. "I've been stuck behind the cordon for the last hour, but couldn't get to you," she said, and gave me a hug that the watching Scots Guards appreciated until their sergeant told them how to behave with a lady present.

And just then, just to add to the fun, Kell, who must have finished taking his long route from the back of the house via Commercial Street or thereabouts, joined our jolly gang. "Home Secretary," he said with great solemnity, "I have information that makes me believe that this man is an anarchist."

"Oh for goodness sake," I said, and Mr Churchill turned to Kell and told him rather briskly that this was not the case and that I had saved his life at the height of the firing by knocking him down as the shots rained above, at great risk to my own life.

They were still debating the finer points of my loyalty when Norris turned up, clearly believing that as part of the whole conspiracy he now had the ear of the Home Secretary. "A word or two if you have a moment, sir" he said to Churchill on spotting me, and reported that he had it on good authority that I was an anarchist. I put my arm through Churchill's – a cheeky move if ever there was one – and manoeuvred him a little away from Norris and Kell. "What happens to Woolwich Arsenal now?" I said.

He shrugged. "The club was just another diversion in case we needed it to stop people noticing the removal of the torpedo factory. Norris has it, and as far as I am concerned he can keep it. Don't know what he'll do with it though, it's going to cost him a fortune to run."

I took Marie's hand, and we turned in the opposite direction, toward Bethnal Green Road, but as we went Churchill called us back. "Lord Willoughby's hands," he said. "I think I owe you for that. Come and see me when this settles down."

In Fleet Street we checked Edward's pictures of the back of Damien Street and the gunshots. He had both – the man is an utter genius, and if I have my way will go down in the history books as the greatest newspaper photographer of the era. A photograph showing six points of light as separate shots were fired from within number 100. Six "anarchists" with the highest grade of weaponry and not a single dead policeman? No one would believe that. And from round the back, a man identified as a rapist and passer-off of fake coinage, limping towards the sergeant with a message.

My insurance policy. Complete.

"Finally," I said, "we connected. And it certainly wasn't dull."

Marie took my arm. "This is us," she said.

Postscript

On 4th January 1911 it was announced in Parliament that the bodies of two men, identified as Fritz Svaars and William Sokolow, had been recovered from the ruins. Not your typical English anarchist names, I thought, but not bad as the names of dangerous foreign spies.

I wrote a piece suggesting that as the shooting had come from six different points within the house, as Edward's pictures of the guns being fired clearly showed, therefore there were at least four more men missing.

One of them, I said, was the ringleader. I wanted nothing to do with Churchill's supposedly Latvian names, so I went for "Peter the Painter". By the next editions every paper in Fleet Street agreed that Peter (whoever he was) had been at the scene, had masterminded the affair, and had escaped. Within the story was a simple message to Churchill. I'm still here, and I'm not giving up – and others know what I know.

I estimated in my piece that there must have been something like 1500 police, firemen and military personnel in the road by the time it was all over. All to capture two suspected anarchists. Surely money was needed to bring the police force of London up to scratch – to give them proper training, and to ensure their officers know how to conduct operations. ("I'm still here, Mr Churchill, and I can play this any way I want.")

Ten days later Lord Cortney informed me that Mr Churchill had attempted and failed to convince the Prime Minister of the need for sterilisation of the poor who inhabited the vortex. His call for a party-free vote on the topic was also rejected.

As for the Liberal budget, that was finally allowed through by the Lords later in 1911 along with their plans for the introduction of old age pensions and unemployment pay.

There never was any evidence of German spies, of course, and war, when it came in 1914, was fought in Europe and not in the German Sea. The Suffragettes did not get their vote, and when war broke out the whole debate was once again held over for the duration.

The miners of Tonypandy also failed to win their demands. They stayed on strike until October 1911 when they finally returned to work on the employers' terms.

As for Woolwich Arsenal it took them until the end of February 1911 before they won another game. But they ended the season with an eleven match unbeaten run which took them away from the relegation zone and they finished the campaign a very respectable tenth. The crowds rose as well, reaching a record (for Plumstead) of 24,000 for the home game with Tottenham Hotspur on April 8th. Henry Norris retained his control of Woolwich Arsenal, and he allowed the club to stay in Kent – for the time being.

Norris finally laid the grounds for the new Arsenal by investing around half of his fortune in building a new stadium opposite the Gillespie Road underground station. On 6th September 1913, 20,000 turned up at Highbury to witness the start of the new era. But that story is, perhaps, best left for another day.

ABOUT THE AUTHOR

Tony Attwood is a season ticket holder at Arsenal, having been a supporter since being taken to a match at Highbury by his father in 1956.

Tony is also the editor of the highly popular daily blog, Untold Arsenal. You can read Tony's daily account of the happenings at the modern Arsenal at www.blog.emiratesstadium.info

He is also a committee member in charge of "Arsenal History" within Arsenal Independent Supporters' Association.